The Mozart Masquerade Gala

Book One

of the

Dr. Elizabeth Stone
Travel Adventure Series

by Wanetta Hill

The Mozart Masquerade Gala by Wanetta Hill

Published by Wanetta Hill

www.wanettahill.com

Copyright © 2017 Wanetta Hill

Cover design by Damian Hill. Editing and formatting by Damian Hill. Printing and binding by CreateSpace.

ISBN-13: 978-1977874511
ISBN-10: 1977874517

This book is dedicated to Laszlo, my real-life dog guardian. He saw me through to the end. He'll be with me always. 2005-2017

Acknowledgements

Travel journals piled high, full of words, are meaningless unless shared.

The Mozart Masquerade Gala, the first in The Dr. Elizabeth Stone Travel series, comes to life from journals kept over the years of my own adventures. Journeys come in many forms - including the journey to completing this first novel. Weaving together a story from my own true-to-life mishaps has been a labor of love that could not have taken place without the help of many.

To my husband, Richard, for believing in me as well as pushing me to believe in myself.

To my son, Damian, for being the amazing editor and cover designer of this book. A compass in a storm, he has helped me hone my own writing skills by sharing his knowledge of writing and publishing.

To my daughter, Megan, for reading the book and loving it. It means a lot to me that you learned more about your mother through reading her stories and experiencing her imagination first hand. You believed in me from the very beginning.

To my youngest son, Nathanael, for designing my webpage and teaching me how to promote my dream. May you continue to use your creative mind in your own works one day.

To my friends Jan, Brenda, Mary Jane, and Pam for allowing me to include you in my cast of characters. You are my faithful friends who trust my imagination enough to let me introduce you to my readers in caricature form.

To my numerous traveling companions who have followed me all over Europe, helping me create real-life adventures fun enough to become stories. Thank you all for encouraging over the years to write a book.

To my buddy, Laszlo, who has laid by my feet, under the table, in the upstairs office - wherever I choose to write, no matter what time of day or night. His loyalty and love are the inspiration for the dogs in my stories.

To Matt, Laura, Emily, and Lois for reading the draft with critical eyes. Your feedback made this book better.

To my readers, thank you for getting to know Dr. Elizabeth Stone. I hope you fall in love with the characters in this book and love them as much as I do, for they will appear throughout the series. This is the first of four planned adventures. The second one, *The Pearl Overture*, will be released in 2018.

Please follow me online for updates: www.wanettahill.com

This has been a family affair - a journey of trust, music, integrity, laughter, and strength. Don't ever suppress your dreams. Grab a journal and write!

Preface

Travel has been an integral part of my life for the past twenty years. Taking students abroad to expose them to the world they live in is important to me as an educator. I have kept a journal recording my adventures for each and every trip—some inspiring, some adventurous, and many amusing, as I make lots of mistakes along the way. Friends who have joined me on tour have asked me for years to put these adventures into a book. Instead of an ordinary travel book, I created Dr. Elizabeth Stone to guide you. A modern-day Miss Marple, she encounters mysteries that require her to trust her intuition and find her inner strength.

In addition to drawing on my personal experiences, I have woven this tale with a bit of real history, a bit of historical fiction, and a bit of humor. What is real and what is imagined? That is for you, the reader, to discover as you experience the world through the eyes of Elizabeth Stone.

The Dr. Elizabeth Stone series hopefully will leave you laughing, crying, and excited about exploring the real cities and histories referenced in the stories.

Book One, *The Mozart Masquerade Gala*, takes you to Vienna, Copenhagen, and Prague. Future books in the series will travel to France, England, Ireland, Scotland, Greece, Germany, Italy, Japan, and destinations in Africa.

The Mozart Masquerade Gala is not just a mystery—it is about family, lifelong friendships, and integrity. Come along! Join us on this journey!

க✳෨

A timeline of Mozart's life, annotated with notes from Elizabeth's research during the Mozart Masquerade Gala adventure, can be found at the back of the book.

Music, even in situations of the greatest horror, should never be painful to the ear but should flatter and charm it, and thereby always remain music.

— *Wolfgang Amadeus Mozart*

1

Vienna, Early Spring

The cobblestones were uneven and hurt my knee, but I kept moving right along with determination. I only had a few minutes to attend to my enigmatic rendezvous here in Vienna, and those minutes were ticking away. St. Stephen's was in my view, so I wasn't far from my destination. I was to meet the curator of the Mozarthaus Museum at 3 p.m. The bells on the cathedral began tolling — *one, two, three* — just as I rounded the corner and stepped into the lobby of the museum. I had explained to my students that I was meeting an acquaintance for coffee during our free time, so they sent me off on my merry way without any questions. They knew I loved my friends — and my coffee. Here I was in my 60s, widowed, tenured at my university as a Choral Director, happy with my teaching, and traipsing about on a secret mission in Vienna.

I looked around. The museum was located at Domgasse number 5. The queue for tickets was short, the museum shop to my right had a few visitors browsing the merchandise, and several tourists were exiting the museum after their visit of Mozart's last known apartment in Vienna. Mozart had lived in several apartments around Vienna, but this is the only one that has survived. Having penned *The Marriage of Figaro* while residing here from 1784-1787, historians write that it was here he was the happiest. I had visited the museum several years earlier on a previous tour to Vienna, finding them to have an excellent display that was very tastefully done.

⇛ ✱ ⇚

I must admit, when I received the email a few weeks ago from the curator, a Mr. Peter Schultz, I was more than curious. In the email, he mentioned that he had received an anonymous gift at the museum, and that the gift had been traced back to my family in the 1700s. He also asked if I might be visiting Vienna in the near future, because he needed to discuss this all with me in person.

After reading the email, I leaned back in my cozy office chair, perplexed, and then leaned forward to read it again, my heart pounding. My family? 1700s? Was this a scam? Instead of replying to the email, I did an internet search for the Mozarthaus Museum on Domgasse. Yes, there was a curator named Schultz. Still unsatisfied, I checked what time it was in Vienna, then dialed the number of the museum. A pleasant-sounding woman answered the phone in polite German. I wrinkled my nose — I was a singer, and German diction was not my forte.

"Sprechen Sie Englisch?" I timidly said, knowing full well the woman on the other end of the phone was rolling her eyes about now.

"Yes, I do. May I help you?" she said in flawless English, though very different from my thick Southern drawl.

"Thank goodness! Yes, may I please speak to Mr. Schultz?"

"He is out of the museum for the day. May I ask who is calling and take a message?"

"No, that is okay. It isn't important. I will try again later. Thank you and have a very good evening." I was praying she didn't notice the nervousness in my voice.

"You are welcome. If you change your mind and want to leave a message, just call me back. I will be here for a few more hours."

I ended the call, my curiosity satisfied — Mr. Schultz existed, and he did indeed work at the Mozarthaus Museum. But what did he want to tell me about my family? My parents were both deceased, but my father had always told me we were of English descent. How were we possibly connected to this curious object in Vienna — an anonymous gift to a museum that housed artifacts of my favorite composer, Mozart?

I was interrupted by a quiet knock on my office door. "Dr. Stone? We were just wondering if you wanted us to go ahead and warm-up?"

I had been so engrossed in my phone call that I didn't even hear the choir come in. Suddenly, the sound of happy chatter, book bags being thrown on the table, and someone playing on the piano became amplified to my senses.

"No, I am on my way out."

I walked toward the piano, began the warm-ups with the choir, but my mind was far off in Vienna with a curator named Schultz. How did Mr. Schultz know we were touring Europe this spring, and that one of our stops was in Vienna?

I kept my phone on the piano by my music folder and tried not to act distracted when it lit up. I glanced down and saw that it was a new email from the curator in Vienna, confirming that his co-worker informed him that I called. The rehearsal would not end for another hour, so the email would have to wait. As I worked out pitches, tuned chords, unified vowel sounds and made beautiful phrases out of the Mozart piece we were preparing for our tour, my mind kept wandering to the Mozarthaus Museum behind St. Stephen's Cathedral in Vienna.

After rehearsal, and after all the students had left, I sequestered myself in my office and opened the latest email from Schultz. It read:

Dr. Stone,

My colleague said I received a call this afternoon from an American woman who left neither her name nor a message. I believe your accent gave you away. I assume you must have called to verify my identity and position. I don't blame you—there are so many scams these days. I can't discuss the details of this matter with you over email or phone. Just know that you will be very interested in what I have to tell you—and give you. I was able to see (on your very informative website) the dates of your choir's upcoming tour in Vienna. I hope we can find a time to meet while you're in town.

Sincerely,
Peter Schultz

ঌ✳ঌ

I don't know how long I stood in the lobby of the museum, recalling how I arrived at this very moment in the Mozarthaus Museum, before a familiar voice said, "Dr. Stone?"

My ears perked up. Although my back was turned, there was no mistaking that this was the voice of the woman I had talked to on the phone. My ears are like finely tuned instruments, due to a lifetime of musical training and practice. In fact, my son, having learned early on he couldn't easily escape my earshot, used to jokingly tell me I have "bat ears."

I smiled as I cautiously turned to face the woman behind the voice. The young woman was blonde, with big blue eyes, and very beautiful. However, based on my quick initial once-over, something didn't feel quite right. For one thing, her outfit, a low-cut blouse with a very tight pencil skirt, didn't seem to match her job description. I honestly had pictured an older German woman in a stiff ruffled blouse and tight bun, but I didn't let this image throw me out of the moment.

"Sophia," I said, startling her. "I would recognize your voice anywhere." I extended my hand, but Sophia lifted her chin in defiance, clasping her hands in front of her. *Well, so much for a warm greeting!* I was amused and quite pleased that my keen sense of hearing had not let me down. I enjoyed seeing the look on her face.

"Peter is waiting for you in his office. He asked me to show you there. Could you follow me please?" she said stiffly as she turned on her heels to lead me to the stairs. I was impressed she could turn that quickly without falling.

I was afraid she was going to throw her back out, as stiff as she was walking, but she loosened up a bit when the toe of her very high heels caught on the first step. She never missed a beat, corrected herself, and kept right on going. I was glad I was behind her so she couldn't see me smiling. I admit, as I watched her, I was a bit jealous. I could lose twenty pounds and never look that good in what she was wearing.

I tried to regain my focus on the meeting, since I really had no clue what awaited me and needed to keep my wits about me.

Trust, I kept saying to myself. Trust that I am being led to an office to meet a nice man named Peter Schultz, and not being led into a trap. I did find it interesting that Sophia called her boss by his first name. The office Sophia was taking me to was located on the second floor of the museum behind a door that I had noticed on my first visit there several years earlier. How different that visit was! A casual couple of hours viewing

Mozart's apartment, seeing handwritten manuscripts, and reading well-written historical accounts of his life while he and his wife Constanze resided there. Hopefully this visit would be as delightful, but currently my stomach was churning.

Sophia opened the big wooden door, shooting darts at me with her big baby blues. "After you, Dr. Stone."

I shot darts right back at her with my big emerald greens. "Thank you, Sophia. Again, a pleasure to finally meet you."

I don't know what I was expecting Peter Schultz to look like, but he looked nothing like what I had imagined. As I entered, the graying head of Mr. Schultz rose from behind the beautifully carved desk where he'd been seated, revealing his tall frame and nicely tailored suit, with reading glasses still perched on the end of his nose.

"Finally, Dr. Stone, I have the pleasure of meeting you in person" he said, as he took the glasses off. Laying them carefully on the book he was reading, he came to the front of his desk to shake my hand.

His English was impeccable.

"Please, be seated. You must be very tired. When did you arrive in Vienna?"

Being polite, I sat quietly, somewhat relieved we were starting with small talk, but also anxious to learn what all of this was about. "Yesterday afternoon. We had a successful concert in Salzburg, and the coach ride was uneventful."

The suspense was killing me. I really wanted to scream "Cut to the chase, Mr. Schultz!" – but my inner voice told me to keep my game face on. It was hard to fully judge the situation, and in the event that things came to some sort of negotiation, I didn't want to ruin my position by seeming overly eager.

"That is good to hear, Dr. Stone. You will have to tell me more about your time in Salzburg sometime. It is one of my favorite cities to visit."

"Mine too. My students were fascinated with being in Mozart's birthplace. We took *The Sound of Music* tour, which was a lot of fun." *When is he going to get to the point?!*

"So, Mr. Schultz..."

"Please, Dr. Stone, call me Peter."

"Of course, Peter. Thank you. And, please, call me Elizabeth."

"Elizabeth, I know you're on a tight schedule today, so if I may, I'd like to move on to the real topic of our visit."

"Yes, thank you. Unfortunately, I don't have much free time today. I must confess, ever since I received your email, I have been very curious how my family is associated with an anonymous gift to the Mozarthaus Museum."

Peter smiled as he stepped back behind his desk. He took a key from the middle drawer and proceeded to the bookcase, where he moved a bust of Mozart in order to access a sliding wooden panel that hid a wall safe. I was rather amused that he didn't hide the fact the safe was there, which meant he trusted me with his secret. Once the safe was open, he reached inside and pulled out a simple wooden box, which I sized up quickly as being about five inches tall and five inches long. I watched as he opened the box and took out a blue velvet pouch, setting it on his desk in front of me. Gently, he opened the pouch and brought out a blue and gold snuff box as well as a letter sealed inside a plastic storage bag.

"What do you know about Mozart's history, Elizabeth?" he asked as he set the items carefully on his desk in front of me.

Not taking my eyes off the items, I began to tell him the typical facts that all music scholars know about Mozart's history. His birthplace, his father, his first symphony, his struggles in Vienna, his marriage, the mysteries behind his death, and the number of compositions he had written. I was rattling off facts as if I were giving a lecture to my Music History class when Peter raised his hand to stop me.

"Excellent! And what do you know of his wife Constanze?"

"Just that Mozart's father was against the marriage and that she was the one who saved his compositions from being destroyed after his untimely death. Not much has been written about her. Everyone who has seen the movie *Amadeus* thinks that she was flippant and flighty. Why do you ask?"

"Well," Peter began after laughing boisterously at my reference to the movie *Amadeus*, "it seems that you are tied to Constanze through family connections."

"You must surely be mistaken, Peter. My father always told me we were English, not German."

At this point, I glanced at my watch. My students were expecting me at Café Sacher in thirty minutes, and I couldn't be late.

"Mr. Schultz, I am totally confused. I am hoping that you have some sort of paperwork that explains all of this. I need to meet my students soon, and I feel that I am going to need more time to absorb all that you are telling me."

"I am well aware that this information is new to you. However, I have the documentation to back it all up. I want to show you something first."

Peter gently took the golden gilded box, which was approximately 2 inches by 2 inches and very ornate, in his hands. "Do you know what this is Elizabeth?"

Not wanting to sound totally ignorant, and inwardly disliking the implication that I didn't know what he was showing me, I replied that it was similar to the snuff boxes that royals gave to Mozart as a young prodigy touring Europe with his father. But surely...

"How clever you are, Dr. Stone! And absolutely correct! His father was hoping for money, but Mozart was paid in gold snuff boxes and other trinkets. When he and Constanze were struggling financially, it is rumored that they would sell these for money or barter the rent. We have several others upstairs in the showcase that survived that fate. But this one is special."

"And why is that, Peter? It resembles all the others I have seen here and in the books I have read while researching Mozart."

"Look on the bottom, Elizabeth. Look at the inscription closely."

He gingerly handed me the tiny snuff box. Taking it in my hands, I carefully turned it over. Good grief, my contacts were not adjusting properly for the tiny inscription. Peter noticed, offering me his reading glasses. There, in tiny engraving were about two lines of writing — in German.

I read it out loud in rough German dialect, but two words were clear to me: Marie Antoinette. I stopped in mid-phrase. *Oh my gosh, was this given to Mozart by Marie Antoinette?* History tells a story from Mozart's Grand Tour — a performance for the Imperial Court at the famous Hofburg Palace. When young Mozart, who was only 6 at the time, slipped on the marble floors, it was Marie Antoinette, around his same age, who comforted him. Marie Antoinette was the fifteenth child of the Empress Maria Theresa and Emperor Francis I of Austria. Smitten by her kindness, Mozart looked up and said, "When I grow up I want to marry you." Those probably weren't his exact words, but you get the general message.

I don't know how long I was suspended in time, frozen, holding this tiny artifact in my hands before Peter said, "Do you understand the significance of this?"

Gee, Mr. Schultz thinks I am a ditz. My instincts were warning me not to reveal too much of what I knew. *Play along, Elizabeth, play along.*

"Oh yes, this is a part of history the whole world knows. I wasn't aware that she gave him anything, however."

"Evidently it was a gift after his performance that day. It was probably common practice to have her name engraved on gifts, or Mozart's father had it engraved to identify the giver. What is unique, however, is that none of the other snuff boxes given to Mozart are engraved — only this one. Open it..."

"Open it?" I asked.

Peter nodded, and I carefully raised the top. Nestled among a gold satin cloth was a beautiful, but small, gold locket. "Go ahead. Take it out. It is yours."

My head jolted up as I took in Peter's words, but then looked back at the dainty locket inside the snuff box. I gingerly lifted it out, and held it in my hands. "Mine? But how can that be?" I asked, my voice shaking in disbelief that this locket inside a snuff box given to Mozart by Marie Antoinette was mine.

"It seems that Constanze was not as flippant or flighty as the movie producers portrayed her. When Mozart died, she became a smart businesswoman — publishing her husband's manuscripts and becoming very wealthy. It is because of her keen business sense that this particular snuff box was not sold off during their difficult days. In fact, she kept it with her at all times, secured in this small wooden box. She was afraid someone would try to steal it once they found out the identity of the benefactor, and she was right. Open the locket and you will see why."

I was shocked and overwhelmed, but my shaking fingers finally got the delicate locket open. Inside, much to my delight, was a tiny miniature portrait of a young Marie Antoinette. You have got to be kidding. I drew the locket closer to examine the tiny brushstrokes that made it one of the finest miniature portraits I had ever seen. I looked up in disbelief at Peter, still holding the locket delicately in the palm of my hand.

"Is this what I think it is? Did Marie Antoinette give Mozart this special locket on that fateful day when she scooped him up from his fall?"

"You assume correctly. It seems the one-day Queen of France exchanged gifts with Wolfgang Amadeus Mozart on that day in 1762. Luckily, his father put the locket in a safe place — inside the gold snuff box received on that same visit. Both have survived to this day."

"I am still a bit confused about how this is mine, Peter. A lot of questions are going through my head right now, and I am a bit overwhelmed. I hate cutting this meeting short, but I really need to go and meet my students. Our concert is tomorrow in St. Stephen's at noon. Could you attend and have a coffee with me afterwards to finish discussing this? You indicated in your email that these items were going to be displayed in the museum, not a gift to me."

"I knew you would need time to absorb all of this, so I didn't mention that this was a gift. I can attend, and yes, we can have coffee afterwards. In the meantime, I want to give you a transcription of what is documented about these items — captured in this fragile letter written by Constanze to her sister, Aloysia. Read it tonight, and we can discuss it further tomorrow over a coffee."

Peter handed me a copy of the transcription, but kept the original letter for obvious reasons. I handed him back the gold snuff box containing the gold locket with a miniature portrait of Marie Antoinette — all of which Peter was telling me now belonged to me.

The transcription was in a nice letter-size envelope so it fit neatly into my cross bag. I rose to let Peter see me to the door.

Bidding me a good evening with the promise of seeing me tomorrow at the concert, he took my hand in both of his. "It is a pleasure to meet you. I look forward to further discussing the snuff box and locket with you tomorrow."

As I left his office and headed down the steps, I noticed Sophia locking up the museum store, as it closed at 4 pm. Seeing me, she headed with her keys to the main entrance.

Opening the front door for me to exit, Sophia said rather frigidly, "Bundle up, Dr. Stone, the weather is rather chilly this afternoon. And be careful — you never know what the weather will bring."

Buttoning up my coat, I interjected, "Thankfully, Sophia, as women get older, we handle the cold better than we do the heat. Have a good evening, and you best bundle up, too. You don't want to catch a chest cold."

Touché, Elizabeth, I thought as I stepped outside. I tightened my neck scarf and tucked it into my coat. There was truth in her statement — it was rather chilly, but it wasn't just the weather that I was concerned with.

⁞ ✳ ⁞

From the gift shop windows, Sophia watched as Dr. Stone adjusted her scarf and headed off towards St. Stephen's. Once she was out of view, she climbed the stairs to Peter's office and knocked lightly on the door as she opened it. Peter was leaning back in his chair, his hands locked behind his head, with a pensive look on his face as she entered.

"How did she take the news?"

"Dr. Stone is in a bit of shock, but if I trust my judgment about her, she will review the document I gave her and will be ready to talk more tomorrow."

As he spoke, he got up and placed the box that contained the Mozart artifacts back in the safe. Closing the door, he put the key in his pocket.

Sophia nodded, and they bade each other a good evening. Peter couldn't take his mind off Dr. Stone and the artifacts. Ever since the mysterious stranger showed up requesting that he find her and give her the valuables, he had been cautious with every move he made. Beyond the legally binding aspects of their agreement, Peter couldn't shake the feeling there was real danger there as well.

Alone in his office now, he opened the safe again and took out the wooden box. He then touched a book on the shelf, which opened a panel on the wall and revealed a much larger and stronger safe. He didn't trust anyone — even Sophia — with the knowledge of this safe's existence. Peter dialed the number combination for the lock, and gently put the wooden box on the top shelf, alongside other Mozart artifacts he had withheld from the museum.

Going to his window, he looked below to the street level just in time to see Dr. Stone briskly turning the corner.

"Ah, Dr. Stone," he said. "You will be an easy one, for sure."

With that, he drew his curtains, put his hands in his pockets, and laughed as he rocked on his heels.

2

The Letter

I quickened my steps as I left the museum. I had about a ten-minute walk to get to the Café Sacher to meet my students for a late afternoon cup of Viennese coffee and a piece of Sachertorte before the coach picked us up. Getting out of the narrow passageway and into a more open pedestrian area with a crowd helped take a little chill out of the air. Vienna was still cold in March, especially once the sun started going down. I couldn't wait to get back to the hotel to read the mysterious transcription, but as far as my students were concerned, I had spent the last few hours having a cup of coffee with an old acquaintance.

Walking among tourists made the journey to meet my students a little chaotic. People were casually stopping to look in the windows on Kartner Strasse, admiring the delicately designed pastries and buying the famous Mozart candy, *Mozartkugel*, to take home to their families. I also noticed, now with renewed interest, the multiple snuff boxes in the shop windows with Mozart's face staring at me as I made my way down the street. Was the one Peter showed me just a cheap imitation, or was it the real deal? I had so many questions to ask him! Weaving through the crowds, I finally arrived to find a group of happy college students waving me to their table.

"Dr. Stone! Vienna is amazing! We have had the most fabulous afternoon."

I listened as they recounted all they had done in the few short hours since I left them. I tried to enjoy my coffee and cake as I engaged in their storytelling, never letting on that my mind was elsewhere. As I sipped my coffee, I noticed a familiar face looking at me through the café window. Even through the café glass, I could see how handsome he was. Dark curls showed under his homburg hat, framing his chiseled features. His scarf was tucked into a dark wool coat, adding to his elegant looks. He was looking straight through me, as if he knew me quite well. It's vaguely possible he's a former student, given his approximate age. However, a former student would have come barreling into the restaurant if they had seen me, so who is this young man? We were staring right at each other, expressionless, and I felt as if time had stood still. Where had I seen him? Instinctively, I drew my cross bag with the document closer to my side. When I looked back, he was gone. Unnerving, to say the least, but I hid my uneasiness as I listened to my student's exciting narrative of their day in Vienna.

The coach picked us up by the Vienna Staatsoper House on Ringstraße, and we cheerfully made our way to a restaurant to enjoy some wiener schnitzel. I thought I had seen the same man from the Café Sacher on the street as we drove off, but surely that was just my imagination. I looked back, but he was gone.

Once back at the hotel, and dinner was done, I finally excused myself from the card games and social networking in the hotel lobby, stating that I needed to do some score study before tomorrow's concert. Out of caution, I looked both ways down the hall as I departed the elevator, fumbling with the key until I was in my room. Leaning my back up against the door, I took a big breath to calm my beating heart. Turning, I latched the door and then drew the curtains.

The room was small but functional, so I didn't have to go far to plop down on the bed to open my cross bag. I anxiously pulled out the transcription that Peter Schultz had given me and began to read. It was a copy of a letter written by Constanze to her sister Aloysia.

My heart started pounding again — Aloysia was the Weber sister that Wolfgang first fell in love with!

September 1824

Salzburg, Austria

My Dear Sister Aloysia,

> *Winter will be here soon. The leaves on the trees are changing, and the shadows over the mountains tell me the cold weather will soon arrive. Georg and I are comfortable here in Salzburg, and Wolfgang's memory lives on through his music in the Cathedrals and*

Theatres. How thrilling it has been to hear his musical efforts interpreted and enjoyed by all. So different from when he was alive and we were struggling to find a patron to support his work.

I am writing to let you know about a huge discovery I made as I was packing up to move here to Salzburg. Remember the gold snuff boxes that Wolfgang was given as a child on his Grand Tour of Europe? We had to sell most of them when we first were married, but for some reason he kept a few choice ones that seemed to be his favorites. When he died, I placed his favorite suit, hat, and two gold snuff boxes in a trunk as keepsakes alongside a few other personal items. I put the trunk in the back of a wardrobe, and hadn't gone through its contents until right before we moved. I pulled out the small trunk and sat in the middle of the floor. As I opened it, I could hear the strains of his music as if I were hearing them for the first time. I held each item in my hand, but when I picked up the blue and gold snuff box, something told me to open it. I had always been much too busy to look inside these tiny little tokens. Much to my surprise, there was a gold locket nestled inside! I had never seen this before and wondered when he had put it in the box, or if it had been in there the whole time.

Nervously, I opened the locket and let out an audible "Oh my" that made Georg come running into the room. He sat down beside me as I was clutching the locket to my heart — he thought something was wrong, but I slowly brought my hand out for him to see what I was holding so gently. He let out an audible gasp as we both realized what we had discovered that day. The locket holds a tiny miniature portrait of Marie Antoinette — Queen of France! She must have given this box and locket to Wolfgang when he met her in Vienna as a child.

This is a wonderful discovery, and I wanted to share it with you! I have placed it back in the trunk where it remains safe with Wolfgang's belongings. If something ever happens to me, please make sure that this box and locket remain in our family — that it always

be a reminder of how special Wolfgang was to everyone he met —
even the future Queen of France, Marie Antoinette.

Sincerely,
Constanze

Letter translated by Peter Schultz, Curator of Mozarthaus, Vienna

My hands were shaking and my heart was still pounding. This letter was proof of everything Peter had told me in his office, but of course, he has the original, written in German locked up safely – I hope.

So, if this had been written by Constanze in 1824, what had transpired with the box between that time and now? I went to the desk and got my tablet to do an internet search about Constanze. Luckily there was plenty of information about her. She had died in 1842 at age 80. One fact caught my eye, though – she and Georg had lived in Copenhagen from 1810-1820. My brother lives in Copenhagen and I will be there in the Fall for his birthday! Maybe I can make more of a connection with all of this while I am visiting. Surely there is evidence of her time in Copenhagen, perhaps at the library. For now, however, I only have more questions about how all these pieces fit together.

There was a knock on my door. I jumped, tossing my tablet in the air. Clumsily catching it, I put the letter back in its envelope, hiding it under my pillow. I laid open my music notebook, since I had told everyone I was going to be doing score study. Just in case.

Normally, I am not so jumpy on tour. With students and parent chaperones traveling with me, there is always a knock on my door. Why should this time be any different? I had to be careful and not show my nervousness or excitement until I knew all the details.

Through the closed door I heard, "It's just me, Dr. Stone, wondering if you are ready for our group meeting."

I opened the door to see my wonderful assistant and accompanist, Bradley, standing in the hall.

"Is it already 9:00? Good grief. Let me get my notebook." As Bradley waited for me in the hallway, I quickly took the envelope from under my pillow and placed it in the front pocket of my music binder.

"Ready. Let's go do this. Are you excited for the concert tomorrow? As I passed St. Stephen's today, I noticed a poster announcing the concert was taped to the front door. I hope we have a great crowd."

"I went in today to see where we will be singing," Bradley said excitedly, "and the priest in charge showed me around. Did you know that there are catacombs underneath the sanctuary and that you can take a tour? I think if there is time after the concert tomorrow I will go. What about you, want to come along?"

"Let me see how I feel after the concert — my friend may want to have coffee afterwards before we leave for home." I was sure hoping that Peter would meet me and answer a few questions afterwards.

We were met by the sound of laughter as we entered the hotel lobby for our meeting. My students were proudly and loudly sharing stories of their afternoon adventures around Vienna. I knew they would love it here.

The meeting consisted of going over the details for tomorrow's concert — time to meet in the lobby, uniform, music, etc. Afterwards, Bradley and I sat in the lobby and went over musical details.

When I was finally back in my room for the night, I fell asleep with the transcription under my pillow with my hand clutching it — just in case.

3

The Concert Encounter

My phone's alarm gently woke me up. I had set it an hour early so I could go down and enjoy a long cup of coffee and small breakfast before departing for St. Stephen's. Dressing in my concert attire – the usual black on black, with pearls of course, I suddenly remembered what was under my pillow as if it were all a dream.

The phone rang, and I jumped. It was just the hotel wake-up call, but I couldn't afford to be jumpy today. I gently moved my pillow, seeing that the transcription was safely there, secured in the envelope Peter had given me just yesterday. Several questions were still going through my mind:

1. Who had given all of this to him?
2. Was Peter's transcription accurate? And, does he even have the actual original?
3. What did the treasures have to do with me?
4. What is in it for Peter?
5. Where do we go from here?

Slipping the document into the pocket of my music binder, knowing I would have it with me at all times, I tucked the binder in my tote. As I started to walk out the door of my room, I suddenly turned and decided to take a careful mental picture of what it looked like – just a precaution, of course. Clutching my bag as if it were a baby, I sighed and headed downstairs. *What would this day hold?*

I wasn't the first one in the lobby. Bradley greeted me in his concert attire, looking up over his cup of coffee and giving a hearty wave as I entered the breakfast room.

Still clutching my bag for dear life, I juggled my cup of coffee as I sauntered carefully over to the table to join him.

"Good morning, Bradley! Your first concert in Vienna. How are you feeling?"

"Nervous," he replied. "I couldn't sleep, so I kept conducting my piece. And, I kept hearing things out in the hall all night. I thought it was the kids, so I would crack the door open to tell them to get some rest, but it wasn't them at all — just some hotel guest walking the halls. He passed my room several times because I began to recognize his footsteps. Strange, don't you think?"

By now, I was listening more intently than ever. Bradley's room was next to mine! I had left the television on last night for white noise, so it must have obscured the sounds of footsteps in the hall. *Was this so-called hotel guest after what I was carrying in my bag? Was this the man I saw in the window of the café and on the street as we drove off?* Not to cause alarm with Bradley, I acted nonchalantly about the whole thing — but my coffee suddenly tasted bitter.

Calmly I said, "I guess some people's jet lag disturbs their roommates, so they have to walk it off. I'm sorry it kept you up."

By this time my students were excitedly joining us, and before I knew it, we were loaded up and ready to go to our rehearsal at St. Stephen's. The morning was beautiful. I was determined to make it a beautiful day.

The priest, named Father Johann, met us at the side entrance, per his directions in his email. A jolly, happy young priest, he greeted me with a firm handshake and big smile.

"Dr. Stone, my pleasure to see you this morning! We are looking forward to your concert at noon. I will show your students where to store their bags. May I take yours for you?" he kindly asked as he reached his hands towards me to take my bag.

"Good morning to you as well, Father Johann. I would prefer to keep my bag with me, if that's alright. It has my music and other necessities." *If only he knew what I was really protecting! And, could I trust even a priest?*

I turned to Bradley, asked him to organize the students and their belongings with Father Johann, and said I would meet him at the main altar where we would sing. Confident he would handle it all beautifully, I walked to the front of the church. I turned in a circle while I gazed at the magnificent ceiling, and then lowered my eyes towards the entrance. *There he is again!* This time I smiled as our eyes met briefly, and he smiled back with a nod of his head and a tip of his stylish homburg. I kept staring as he moved deftly into the queue to visit the catacombs. I wanted to follow him and talk to him. I felt a connection, like he had known me all my life. Yet how could that be since he looked to be about forty? And then he was gone. I looked and looked, but never saw him.

We finished our rehearsal, which consisted of several works of Mozart: the *Te Deum*, which he wrote before leaving on his first journey to Italy with his father in 1769; the *Regina coeli in C Major*, 1771; and *Ave Verum Corpus*, written in 1791. Sung in this beautiful Gothic cathedral, the pieces sounded both sacred and haunting.

After the rehearsal, Father Johann wanted to give us a guided tour of the cathedral. I bowed out to unwind, choosing to walk silently around by myself. I really wanted to wander about and see if I could find my mysterious man. The last time I saw him, he was headed towards the catacombs, so off I went. We hadn't rehearsed for long, so surely he was still in the cathedral. I was sad to see when I arrived at the entrance that you could not go into the catacombs except on a guided tour. The next one was in thirty minutes. I headed back to find our group. Maybe Bradley was still interested in going to see them and would go with me.

I stopped behind our group just as the jovial priest was telling them about the statue lovingly called *Christ with a Toothache*. He had the students hysterically laughing, and I was enjoying seeing their excitement, grinning to myself, when I felt a hand on my shoulder. Turning, expecting to see someone from my group, I was surprised to see Peter standing there.

"Peter! How nice to see you. The concert doesn't start for another hour, so I hope you are still planning to stay and enjoy it." Something about his presence was unnerving, but I told myself to relax. I prayed he either didn't notice my nervousness or chalked it up to pre-concert jitters.

"Ah, Dr. Stone, unfortunately I have had a last-minute meeting come up with some museum benefactors and will not be able to attend after all. I believe you are departing for home tomorrow, so I wanted to bring you something before you left — a souvenir of your visit to Vienna."

I watched as he gently pulled a small wooden box from his briefcase and handed it to me. I hesitated before taking it, because I knew what was in that box — a velvet pouch with a small blue and gold snuff box containing a gold locket which had a miniature portrait of Marie Antoinette. Peter was entrusting this to me? I blew out a sigh and slowly took the box in my hands.

"Peter, I still don't understand. I read the letter, and as exciting as it is, I still don't see where I fit into this incredible picture. This is a priceless artifact, and in no way should I be the keeper of something so valuable!" I hadn't budged. I was holding on for dear life to the fragile wooden box, my eyes fixated on it the whole time I spoke.

"Don't shoot the messenger, Elizabeth. This is a gift to you from an anonymous donor. But I have a feeling this isn't the end of the tale. Your curiosity will get to the bottom of this mystery, and I have complete faith in your detective skills," he said with a grin.

With a tip of his hat towards me, he said, "Auf Wiedersehen, Dr. Stone. Perhaps one day our paths will cross again." Turning to go, he looked over his shoulder at me and said, "Keep me informed, Dr. Stone. Keep me informed."

Peter Schultz made me uneasy. I watched him casually leave the cathedral, then looked down at the wooden box he had just handed me — as if this were a common trinket bought off the street. I felt so conspicuous, and more than a little unworthy of such important items. Realizing I was in a public place with the treasures right out in the open, I quickly, but carefully, placed the box in my bag. Acting nonchalantly, I walked over to where Bradley was standing with the students.

"Say, how about if I treat all of you to a visit to the catacombs? We might as well see them while we are here. The next tour starts in just a few minutes, so I will meet you all at the entrance."

The students were so excited, and I think Bradley was even more so. I got out my trusty credit card, paid for the group, and then suddenly we heard the extremely loud voice of the guide calling us to him. After establishing that we were English speaking, he began to lead us down the steps into what he explained as the refurbished part of the catacombs, directly underneath the cathedral. Our guide was good, worth every euro I paid, but at first glimpse I couldn't see what the big deal was about the catacombs. Whitewashed walls, bright lights, and where were the crypts?

Leading us into what is called the Ducal Crypt, the guide finally revealed to us what was in the urns lining the shelves. This crypt was not actually for the bodies of the clergy and bishops, but for their internal organs.

The students made all sorts of shocked or grossed out noises as we learned the crypt housed more than 60 urns with the entrails of Habsburgs who died between 1650 and the 19th century. But the tour got even better as he led us to a newer — yet older looking — part located under the square next to the church.

Bones! The bones of over 11,000 people taken from surrounding cemeteries to make room for plague victims in those cemeteries after a horrible outbreak of the bubonic plague. Hardly any light in here, so it appears dark and sinister. You could look up into the ossuary caverns and see bones and skulls stacked high.

I was at the back of the group, waiting for a turn up front to get a better look, when out of the corner of my eye I saw a familiar homburg. Hoping it was my mysterious man, I walked toward him, only to be disappointed when he wasn't there. I hung my head, shaking it in disbelief that I missed him yet again, when a small folded piece of paper on the ground caught my eye. *Seriously people*, I thought, *can't you pick up your own trash?* I bent down to pick it up, and let out an audible gasp.

"You have a question back there?" the guide asked, "or did the ghost of the catacombs scare you?" He laughed so hard I thought he was going to rattle all the bones out of place, and my students just shook their heads.

"No, just truly amazed at how well these bones are laid out." I let out a nervous giggle, which made everyone just shake their heads more.

I calmly put the slip of paper in my pocket so I could look at it in better light. What had made me gasp was that my name, Dr. Elizabeth Stone, was on the piece of paper! I wrapped my hand around it inside my pocket, not wanting to let go of what might be a clue to my mystery man.

What seemed like hours was only five minutes before the guide led us back up the stairs into the cathedral. The students dispersed to get changed into the uniforms for the concert, and I found a nice quiet place by myself.

My hands were shaking when I pulled the note out of my pocket. I stared at the handwriting. A beautiful calligraphy style I was unaware of. One of my hobbies is calligraphy, but this was unlike anything I had ever seen. The strokes spelling out my name were ethereal in nature, unconnected and just looking like feathery lines to the ordinary eye, but I could see they spelled my name.

Stunned, I opened the note, which had just been folded once. It said, simply:

You will remember me. M

4

Copenhagen, The Fall

"Dr. Stone? Dr. Stone?"

I felt someone shaking me gently, but I was so disoriented from jet lag and change of scenery that I didn't quite know who was shaking me or why. I looked up to see the waiter staring at me with a puzzled expression. And, even more surprising to me, I didn't see Sherlock or Holmes anywhere. Was I still dreaming?

"Dr. Stone, are you ok? You came in an hour ago, said you didn't want anything but a glass of water, and you've just been sitting here quietly. When you fell asleep, I began to worry. The bar is about to close."

"Thank you, Jesper. I came in with a man and his dog. Did they leave earlier?" I was looking around for any signs that they were still in the bar area, but both were not anywhere to be seen.

"I'm sorry. I'm a little confused... You came in alone. I haven't seen a man or a dog with you this evening."

Not wanting to seem any crazier than Jesper thought I already was, I quietly said good night. But, on the table was a red scarf — one that did not belong to me — which jolted my brain into recalling earlier events of the night. My head started to spin.

Clutching my bag and the scarf, I bade good night to the other staff busily putting away glasses, cleaning the bar area, and wiping down tables. After exiting the bar area, I made my way as quickly as possible to my room.

I was still trying to figure out what exactly had transpired that evening. I plopped down on the bed, shaking my head in confusion, retracing what I could remember of my steps from the day. Just then, I heard a dog bark. It sounded really close, like maybe it was just outside on the street. But, when I looked out the window, there was no dog in sight. It barked again. The bark was coming from the hallway! *Good grief! It's late, and the management is going to come knocking.* I took the night latch off the door and there he was

— Sherlock, the big, black beautiful dog that had saved my life earlier that evening.

My memories of the evening started flooding back.

∾✳∾

The evening began simply enough: a craving. The hotel bar was very cozy, and the menu looked great, but I had my heart set on an encore of the sandwich I had at lunch. The shop was just one block away, and well, I was traveling. However, the moment I stepped out onto the side street by the hotel, something told me it was a mistake. Chances were the shop was already closed, so why was I stepping out into the darkness?

The chill of the night air hit me the instant I stepped outside, so I paused to pull my wool scarf up over my nose and mouth before tightening it around my neck. I stuffed my gloved hands in my pockets, hugged my jacket closer to my body, and headed south toward the intersection where the sandwich shop was located. As I watched my feet to avoid falling on the uneven surface, I noticed the cobblestones made no sound beneath my black suede boots. *Only one block*, I repeated.

Suddenly, out of nowhere, someone grabbed me and threw me to the cobblestones. Realizing the possibility that I was meeting a fateful end brought tears to my eyes, but I was not ready for the gleam in my attacker's eyes as he prepared to strangle me. I tried to scream, but I struggled to make a sound between the paralyzing waves of terror and my attacker's choking actions against my scarfed neck. I instinctively started to say my final prayers. "*Dear Lord, thank you —* " was as far as I got before this evil man was knocked off of me by the biggest black dog I have ever seen. As this monster was chasing my attacker away, I sat up as best I could and scooted over to lean up against the building. Rubbing my neck, I heard a man at the corner yelling, "Sherlock!" and holding an empty leash. I managed a weak, "Help," as the dog's owner ran towards me.

"Are you okay? My God, what happened?"

"What happened is your dog saved my life. He went that way, by the way. What kind of dog is that? And seriously, his name is Sherlock?"

I was still rubbing my neck as this gentle giant of a man stooped down next to me. I was shaking, but not from fear. I was mad. Mad at myself for leaving the hotel alone, and mad that I let my guard down. And, all of this was because I had a craving for a sandwich! I have to quit letting food run my life. Before I brushed myself off, I made sure my cross-body bag was still under my coat and on my shoulder. At least this giant dog named Sherlock scared the robber before he took my valuables. I knew that if my passport was stolen, that was a relatively easy fix — I learned that much on an earlier trip to Barcelona. I was more concerned with other things in my bag tonight.

"Yes, his name is Sherlock," the man said, as Sherlock was bounding towards us with a black plaid wool scarf in his mouth. "Good job, boy!"

Sherlock's tail was wagging so hard and so fast that I almost found myself on the cobblestones again. I reached down and gave him the biggest hug I could as I said gently in his ear, "Thank you, big boy, for saving my life."

I turned to the man, who was dressed in a black wool overcoat with a red scarf, and flippantly asked, "With a dog named Sherlock, I suppose your name is Holmes?"

I expected him to laugh, but instead he gently said, "Yes, but don't judge me just yet. Right now, we need to get you out of this cold. Where are you staying?"

My body hurt too badly to stop and rationalize or worry about this man wanting to know where I was staying. My voice of reason told me he meant no harm and only wanted to get me to safety. Besides, at my age, I pose no threat to a handsome young man.

"Right here at the Phoenix." Helping me up was a chore, but the young man who called himself Holmes was strong. Lifting me was not a problem for him. He gave me time to steady myself after standing, then we turned and headed the short distance back to the corner where the side entrance of the hotel was. Sherlock was leading the way with Holmes right by my side. He was even so kind as to offer me his arm. I was still in shock, but I stubbornly didn't want to admit it as I gallantly limped the short distance back.

"Does the hotel allow dogs?" Holmes asked.

"I believe so, especially for dogs that save people's lives."

We entered the hotel, where I instantly found comfort in the warmth that greeted us.

"The restaurant is closed, but the bar is open," I said, as I led the way down the stairs. The hotel staff knew me by now, and they greeted me by name — yet looked at me with a strange curiosity. I nodded, a silent show that I was okay, and they went on about their business serving the other guests.

"There's a table in the corner." Sherlock was on his leash by now, and Holmes guided him through the crowded bar to the empty table. Once we were settled in and had ordered a drink, Holmes turned to me.

"Now, tell me why someone attacked you."

As if Sherlock knew the cue, he lay down and rested his giant head on his front paws.

I had to make a quick decision to either trust this man named Holmes or avoid telling him the truth.

"Well, it all began last spring ..."

It was going to be a long night.

&* *&

Sherlock barked again and brought me back to the present.

"Get in here, big boy, before you get us both kicked out!" Wagging his tail, Sherlock bounded into the room like he had been lost from me for days. Plopping down on the extra twin bed, he looked very pleased with himself. I turned to shut the door when Holmes appeared in the doorway, startling me.

"And, just what makes you think I am going to let you in after you two abandoned me in the bar, leaving me to look totally insane to the staff and scaring me to death just now?" I was flustered, and I believe I got my point across, but all Holmes did was smile.

"I totally agree. We saw how the staff reacted, so we thought we would come by and explain it all to you in person. May I now come in? After all, you do have my dog."

"Oh, alright. But you can't stay long. I have a full day tomorrow with meetings..." I stopped myself, because my meeting concerned the treasures I was carrying around. I had little recollection of everything I had told him in the bar, so I played it safe and didn't mention them.

"I guess the meeting is about those little prizes you are carrying around in your black bag, huh?"

My face showed it all – disbelief, shock, betrayal. "And, Mr. Smartypants, how do you know this? Did Peter send you to fake an attack to steal the treasures, send in this big beautiful dog to rescue me, and send an angel to protect me?"

"Peter did not send me, the attack was real, you told me about the treasures in the bar, and I am an angel.

I was staring straight into Holmes' eyes, when suddenly it dawned on me.

"Oh, my goodness. Oh, my goodness. You are the man in the café window, the bus stop, the cathedral..." Surprisingly, the attack on the street was not the most shocking event of the night. This revelation was startling.

I had to sit down – or I should say I partially fainted on the bed. Sherlock was licking my face, and I was finally getting my breath back after that last statement sunk in.

"This just gets more bizarre by the minute," I said in curious exasperation. "An angel? I'm just supposed to believe you? What, I suppose Sherlock is an angel, too?"

"How did you guess? I was hoping to keep that a secret for a little while longer." Holmes was mocking me now, and all I could do was just sit there and shake my head.

Gaining my composure, I finally managed to say, "I think you better start from the beginning."

Holmes began. It was a lot to take in, so I just listened.

ॐ ✳ ॐ

"I have had many names. It all depends on who I am guarding. I am Holmes to you because you love a good mystery. Sherlock is with me because you have a big heart for animals, especially dogs.

You have been given the very special gift of being able to see angels. Normally, I would have introduced myself more formally before we had any significant interaction, but I'm afraid the attack forced my hand. I'm sorry this made you feel like you were losing your mind. I imagine it was very disorienting. That's why, after you fell asleep in the bar, I left the scarf behind as a sign that we are real to you, if not to anyone else.

For the moment, only you can see or hear me and Sherlock. That is why the barking didn't bring the hotel management, and why they didn't see us in the bar. Additionally, if we are carrying on a conversation in public, you will not appear to be talking to yourself. We will be communicating with our minds — our 'spirit' voice. So, the staff earlier didn't think you were crazy, and you handled it like a champ.

You are correct that I am the man in the homburg, and the one who left you the note in the catacombs. I began actively guarding you the moment you stepped out of the Mozarthaus Museum that day. You have been special all your life, Elizabeth, and when we saw Peter Schultz give you those Mozart treasures, a decision was instantly made to protect you, for we felt something wasn't quite right. Since then, I have been keeping an eye on Peter, Sophia, and several other key players you will meet soon — to gauge the level of danger.

Being an angel does not mean that I'm omniscient. Like you, I must also gather clues and information through means available to me, but I will share as much as I can, when I can. Keep in mind, though, I don't have the ability to give you all the answers you seek — I am here mainly to protect you in your quest and keep you on the right track. You must work this out for yourself. I have faith that you are clever and resourceful enough, and your journey will be as important as the answers you'll ultimately find.

So far, I have been able to determine that Sophia is Peter's girlfriend, and has been since right after she began working at the museum several years ago. They are working together as a team to steal the snuff box and miniature from you, sell to the highest bidder, and then take the money and disappear. Their end goal might seem straightforward enough, but there are still many questions about how many others are involved and who this mysterious benefactor is. I don't yet know who the benefactor is – and neither does Peter. That is one of the things you will need to find out, and it's one of the main reasons Peter has even bothered involving you instead of simply trying to run off with the artifacts. At least Peter was honest and got the gifts to you, but he and Sophia think you are a weak woman who can be duped easily. You should use that to your advantage.

They will try to charm you and keep you just close enough to trip you up. You should do your best to play along for now, but pay close attention to your surroundings at all times. They won't be acting alone. The broker you are seeing tomorrow will be sincere at your meeting, but I am unsure at this point if he is in with Peter and Sophia. I have my reasons to believe he is.

They have been avoiding you, but Peter and Sophia are in Copenhagen. Peter somehow knows your schedule. Do you post it on your website or something? Perhaps you should keep your travels private, and just tell your students until this all blows over. Warn Bradley not to answer any questions if anyone out of the ordinary calls to inquire where you are.

I won't be able to be by your side constantly, due to other obligations, but I'll never be far away. Sherlock is going to stay with you full time, to give you comfort and support – similar to what you might call a service dog. If you ever need me just call for me or send Sherlock.

One last thing I want to warn you about so you're not caught off guard: You occasionally will receive visions from the past relevant to this mystery. Visions are sometimes a more efficient way of communicating because they can convey so much more context than static documents alone. The clues from these visions will ultimately help you put all the puzzle pieces together. Sherlock will try to alert you that a vision is approaching – with a whimper, for example – so don't be alarmed.

As the old saying goes, *'don't be afraid, be aware.'* You are about to embark on a fabulous journey, but there will be many dangers and pitfalls to avoid along the way."

ȣ✳ȣ

Sherlock was resting his head in my lap. I felt such peace as Holmes was telling his story. Whether this is a dream or not, I believe what he is saying. Someone definitely tried to hurt me tonight — maybe even kill me — and they knew what I had in my bag. I am alive, unharmed, and I believe in guardian angels. I have believed all my life. So why change now?

"Holmes, or whoever you truly are, thank you for saving my life tonight — and potentially other times since Vienna that I might not have been aware of. I'm still trying to wrap my mind around all of this, but I feel much better knowing I have you and Sherlock on my side."

Holmes was watching me with Sherlock and smiling. Here I was, with a beautiful angel and a beautiful angel dog looking after me. I started crying and both looked at me with great concern.

"Don't worry — I am just thinking of my late husband and how happy he must be that I have you two protecting me. I am tired, and I hate to bring this slumber party to a close, but if I am going to be mentally prepared for my meeting in the morning, I need to sleep."

"I think sleep is exactly what you need at this point. I will take my leave. And if you don't mind, I won't pretend to use a human method this time. Remember — I will be nearby at all times." With that, in the blink of an eye, he was gone.

"Sherlock, big boy, it's just you and me now. Thanks for keeping an eye on me." With that, I turned out the lights.

Page 31

5

Peter and Sophia

"This is going to be too easy," Peter thought. He knew that Elizabeth was staying at the Phoenix. Her assistant was quick to give out her schedule when he called her office, and her website always conveniently noted when she was going to be away. Peter was quick to book a room at the same hotel once he found out, and he made airline reservations for himself and Sophia.

Ever since the benefactor's representative came to the museum last March asking him to find Elizabeth and deliver the Mozart treasures to her, Peter had been devising his scheme to get them back. When he first laid eyes on the miniature, he knew it was one-of-a-kind and worth millions. Before contacting Dr. Elizabeth Stone, he researched her completely. She was from a small town in Texas, received her undergraduate degree from a large Texas university, and then continued on to receive her master's and doctoral degrees in conducting. Sixtyish, active, not bad looking, recently widowed, a popular clinician around the United States, and well loved by all.

Peter kept his word and passed on the artifacts to Elizabeth. It pained him to do so, and he had become obsessed with getting them back. While they were in his possession, before he delivered them to Elizabeth, he would take them out and admire them several times a day. He would turn the snuff box and locket over and over in his hand, dreaming about the millions he would receive when he sold them. He already had a buyer, but the buyer wanted answers that he could not give him. These artifacts appeared to be completely off the grid, nowhere to be found in any historical documents. Who had them last? How did they acquire them, and at what price? How was Elizabeth related, and why did the benefactor want her to have them? Peter was so frustrated he couldn't find the answers, but he knew Elizabeth was the key, and that she would find out everything he needed to know. Since she lived alone, she would be easy to watch and easy to wear down. Her age played against her as well — what harm could a sixty-year-old do to a young man like him? Well, he still considered himself young at forty-five.

Peter hadn't originally planned on bringing Sophia onto the scene. A lovely young woman, they had become romantically involved after she began working at the Museum with him. He had tried to keep the fact that he had the artifacts a secret, but she barged into his office one day while he was admiring them. Gasping, she ran to his desk asking all sorts of questions, and he just couldn't lie — not when she was always so sweet to him when they were alone. At first, they hadn't really considered scheming to get them away from Elizabeth, but the more they talked, the more it grew into an elaborate heist. He couldn't wait for it to be over. They would then deposit the money into a Swiss bank account and head off to start a new life in a new country. He couldn't wait to be away from the museum — what a boring job! Little did the benefactor's representative know how he had changed Peter's life when he walked into the museum that dreary afternoon.

Peter remembered that day well.

⇛ ✱ ⇚

It had been a slow morning, which had started off with a great cup of coffee and a pastry, and now he was reading the news on his computer. His phone rang. "Yes, Sophia?"

"There is a gentleman here to see you. Says he has something important relating to Mozart that he needs to discuss with you. However, he won't tell me his name. Can I send him up?"

"Sure, go ahead." This happened all the time. People came in thinking they had priceless Mozart items that relatives had left in their estates or that they found in antique shops. Peter was always kind, always took them and researched them for authenticity, and sometimes the patrons were right — they had a Mozart treasure. From there he would ask if they wanted to donate them to the museum. Sometimes yes; sometimes no.

But, these transactions were never beneficial to Peter. Just a lot of work for a modest government salary.

A knock on the office door. Peter opened it to reveal a very well-dressed man carrying a leather briefcase. From head to toe this man looked like money. Lots of money.

"Come in. I am Peter Schultz, the curator of the museum. And you are...?"

"Nice to meet you. I have something to give to you and a request. I am merely the messenger, and that is all you need to know me at this time. May I sit down?"

The gentleman spoke impeccable German, and wasn't wasting any time on casual niceties.

"Please." Peter was shocked at the bluntness of the man in the expensive suit. He had piqued his curiosity, and his heart was pounding in his chest. "How may I help you?"

Peter watched as the gentleman took a small wooden box from his briefcase. Gently placing it on Peter's desk, he opened it with caution. Inside the box was a velvet pouch. Slowly pulling on the drawstrings to open the pouch, he lifted out a blue and gold snuff box. *A snuff box? That's what this is about?* The Museum had dozens of these that were displayed in a glass case with special lighting designed to show off all their details. However, the suited messenger then opened the box and lifted out an object that made Peter's pounding heart stop. It was a gold locket.

"Do you know what this is, Mr. Schultz? Of course you do, but do you know what is inside the locket?" He reached into his briefcase and took out a pair of white gloves. It seemed like an eternity before he had them on, making sure the material was wedged between each finger just so-so. Finally, he carefully opened the locket and turned it towards Peter.

Peter let out a gasp and said, "Marie Antoinette? Does this mean?"

"Yes, Mr. Schultz. It means that the young future Queen of France gave this to the young Mozart. Look at the engraving on the bottom of the snuff box."

The mysterious stranger handed Peter a pair of white gloves to put on before he handled the treasures.

Peter quickly put them on before he turned the snuff box over. His hands shaking, he saw for himself that Marie Antoinette's name was engraved on the bottom. Peter felt his heart in his throat now. Never had anything like this come across his desk, and he had seen a lot during his time at the museum.

"And may I be so bold to ask what it is you desire of me? Why have you entrusted me with this treasure?"

Before answering, the gentleman took the snuff box away from Peter. He placed the locket carefully back inside before placing the snuff box into the wooden box. Taking what seemed to Peter to be an eternity, the gentleman slowly removed his white gloves.

"I have been instructed to have you locate Dr. Elizabeth Stone, a Choral Professor at a university in Texas, and give this to her. My client has discovered that this legally belongs to her, and in order to retain his own anonymity, he feels it is wiser for the museum to contact her. I also have documents that verify these artifacts belonged to Mozart, identify this is Marie Antoinette's portrait, and give clues to why Dr. Stone is heir to the treasures. I will keep these, of course, but please be aware that I have them and will use them against you if any harm comes to Dr. Stone. You may quit drooling, Mr. Schultz. It isn't becoming for a gentleman in your position. I have an agreement you need to sign, verifying that you received the treasures and will deliver them to Dr. Elizabeth Stone within the next month. We are aware she is traveling here in the spring to give a concert at St. Stephen's — so we will be watching you."

Reaching back into his briefcase, the mysterious gentleman then retrieved a two-page document, which he checked over quickly before handing to Peter. He also drew a pen out of his inside coat pocket for Peter to use. Peter was convinced the pen was made from high quality gold, and took it gingerly out of the gentleman's hand. This was all so bizarre, but he complied without hesitation, knowing that any questions he asked concerning identity would be ignored. Taking a few moments to peruse the document himself, confident there was no funny business in fine print, he slowly signed his legal name – Peter Heinrich Schultz.

After Peter returned the document, the messenger looked to make sure Peter had signed his real name, and then stored the document back in its embossed folder. Tucking it into his leather briefcase before snapping it shut, he said, "Thank you, Mr. Schultz. It has been a pleasure doing business with you. Just remember – the delivery must be made while Dr. Stone is in Vienna this spring on tour. I suggest you try to contact her immediately. I trust you will put the treasures somewhere safe until then. We wouldn't want anything happening now, would we? I will see myself out."

With that, he stood, put forth his hand for a final gentlemen's handshake, and then moved towards the door.

Peter leaned up against the door as it closed behind him, staring at his desk where the small wooden box was sitting, uncertain if the past several minutes even happened or if it was a daydream.

He regained his composure and made a move to store the objects. Luckily, he had a hidden safe in his office that only he knew about. He would be putting the objects in there.

In fact, he had a second hidden safe in the office – a decoy of sorts – which he allowed others, including Sophia, to see him access. This kept Sophia feeling as though she was "in the know," but he always moved the best pieces to his private safe after she left the room.

Going to his bookcase, he pulled out the Sherlock Holmes novel, *A Scandal in Bohemia*, revealing a small wall safe with a combination lock. Entering the number combination, he opened his private safe and shifted some things around to make room for the new items.

Inside already was an assortment of jewels and other quaint pieces he had managed to pilfer from the museum without anyone ever knowing. Picking up his previous favorite piece, a diamond brooch owned by Mozart's mother, he sneered as he thought about what a trinket this was now that he had the new treasures. He picked up the new wooden box from his desk and opened it before putting it in the safe — *just one more glimpse before putting you away, my sweets!*

Settling in his comfortable office chair, he swung around to boot up his computer.

"Now, Dr. Elizabeth Stone — let's see what is so special about you."

There was a quiet knock at his door that he recognized as Sophia's. "Bitte."

Sophia came around to Peter's computer and began rubbing his shoulders. "So? What did this mysterious gentleman who came to visit you today want?"

A little annoyed that she was standing over his computer, he gently took her hand and turned to face her.

"A little research on some new Mozart treasures that evidently have been bequeathed to an American named Dr. Elizabeth Stone."

Taking the cue to stop invading his personal space, she walked around and sat in the chair facing him across his desk — the same chair that the well-dressed gentleman had just sat in. She could still pick up a hint of his cologne, which smelled expensive. Money, she smelled money. Settling more comfortably in the chair, she began to question Peter more about the visit. Sophia knew Peter couldn't resist her charms, for she rewarded him nicely whenever they were alone. By the end of the conversation, Peter had filled her in on several facts:

1. Dr. Elizabeth Stone had been willed some valuable Mozart artifacts.
2. Dr. Stone was coming on tour with her university choir in the spring. Peter was to contact her beforehand and then have her meet him at the museum to discuss the inheritance.
3. Dr. Stone was in her early sixties, widowed, and a well-known musician in the States.

What Peter didn't mention were the treasures. He wasn't sure he wanted to share them.

۶✳۷

Looking back on the day he received the treasures at the museum made him even more determined to get them back from Dr. Stone. He sincerely hoped this escapade would all end in Copenhagen. He turned to face Sophia, who was sleeping peacefully next to him in their comfortable room at the Phoenix.

"Tomorrow. I hope this all ends tomorrow," he whispered to himself to keep from waking Sophia.

6

A New Day in Copenhagen

I awoke to the sound of my alarm. When I opened my eyes, I was staring right into the face of Sherlock, who was staring right back at me.

"Good morning, buddy," I said, as I tussled his big head. His tail was wagging energetically, and I wondered if he had physical needs like earthly dogs. I sat up and put my glasses on to make sure I had set the alarm right.

My meeting was in a couple of hours, and I wanted time to enjoy the incredible breakfast buffet the Phoenix offered. I'd better get hopping. The Danes have wonderful breads and cheeses galore, so I planned on indulging a bit before heading home tomorrow. It had been a wonderful trip, seeing family and celebrating my brother's birthday.

Last night, after the party, I filled my brother in on what was going on. I needed to explain why I was spending the extra day in Copenhagen, especially since he was leaving town (traveling to his favorite Greek island, Lesbos). He was intrigued, wished me well in my search for the right answers, and promised to check his email regularly in case I needed his help. It was after our conversation that I left to get the fateful sandwich. I shuddered and rubbed the back of my head, remembering the attack. It all still seemed to be a dream — the attack, Holmes, Sherlock.

Hopefully, I would get some answers about the treasures when I met with the broker this morning. And then after my meeting with him, I plan to go in search of more information about the time Constanze and her second husband spent here in Copenhagen.

I felt a nudge and realized Sherlock was encouraging me to get out of bed and get moving if I wanted to enjoy the buffet. Putting my phone down, I swung my feet to the floor. This was a beautiful room with old world charm. Soft blues and gold trim, with furniture and wall art that was more Classical than modern. However, the girl in the painting above my bed appeared in the hall, the restaurant, the lobby — she followed me everywhere. Lately, however, I feel everyone is following me, so she is the least of my worries.

On with the make-up, and then choosing just the right outfit to greet my day. I chose to go business chic: a long black dress, smart cardigan, black boots, and a colorful scarf. I turned toward Sherlock, did a spin and said, "How do I look, big boy? Okay?"

Sherlock sat up and wagged his tail in approval of my outfit. He was ready to go and headed to the door. Grabbing my bag, I looked inside, as I always did, to make sure the large cosmetic bag was still in place – the one I had bought to hold and conceal the small wooden box holding the velvet pouch with the treasures. The black plaid scarf that was still in my bag reminded me that my frightful attacker was still out there somewhere. The red scarf Holmes left behind was nestled in the bag as well, giving me some reassurance. I have questions for Holmes when I see him next – if I am the only one who can see him and Sherlock, why did the attacker get scared away? And, how was Sherlock able to bring back the scarf?

Locking the door behind me, I gave an extra turn of the doorknob to make sure it was locked. When I turned around, I caught a quick glimpse of movement at the end of the hallway. Whoever it was ducked into a room before I could see them. I sensed it was probably Peter. *What a rat!* My heart might have skipped a beat if Sherlock had not been there, leaning on me to remind me he was there to support me. Instead, I felt empowered that I had backup in the case of trouble. My job – solve this mystery!

"Thanks, buddy, you're the best rat hunter ever. We are going to make sure that no one gets ahold of what's been entrusted to me!" I did take note of the room I thought I saw Peter slip into. He had a lot of gall requesting a room on the same floor. How did he plan on explaining that one to me? A chance trip to Copenhagen, and surprise – *"Hello, Elizabeth, what are you doing here?"* If that happens, I will just act surprised instead of letting on that I am fully aware of his and Sophia's antics to steal the Mozart treasures.

By this time, I was at the door of the restaurant, and my favorite waiter was approaching me with a big smile. "Good morning, Dr. Stone! Let me show you to a table – and as usual, coffee right away? "

"Yes, Jesper – coffee first." I had to keep track of all the Jespers at the hotel, as it was a very common Danish name. There were at least three I had met so far, but this Jesper had been the most attentive.

I was curious, after being seated, if Peter and Sophia would just casually stroll in, or if they had already eaten breakfast. Sherlock stayed outside in the corridor watching the entrance, and I could see his big head from where I was sitting. I made sure my back was not to the door. I took out my phone. In my notes, I found the address of the broker I was meeting today: Mr. Arthur Adderly, an independent art broker who was recommended to me by Peter – surprise, surprise. I had mentioned that I wanted to get the items appraised, and he didn't hesitate to give me Mr. Arthur Adderly's name and contact information. After my conversation with Holmes, I now know my meeting with Mr. Adderly is a set-up, but I will go and visit with him and act like I don't know they might be connected. He had an office on Nyhavn – convenient for me, as it was within walking distance of the hotel. And I was going to need to exercise after the feast I was enjoying!

I was savoring my last few sips of coffee when I saw Peter and Sophia come into the restaurant. I heard a faint "grr" from Sherlock when they walked in. Jesper greeted them, and as they followed him to a table, they saw me.

"Elizabeth?" Peter gasped as if it was the shock of the century to see me in a hotel where he knew I was staying.

"Peter? Sophia?" I answered as if I didn't already know they were staying at the same hotel and pretended we were shocked in the same century. "What a pleasant surprise to see you in Copenhagen! Vacation?" I said as I sheepishly winked, leading them on like I didn't know they were already an item.

When Sophia picked up on my wink, she made more space between her and Peter. *Come on,* I was thinking, *how stupid do you think I am?* I was definitely smart enough to lead them on, but I must not let my guard down. I especially felt that Sophia could be vindictive — she was in it for money, mostly, and was not going to let me get in her way. If my intuition serves me, I suspect Peter will probably ditch her when this is all said and done.

"Business," Peter said, as Sophia nodded in agreement. "Sophia was promoted to Historian at the museum, so she now accompanies me on business trips to document and record our new findings. Her research skills are also quite impressive, so I find her quite valuable to have with me on these types of trips."

Oh, come on, I'm thinking, *valuable in what manner? Historian?* What a bunch of malarkey. It took all my willpower not to throw in a couple of *"Bless your hearts!"* at this point in the exchange. I'm sure they sat in bed and scripted this meeting. *Okay, Elizabeth, play along.*

"Sophia, how wonderful for you! Congratulations! Well, I hate to run but I have somewhere to be. You will love the breakfast here. The Danes sure know how to do it right! Perhaps we can meet for a drink later this evening? In the hotel bar?"

"Unfortunately, we will have to take a rain check on the drink. We are taking the 16:00 — sorry, 4:00 afternoon train back to Vienna today via Berlin, where we also have business to do," Peter responded.

Sophia again was nodding in agreement like a puppet. She had not yet uttered one word to me, so I suspect she is gritting her teeth behind that fake smile and can't pry her mouth open.

Jesper was still waiting patiently by the table he had chosen for them, and pulled out the chair for Sophia when they finally walked away from my table. Such pleasantries they exchanged! I imagine when they see me leave they will sick their hounds on me.

I noticed Peter watching me when I picked up my bag, so I didn't make a big deal of it. He knew why I was in Copenhagen, so he knew the treasures were in my bag. I turned back to the table, taking one last swig of coffee before I waved goodbye to Peter and Sophia — just to be nice, of course. Jesper stopped to chat with me, bidding me a good day, and then I walked calmly to the door where my faithful Sherlock was waiting for me.

Walking one flight up to the lobby, I paused at the top of the marble stairs leading down to street level. I took my phone and pressed the home button to ask for directions.

"What can I help you with?" popped quickly up on the screen.

"Mr. Arthur Adderly, Nyhavn." Once the map was up, I pressed Start, and walked out into the street.

It was a beautiful fall morning. The city seemed to glow after the rain that had gently fallen during the night. The air smelled clean, but then, Copenhagen always smelled clean to me. I wanted to take it all in and go to the park instead of the meeting, but the navigation command, "Turn right and proceed down Bredgade," brought me back to reality.

Turning to the right, I noticed a man coming my direction from the corner to my left, and Sherlock growled as he leaned more into me. Mentally I began calling for Holmes, but before I had said his name he was by my side.

"Good Morning, Elizabeth. Keep walking toward your destination and don't look back. I have you covered. Peter and Sophia indeed have goons after you, but all they are doing is following you to keep you under surveillance. Their job is to report back. I don't think this one is the man who attacked you last night, so don't be afraid."

We continued up the street, and I kept my head held high while stepping cautiously on the cobblestones. I have a love-hate relationship with cobblestones as I get older. I love the old-world charm of them; I hate having to ice my knees down after a day of walking on them. When I was younger and traveling, I never had a problem with their unevenness. Oh the joys of aging.

Already on edge, my sensitive ears were on high alert today. It might drive my family, friends, and choir crazy because I hear everything, but it's also pretty hard for anyone to sneak up on me. Typically, I can even tell which of my colleagues has entered my choir room, just from the sound of their footsteps. Right now, behind me, I can hear footsteps getting closer and closer — and they don't sound friendly. Instinctively, I tightened my grip on my bag, sensing what was about to happen.

I saw Sherlock running ahead in the rain-filled ditches, drinking in as much as he could as he barreled along. I turned to tell Holmes what a crazy dog Sherlock was, but he was nowhere to be seen. I panicked, because I was alone with the footsteps getting closer and closer to me. I kept mentally calling for both, but Sherlock was now distracted by a standard poodle walking ahead of us. Where was Holmes when I needed him? I quickened my steps, but the cobblestones and a bum knee made it difficult to gain much speed. My thoughts returned to the attack last night, praying this was not the same person stalking me in broad daylight now. All I could hear now was the pounding of my heart.

"Hey! Watch where you're going, jerk!"

I turned to look, and the goon following me was completely wet. A car had sped past, splashing him with water from the street. I died laughing when I realized it was Holmes behind the wheel of the vehicle that had just splashed him! He had stopped and was brushing the water frantically from his suit. He should have worn a trench coat – I thought all goons did. He must have failed Goons 101.

Holmes was back, laughing. Sherlock, ignored by the finicky poodle, was once more beside me. His tail was wagging so hard it hurt my leg.

"Told you I had you covered!" Holmes was still laughing.

"Not before I about had a panic attack when both of you abandoned me! And since when could you drive a car?"

We continued the short distance to Nyhavn. Once again, the beauty of Copenhagen took my breath away as I turned left from Bredgade onto Nyhavn. Copenhagen is a gem of a city. I love visiting! Full of rich history but also vibrant new ideas, I love making new discoveries every time I visit.

I knew that odd numbered addresses were to my left with even numbers located across the canal. The address I was searching for was an odd number. The colors on the buildings were so vibrant after the rain, and the boats seemed to glisten as they gently moved along the canal. Locals and tourists were enjoying the outdoor café areas, some alone, some in groups, but all were starting the day off with a great cup of coffee. The tourists had their maps out charting their day, and the lines to buy tickets for the canal rides were already getting long. I detected several languages: German, French, Danish, Dutch, English... Catching a bit of the rhythm of each as I walked by made me smile — happy tourists chatting away with no cares in the world. I took in the contrast with my own appearance. Perhaps I looked to them like a lonely, aging American woman. Nothing could be farther from the truth.

My phone startled me when it called out, "In 200 feet, the destination is on your left." I stopped, turned to my left, and looked at where my phone had said my destination was. *A restaurant? He wants to meet me in a restaurant?*

Sherlock and Holmes both were staring at the restaurant with me: Holmes on my left, and Sherlock on my right. What a picture we made — if only others could see it.

"Elizabeth, be cautious," Holmes said as he continued to stare at the multi-storied restaurant. "We can't be sure this isn't a trap — that Peter and Sophia or other goons aren't lurking nearby."

"You're telling me... Are you going in or staying out?" I was clutching my bag and still staring at the restaurant, hesitant to go in just yet.

"Sherlock will guard the door. I will be roaming the restaurant, keeping guard and eavesdropping on conversations. I will signal to you if I see or hear anything out of the ordinary or dangerous to you."

Taking in a deep breath and letting it out slowly, I said, "Okay, I am going in." I felt a slight brush on my arm, a gentle touch from Holmes, as Sherlock started walking me to the door.

"Let me go ahead of you to make sure the coast is clear." Holmes swiftly disappeared, and within seconds I heard a knock from the upstairs window. Looking up, I saw Holmes giving me the signal that all was okay, and come on in. By doing that, I figured that Mr. Adderly was sitting by the window, and therefore Holmes was giving me a heads up where I would be sitting.

Stepping inside the threshold of the restaurant, I was greeted by the smell of fresh baked rye bread, fish, and the sweet aroma of coffee. For a moment, my senses took me away from the confrontation I was expecting with Mr. Adderly.

"Good morning. May I help you?" The hostess at the counter drew me out of my sensory trance, and I quickly turned to her, returning the greeting.

"A good morning, indeed!" followed by a nervous laugh — good grief where did that come from. I faked a cough, followed by a high-pitched, "I am meeting Mr. Arthur Adderly. Has he arrived here yet?" I cleared my throat, hoping it would settle my voice back down to its normal speaking tone. She was grinning and — oh my gosh — she thinks I am meeting him as a date!

I quickly replied, in my normal tone, "I have a business meeting with him, and I fear I am very early."

"Mr. Adderly has indeed arrived! He is seated at his favorite table upstairs by the window overlooking the canal. Follow me, and I will take you up."

The restaurant was quaint, with a cottage feel. Wood beams, chandeliers, and Danish memorabilia on the walls — beautiful plates and artwork that depicted earlier eras of Danish life. The stairs to the second floor creaked under each footstep. They were very narrow and made a sharp turn to the right. Luckily the handrail was sturdy, and I did my best to keep up with the waitress who was in much better shape than me. Once we got to the top of the stairs, the waitress, whose name badge read Alma, turned and escorted me to a cozy table by the window. It had a great view of the canal, and two candlesticks in the window. On the table was a bouquet of fresh flowers — but nothing compared to the gentleman sitting at the table waiting for me.

7

Mr. Arthur Adderly, Art Broker

Arthur Adderly was an Englishman who had moved from London to Copenhagen after falling in love with its charm during a summer vacation about 10 years earlier. Arthur had never married and was mostly content with his work, his art, and his research. Known among the expats for throwing great dinner parties, he lavished his guests with exquisite meals and desserts — all of which he had prepared himself. Also a wine connoisseur, he enjoyed exploring the wine-producing regions of Europe. He was partial to French wines from the region of Provence. He would travel there at least once a year, and he always came home with enough for several dinner parties.

Arthur loved classical music, especially Mozart and his contemporaries. He prided himself on being a Mozart expert, having researched and read every book he could find about the great musician. His music library contained an extensive collection of Mozart recordings. He often spent hours listening to his LPs — conducting from his comfy arm chair as he sang along. He even had a conductor's baton, with a magnificent, hand-carved handle. He liked to hold it with his thumb and index finger while spreading the other fingers delicately in the air. Oh, the ecstasy he felt when conducting a Mozart symphony! But his favorite was the *Requiem* — such haunting melodies, and mystery, in Mozart's famous last piece.

In fact, Arthur was such a Mozart fan that he even named his white Persian cat Stanzi — reportedly Mozart's nickname for his wife, Constanze. The cat called Stanzi would curl up in Arthur's lap and purr softly to the music, a perfect picture of queenly elegance. No wonder her breed was the favorite of Queen Victoria! Arthur acquired her when she was a kitten, and they had been together for 12 years now. Answering an ad he had seen in the *London Evening Standard*, he was enamored at first sight. They have been inseparable ever since that moment. Stanzi was always at the door greet him when he arrived at home, and she always seemed happy to sit in his lap and listen to Mozart for hours. Such a life for a cat!

❧✳❧

Arthur had graduated with an advanced art history degree from Oxford. For a time, he was a curator at the V&A — the Victoria and Albert Museum in London — a job he loved, as it enabled him to be surrounded every day by great art and interesting people. His favorite part of the job was meeting with donors and evaluating their gifts to the museum. He loved the pride they had in their collections and their dedication to sharing their art with the public.

However, he also wasn't getting any younger, and his tastes weren't getting any less expensive. One day, a donor made mention to him that he planned to donate his collection even though an art broker estimated it could fetch £5 million if he sold to private buyers. At the time, that was an awfully large sum for an art collection. Arthur silently thought about the fee a broker would make on that transaction. As soon as the donor left, Arthur decided he was going to make a career change. He went to work researching what it took to become an art broker. He was surprised to learn that he had most of the qualifications already — an art degree and the vast knowledge he had gained while working at the Victoria and Albert.

He began planning and networking right away — taking advantage of his experience and position at the V&A to gain access to exclusive events where he could quietly woo art galleries and individual collectors. He also reached out to up-and-coming artists who might be ready to work with an independent broker as a way to avoid high gallery commission rates.

It took about a year, but *finally* he was starting to see results from his hard work. He was happy with his clientele, and they loved his knowledge and charm. He knew they were happy as well because they referred new clients to him when they could. However, the rewards will still fairly modest.

Working with wealthy and influential people was very addictive for him. He grew even more accustomed to fine things — and the money it took to buy them. He was happy enough from day-to-day, but he was always on the hunt for the sale that would set him up for life.

❉

The phone rings.

"Hello?!" Arthur said into the phone, perhaps a bit too energetically, in his attempt to be heard over his Mozart recording. He fussed with the stereo remote, finally finding the mute button. Stanzi looked up at Arthur, annoyed when he shifted her.

"Mr. Adderly? This is Peter Schultz. I would like to meet with you and discuss some art I would like to sell. Do I have the correct Arthur Adderly?" The gentleman on the other end of the phone spoke with a German accent, but perfect English.

"You do have the correct Arthur Adderly, and I just might be available to assist you. Pardon me, Mr. Schultz, but do I detect a German accent? Are you currently here in London?" Arthur was sitting on the edge of his chair by now, and Stanzi was even more annoyed.

"Yes, actually. I was here on other business when I heard you might be taking on new clients. Is there a time in the next few days we could meet in person to discuss?"

The stranger on the other end of the phone was unaware that he was causing Arthur a great deal of excitement. A potential sale had just fallen through unexpectedly, so he hoped his luck was changing.

"Sorry, give me just a moment while I check my calendar..." Arthur said, loudly flipping the pages of a nearby schedule book so Mr. Schultz would think he had more appointments than he actually had.

"Here we go. It looks like Wednesday is open. Since it is an evening meeting, should we discuss the matter over dinner?" Arthur didn't invite clients into his home, and couldn't meet him at the museum, obviously, so he hoped that Mr. Schultz would agree to the dinner meeting.

"That will work, Mr. Adderly. Where shall I meet you?"

Arthur was so excited that he quickly stood up, forgetting that Stanzi was in his lap. Startled, she was hanging on to his pants leg for dear life and trying to climb her way up to his shoulder.

"There's a lovely Italian restaurant right behind the Victoria and Albert Museum — on Thurloe Place. I will make a reservation under my name for, say, 6:30 p.m.?"

"I look forward to our meeting, Mr. Adderly. I believe we have a bright future together. See you then."

Arthur heard the click on the other end indicating that Mr. Schultz had hung up, but he listened to the dead tone for a moment before placing his phone back on the cradle. Sitting down, Stanzi was thrown off his shoulders to the back of the chair, to which she finally voiced her opinion with a loud "meow!" Calming down now, Arthur realized he had terrorized poor Stanzi. He picked her up and placed her back in his lap. He stroked her head gently and kept telling her he was sorry.

"Stanzi, what did he mean, 'we will have a bright future together'? What is this Mr. Schultz bringing to the table on Wednesday?" Arthur had a good feeling about this meeting.

❧ ✳ ☙

Arthur and Peter had been in similar positions, each helping wealthy donors bequeath expensive gifts to museums. Likewise, they both had loftier goals in life — and weren't afraid to break the rules now and then to achieve them.

Peter was happy to stay on at the museum, for now, in order to keep a steady flow of potential targets. He got very good at determining if a donor was open to participating directly in the sale. Sometimes, all it took was a discussion about money over a nice meal. However, sometimes Peter had to take matters into his own hands — and into his own safe — in order to get what he wanted. It was a very fine line he had to walk, though. If a donor was committed to donating rather than selling, he didn't want to make them suspicious about his motives.

The downside to Peter's plan was that he never could get away with looting the really big or important items. Those would be missed from the museum or would be noticed too obviously in another private collection. He had to limit his plunder to small pieces or the occasional artifacts that didn't have clearly documented provenance. In other words, he was making some money — certainly enough to be comfortable — but not as much as he'd like.

Peter realized along the way that he needed a business partner to handle the covert transactions. He hadn't wanted to share his meager takings, but it was becoming harder and harder to do it alone. A former client had recommended a gallery in London he had worked with in the past on a "quiet" sale. Following up on the lead, Peter went to this gallery in London and spoke with the contact he'd been given. To his chagrin, she was hanging up her hat and getting out of the business. She did, however, drop the name of a man she had recently met at the opening of an exhibition. She said this sounded like his cup of tea and that he worked at the Victoria and Albert museum in his "regular capacity."

That afternoon, Peter wandered into the V&A in search of this potential broker. As he was admiring *Stonehenge*, an 1835 watercolor by the English artist John Constable, he heard a distinguished voice giving a very detailed description of a nearby painting to a small group of well-dressed philanthropists. He liked what he heard. This guy had charm and charisma, and he clearly knew his stuff. He noticed the name on the gentleman's official V&A ID badge: Arthur Adderly. It just so happened that he had heard that name from a certain London gallery owner only this morning.

Peter had a good feeling about this coincidence.

&❋&

That first meeting was about 10 years ago, not long before Arthur moved to Copenhagen. At that meeting, Peter proposed a business partnership: He would acquire Mozart artifacts and other art, by whatever means necessary, and Arthur would locate buyers and broker the sale of those pieces.

It was because of that successful meeting with Peter in the restaurant, nestled in a cozy corner of the Italian restaurant on Thurloe Street, that Arthur decided the best deals were made away from offices.

8

Brunch Extraordinaire

I was staring at a character from a movie, surely, as Alma seated me across from Mr. Adderly. A big round face to match his physique, a nicely trimmed mustache, hair slicked down, a brown tweed jacket with suede patches on the elbows, and a brown bowtie adorning his freshly pressed white oxford dress shirt. Standing as I was seated, he extended his hand to me warmly. I noticed on the coat rack behind him that a beautiful brown fedora hat was perched perfectly, waiting patiently to be placed back on Mr. Adderly's head. I was bit disappointed that it wasn't a bowler hat, for he reminded me of an aging Charlie Chaplin.

"Dr. Stone, a pleasure to meet you at last!"

I wasn't prepared for his articulate English accent.

"A pleasure to meet you as well, Mr. Adderly." I placed my bag cautiously in my lap, took my napkin from the table, popped it open and placed it over my bag. Not setting it down for a second — nope. Mr. Adderly is far too charming to be trusted.

Seeing a slight movement to my left, I looked over and saw Holmes holding up a cue card with the words **BE CAUTIOUS** written boldly so I could read without squinting. I laughed silently at his choice of materials — a cue card and marker? Looking back at him, he held up another one saying *HE IS IN ON IT.*

I still wasn't quite sure what others might see when I was interacting with Holmes. Realizing my movements might be conspicuous, and not wanting raise suspicions, I smiled pleasantly and said, "So, Mr. Adderly, are you originally from Copenhagen? I detect a wonderful English accent — London perhaps?"

"You are quite clever, Dr. Stone. Yes, London is my birthplace. I lived there until about 10 years ago when I fell in love with Copenhagen." With a confident wave of his hand, he summoned a waiter to our table.

"Ah, Mr. Adderly, your guest has arrived. Would you care for something to drink?" he asked as he poured me a glass of water. By the way he greeted him, I could tell the waiter was more than familiar with the eccentric Mr. Adderly. He must meet all his clients here. No overhead, how clever, and good for the restaurant.

"Coffee, please. No cream or sugar. Thank you. I am a cheap coffee date," I said with a nervous laugh, trying to lighten the conversation.

Both men gave an obligatory laugh before the waiter turned to go fetch my brew. I didn't get his name, but I wondered if he was another Jesper.

Smoothing the napkin in my lap, I continued my conversation with Mr. Adderly. I couldn't bring myself to call him Arthur — I didn't plan to get to know him on a personal basis.

"Well, your accent is delightful. And, I certainly don't blame you for wanting to move to Copenhagen — I fall in love with it more every time I visit. I was thankful you were available to see me on this visit."

The waiter appeared with my coffee — smelling freshly brewed and served in a beautiful blue china cup. I wanted to hold it up and look on the bottom to see its maker, but kept my cool as I said a polite thank you. I knew without looking that it was Blue by Royal Copenhagen, and I knew the pattern was Blue Fluted Plain. The first day I was here, I had some free time before dinner and had gone shopping. I spent a lot of time looking at this exact pattern in one of the shops near the Phoenix. Now that I am seeing it set on the table, I think I'll go back and buy a set of eight to have shipped home. I loved the high handle, and the fluted sides felt comforting in my hand.

I was anxiously anticipating the part of our conversation about my treasures, but the warm coffee gave me a little confidence. When I took my first sip, I glanced back over to Holmes. This time the cue card read: *LOOK AT THE OTHER CUSTOMERS' COFFEE CUPS*.

I made a casual look around the room with that sip. *What?!* No one else in the restaurant was drinking their coffee from a Royal Copenhagen Blue Fluted Plain porcelain cup except for Mr. Adderly and me! The goons. The goons reported back to him after they saw me shopping yesterday afternoon! *He's trying to impress me*, I thought, so I decided to play along with it.

"I love Royal Copenhagen china! This pattern is very special to me. My mother had a set of cups that she purchased on a visit here back in her younger days, and she willed them to me when she died. I have my coffee every morning in one of them." I took another small sip so as not to dig myself deeper into the story. My mother is probably shaking in her urn now with this little white lie.

I saw Mr. Adderly grin sheepishly, implying he was pleased with himself, and probably thinking, "I have her now."

"Are you ready to order, or do you need more time with the menu?"

Our waiter wasn't another Jesper after all. His name was Kristoph, according to his badge. Clean cut, young, tall like so many Danes, and very blonde. His thin black tie was meticulously tucked in his white apron which was tied perfectly at his waist. Nothing was out of place.

Hmm..., I thought. Usually waiters had some bit of food on their aprons or some other sign they had been working around food. *Oh, another cue card!* It read: **HE IS ADDERLY'S ASSISTANT, SO BE CAREFUL.**

"I had a huge breakfast at the hotel before I came. Could I see a dessert menu? Or, perhaps you could just tell me what you have?" As I grinned my most charming smile, I added, "preferably chocolate."

"Our desserts vary from day-to-day. Let me go and check with the chef to see what the specials are today. In the meantime, let me refresh your coffee." I noticed he glanced at Mr. Adderly as he was leaving, looking for guidance in his eyes. "And you, sir? Will you have your regular lunch today, or would you care to look at the menu?"

Adderly had been silent during all of this. I could tell he was getting antsy to get the chit chat out of the way and get down to business.

"I will have my regular, Kristoph. Dr. Stone, I am very curious about your Mozart items — your email intrigued me immensely."

"You come highly recommended to me by Mr. Peter Schultz at the Mozarthaus Museum in Vienna. Have you met him?" I was curious to watch his reaction when I mentioned Peter's name, but Adderly was good.

He must have taken acting somewhere along the line to keep such a straight face.

"Only through email," he quickly replied. "He found me online and has recommended me to several of his clients who choose to sell their art instead of donate. I have tried several times to meet up with him when I travel to Vienna, but our paths never cross. He is a very busy curator."

"Oh, I am not interested in selling my items, Mr. Adderly." This time I got a reaction. My turn to stir the pot. "I am interested only in authentication and finding out who wanted me to have them and why." I looked him straight on as I said all of this, and it took everything he had within his power not to overreact to this news.

"I see," he calmly said, putting his elbows on the table and clasping his hands together, nervously twiddling his thumbs. "I was under the impression from Mr. Schultz that you wanted to speak with me about potential buyers. It sounds as though you have had a change of mind somewhere along the way?"

"I am so sorry if you have been misled, Mr. Adderly. I don't believe I ever mentioned to Peter why I would like to talk to an art broker. These items were given to me in trust to preserve — not to sell for individual gain. I want to solve a mystery, not get rid of one. Surely you understand, Mr. Adderly? I thought everybody loved a good mystery."

I picked up my coffee cup to take a victory sip, and looked over to see Holmes' latest cue card: **WELL DONE! ELIZABETH: 1, ADDERLY: 0.**

Kristoph showed up with my pastry and Adderly's sandwich, but I fear he has lost his appetite. Feeling empowered but cautious, I continued. "I certainly intend to pay a fee for your services, and who knows — maybe once I have all of the clues in place things will change. I feel like the first thing I need to know is whether these heirlooms are real or fake. There are so many shops in Vienna that sell replicas of Mozart's snuff boxes, but this is the first I have ever heard of a locket."

Adderly was eating like it was his last meal, taking tiny bites and chewing them ever so slowly, which led me to think I was either making him extremely nervous or he was furious at Peter and trying to contain himself. Perhaps he's gritting his teeth so hard he can't swallow. At least he is a gentleman and is keeping his cool. We continued in silence for a moment before he finally spoke.

"I totally understand, Dr. Stone, and I admire you for not wanting to sell. I honestly wish all my clients had the passion for understanding the master behind the art before trying to profit. If what Peter told me is true, the locket is indeed rare – and the two items together would bring millions."

"I would have retirement made for sure," I smiled. He surprised me by busting out in a hearty belly laugh, which got me tickled, but also quickly got everyone in the restaurant looking our way. We cleared our throats at the same time, stifling our laughter, making me think that in another time and a different situation, we could become friends.

"So would I, Dr. Stone, so would I! Oh well, I appreciate your total honesty and that you didn't lead me on until the ticket arrived!" He winked, and I took that as my cue that this meal was on me now.

Kristoph came and cleared the table, poured me some fresh coffee, and brought Adderly his hot tea. Now that the table was cleared, I suspected the next item on the agenda was looking at the snuff box and locket. The weight of my bag on my lap had been comforting, but I anticipated his next move.

"Dr. Stone, is it at all possible for me to see the items now? If you want a clear picture of what you possess, I do need to examine them."

Unbelievably, he reached into his briefcase and pulled out a velvet cloth as well as hand sanitizer. Clearly a professional, prepared for every situation. He reached across the table and offered me the hand sanitizer. Smooth move.

I looked over to Holmes for guidance, but he was nowhere in sight. *You've gotta be kidding me. Where is he now?* Obviously, there were going to be times when he is not around, but I don't know how I felt about his timing. This was on me now. I had to learn to trust myself.

While I kept my left hand securely on my bag, I extended my right hand toward Adderly. He squeezed a dime-size blob of hand sanitizer onto it. No scent — just a clean alcohol smell. I quickly rubbed my hands together. The thought suddenly crossed my mind: *What if this is drugged, giving Adderly the perfect opportunity to run off with the goods?* I reassured myself: *Faith. Trust. Keep my mind. Stay on script.*

In the meantime, Adderly had put on pristine white gloves and was smoothing the velvet cloth onto the table in front of him. His patience was wearing thin as he waited on me to retrieve the objects. He must have smoothed out the velvet cloth at least five times while I stalled. Only Peter, Sophia, and I have seen the snuff box and locket in person, so this was a huge leap for me to show them to a man I had barely met — and a conniving art broker at that.

Finally, after what seemed an eternity, I opened my bag while it sat on my lap. But, before I could reach inside, I saw a flash out of the corner of my eye. Holmes was back; this time holding a gigantic cue card. *BE CAREFUL. GOONS IN THE HOUSE. TABLE TO YOUR LEFT.*

I looked, and sure enough, there was the man I'd encountered on the street earlier — the one who had been doused with gutter water. He was having lunch with a woman who looked as if she could be Sophia's sister. They were engaged in a lively conversation, acting as if they were long-lost lovers getting reacquainted. A chill went through my body, and I realized I had two choices. 1) Lie about having the items with me, or 2) Trust that Holmes really did have my back. I looked at him and saw that he was closing in on the Goon Table for Two, so I took a leap of faith and went with my option number two.

Cautiously, I lifted out the cosmetic bag and then removed the wooden box that had been hidden there. Slowly, I moved it onto the velvet cloth, but had not taken my hands off it. Adderly was tapping his fingers on the table in anticipation, a habit I always found annoying in people. At least with his gloved hands, the tapping was silent and less annoying. *Focus, Elizabeth.*

Before I let go, I heard a loud scream from the male goon at the next table. "How can you be so careless?!" He was screaming at Kristoph, who looked horrified that he had poured hot coffee in the goon's lap. He was standing now, wiping furiously with his napkin and dipping it in the cold water so the coffee wouldn't stain his suit. "First, I get anointed in the street with dirty rain water, and now this incompetence! Come on, we are leaving. Get your things, Karina."

Poor Karina was mortified. She dug through her purse to find some kroner to leave on the table to pay the bill, and then she quickly left to catch up to the male goon. Before she descended the stairs, however, she paused and caught my eye. It was as if she was warning me to be cautious. Then, just as quickly, she disappeared down the stairs.

Kristoph looked bewildered, wondering how in the world the coffee he was carrying so carefully had ended up in the man's lap. If only he could have seen Holmes give him a gentle shove, he would have understood. Holmes was laughing, holding up another cue card: *GOONS: 0, HOLMES: 2.*

I still had not taken my hands off the box. I couldn't seem to move them, feeling almost frozen in time as I watched Holmes causing the coffee commotion. He finally gave me a thumbs-up. Now I knew what would have happened. The moment I turned the box over to Adderly, the goon would have distracted us and stolen the box. *What a scam!* He and Peter needed to hire a new goon — this one was too OCD about his clothes. They must have him on a tight budget.

I needed to decide quickly now: either let go of the box or take it back. Holmes had moved directly behind Adderly, so I let go. When I looked in Adderly's eyes, I detected a bit of disappointment that the Great Goon Caper hadn't gone as planned. It was a lame plan anyway, as I would have put up a fight, with or without Holmes.

"Mr. Adderly, I trust you to inspect the treasures in this box with dignity and respect. All I want from you is verification that they are indeed authentic so I can continue in my quest to find the truth."

"Of course, Dr. Stone. Why would you expect anything else? I am respected in my field and wish to stay that way."

By this time, he was salivating and wringing his hands, eager to behold what was inside the antique wooden box. I was sad that I couldn't trust him enough to ask the many historical questions I had — questions he might well have been able to answer. But, perhaps by seeing the treasures, he would inadvertently share some of the information I seek.

Adderly gently reset the wooden box on the velvet cloth in front of him, so the interior would face him when he opened it. He opened the latch, revealing the blue velvet pouch within. The box itself was lined in black velvet, and the blue looked striking against it. Loosening the drawstring on the pouch and reaching inside, he let out a small gasp as he gingerly exposed the snuff box. I kept my eyes on his hands, fully expecting another goon to appear out of nowhere to steal the objects I've been protecting.

"My dear Dr. Stone," he said breathlessly, "you do indeed have one of the rarest snuff boxes I have seen to this date. In fact, I have never even seen one as exquisite as this."

He took his gloved hands and lifted the snuff box out of its cradle as if it were a fragile newborn being exposed to the world for the first time. Interestingly, he lifted it above his head. This made me smile because I saw the same twinkle in his eyes that I see in my granddaughter's when she experiences something beautiful for the first time.

"Authentic, madam. Authentic beyond words. Empress Maria Theresa had a special seal that her jewelers and craftsmen used — and here it is, engraved right on the bottom of the box! I have only seen it one other time, on a jewelry box that a client had inherited. Very, very rare, Dr. Stone."

Adderly tilted the snuff box and let me see the engraving. I had seen the mark before now, when inspecting the items in private, but I was curious to see what new information he might share.

"See — there is the crown, and the stars represent all of her children. You know that she was a very fine politician who strategically married her children to leaders of the world so that Austria would remain well positioned? A very wise ruler. Ahh, and there is Marie Antoinette's name as well!" Adderly was giddy telling me this, delighting in holding a piece of history.

"Fascinating!" I exclaimed and leaned closer, even though I knew some of this already. Leaning in also allowed me to be closer to his hands in case he tried any more funny business.

"Mr. Adderly, I fear you should set the snuff box down before you open it to see the real treasure inside." I was holding my breath, unsure what reaction he would have to the locket.

Holmes had both hands on the table by now, leaning in closer to Adderly. We both held our breath as Adderly lowered it to the table.

I spoke softly, "The latch is fragile, so please be careful." I know I probably offended his professionalism with the comment, but I was protecting my interest. This next step is crucial – the moment he sees the miniature of Marie Antoinette inside the locket.

Carefully he lifted the lid to the snuff box. It was as if time had stood still again – for the second time in this meeting. Finally, there it was: the locket.

Silence.

Adderly was completely silent, and his gaze was locked on the locket. His hands shook as he picked it up and placed it gently in his gloved left palm. He lifted his right hand to his mouth and, one-by-one, removed each finger from the glove using his teeth to help. He then placed the glove on the velvet cloth he had laid out. His hand was shaking even more now, but I didn't bring that to his attention. I merely said, "Exciting, yes?"

He looked up at me with eyes glazed over, as if I had just awakened him from a wonderful dream.

Having trouble finding his voice, he finally managed to squeak, "More than exciting, Dr. Stone – this is a highlight of my career being able to see this magnificent work of art in person."

He truly was ecstatic; but, as I suspected, he seemed to have prior knowledge of what was inside the locket. No doubt about it, Peter had informed him. In my communication with Adderly, I had never mentioned the miniature, just the snuff box and locket. Holmes and I turned to each other, noses almost touching, both lifting our eyebrows in an *Aha!* expression.

He was still sitting with his eyes transfixed on the locket in his left hand. Finally, he slowly set it down on the velvet cloth and removed his left glove. I was beginning to think it would be dinner time before Adderly opened the locket.

I thought the man was going to have a heart attack when at last he saw the miniature. He started crying! Not just a tear trickling down his cheek — no, he started sobbing! Good Lord, he is going to get the locket wet, so I touched his arm to bring him back to reality.

"Mr. Adderly, the locket has survived hundreds of years. Let's don't let the tears of a happy man be its demise."

He burst out laughing and kept muttering "Oh my!" over and over again, shaking his head from side to side. At last, he cleared his throat in an attempt to dignify himself again.

"Dr. Stone. If you ever do decide to sell, I will sell all my belongings to purchase this rare gem from you! You have in your possession what I believe to be one of the earliest and finest miniatures of Marie Antoinette I have ever seen or read about. It's also been incredibly well preserved. Do you know the artist?"

"I believe I do, thanks to an internet search — but what are your thoughts? You are the art expert, after all."

Still in a daze, Adderly finally took his eyes off the miniature and looked me square in the eyes. I got a chill up my spine from that look, for I saw a man with a mission in mind: he wants this miniature.

"I do, Dr. Stone, I do. Jean-Étienne Liotard. He was born in Geneva in 1702, and was trained first of all as a miniature painter. Pastels were his hallmark, and his nickname was 'the Turkish painter' after living in Constantinople for four years. Lord Byron even had him paint a portrait of him in Turkish clothing. A very interesting character, indeed. Maria Theresa had him paint the Imperial family in 1742, and loved him so much that she invited him back in 1762 to paint them again. Remember,

Marie Antoinette was the 15th child of the Empress, so she was about 7 in this picture. But, this miniature is not the one that Liotard is famous for. I have never seen this one. Never. Seen. This. One. So, do you know what that means, Dr. Stone? "

"If this isn't the one the world knows about, then why are you certain that Liotard is the artist of this miniature?" Adderly was now piquing my curiosity.

"The style is the same," he replied, "sanguine and black chalks, graphite pencil, watercolor and pastels on white paper. Realistic and masterful details surrounded by a very naturalistic glow. His style is in distinct contrast to Martin van Meytens, the Imperial Painter for the Empress Maria Theresa. Van Meytens portraits of Marie Antoinette and the imperial family were a bit more idealized and the color choices tended to be more vivid against darker backgrounds."

Adderly was on a roll, and my mind was jumping in all directions with questions about the locket. For obvious reasons, I had decided not to voice these questions, but to research them on my own. I decided now was the time for me to make excuses and leave.

"Mr. Adderly," I said quietly, so as not to jolt him out of his stupor. He was still staring at the miniature. "I am afraid I need to leave now, as I have some other obligations to attend to before my flight home. You have been most informative and helpful. You have covered all the questions I had for you today."

Realizing my words, Adderly finally began acting more like himself. "Of course, Dr. Stone. I know your time is valuable. Please, please, let me know if you change your mind about selling. It was lovely to meet you, and it was a tremendous pleasure to be in the presence of such a wonderful work of art."

He began gently closing the locket and laying it on the velvet cloth. Putting the pristine white gloves back on his delicate hands, he placed the locket back in the snuff box. The final step of putting the two items back into the wooden box seemed to drag on — as if he didn't want to let go of this moment. My eyes stayed glued on him the whole time, and I was getting a bit antsy by the time he let me pick up the wooden box with all the items. I was leaning on my elbows, which were perched on the table, and my legs were jiggling so hard that the table was shaking. I was so glad when I had everything back in my possession, back in my bag, and away from the criminally greedy Mr. Adderly.

Kristoph suddenly appeared from somewhere, which refocused my attention my physical surroundings. I noticed my guardian had changed positions in the room as well. I asked Kristoph for the bill, much to Mr. Adderly's protest, but I knew he had this down to a delicate art. He kindly accepted and thanked me as I handed Kristoph cash for the meal. "No change, Kristoph. You were wonderful," I said as I rose from my chair. Adderly stood as I did, but made no move to gather his things or walk out with me.

He reached out to shake my hand, but I offered just half an arm since I was clutching my bag to my chest. I wasn't taking any chances here. Grab the bag, you get the girl, too! Kristoph made a polite bow-type gesture as I began to make my way down the stairs to the main floor. I looked over at Holmes, and he shooed me on — letting me know he was going to observe Adderly after my departure.

9

The Aftermath

Kristoph quietly sat down in the chair Dr. Stone had occupied during the brunch. Adderly mopped his forehead with his handkerchief, making large dramatic motions as he did so, before folding his arms on the table and dropping his head down sobbing.

"Mr. Adderly, I know you're disappointed that Dr. Stone does not want to sell the locket and snuff box, but surely you know that this is not over yet, right? You and Peter will find a way to convince her that she needs to sell, and then you will have the locket and a profit." Kristoph was speaking softly, at about the same dynamic as Adderly's pitiful sobs. He had not ever seen his boss like this, and he had been employed by him since he came to Copenhagen ten years ago.

*

Kristoph had been struggling to make ends meet with odd jobs when one night he met Adderly a local restaurant where he was bartending. Adderly sat at the bar, drinking a significant amount of chardonnay and talking freely about his art dealings. Kristoph listened, and when the opportune moment came, he asked if Adderly needed an assistant or body guard. Adderly got very excited and handed him his personal card.

The next day, he ventured to Adderly's very nice apartment to discuss the matter. By the end of his visit, he was Adderly's assistant — surely helped by the fact that Stanzi immediately took a liking to Kristoph. The title of assistant covered the duties of chef, butler, body guard, chauffeur, and any other job Adderly needed him to do. He was paid well, and he enjoyed the day-to-day adventures he and his odd boss shared. But, above all else, Kristoph appreciated that Adderly had always been an optimist who tried to find every silver lining.

*

Adderly finally looked up and mopped his face again. "I know, Kristoph, I know. I was just hoping we would be able to convince her right away. She is a very smart lady, and we will be fortunate if she changes her mind. I have my doubts."

Kristoph gently patted his boss's arm to reassure him that all would be fine. He said he would make sure of it.

Holmes sat on the windowsill and listened to these two oddly paired men talking – Adderly, an eccentric English gentleman, and Kristoph, a very fit Dane. Holmes was curious how Kristoph would make Dr. Stone change her mind, so he decided he needed to watch him very carefully. With the growing list of people after the treasures, Holmes was determined to keep Elizabeth safe.

10

Small World

The fresh air washed over me as I stepped outside the restaurant, clearing away the heaviness that had surrounded me inside with Adderly. The rain had left the air crisp and clean, and it reminded me to breathe. However, I had only made it a few steps before a chill set in. Adderly, Peter, Sophia, the goons... *Was that the end of the list, or were there more adversaries I had yet to meet? Who else was waiting for me?* I tightened my scarf and buttoned my coat. Suddenly I felt Sherlock's warmth as he pressed up against me in a sign of reassurance. A welcomed relief. I had not seen him when I first entered the street.

I found a bench along the canal and sat for a moment to consolidate my mental notes. I now knew:

1. Adderly and Peter were partners.
2. Sophia was in on the escapade, but in what capacity? And, what was she holding over Peter in order to be a part of the team?
3. Kristoph worked for Adderly, but I wasn't sure of his job description. He appeared to be very loyal, yet very protective of his eccentric boss.
4. Adderly and Peter had several goons following me. Who could I trust now?
5. I definitely was not going to let go of the snuff box and the locket — not for anyone — but how safe was I if I was carrying them? I shuddered as I remembered the goon who tried to strangle me just last night. My attacker last night seemed very different from the other goons I'd encountered.

Deep in thought as I recalled recent events, I was brought back to reality when I heard someone call my name.

"Elizabeth? Dr. Elizabeth Stone?"

Standing before me in utter surprise was Dr. Benjamin Watson, a world-renowned choral conductor from Boston, and my very dear friend.

He is also a Mozart expert. *Good grief*, I thought, *I have Sherlock, Holmes, and now Watson?*

"Benjamin! What a surprise to see you here in Copenhagen!"

I immediately stood and hugged him tightly, the type of hug you reserve for your closest friends. Plus, it was just so good to see a familiar face at that moment.

Benjamin had been my friend and mentor when I studied at Oxford several years ago, where I was getting my doctoral degree. We had stayed in communication all these years, but even more so after I became a widow unexpectedly two years ago. Benjamin had phoned, invited me to Boston to regroup after my loss, and had treated me like a queen. A widower himself, he knew how to guide me through my grieving process. However, I had been so preoccupied with this new adventure that I hadn't called him in a while, so I was truly surprised to see him on the streets of Copenhagen! He looked handsome today in his black overcoat with his perfectly tied plaid scarf.

We both started asking questions at the same time, then burst out laughing with delight at running into each other.

"You first, Elizabeth — what are you doing in Copenhagen? Why didn't you tell me?"

"Oh, Benjamin, I am so sorry. I have been busy at school, I was helping my brother with some details for his party here, and I knew you were on your European tour. I leave tomorrow. Now you — what are you doing in Copenhagen?"

He smiled that million-dollar smile that was splattered all over the magazines. He suggested we grab an outdoor table at the restaurant that was just behind us. Before I knew it, we had two very good-looking cappuccinos in front of us, and we were both talking a mile a minute.

It seems his tour ended in Amsterdam the night before, but instead of staying there, where he might encounter fans and reporters, he took a very early morning flight to Copenhagen. He had just checked in at the Phoenix, his favorite hotel in Copenhagen, and was enjoying his walk along Nyhavn.

"You cannot believe what a sight you are for these sore eyes, Elizabeth! This tour was successful, but very tiresome — 8 different cities in 12 days. All the concerts were sold out, and the reviews were kind, but I am exhausted. You of all people understand how emotionally draining, yet exhilarating, conducting can be. It stirs your soul, but also empties you. I came to Copenhagen to refill my tank!"

I had set down my cup when he mentioned the Phoenix. "Benjamin, I am staying at the Phoenix as well! That is where I stay every time I come to visit my brother. It's a lovely hotel — charming, great staff, very close to city center. I am so glad you are here. I have so much to tell you, and I actually need to pick your brain about a few things."

Sherlock was nudging me. I was so excited to see Benjamin that I had forgotten my beautiful canine companion was with me. I scanned the area for Holmes, whom I found seated at the next table. He was giving me two thumbs up about Benjamin. I was so relieved that Benjamin was the real thing. I'm not sure I could have handled it if he had been in cahoots with Peter and Arthur.

Benjamin's ears perked up when I mentioned I needed to pick his brain. His knowledge of Mozart will be a real asset to my research efforts, but we had so much to catch up on that the topic was buried in conversation for the moment. I was anxious to hear about his tour, his choir, the cities he visited, as well as his repertoire. He asked me questions about my tour last spring in Vienna, my current school year, and my repertoire as well. It's such a nice feeling to have that mutual understanding that comes from having similar careers.

Caught up in the conversation, I lost track of time. I glanced at my watch. *How did it get that late already?!*

"Benjamin, I have one last matter of business to attend to today. Would you like to come with me? You might find this interesting. If you are busy, I totally understand."

Piquing his interest, Benjamin set his cup down immediately, replying, "Nothing would please me more than going on an adventure with you." He raised his hand to get the waiter's attention, and paid the bill as I stood to gather my things.

Still not knowing who to trust, I looked around to see if Sherlock and Holmes were scouting Nyhavn for trouble. Sherlock nudged my hand, appearing from out of nowhere. Holmes was standing with his back to the canal scoping the crowd. I instinctively felt Benjamin was on my side and totally unaware of my inheritance, but I was going to step cautiously into the story with him as it unfolded.

We began walking towards the corner, where I could hail a taxi. One pulled up to the curb, and Benjamin opened the door for me as I gave the driver the address.

"Lavendelstræde 1, please."

As we set off, Benjamin immediately began asking where we were going and why. Our destination was not far, and we probably could have walked, but I didn't want to risk meeting any goons along the way or put Benjamin's life in danger. As I looked out the front window of the cab, I nearly cracked up. It was all I could do to keep my composure. Sherlock and Holmes were both sitting on the hood of the cab — like hood ornaments! Funny as it was, it was also touching to see Holmes' arm around Sherlock. I reminded myself to take Holmes and Sherlock to NYC sometime.

In an effort to contain my laughter, I turned away from the amusement of watching my guardians and towards Benjamin to explain where we were going.

"We are going to the residence where Constanze Mozart and Georg lived here in Copenhagen. I am curious to see if it still exists in its original state or if something else has been constructed there."

"And why, Elizabeth, must you know this?" Benjamin quipped. "I knew she and Georg resided here from 1810-1824, but why so interested? I thought they led a peaceful and quiet life here."

"I know, I know, but I just want to cross it off my bucket list. I know so much of Mozart's history, but I also know that Constanze was instrumental in getting his music organized and published after his death. The world owes a lot to her, so I just want to see where they lived before moving back to Salzburg. Did you know some have speculated that Georg was Mozart? That his death was faked in Vienna so that he could escape the political scene?"

"Mozart has had a lot of historians rewrite his history," Benjamin said. "If only we could travel back in time to see the man behind the world's most beloved music. And, I do admire Constanze and all her hard work. Behind every great man there is a woman. Just think about Napoleon and the sacrifice Josephine made. At least he didn't have her beheaded like Henry VIII did when his wives didn't produce a male heir."

We were nearing Tivoli Gardens, which was outside the city walls when it was first built, and I knew Lavendelstræde was close to this famous amusement park. It was also right around the corner from Grand Teatret (The Grand Theatre) — one of the oldest cinemas in Copenhagen.

"I have yet to visit Tivoli," I sighed. "I want to come at night and see the lights. I hear it looks like a fairy tale. You know Hans Christian Andersen visited many times. I wonder if it influenced his writings. And, Walt Disney, one of my heroes, fell in love with Tivoli and was inspired by its magic when he built Disneyland."

I was lost in thought when Benjamin said, "Do you want to go tonight? I hear Tivoli in October is fun and enchanting."

"Seriously?" I jerked my head around towards him and quickly said, "Yes!" I started talking a mile a minute and Benjamin was laughing at my exuberance. I could see the taxi driver smiling at us in his rear-view mirror.

We were interrupted as the taxi pulled up to the curb, indicating that we had arrived at our destination. I insisted on paying the driver, and I couldn't help but notice that Sherlock and Holmes were already scoping the neighborhood. I wouldn't put it past Peter's goons to be nearby.

Two male pedestrians were approaching us as we walked away from the cab. One of the men bumped into Benjamin, and I felt someone grab at my purse. I held on with all my might and shoved him really hard with my elbow. This seemed enough to send him on his way for now.

I was glad to see Sherlock following them down the street. The giant dog nudged one of them with his nose, pushing him forward. He lunged forward from the force, falling flat on his face. His partner reached down to help him up, but Holmes, right behind him, pushed him forward as well, causing the two would-be perpetrators to fall all over each other instead. The scene they created was comical, and passersby were snickering as the two tried their best to cover up the fact that they had just fallen. They were arguing, blaming each other for the fall, creating even more of a scene. Peter would not be happy knowing the goons that he hired always ended up looking like clowns.

"Well, that was rude," I said as I brushed off my coat.

"What was that about?" Benjamin uttered as he straightened his wool coat.

Since I'd just had another attempted theft, I decided here on the street was not the time to tell Benjamin the whole story.

"So, this is where Constanze and Georg lived..."

Lavendelstræde is just inside the old Western gate of the city. Copenhagen was walled at the time, which meant Constanze and Georg lived within the walls. In fact, until later in the 1800s, no one lived outside the walls.

I looked at the building, which I suspect had been remodeled, but it still held most of its charm from the 1800s. I imagined Constanze and Georg organizing manuscripts and beginning their talks of writing Mozart's biography. I wondered what the neighborhood was like then. They had moved to Salzburg in 1819, but Tivoli didn't open until 1843. Curiosity would lead me to research this, but for now, I just wanted to see the area and get a feel for their time here in Copenhagen. I wish there had been a plaque on the outside saying "Constanze Mozart Nissen Lived Here."

Benjamin broke my concentration. "Elizabeth, is there something you're not telling me? This is interesting, but why do you want to know more about Constanze?"

Holmes had come back and was giving me the sign not to talk to Benjamin about anything yet. On the street was not the place, and now was not the time.

I turned to face him. "I just hadn't realized until recently that she had married a Danish diplomat, and I find that interesting. I was doing some research before our spring tour to Vienna, and I came across an article about her and Georg. When I visited the Mozarthaus Museum in Vienna, there were several items of hers that drew my attention, so I began wondering more about this incredible woman who was Mozart's only wife. Once I knew I was going to be in Copenhagen this week, I decided I wanted to see the house where they lived. She intrigues me, and I wish there was more written about her. Maybe when I retire I will write a book about her."

My trip to this neighborhood today hadn't accomplished much of anything, aside from checking this off my bucket list, but it did give me a visual. There has to be something about her life here in Copenhagen that ties into this mystery I'm now a part of.

We had begun walking down the street by now, and I had hooked my arm in Benjamin's. Sherlock was on the other side of me leaning in, so I felt safe on both sides.

"It's the historian in you, Elizabeth," Benjamin quietly said. "But it's also just the incredible woman you are — reaching out to gain strength and knowledge from those who went before you and then passing that on to the next generation. It wasn't easy for Constanze. A woman doing business in the 1800s was almost unheard of, but she managed to get his works published and performed and his honor restored and recorded by historians."

We had reached the Grand Theatre. I began to think of all the movies that had played here and all the people who had walked this street. I was starting to relax again.

While Elizabeth and Benjamin were looking at the movie posters that lined the outside of the theater, Holmes noticed a man taking photos of them from across the street. He walked over to where the man was standing. The gentleman was sporting an expensive looking black leather jacket with a black turtleneck sweater, black jeans, and black leather Nikes. He wore a black leather Ivy Cap with a large bill that covered his eyes, so Holmes couldn't get a good look at his face.

I guess he is trying not to stand out in the crowd, Holmes thought, as he looked the man in black over from head to toe.

Standing behind him unnoticed, Holmes watched him focus his phone's camera on the couple as they ventured down the street. Once they were out of his view, the stranger sent the pictures to a number on his phone, and then began walking in the same direction as Elizabeth and Benjamin. As he followed them, he dialed a number on the phone and said only one word when the person on the other end answered: "Proceed." Smiling, he continued towards the Royal Gardens with his hands in his pockets.

Holmes swiftly made his way to Elizabeth.

11

Paparazzi

They make a nice couple, thought Elizabeth's covert Paparazzi in all black. *A dignified couple for sure. And, they are perfect for each other.*

He never dreamed that Benjamin Watson would turn up in Copenhagen and become a part of this adventure, but he is perfect for it: a Mozart historian, a highly accomplished conductor, and a great friend to Elizabeth. From the looks of Benjamin's actions, he is hoping for more than friendship. Hopefully, Elizabeth will realize how good they would be together.

The more this fellow observed Elizabeth, the more he liked her. He wished he could get to know her as more than just a subject on the other side of his camera lens. But, he's only been hired to stay behind the scenes for now.

He took pictures for a man who only called himself "The Benefactor." The Benefactor asked him to follow Elizabeth, take photos, and then send the photos to him each day. He was provided travel money, lodging, and a stipend for food. This was one of the easiest jobs he had ever had.

His boss was not happy about the goons who had been following Elizabeth, nor the outcome of her meeting with Mr. Adderly. Paparazzi did not know what was going on. He was just asked to keep tabs and report back. However, he was growing fond of Elizabeth and finding himself feeling more protective of her. He just needed to stay low and not blow his cover.

The couple had reached the Royal Library Gardens now, and were sitting on a bench chatting away.

Click. Click. Click. *One more for good measure...* Click.

After taking pictures of the couple, he began casually taking pictures of the gardens. He sat down on a nearby bench to email the photos to The Benefactor. Paparazzi had also followed through with his orders to set up a scene unveiling the next clue to Elizabeth. Now, he just had to wait until her sleuthing instincts lead her to it.

12

The Royal Library

Holmes got the feeling the man taking the photos was an ally, intending no harm towards Elizabeth. But, who was he taking the pictures for? This assignment kept getting more and more complicated as new characters came into the picture. Elizabeth was due to fly home tomorrow, so Holmes was praying that the rest of her time in Copenhagen was without incident.

He was lost in thought when he felt Sherlock's head nudge his hand, bringing him back into focus. He saw that Elizabeth and Benjamin had sat down on a bench in the Royal Library Gardens. Elizabeth was animated as she relayed some story to Benjamin — waving her hands and being very dramatic. Benjamin was laughing and hanging on to every word she said. Sherlock bounded back over to Elizabeth, and sat down in a stately manner as he too listened to her story.

The garden was lovely, tranquil, and secluded, but Holmes was watching every entrance to make sure no one else had followed Elizabeth and Benjamin. Just when he thought the scene was all clear, a man entered and started walking towards them. His hands were in his pockets, his head was down, and he was walking as if something was on fire nearby and he had to evacuate the area. Elizabeth was still waving her hands, so her bag with the treasures was vulnerable, even though she had the strap around her neck. The man approached, slowed down, and brought his left hand out of his pocket. Holmes whistled, alerting Sherlock, and the big black dog sprang into action. He jumped on the man, knocking him down.

Elizabeth and Benjamin saw him fall, and Benjamin quickly went over to help him up. The man, however, ran off before Benjamin could even offer him his hand. With Holmes now by her side, Elizabeth realized that Sherlock had knocked down the foiled assailant. She had let her guard down, and almost paid dearly for it. She was very curious if Holmes had any more dirt on these goons yet.

Benjamin was shaking his head in disbelief. "Well, I don't know why he ran off like that. I guess he was embarrassed after falling. I don't understand how he fell, though. There doesn't seem to be anything obvious on the path here that might cause a person to fall."

"Maybe he's just a klutz like me and falls over his own two feet," Elizabeth said, but she was hoping Benjamin didn't hear the fear in her voice or see her hand shaking as she clutched her bag. This was getting old. She couldn't do anything without Peter and Arthur's goons following her. She almost messed up this time, but thank goodness she had Holmes and Sherlock looking out for her.

"We need to get a move on if we are going to Tivoli tonight! I have some business I need to take care of from the hotel — follow-ups on the tour, etc." Benjamin stood and extended his hand to Elizabeth to help her up.

They had just turned to go back down the path when Elizabeth suddenly had a thought. She stopped dead in her tracks, causing Sherlock to run into her from behind.

"Benjamin! Let's go into the Royal Library while we're here. I wonder if they have any record of Constanze's time in Copenhagen?!"

"You really are on a Constanze kick!" Benjamin laughed. Inwardly he was reveling in being with Elizabeth. He hadn't laughed so much in months.

Elizabeth opened the door to the library and looked up as she walked inside. The beauty of the library took her breath away. At first glance, it reminded her of the Trinity University library in Dublin. The green glass lamps at the wooden reading tables cast a green glow that mingled with the light coming through the windows. The smell of polished wood and lemon oil filled her senses. Elizabeth just wanted to stand and gawk, but the afternoon was getting away from them. She walked to the information desk, where a young man sat quietly behind the counter.

He politely looked up from his work at the computer and greeted them in Danish. Elizabeth chuckled and asked him in English where she should look for information on Constanze Mozart Nissen.

"I can look that up for you here at the computer," he said in proper English, as he began typing away. While he was looking at the screen, Elizabeth glanced around the library. She noticed Holmes sitting at one of the desks across from a gentleman who looked familiar. *Wasn't he just in the gardens taking pictures near us?* Holmes wasn't taking his eyes off him, as if he anticipated a sudden move. Elizabeth clutched her bag closer. She turned back to the young man behind the desk, whose nametag said 'George.' Strange name for a Dane.

"Here we go — the files show that there are photocopies of some of her letters and correspondence. Not a lot, but you are welcome to view them." George stood up and walked from the behind the desk, asking them to take a seat while he collected the documents.

Elizabeth and Benjamin sat down, but not at the desk near the man she had seen in the garden. It didn't take George long to lay a leather-bound journal in front of Elizabeth. She felt like someone had just handed her a bag full of gold, and paused for a moment before she gently turned the cover page.

LETTERS AND CORRESPONDENCE OF
CONSTANZE MOZART NISSEN
COPENHAGEN YEARS, 1810-1820

Below the title was a badly Xeroxed picture of the 1782 portrait of Constanze. At least someone had made an effort to give her a decent journal. The pages crinkled as Elizabeth turned them. There was even a prologue with a brief biography of Constanze, which included Georg — after all, he was a Danish diplomat. The next page contained an index of the letters, with the corresponding dates when they were written. There were quite a few — about fifty — and Elizabeth got even more excited as she turned to the first letter. Benjamin had been just as excited once he saw that the letters existed. However, she really wanted to read these by herself, in the privacy of her hotel room or office, so she looked at George.

"George," Elizabeth said, "is there any way to get these letters copied? I am willing to pay." She said this ever so sweetly, hoping she could talk him into it.

"Well, since these are copies of the originals, and not very many pages, I suppose I could get my office aide to copy the journal for you. I am estimating the cost at about 350 kroner. Is that alright for you?"

Elizabeth's heart was racing, and immediately gave him the go ahead to copy the book. That converted to a little over $50 for this gem, which was totally worth it.

George disappeared with the book. Benjamin asked her if she would like to look around while they waited. The library was a treasure trove of every Danish publication since the 17th century. They even found a display case housing the first published Danish book, from 1482.

As they were standing there admiring it, George appeared again. He was carrying a handful of white papers, which he had secured with a binder clip. Elizabeth followed him back to the main desk, where she handed him 400 kroner. He started looking for change, but Elizabeth told him to keep the change — that the time he spent copying the journal meant a lot to her. He smiled and thanked her, and then stood to shake hands with her and Benjamin.

Elizabeth placed the papers in her bag, careful not to make a sound as she maneuvered them to fit next to the pouch containing the Mozart treasures. Confident that she was successful, she and Benjamin thanked George again and headed back outside into the fading sunshine.

"Wow! Just wow! That wild hunch sure paid off. I am so excited that he could copy them for me. This will help so much in my research!"

Elizabeth was grinning from ear-to-ear. At that moment, Holmes passed by her and whispered in her ear, "We need to talk."

Elizabeth stiffened, but didn't give Holmes away.

"Are you ok?" Benjamin noticed her sudden reaction.

"I just feel like a kid in a candy store right now — and it gave me the shivers for a moment." She laughed a silly laugh, trying to cover up her concern, wondering what she and Holmes needed to "talk about." *What did he hear and see in the library?* She didn't think she could hold on to her bag any tighter, but she did.

"The day is getting away from us, and I am so excited we are going to Tivoli tonight! Of course, I also need to check on my classes from my computer at the hotel... And, perhaps we can grab a sandwich — I know a wonderful place just around the corner from the hotel."

They walked to the street and hailed a taxi back to the hotel, just to save time. As the door shut on the taxi, Sherlock took his place on the hood, but Holmes stayed behind to observe the men in the library.

Benjamin told the driver they were going to the Phoenix, and away they went. *What a strange day this had been*, Elizabeth thought to herself, and it wasn't even over yet.

&⁕&

Meanwhile, in the library, Paparazzi walked to the information desk.

"Well done, George!"

Paparazzi reached to take the leather-bound journal from him, placing it back into the black messenger bag concealed by his jacket. Paparazzi had received the Constanze letters that morning at the hotel, with a note from Elizabeth's benefactor: *I trust that you will find the right time to get these to Elizabeth.* Paparazzi thought he had timed it perfectly; and George, for the right sum, was happy to play along.

George responded, "Thank you, sir. I am glad I could be of some help." Counting the kroner that had been handed to him, he looked up in shock. "Anytime, sir, anytime."

"I am certain that you are a reputable young man who knows that the right thing to do is take Dr. Stone's kroner and donate them to the library... I more than made up for that, as you can see."

"Yes, sir, a donation was made today in the name of Dr. Elizabeth Stone."

They shook hands, and then Paparazzi stepped outside of the library. He took out his phone and sent a quick text:

> Elizabeth now has the documents and was very excited. I will be at Tivoli tonight and will send pictures.

Paparazzi looked both ways before heading towards the street to hail a taxi back to the Phoenix.

13

Revelations

The taxi dropped us off at the hotel, and then we walked to the sandwich shop on the next street over. I wasn't disappointed. The sandwich was delicious, partly due again to the fabulous Danish bread. We sat at a table looking out on the street, enjoying watching the crowd. On the way back to the hotel, a shiver went down my spine remembering the events of last night when I was attacked. I could still see the look in my attacker's eyes. I kept the conversation light, but I quickened my step. One day I would tell Benjamin what happened, but the time wasn't yet right.

We set a time to meet in the lobby to go to Tivoli, and then we headed off to our respective rooms. I shut my door, leaning my back up against it. As I did, I breathed a sigh of relief to be safe in my room again. I felt confident that no one would harm me here — especially when I saw Sherlock sitting in the middle of the bed, happily wagging his tail in a way that seemed to say, "What took you so long?"

Smiling, I went over and sat down next to the big dog. He nestled up against me, putting his head under my hand. I ruffled his head a bit before grabbing him around the neck to give him a big hug. He laid his head in my lap, and I began recapping the events of the day aloud: seeing Peter and Sophia in the restaurant, meeting the eccentric Mr. Adderly, running into Benjamin, visiting Constanze's residence here, and scoring copies of her letters from her years here in Copenhagen.

I only had a few minutes, but I thought I might steal a quick look at the journal. I reached for my bag — careful not to disturb Sherlock, who was snoozing peacefully with his big head in my lap. Just as I was pulling the journal from my bag, there was a knock on the door. Sherlock lifted his sleepy head and wagged his tail, so I knew it wasn't a stranger.

Going to the door, I slowly cracked it open and asked, "Who is it?"

"It's me — Holmes."

Opening the door, I put my hand on my hip and said, "Why bother knocking? Can't you just appear — you know, walk through walls and such?"

"Sometimes it is nice to act human. And besides, I didn't want to startle you. Are you going to let me in, or do I have to stand in the hall where people will think you are crazy?"

"I suppose you can come in. I am anxious to read the letters, but more anxious to know what you needed to talk to me about. What's up?" I plopped back down on the bed, and Holmes sat in the chair at the desk across from me. He leaned his elbows on his knees, clasping his hands. *Uh-oh, this is serious.*

"Today has been interesting," Holmes began. "I have been observing people all day, and this adventure is becoming more and more complicated. Let's recap. Adderly: He's very much in on it, but I feel there's more to the story there. Adderly desperately wants the treasures — but not for just for personal gain. He loves that they are one of a kind. He was very upset — sobbing — after you left him. His personal assistant, Kristoph, assured his boss that you *would* change your mind about selling the snuff box and locket. And, all of the goons we have encountered have been hired by Peter and Adderly, but are friends of Kristoph's."

"Is Kristoph dangerous? Do you think he is the one who attacked me outside of the Phoenix?" I really liked Kristoph today, so this thought shocked me.

"I don't know," Holmes continued. "You were the one who saw your attacker's eyes. All I gathered was that Adderly wants the treasures, and Kristoph promised to make it happen. I am glad Benjamin showed up. That was a pleasant surprise. Rest assured that he is in no way involved in the conspiracy to rob you."

That was music to my ears. I had enjoyed being with Benjamin all day, but couldn't help doubting my own judgment at this point. Holmes had given me a thumbs-up earlier, but his verbal confirmation just now was reassuring. That would have devastated me.

"When you and Benjamin left Lavendelstræde 1, I noticed a man across the street casually taking pictures as if he were a tourist. When he began following you and Benjamin, I walked beside him. He was checking his pictures on his phone. Elizabeth, there were *a lot* of pictures of you – and not just here in Copenhagen. He has some of you at school, and at home."

I shuddered.

"He sat near you and Benjamin in the Royal Library Gardens. He would act like he was taking pictures of the plants, but he was taking pictures of you. Do you remember the man who sat at a reading table in the library while you and Benjamin were talking to George?"

"Yes," Elizabeth said. "I noticed you sat down across from him, so I figured you were scouting him out."

"While you and Benjamin were still out on the bench talking, he went into the library, so I followed him. He spoke briefly with the librarian, George, and then handed him the leather journal with Constanze's letters. He explained that you would be coming in to ask for information about her time here in Copenhagen. He was then supposed to go back to the office to Xerox them for you. After you left the library, George gave the journal back to him, and the man paid him a hefty sum of money for completing the task. I don't get the feeling he means malice towards you... He almost seems like a messenger of some sort."

By now I was frenetically rubbing Sherlock's head, but my heart was beating even faster. *What did all of this mean? When would it end?* I was mentally and physically exhausted from the last few days, but I was also more determined than ever to find out who bequeathed these items to me and how I was connected to them. I was reminded again how grateful I was that Holmes and Sherlock had appeared on the scene as my guardians. I'm not sure I would have made it this far without them.

"Holmes, I appreciate beyond words everything you're doing for me, but how are we ever going to end this? It seems it's just getting more complicated. The more clues I uncover, the more questions I have. I hope I will find some answers when I read Constanze's Copenhagen correspondence. For now, though — and I hope you don't mind — I just really want to be alone to get ready for tonight. I need to clear my head."

Sherlock looked up at me and then started to get down. "Not you, Sherlock. You can stay. No offense, Holmes…"

I looked to where Holmes had been sitting, but he was already gone. Hopefully, he was out scouting for more answers.

As much as I wanted to curl up and read through the letters, the clock told me that I only had an hour before meeting Benjamin downstairs. I went to the dressing mirror to take survey of my makeup and decide what to wear that evening. This was taking a toll on me, and the mirror agreed.

Sighing so heavily that it woke up Sherlock, I made my way to the bathroom to touch up my hair and makeup. I dragged the dresser chair in with me so I could sit while I worked. Putting my elbows on the counter and planting my face in my hands, I shut my eyes. This was beyond repair, but I was willing to give it my best shot.

Opening my eyes, I looked into the mirror, which was suddenly all fogged over.

"What is this…?" I stood to wipe off the mirror with the hand towel next to me.

Sherlock was whimpering.

"A vision! Holmes said Sherlock would let me know!"

As I began rubbing the mirror, a scene emerged as if I was watching a movie. In disbelief, I sat down firmly in the chair. However, I very quickly found myself caught up in what was unfolding in my bathroom mirror.

I was staring at the back of a man who was walking down an unpaved dirt street, coat pulled tight, head down, and humming as he walked against the bitter cold. I heard church bells, and I recognized St. Stephen's in Vienna as the gentleman approached its Gothic spires. I felt chills up and down my spine, but I leaned in further so I could see every detail — for I realized I was with Wolfgang Amadeus Mozart, walking down the streets of Vienna, as he made his way home to the apartment that was now the Mozarthaus Museum!

ॐ ✳ ॐ

Snowflakes began to fall. Mozart lifted his head to feel them fall on his face. He smiled, for he knew Constanze would be waiting with a cup of hot chocolate. A nice fire would also be waiting for him to warm his hands and feet. He held his manuscript tighter under his coat so the ink wouldn't smear from the moisture. Quickening his steps, he rounded the corner as the bells stopped chiming five. Already getting dark, Mozart was thankful that the rehearsal had gone as smoothly as it did so that he could get home earlier than usual.

Wiping his feet on the mat inside the door, he called out as he took off his coat and hung it on the wall peg.

"Stanzi! I am home!"

He heard footsteps on the stairs as Constanze ran down to greet him.

"Come upstairs, you silly goose! This hallway is colder than it is outside!" She pulled her shawl closer around her as she took his hand, and then, giggling, led him upstairs. She opened the door to the sitting room, where a small fire was gently burning to provide warmth to the only room they could afford to keep heated during the winter. She hushed him gently because the baby was sound asleep. Born in September, Karl Thomas was just a few months old.

Mozart had pulled a stool nearer to the fire and was rubbing his hands together to banish the cold from them. Constanze called him to the small table to eat a bowl of soup. She placed a basket of hard rolls in front of him, and Mozart voraciously tore one apart and began dipping it in his soup.

"How I have dreamed of your soup all day, Constanze! It warms my soul that I married such a fabulous chef!"

They both knew that their meager income couldn't keep them in fresh vegetables and meat every day, but Constanze was frugal and made their food budget stretch as far as possible. Today she had made a potato soup, and it pleased her to see Mozart enjoy it so much.

They made small talk about the rehearsal, the baby, and enjoyed a warm cup of chocolate by the fire with dainty little butter cookies. When Constanze had gone to the bakery with little Karl to get the bread for the week, the baker had given her some chocolate and a dozen of the cookies out of kindness.

The baby woke up, and Mozart picked him up out of his cradle. After cuddling and talking sweet baby talk with him, he handed him to an admiring Constanze who nursed him. Mozart sat with her and rattled on about the rehearsal. She could tell he was pleased, and she was very proud of her husband. Now, if they could just bring in more income and her husband were more appreciated... She knew he was brilliant, but Vienna needed to acknowledge this as well.

After changing the baby and putting him back down to sleep for the night, Constanze and Wolfgang pulled the mattress off the small bed in the bedroom, drug it to the sitting room, and settled in for the night as well. Wolfgang waited to make sure Constanze was sound asleep before he tiptoed to a chest in the corner of the room.

Lifting the lid ever so quietly, he reached his hand down to the bottom of the chest. There he pulled out a small wooden box and opened it to reveal a small velvet bag with a drawstring. He opened it and took out a small blue and gold snuff box which contained a small locket. Taking the locket into his hand, he delicately opened it to gaze at the tiny portrait of Marie Antoinette. He smiled, remembering the day she had given him the box and locket.

Whispering, he said, "One day, Marie Antoinette, this portrait of you will change Constanze's life. Thank you, dear friend. France is fortunate to have you as their Queen."

ॐ ✳ ॐ

With that final statement, I was again staring at myself in the mirror. The scene had disappeared, and I sat there in shock realizing what I had just witnessed. The vision had presented itself to me in English, and not Mozart's native German, so I was able to savor every moment and understand what was being revealed to me without relying on my mediocre German skills. I wanted more. It was like a good book that finished too soon, and I couldn't wait for the sequel.

I sat there in stunned silence.

14

Tivoli Gardens

I stood like a child outside the Tivoli Gate when Benjamin and I got out of the taxi. Twinkling lights were everywhere, giving me the feeling I was about to enter a fairyland.

"Ahem."

I jumped and turned to see Benjamin, who had cleared his throat to get me out of the trance I was in.

"I'm sorry, Benjamin. It's just so...beautiful — like the stars have come down from the heavens to join this small portion of the earth, a chorus of bright lights to guide our way. Oh my, listen to how silly I am. I haven't written lyrics in a while. Maybe Tivoli will inspire me tonight."

Benjamin chuckled and led me to the ticket gate, where he purchased two entrance tickets. I was still gawking when we walked through to the main park area, where the scene was brighter and livelier than we both had anticipated. Guests were in costume — super heroes, movie characters, Disney characters, scary Halloween costumes — you name it, it was there. Pumpkins and jack-o'-lanterns adorned nooks and crannies. Benjamin and I made our way carefully through the crowd, doing our best to stay together and not bump into anyone. We had looked at a map, so we knew we were generally headed to the area where a ballet, called *The Witch Show*, was being performed. I wasn't a fan of rides, so we had decided to enjoy the ambience of the season through the various performances in the gardens.

On the way to the venue, I noticed they had a House of Mirrors. There was a very artistic sign in front, indicating this was a special edition to Tivoli this year — especially for Halloween.

"Let's go in, Benjamin! We have time, and I haven't been in one of these for years!" I was practically dragging him into the queue before he had time to protest. The night air's magic and my enthusiasm were contagious, so he had no choice but to follow.

Once inside, there were two ways to go. I had planned to head one way, but a noisy group of teenagers pushed me along with them the other way. Suddenly, I realized I was separated from Benjamin. Don't panic, I told myself. I began sending messages to Holmes and Sherlock. I closed my eyes and took a big breath, and when I opened them again, I found myself in a room surrounded by mirrors — and no visible exit anywhere. I turned in a panic, and then froze as I looked more closely into one of the mirrors. I wasn't seeing myself — I was seeing another scene unfold before me. *Why was another vision coming so soon after my first? Without a warning from Sherlock?* This didn't feel good. Not at all.

⇛✳⇝

Mozart wasn't feeling well. He was tired, and he was working by candlelight, wrapped in a shawl for warmth against the cold dankness of the room. Constanze and the baby were asleep in front of the fireplace, where the embers were slowly dying out. He was desperate to finish his opera so that they wouldn't have to freeze like this for the rest of winter. There was a knock on the door, and it startled him out of his musical daze. It was a light rap, as if the visitor knew his family was asleep. He feared he knew who it was — the stranger, wanting more music from his strange commission. "Write a Requiem, and let me put my name on it," the stranger had requested. Being desperate for funds, Mozart agreed, against his integrity. He quietly and cautiously opened the door, just a crack, and sure enough, there stood the stranger. He once again hid his true identity by wearing a white mask and a three-cornered hat. Mozart looked him in the eyes...

⇛✳⇝

Just as I was watching Mozart stare into the stranger's eyes, I saw that same stranger in the mirror behind me.

"No, no... this can't be..." I whispered as I froze.

The masked man came up behind me, put his hand over my mouth, and said quietly in my ear, "Give me your bag, Dr. Stone, and I won't harm you. I will quietly lead you out of this room and back into the arms of Dr. Watson if you just give me the bag. Your cooperation is all I ask."

I saw my expression in the mirror — it was that of sheer fear, and I had no voice. I was so frozen that I couldn't fight back or even bite the stranger's hand. So, I did what he asked.

I mumbled, "I need to unbutton my coat to retrieve the bag off my shoulder, but I am going to cooperate."

When the stranger in the three-cornered hat and black cape took his hand from my mouth, I began to very slowly unbutton my coat. My hands were shaking so badly, but I managed to get it off. I was shivering, but not because I was cold. I was afraid for my life, even more so than I had been last night outside of the Phoenix. I knew if I could see this stranger's eyes, they would be the same eyes I looked into last night. The scene in Mozart's apartment had gone away, and all I could see in the mirrors now were multiple images of a frightened woman standing next to a stranger in a costume straight out of *Amadeus*.

I took my bag off my shoulder. "May I keep my passport please? I need to get back home tomorrow, and I know you are more interested in what I have hidden in the bottom of my bag. Here, I will let you get it for me — it's in the inside pocket, the blue case."

I was surprised when the stranger did as I asked. He reached inside, handed me my passport, and then firmly grabbed me by my arm. He began leading me out a hidden door I hadn't seen, but one the stranger obviously had scouted out beforehand. Once we were back amongst the noisy group of teenagers, the stranger ran off from me, leaving me shaking. *Where had Benjamin gone? Why hadn't Holmes and Sherlock heard me? Why is any of this happening? Why? Why?*

15

Angels Amongst Us

Holmes liked Tivoli Gardens. He could see why Elizabeth was so enamored with it. The frivolity was infectious, and the laughter of children filled the night air. He and Sherlock were enjoying the sights when he suddenly heard his name from behind.

"Michael, funny meeting you here."

Holmes turned around slowly. Only another angel would call him by this name — his real name, as he was known in the heavens. He straightened as he faced his archenemy Simon. Ever so confidently he replied, "Fancy meeting you here. Let me guess. You are working with Schultz. How convenient that we are paired together — again."

Simon laughed a laugh that shook the ground. "I have been watching in amusement, Michael — or should I say 'Holmes.' You get the little old ladies, big dogs, and simple musicians. How boring your guardianship must be!"

Little old lady, my foot, thought Michael. Elizabeth was a strong woman, who was facing these dangers with confidence and intelligence. It was best to let Simon keep thinking she was weak. Just knowing she was strong would make him work harder at tricking her.

"And just where is your little Elizabeth right now, Michael?" Simon was crossing his arms, and seemed to grow a foot taller and wider as he spoke these words, which only amused Michael. In retort, he made himself match Simon's size, so they were standing face to face.

Simon continued. "She was calling for you just now, and you didn't hear. Want to know why? I put a shield around her in the Hall of Mirrors so her voice wouldn't reach you. You might want to go and make sure she is still alive after the encounter that just took place there."

Laughter filled the heavens — a big, ugly, deceiving laughter that made Michael turn and fly swiftly towards the Hall of Mirrors. Simon's laughter was echoing as he got farther away.

Michael spotted Elizabeth and Benjamin below and made a soft landing next to her. This was the first time he had appeared to her in angelic form, but he was too worried about her right now to care about appearances. Elizabeth heard the rustle of his angel wings, but was too shaken to react. When she turned to look at him, he almost fell to his knees. Elizabeth was in shock, and Benjamin was trying his best to console her. Sherlock was leaning up against her leg, whining, as if he was also trying to bring her back to reality.

"Elizabeth! Elizabeth!" Benjamin was softly saying.

While in Benjamin's arms, Elizabeth quickly used her thoughts to tell Holmes what took place in the Hall of Mirrors. Holmes instantly disappeared, promising to meet up with her later.

"SIMON!" Michael cried as he flew back to where he had last seen his archenemy.

Simon was nowhere to be seen. Michael did, however, see Peter and Sophia exiting a carnival ride, laughing and looking way too happy as they made their way to another attraction in the park. Michael was furious, but hadn't lost faith that he and Elizabeth could outwit Simon and friends in the end. Michael decided to follow Peter and Sophia for a bit to see if he could learn anything else. He flew in closer and began walking behind them.

"Almost ours, Sophia! We're finally about to be done with this nonsense! I believe this time we have succeeded in getting the Mozart treasures!"

"I am growing weary of waiting, Peter," Sophia said. "This has taken too long. Dr. Stone should have been a pushover. If we don't get the transaction completed soon, I'm moving on. You promised me money, Peter – a house, nice jewels, travel – and you have yet to show me anything but Copenhagen."

"I will fill your world with riches, dear Sophia. But, if you leave me, then I will reveal the little secrets I know about you to the authorities. So, if I were you, I would be more than grateful that you have at least seen Copenhagen instead of the inside of a jail cell."

Michael was amused. These two were a match made in heaven. Little did they know they were both being used as pawns in someone else's game — someone with much bigger game pieces.

ও✳ও

Holmes had swiftly left me after I relayed to him what had happened in the Hall of Mirrors.

"Benjamin," I said with a shaky voice. "Let's go see the ballet. I hear it is wonderful."

"Are you sure you up to this, Elizabeth? You obviously just went through a shocking experience, which by the way, you have not explained to me. What in the world happened in the Hall of Mirrors? I was with you one moment, and the next, you were gone! Where is your bag?"

I wasn't worried about my bag or most of its contents. I could replace most things easily from any number of shops. My phone would be a different story, though. Luckily, it had been in my coat pocket and not my bag. I stuck my hand in my coat pocket and touched my phone, just to confirm.

"Benjamin, it's a long story, and I'm not sure you'll even believe. While we are at the ballet, please keep your phone out. I am going to text you to explain. After the show, we need to hail a taxi and then talk in the downstairs bar at the Phoenix. I leave early in the morning, and I need you to be aware of a dangerous situation — just in case something dreadful happens to me."

Benjamin's face tightened with my words, and he just nodded as he led me through the crowd. We found a seat amidst a group of very noisy kids dressed as Harry Potter characters.

Perfect, I thought. As soon as the conductor lifted his hands, I began quickly texting Benjamin a shortened tale of the Mozart treasures.

After we left the theater, we were laughing and walking arm-in-arm, putting on airs that nothing had happened. I was still in shock, but my wits were returning. Two actual attacks and several attempted attacks in two days had not been on my carefully planned agenda for this trip. I knew this last vision had not been brought on by Holmes. It had a wicked feel, like it was some unknown power I hadn't ever encountered. However, the attacker seemed uneasy, not evil at all. He was too concerned about my well-being, and he did not have the look of murder in his eyes like the first attacker had. In fact, they weren't the same eyes at all, so I am pretty sure the two attackers were different men.

I patted Benjamin's arm so that he would release the very tight hold he had on me. He was scouring the crowd for anything out of the ordinary. Feeling my touch, he let up.

"That was a lovely presentation," I said. "I loved how they used the *Dance Macbre, Night on Bald Mountain,* and *In the Hall of the Mountain King.*"

"And, did you notice how lively the conductor was!" Benjamin began conducting the air and singing loudly at the top of his lungs. We were laughing hysterically by the time we stopped to buy a cup of hot chocolate. The vendor gave us a very quizzical look, as if saying, "Crazy Americans."

I saw Holmes in my line of vision and gave him a quick thumbs-up to let him know I was OK. I also shot him a 'message' that I had filled Benjamin in on the treasures. Benjamin and I kept acting as if nothing had happened, yet we were totally aware that we were being watched by someone. Before flying off again, Holmes told me that he was anxious to hear what had really happened in the Hall of Mirrors. He let me know that he would be waiting for me back at the Phoenix.

We casually made our way to the taxi stand and hailed a cab. Once inside the taxi, I pointed to my phone. I certainly wasn't going to assume at this point that our taxi driver was safe. So, I texted quickly while I tried to keep a vocal conversation going about the ballet and the lovely time we had at Tivoli Gardens. I just love multi-tasking. As we pulled away, Tivoli's fireworks were starting, lighting up the sky.

E: When we get back to the hotel, let's go immediately to the bar.

B: Ok. Do you think we will be safe there?

E: Sure, as long as we keep an eye on the door.

B: Bizarre, just bizarre. These attacks have me extremely worried about your safety.

E: I will be cautious, so don't worry.

I chose not to tell Benjamin the whole story. I conveniently left out the part about Holmes and Sherlock being my guardians. I wasn't comfortable telling him everything — not yet. And, will he even believe me if or when I do tell him?

The taxi had pulled up to the hotel. True to his word, Holmes was sitting on the steps, watching as Benjamin quickly guided me into the foyer and up the marble stairs to the main lobby. We paused for a moment at the desk to check if either one of us had any messages.

"Good evening, Dr. Stone and Dr. Watson. I hope you have had a lovely evening in our beautiful Copenhagen!"

The night clerk's name was Hans, and he handed each of us a note with several messages written down. We both reached our right hands towards the notes and looked down at our respective messages.

"Benjamin," Elizabeth started, "do you have time for a nightcap before I head to my room to pack for my trip home tomorrow?" I made sure I was loud enough for those around us to hear. That might help us spot any goons in the bar with us. *I am catching on to you, so you better watch out!*

Playing along, and taking part in the script we had practiced through texts in the taxi, Benjamin agreed that he indeed did have time and that he also had an early flight to Boston in the morning.

We both said goodnight to Hans, and then headed arm-in-arm towards the downstairs bar. We had taken just a few steps when Hans exclaimed, "Dr. Stone! I almost forgot! This arrived for you today via courier." He reached under the desk and produced a small box wrapped in gold foil paper with a royal blue ribbon.

Startled, I gingerly took the package, wondering if this was some kind of joke. The package didn't have a tag, so I had no idea who it was from. Hans said a courier brought it in without any kind of documentation.

"What did the courier look like, do you remember?" I quizzically asked.

"Tall, nice looking, and come to think of it — very nicely dressed for a courier." Hans looked perplexed as he relayed this bit of information to the confused couple on the other side of the desk.

I thanked him, and then Benjamin and I continued on our way to the bar. Careful not to look too puzzled about the gift, we maintained the appearance of a happy couple on our way for an after-dinner drink. Out of sight, we both relaxed a bit and gave each other a concerned look of '*What just happened here?*'

I was cradling the gift carefully as we took a seat at a corner table in the bar. My favorite Jesper was working tonight. He made his way happily over to the table.

"Good evening, Dr. Stone and Dr. Watson! I didn't realize you two knew each other! What can I get you tonight?"

I laughed, "We go way back, Jesper! Imagine my delight and surprise when we ran into each other this morning on Nyhavn! Goodness, Benjamin — was that just this morning? We have had such a great day catching up and sight-seeing!"

We each ordered a glass of red wine and some appetizers. While we were waiting, we put our heads closely together, again keeping up the façade of two lovers in the crowded bar.

"Do I dare open this now?" I asked quietly. I looked at the tiny package in front of me, which looked as if it could have come directly from a high-end boutique. Then again, maybe it was...

"Personally, I think it's probably safe. If it were dangerous, why leave it at the hotel front desk? It's up to you. You must have a secret admirer, Elizabeth — someone other than me, perhaps?"

I was too startled to reply to his remark, but tried not to show my pleasure in hearing him admit there might be something between us. This was not the time or the place to get romantically involved. I have a mystery to solve and goons to catch.

"I'm going to do it. Here goes."

I held my breath as I removed the royal blue ribbon and laid it on the table. Sighing heavily, I stared at the package once more before unwrapping it completely to reveal what was inside. Before the final reveal, I noticed that Sherlock was under my feet, which caused me to look around the room once more. Holmes was seated at the bar, watching me in the mirror, and he ever so slyly gave me a thumbs-up to indicate that the gift was safe. I now knew what Adderly must have felt as he prepared to see the Mozart treasures for the first time.

Upon opening the box, the first item I saw was a small embossed envelope with one word on the front: *Elizabeth*. Slowly taking the note out of the envelope, I gazed upon a beautifully handwritten message:

My Dearest Elizabeth,

> *You are on the right track. I knew this adventure would bring out your strength, as you have proven several times already — in Vienna, and here in Copenhagen. You have reassured me that you indeed are the rightful owner of the Mozart treasures. Continue finding answers to your questions, and you will soon know who I am. I am giving you another small token of my trust. Enjoy. Remember, it's your integrity that makes you strong. Oh, and — I like this Dr. Benjamin Watson. He is a good man.*

No signature. I turned the note over to see if there were any clues there. I passed the note to Benjamin to read. He had given me space while I read it, and frankly was surprised when I passed it to him.

Underneath the notecard was a beautiful blue velvet cloth, folded neatly to protect the treasure inside. I paused to enjoy the texture of the cloth between my fingers before I peeked inside to find a tiny blue velvet box. I lifted this smaller box out of the gift box. We both excitedly held our breath and briefly shared an anxious glance. After what seemed an eternity suspended in space, I finally opened it. When I did, we both let out a cry of amazement. Nestled inside the box was a beautiful diamond treble clef necklace! We looked at each other with wide eyes — trying not to draw too much more attention to ourselves in front of the other patrons.

Something the note said reiterated what I say time and again in my choir classes: keep the integrity of the music, and always do what you know is right when you perform the piece. My elusive benefactor was sending me a message to keep Mozart's integrity while protecting the treasures in my possession.

As much as I wanted to put it on, I closed the lid and placed it back in its gift box. I wasn't in the mood for an awkward moment with Benjamin helping me clasp the beautiful necklace. Too much too soon. However, I definitely would wear it home tomorrow; and in fact, I would wear it every day as a reminder to always keep the integrity.

Benjamin broke the silence. "What are you thinking? This is quite the gift."

"I'm thinking my benefactor does not want Mozart's musical integrity to be stained with this escapade. He doesn't want the treasures to fall into the wrong hands."

"If anyone can keep this from happening, you can. Besides, you already foiled their little plan tonight at Tivoli." With that last statement, he winked and left it at that.

It was getting late, and it had been a very full day. Hopefully, tomorrow would not be as eventful.

"I hate to be a party pooper, but I need to go and pack. When is your flight?" I was sipping the last of my wine as I asked, and Benjamin was getting Jesper's attention to get the bill.

"My flight to Amsterdam leaves at 8:00 a.m. And you?"

"The same! Let's schedule a taxi to take us to the airport. 6 a.m. okay with you?"

We continued our small talk as we gathered our things and headed for the lobby.

そ＊や

Neither one of them noticed the man in the corner smiling at them as they left. As they walked past him, he snapped pictures of their departure. He immediately sent these in a text, with a simple message:

Mission accomplished.

16

The Night Comes to an End

I was giddy and exhausted when I finally got back to my room. Luckily, I never totally unpacked, so I didn't have a lot to do — which was good, considering it was already 10:30. Sherlock, my big buddy, bounded into the room unannounced, nearly knocking me down on his way to the bed. Holmes was right behind Sherlock, and for the first time since I had met him, he had a concerned look on his face. It's hard to believe it was only last night that he and Sherlock had rescued me on the side street. So much had happened since then.

"What happened tonight in the Hall of Mirrors, Elizabeth?" Holmes asked with a scowl on his face.

"Funny you ask! I practically screamed for you and Sherlock while a stranger in a mask, black cape, and three-cornered hat kept his hand around my neck and stole my bag!" I was scowling back. Sherlock whimpered, and put his paws over his eyes, hiding from his shame.

"You tried to call us?"

I nodded, and Sherlock whimpered again.

Holmes sat down and said, "Start from the beginning, and tell me the whole story."

I didn't leave anything out. When I was finished, Holmes told me his side of the story.

"An archenemy? Simon? And you two don't get along? At all? And he is on Peter's side? Well that's just peachy keen."

"But you didn't get hurt, and he didn't take your passport. These are good things. Of course, they weren't after your passport." Holmes paused. "So, where are the treasures?"

I smiled. "I might be old, but I am not stupid. I figured they would be after me at Tivoli, in such a public place with so many people, so I went prepared. The goons all know by now that I keep the treasures in a box in my bag, which I keep at my side at all times. What they didn't know tonight is that the snuff box and the locket were hidden in a travel pouch under my blouse. Earlier today, I took an empty tea box from the breakfast buffet and put that in my cosmetic bag as a decoy, to feel as though the treasures were still there. The actual wooden box is in my suitcase, but I didn't want to leave the treasures here. Someone is not very happy right about now!"

And with that, we both let out a laugh that shook the heavens.

⇢✳⇦

Elsewhere in Copenhagen, someone was not laughing. The man in the *Amadeus* costume was sitting and looking at an empty bag — realizing he had been duped. There was nothing of importance in the bag. No wooden box containing the snuff box with the locket. Nothing. How could this have happened? Everything had been meticulously planned, and Dr. Stone was supposed to be an easy target.

His phone buzzed, and the call he had been dreading had now popped up on his screen. He answered, and the voice on the other end spoke without a greeting.

"When can I pick up the treasures? You *DO* have them, correct?"

"We've been duped."

The silence that followed was deafening.

17

Home Again

The flight home had been uneventful, but I had taken extra precautions on each leg of the journey. After our shared flight to Amsterdam, Benjamin and I grabbed a quick coffee and then perused the beautiful shops that line the international terminal at Amsterdam's Schiphol airport. Before boarding our respective flights, we hugged and promised to update each other when we arrived home safely. Benjamin had felt guilty sending me on alone, especially knowing the danger I was in, but I had reassured him I was more than capable of looking out for myself.

I had arranged for Matthew Finley, my banker who was also a close friend, to pose as a car service driver when picking me up. He played the part to a tee — holding a sign in the baggage area with "Dr. Elizabeth Stone" typed out in big bold letters. He approached me with a businesslike greeting as he reached to take my bag — yes, the bag with the wooden box — while I went to wait for my luggage to arrive on the belt. Matthew opened the backseat passenger door for me, and then went to the trunk to load my luggage.

"Would you like your bag with you, Dr. Stone?"

Casually I replied, "Yes, thank you." *Man, he was good at this!*

Once the trunk was shut, we were off on the short ride to my home. Following us was an off-duty policeman I had once taught, who was more than happy to see that I made it home safely.

Matthew and I finally broke character after we were safely on the freeway.

"I have never had so much fun in my life, Elizabeth! Now, could you fill me in on what this is all about? Your message was so cryptic that I figured it must be important."

I grinned. My message when I called the bank was a simple one: *Call Bradley, my assistant.* Bradley had all the details, which were relayed to Matthew at the coffee shop near the bank. They made it look like an interview as they sat at a corner table. Matthew didn't know all the dangers, but he had been around me long enough now to know that if I needed help, I would explain later.

As he drove me home, I gave him a very brief synopsis of my plight. His responses from the driver's seat seemed to be a constant string of phrases like, "Wow! Seriously? You have got to be kidding, Elizabeth!" Despite having to remind him to keep his eyes on the road, I actually was loving his reaction to all that had happened in the four days I had been away.

Back in character now as we pulled up to my house, Matthew helped me out of the car, rolled my suitcase to the front door, and waited for me to get into the house. I wanted to make sure he was seen receiving payment, so we stood on the front porch as I fumbled in my bag for the cash to hand him. Matthew added a little handshake at the end, with a small bow, before he got in his car and drove away. My former student, BJ, who had agreed to keep watch over the house from his car for a few nights, was already parked three houses down when I arrived home.

I had thirty seconds to disarm the security alarm after entering my house. Once I did that, I leaned up against the front door, locked it, and gave a huge sigh of relief. I reset the alarm. It wasn't night yet, but I wanted to err on the side of safety after all that had happened.

What no one but Matthew and I knew was that the wooden box with the treasures had stayed in the backseat as Matthew drove off. Here was the plan: To make sure he wasn't followed, he wouldn't immediately go home, but instead would head back to the airport as if he were picking up someone else. Once he was sure he hadn't been followed, he would return to his own house. After lowering the garage door, he would slip the wooden box into a locked tool box on his workbench. He would retrieve it the next morning on his way to the bank, and then put it in a new safety deposit box for Elizabeth under the name Constance Salieri – Constance for Constanze Mozart; and Salieri for Antonio Salieri, Mozart's rival in the Habsburg Court in Vienna.

So far, all was going according to plan. Matthew was home, and the treasures were safe in the tool box. He was having an absolute blast pretending he was James Bond. He sent me a text saying all was well for now.

I couldn't help but laugh out loud. We had pulled it off! Standing at the front window, I watched as a car drove slowly past. I quickly moved away from the window so they couldn't see me peering out. Confident that BJ would keep me informed of any suspicious activity, I then proceeded to my bedroom and started unpacking. If for nothing more than appearance's sake, I wanted to carry on with a normal routine.

Four days! Really? That is all I had been away? I collapsed onto my bed as it hit me just how much had transpired in four short days. I found myself holding the diamond treble clef necklace for comfort, and before it could all sink in, my phone buzzed displaying a text from Benjamin.

Made it home safely, and you?

I texted back: Yes, and it was lovely to see you again. All is well here!

Ok, good to hear. I will check back with you soon. Get some rest. Hope the jet lag isn't too bad.

You too — more later...

Benjamin's text was warming, but I felt we had both played it a little safe with our emotions. The exchange also reminded me that I needed to text BJ to tell him I was fine. After checking in that all was well, I continued to recap the last four days, trying to wrap my head around it all. Zipping up my suitcase, I heard a familiar bark behind me. Sherlock was here! I bent down to give his big head a roughing up before I hugged his neck tightly. Goodness — he felt good, and I felt safe! So happy to see him, I lost my balance and fell on the floor, still holding on to his neck and laughing.

"I sure am glad to see you! Where is your buddy Holmes?" If Sherlock was here, then Holmes was not far behind. Sure enough, before standing up, a pair of boots crossed my line of sight. *What in the...?* Holmes was decked out in blue jeans, a pearl snap shirt, and black boots. I tried really hard not to laugh, but it was a sight to behold, and I could not restrain myself.

"What are you laughing about? What did you expect — angel wings and a long flowing robe? We are in Texas!" He hooked his thumbs in the front pockets, and by this time I was rolling on the floor laughing, with Sherlock licking my face.

"Stop it! Stop it — you both are killing me! Oh, good grief!"

I was trying to get up, but it wasn't a pretty sight. I managed to get on all fours, crawl to the bed, and start to pull myself up. But I couldn't stop laughing at the sight of Michael in boots and jeans, so I kept falling back down. Sherlock would nudge my butt to help hoist me, but it tickled, so I would end up on the floor again. I was laughing so hard that tears were rolling down my cheeks. Getting old was the pits, but it didn't have to be! I reminded myself I needed to work out more to strengthen my core, something I had been telling myself for a while...

After finally standing on my feet and composing myself, I led them both into the kitchen area. I was dehydrated from the flight, and hungry as well. Holmes was really proud of himself, so I tried not to giggle every time I looked his way.

I had a sudden thought and blurted out, "Do you ever eat? Or drink? I just realized I have never seen you do either."

While I was filling my glass at the sink, both of my heavenly guests were looking around the kitchen. Sherlock was sniffing the floor, and Holmes had opened the refrigerator.

"We have our means — just not your way." He shut the refrigerator door, and then went to look inside the microwave and the dishwasher. Sherlock was still sniffing the floor. It was amusing watching them.

"Sherlock, you will meet Charlotte tomorrow. I will pick her up tomorrow after class. I think you will like her!"

Sherlock had stopped, looked at me, and cocked his head to one side when I began talking to him. He gave Holmes a quizzical look, which in turn caused Holmes to give one back to me.

"Charlotte? You have a daughter?"

"No, silly! Charlotte is my dog. I am extremely curious whether she will be able to see Sherlock. Tomorrow will be fun! And, Holmes, you will love Charlotte. She is loyal, smart, funny, and very entertaining."

The grandfather clock struck nine gentle chimes, a reminder that it was important for me to get back to my regular rhythm. Our choirs were rehearsing for their next concert, which was in two weeks, and I was anxious to see how far Bradley had taken them in the music while I was away. The holiday season was also approaching, so I had left music for him to copy and get into their folders. Never a dull moment.

"Holmes, I need to try to sleep so I can get back on my regular schedule. I feel comfortable by myself here with my alarm system. I don't know what your plans are, but hopefully you are just a thought away."

"I am leaving to go check on some new developments, but Sherlock will stay here with you."

"New developments" didn't sound good. Hearing these coded words from Holmes made my stomach a little queasy.

"Elizabeth, I think from here on out you need to call me by my real name – Michael."

"And why is that, Holmes – uh, Michael?"

"It is going to get complicated soon. For now, I hope you continue to trust me, and just call me Michael."

"I am with you, Michael. But, for now I need to unwind and get to bed. I have a little reading I want to do as well. Remember the letters I got at the library in Copenhagen? This is the first chance I've really had to look at those in private, so I'm excited to get started. I had them in my bag to read on the plane, but the lady next to me would not quit talking. Her granddaughter was majoring in music and wanted my opinions on everything. I finally had to close my eyes and put the letters away so she would give me some quiet time."

"I think you are going to be surprised."

Before I could question him about that statement, he was gone – in a flash. Boots and all.

"Gee thanks, Michael Holmes. Leave me curious." I said out loud to a (mostly) empty room. Let's face it, I wasn't going to be able to call him just plain Michael.

I started to move, but I had forgotten that Sherlock had laid on my feet. Grounded.

"Sherlock, big buddy, we need to go to bed — so I need you to get up and let me walk. You have the night shift, so let's get moving."

Sherlock hesitated, but then slowly rose. He stayed by my side while I went to the front porch and blinked the light switch twice — my signal to BJ that I was going to bed. Sherlock accompanied me as I made my nightly rounds in the house. Confident that all was safe and secure, I staggered to my bedroom. Jet lag was beginning to grab a hold of me, and it felt like I was hitting a brick wall.

Barely able to keep my eyes open, I shifted various "unpackings" from my bed to my nightstand: Michael Holmes' red scarf, the attacker's black plaid scarf, the little jewelry box that the diamond treble clef necklace had come in, and the copies of all Constanze's letters.

I went to the bathroom to wash my face and do my nightly routine. Mind fuzzy, I looked into the mirror at the tired woman who had taken over my face and apparently run over it a few times. Facial cleanser, toner...and definitely an extra dab of moisturizer tonight. The air on the plane makes you feel so dry.

Sherlock whined. I froze.

"What is it, boy?" I whispered.

When I turned back to my mirror, I understood. Another vision had appeared. *Great timing...* But, I still leaned in to get a better look at the scene unfolding — perhaps I leaned a little closer than usual, since I had already taken my contacts out.

‬❧ ✳ ☙

Constanze answered the door and greeted the gentleman with a hug.

"I am so glad you are here. Please, come in out of the cold. Copenhagen is having a bitter winter this year, and you must be freezing!"

Stomping his snow-covered boots on the rug by the door, the visitor was rubbing his hands together and blowing on them to shake off the chill.

"Come by the fire. Would you like coffee? Tea?"

Constanze was speaking in broken English, and when the visitor spoke, he spoke with a fluent and beautiful English accent.

"Tea, please. It is nice to see you again, Constanze. It has been too long, dear friend. I still am angry with your rejection, and if Georg ever leaves you..."

She laughed – a hearty laugh that filled the room.

"I will always love you, Lord William – you are my forever love." She grinned and winked as she brought him his tea.

Lord William held the cup in both hands and took a slow small sip of the aromatic tea. "Ah, you remembered how I take my tea. Thank you. The carriage ride from the ferry wasn't far, but it doesn't take long for the cold to chill you to your bones."

He continued to sip his tea while Constanze sat silently watching him. Lord William *was* her forever love. They had met when they were children, long before she had met Wolfgang. His family were patrons of her sister, Aloysia, but William had not been as enamored of her as many others had been. He was immediately attracted to Constanze – the quiet one in the background – and had enjoyed their friendship from the very start. They shared many of the same interests, and that first meeting, at the young age of eleven, began a lifelong correspondence.

William had grown concerned when he received what seemed to be a fairly urgent request for him to come to see her in Copenhagen. Leaving his estate in southern England, near Bath, he came as soon as he could. Traveling this time of the year was not his favorite, but he would do anything for Constanze.

"Surely you didn't call me here just to have tea. I've been so worried since your letter. Please, what's troubling you?" William set the cup down and took Constanze's hands in his, looking her square in the eyes.

Constanze slowly got up and walked over to a locked cupboard in the sitting room. William watched her as she took the key from behind the mantle clock and quickly unlocked the top drawer. She reached in, pulled out a small wooden box, and then turned to him and said...

৯০ ✳ ৽

My head hit the vanity with a hard bang. "Ouch!"

I rubbed my forehead as I leaned into towards the mirror and cried, "No! Take me back! I need to see what she gives him!"

The tired woman in the mirror just screamed back at me, but this time she had a big blob of moisturizer smeared on her cheek. The vision was gone.

"Lord William. William. English. Oh!"

Going to my nightstand, I picked up the folder with the letters and started flipping through the pages.

"Dear William. Dear Will..." each letter was addressed to him! But, Lord William who? The events of Copenhagen had not allowed me to sit and study the letters, or I would have seen that they were all to the same man — Lord William, or Will, as Constanze fondly called him. *That's the connection!* I sat on my bed and plunked the letters into my lap with a satisfying thud.

I looked at Sherlock. "Buddy boy, we are getting closer. But, tonight I am too exhausted. I don't have enough eyeball power left to make it through these letters. It's starting to make more sense now, though. I have English ancestry. Lord William is English. Constanze was giving him the wooden box holding the treasures... But why did she want him to have them?"

Sherlock sat there "smiling" at me. Then, he shook his whole body from head to tail, turned in a circle, and lay down beside my bed.

A thousand new questions were going through my head when I finally curled up on my side to go to sleep. Jet lag hit me like a wave, engulfing me completely. I had no choice but to succumb to the deep.

18

The Invitation

I was awake way before my alarm went off at 5:15 am, thanks again to the jet lag. Coffee made, I sat down in my reading chair to savor the first sip. The warmth of the cup was comforting, and I always relished the extra time I had to enjoy the first cup before getting ready for class. Early morning was the time to clear my head and think about the day.

I love my job. I love getting up every morning to go and be with my students and teach music. Being Monday, it was time for our weekly staff meeting with the Dean of Music, followed by two choral rehearsals, and then Theory 101 – literally beginning music theory, for freshmen who were struggling with ear training and key signatures. The last class of the day was the advanced choir, composed mainly of graduate students passionate about their music and ready to go out and conquer the world.

While I was deep in thought, Michael Holmes plopped down on the couch.

"Well good morning to you, Michael Holmes. You look like you are worse for the wear this morning."

"Ha ha. While you were sleeping, and snoring no less, I was off helping your case *and* averting dangers in another case I am working on."

"What? You are not mine exclusively, Michael Holmes?? And, for the record, I don't snore – I gurgle...musically."

"Whatever. So, before you go out today, did you do some reading last night before you, um, gurgled?"

"If you are referring to the letters, no, but I had another vision last night."

Michael sat up now and leaned in to hear the details. He had the ability to trigger her visions, but he wasn't in control of them and didn't always know what she would see. Additionally, Michael was still on edge after Elizabeth's encounter with Simon and his vision in the Hall of Mirrors. He silently shuddered, and waited to hear if this vision was a planned one.

"Constanze had a lifelong friend named Lord William who lived south of Bath. She gave him the wooden box with the treasures at some point while she was living in Copenhagen. I fell asleep and hit my head on my vanity while I was watching, so the scene didn't play out. When I looked at the copied letters, they are all addressed to Will, as Constanze affectionately calls Lord William. It's the connection to me that I have been looking for."

Michael was nodding his head in agreement. "Good. Seems we're on the right track to your benefactor. If we can identify him, make contact, and keep the goons off our trail, we are going to solve this case."

"I want to know who was in costume at Tivoli, and who sent him," I said. "I am not going to lie. It was a scary moment — even though I knew I didn't have the treasures with me. However, except for that first attack on the street in Copenhagen, I haven't had the feeling that my perpetrators have wanted to harm me. They want to scare me, intimidate me, and steal the Mozart treasures. Well, I just want to state that they have met their match."

"Elizabeth, when I found out I was assigned to you, I seriously thought I was going to have to babysit you the whole time. Boy, was I ever wrong. You are resourceful, smart, and have incredible inner strength."

"Well thank you, Michael Holmes. Coming from an angel of your caliber, I take that as the highest compliment." I winked and tipped my coffee cup towards him. "As much as I would like to sit here all day receiving your compliments, I've got to go to work. It is a very busy day."

I had walked to the coffee pot, and poured myself a much needed second cup. "Yes, very busy... And, I pick up Charlotte this afternoon."

Sherlock perked up. Bending down and ruffling his head, I said, "Oh, just you wait, Sherlock — you will meet *your* match!" I chuckled and went to get ready for work, leaving both Sherlock and Michael Holmes shaking their heads.

I unlocked my office door promptly at 7 a.m. A large area, it was warm and inviting, as well as tastefully decorated. Bradley had his own space, thank goodness. He was the tech geek of the team — his office, setup more like a small recording studio, held more gadgets and gizmos than I could keep up with. He was a genius at arranging music and writing original compositions. He was also an accomplished accompanist and wonderful conductor. I knew I was blessed to have him, so I tried to incorporate his talents into the program at every chance.

Bradley always dashes in here five minutes before our first class, so I was thankful to have some alone time right now to take care of business. The faculty meeting wouldn't take long, but I was dreading having to sit there listening to Dr. Joseph Chamberlain drone on about recruiting and budgets and such. My focus was on solving the mystery of the nameless benefactor, as well as finding the treasures a safe place to live. However, I knew it was important to push forward with normal life as well.

Not surprisingly, there were at least a hundred emails in my inbox when the computer came to life. Gone for four days. Almost lost my life twice. Yet email lives on. Perusing my inbox, I bristled when I saw an email from Peter. I immediately clicked to open.

Good Morning, Dr. Stone —

I hope you had a nice flight home, and that this email finds you calmly sitting in your office. It was such a pleasure to see you in Copenhagen — what a coincidence that Sophia and I ran into you! Our business concluded there, and I came back with several new Mozart memorabilia for the Mozarthaus Museum.

One item in particular made me think of you and the wonderful treasures you inherited. We met with a client who was a distant relative of Georg von Nissen, Constanze's second husband. He asked us to verify that a manuscript about Mozart was indeed authentic. As you recall in your studies, Georg and Constanze were writing a biography about Mozart's life. The book was published by Constanze after Georg's death.

Sophia and I were excited to see this manuscript — handwritten, with comments written in the margins in a different handwriting, probably Constanze's. On one of the pages, written very boldly, we saw the note Marie Antoinette,

23. The corresponding paragraph was about little Wolfgang's visit to Vienna when he was 6. We couldn't decipher, however, why 23 was by her name and not 6. Since you hold the locket with the miniature of Marie Antoinette, we thought you would be interested in our find. The relative did not want to release the book to the museum as of yet, but indicated that it would eventually find its way there.

Sophia sends warmest greetings, and we hope you remain in correspondence with us.

Sincerely,
Peter

Peter Schultz had a lot of nerve. I can't believe his audacity. And honestly, this email doesn't even warrant a response. Not yet. Make him sweat it out. I knew if I responded immediately, Peter would be thrilled. He was trying to get a reaction out of me. I could picture Sophia looking over his shoulder, and could just hear the sarcasm in her voice.

My interest was piqued, though. I leaned back in my chair and pondered why 23 might be important enough for Constanze to write it in the margins. *What did it have to do with the treasures? Was this even legit — or another one of Peter's tricks?* It'll have to wait. I have too many other things to do today.

"Elizabeth! How good to see you!" Bradley burst into the office.

"What brings you in so early? It isn't even 7:30 yet! Don't tell me, let me guess — you missed me so much that you just couldn't wait to see my beautiful face!"

"Man," he said as he spun around. "You have me figured out! I thought you might need an extra boost today." He proudly produced two cups of coffee from our favorite coffee shop along with two breakfast tacos.

"Be still, my beating heart!" Coffee was my guilty pleasure. No sugar. No cream. Just black. Just right.

"I came early to find out about your trip, but I am really curious to find out about the cryptic message and instructions you had me deliver to Matthew." Bradley had unwrapped his taco, waiting eagerly for the story to begin.

Taking a deep breath, I began a recap of the last four days.

As soon as Bradley heard about the first attack, his eyes got wide and he almost choked on his taco. Putting his taco down, he just sat there in a trance while his favorite person in the whole wide world told him of the dangers she had faced in Copenhagen. I already knew I was his hero, but now he will consider me his superhero! He just kept saying "Wow!" every so often and shaking his head.

I told him everything — well, not everything. I didn't tell him about Michael Holmes and Sherlock yet. Everyone already thought I was crazy, and I certainly didn't want to add fuel to the fire. That would come soon enough. Just as I had finished the part about Tivoli Gardens, my alarm went off.

"Time for our meeting, Bradley. Dr. Chamberlain awaits us, and we must walk in like nothing at all has happened, OK?"

Still stunned, Bradley nodded in agreement. We walked in silence down the hall to the conference room — a beautiful room with a huge table in the center. The other professors were gathering, and laughter greeted us as we entered and took our seats. The conference room was like church — everyone had their favorite spots, and no one dared to sit anywhere else but in their place. The normal chatter continued with talk of concerts, rehearsals, exams, and family events that took place over the weekend.

"Elizabeth! How was Copenhagen?" The question came from Ian Taylor, one of the voice teachers.

"It was lovely, just lovely, Ian. Thank you for asking. The trees were turning, and their colors were vivid. Not enough time to truly sightsee with my brother's big birthday celebration taking place, but I had a wonderful time."

At that moment, Dr. Joseph Chamberlain, a prominent orchestra director and our Dean of Music, walked briskly into the conference room. His very presence commanded respect, so we all greeted him and focused our attention to the head of the table. Joseph was a character. He was about six feet tall and probably weighed 150 pounds — wet. Always dressed in a suit with a colorful bowtie, Joseph was so much fun to watch on the podium. His orchestras were sought after nationally, performing in Carnegie Hall multiple times.

"I pray all of you had a pleasant weekend." As Joseph spoke, he began passing around a stapled packet that included the agenda for the meeting and other pertinent information. I flipped through it to see it was mostly what we had discussed at the last meeting, and the meeting before that. Always the same this time of year, but Joseph did a great job keeping us all on track within our special areas.

I was trying unsuccessfully to keep my thoughts from drifting elsewhere, so I jumped when Joseph called my name. *Oh, dear God, I hope I wasn't asleep!* I glared at Bradley as if to say, *"kick me the next time ok???"*

"Yes, sir?"

"I received an invitation for us to do a joint concert of Mozart repertoire on New Year's Eve."

Suddenly wide awake, something told me this was related to the Mozart treasures.

"How fun! I'm game, are you? Who sent you the invitation, how much, when, where?"

"That's the unusual part. The invitation came from a travel company's representative. He said he couldn't tell me who was booking the concert. But wait — it gets even better. The concert is to take place at a Masquerade Gala in Prague at the Estates Theatre."

My heart was pounding. Mozart's *Don Giovanni* premiered at the Estates Theatre in 1787! I had been an audience member there once on tour with students several years ago. It's a small theatre, with a large feel, so I could envision us doing a concert there.

By this time, the other faculty members had grown very quiet — a touch of jealousy perhaps, but more likely feeling a bit left out of the conversation. Joseph could have done this in private, so why is he bringing this to the table?

"On top of it all, our whole trip is paid for, *and* our whole faculty is invited to attend. I figure we could use good chaperones, and since no one knows our students better than the fine group of teachers sitting around this table... What do you say? Do we accept?"

Everyone began talking at once — everyone but me. My wheels were turning about who had sent the invitation...and what their motive might be.

"Joseph, what is the gala for? Do you at least know what the event is supporting?" I started my questioning slowly, even though I had a thousand ideas going through my head at the moment.

Faculty members were discussing the trip amongst themselves, so Joseph leaned in to talk to me directly.

"Elizabeth, it is all being communicated to me through a travel company based in Vienna. The company is called Mozart Travel Company, and the letter said that the benefactor of the tour wants to remain anonymous. They gave me a deadline to accept the invitation, and after I do that, then more details will be explained to me. Have you heard of this company before?"

"No, but that doesn't mean they aren't reliable. We have so many travel companies that offer performance-based tours these days. It is an ever-growing, ever-changing business. I have only used the ones based here in the States. Does the agent have contact information? Company website? And how did the letter arrive — by parcel? Regular mail? Email?"

I could see a bit of frustration in Joseph. He leaned back in his chair before answering. I could tell that he just wanted us all to say yes, without questions. Understandably, I think he was just excited by the fact that someone wanted to sponsor our whole department on an all-expenses-paid tour to Prague — one of the most amazing cities in the world.

"My, my, Elizabeth. You're not usually one to turn down a trip abroad — especially an all-expenses-paid tour." He leaned forward and clasped his hands, "Do you understand what this means to our Fine Arts College? The publicity, the community rallying behind us, the recruitment — think about it! Every US student inclined to be a music major will want to come study here!" He grinned with excitement, just thinking about the possibilities.

My heart had stopped pounding as loudly, and that made me hear Joseph loud and clear — he was not going to turn down this invitation, despite the unanswered questions. I smiled back.

"Just curious is all, Joseph. I think it is a wonderful opportunity, and I have been wanting to go back to Prague. Just imagining us performing in the Estates Theatre gives me goosebumps! Please allow me to look at the repertoire options for orchestra and choir. It would be fabulous to do parts of the *Requiem!*"

This was all Joseph had wanted to hear. Satisfied, he turned his attention back to the whole group. "Ladies and Gentlemen, I do believe you will all be packing your bags for New Year's in Prague!"

They all clapped their hands with joy. They were thrilled to be included in this exclusive adventure.

"Please go back to your respective offices and clear your calendars from December 27th through January 2nd. I hate that your families will not be invited, but if that changes, I will inform you immediately. In the meantime, I will reply back and give them a hearty 'yes!' to this incredible invitation to perform in Prague!"

I turned to Bradley, who was tapping me on the arm in double-time excitement. He had the look of a two-year old who had just discovered ice cream, and I couldn't contain my laughter.

"What?" I laughed.

"Prague! I am so excited! Do you want me to start researching sights to see and things to do?" Bradley literally had his laptop out, ready to browse the web for the top ten things to do in Prague.

"Yes, Bradley, you can. But one thing for sure — don't mention our conversation this morning to anyone. We need to talk further as to how this trip may be part of the plan."

Bradley stopped mid-typing and turned slowly to me. "Oh... That. Yes." He cleared his throat. "Yes," he said deeper, "we must talk about plans. Soon."

Joseph was clinking on his coffee cup to get our attention. "Okay. Clear your calendars, and I will keep you all informed of the itinerary as I get more information. December is not far away, so if you need to get your passport renewed — or get a passport — do that now. In the meantime, you all have your own agendas for the rest of the semester. Remember to support each other during this busy time by attending as many concerts and recitals as you are able. Elizabeth, would you mind staying behind for a moment? The rest of you are dismissed. Have a great day."

I stayed put while Bradley gathered his things, whispering to me that he would warm-up the choir if I didn't make it back in time. One of the band directors had stopped to ask Joseph something about the upcoming football game, and while I patiently waited, my phone lit up with an incoming call from the bank. As was previously arranged, I declined the call — this was Matthew's way to tell me the treasures were safe and sound in the bank's vault.

Joseph was making his way back to me. "This is exciting for our department, Elizabeth! I sense you have reservations about us accepting, so I wanted to make sure we were on the same page."

"I completely agree that it is exciting! I am already planning the concert in my head! It's just — I'm honestly curious about the gala logistics. And, who in the world has enough money to pay for all of us to go? That's all." I forced a smile that hopefully looked natural.

"Excellent! Good to hear! I am going to go and accept. As the letter states, they must know by the end of today. Let's get together soon and discuss the program, okay?" With that, Joseph exited the conference room and hurried on his way to accept the concert invitation.

Following his exit, I sat in the conference room by myself for a moment, sipping the good, strong coffee. This trip to Prague is all about me, or perhaps more accurately — all about the treasures. Two months until New Year's Eve. Sixty days to solve the puzzle so that no piece is out of place when the gala occurs.

Calmly taking another sip of coffee, I smiled. Time to put another plan into action.

19
Charlotte Returns

We stayed busy all day — students in-and-out, phone calls, emails, section rehearsals — a constant stream of activity. Not once did Bradley and I find a chance to chat. At 4 p.m., Bradley reminded me that I only had an hour before the vet closed, so if I was going to go and get Charlotte, I'd better get a move on.

"Holy moly, Bradley!" I exclaimed, quickly shutting down the computer and gathering my things. "Thanks for getting me out of the brain fog I was in!"

Bradley followed me to the car, on my heels, taking notes on his phone as I quickly rattled off business we had to get done the next day. I threw my briefcase in the backseat of my car. Buckling up, I rolled down the window to finish a list item. Poor Bradley was typing frantically as I backed out of the parking space, waving and yelling, "See you bright and early tomorrow!"

Luckily the vet was near the university. The staff loved Charlotte — so much so that when I boarded her, the only time she was in her kennel was at night. Gianna, the receptionist, would put Charlotte's bed in the office area, allowing her to hang out with her during the day. Charlotte became the official greeter when clients came in with their pets, managing to calm the nerves of those poor animals who hated coming to the vet — and calm the nerves of the poor owners who were worried about their pets. I sincerely felt Charlotte's calling was a therapy dog, and I have strongly considered getting her certified to go help in the children's wing at the hospital. For the time being, Charlotte provided the therapy I needed from the stress of the job and the loss of my husband.

I pulled into the vet's parking lot at 4:20. As usual, when I entered the reception area, there were a number of people there to pick up their pets after a weekend of boarding. Anxious pet parents were standing around, waiting for the attendant to bring their fur babies to them. We casually smiled and nodded to each other.

"Dr. Stone!" Gianna greeted me with her usual cheerfulness, exhibiting a true love for her job.

Before I had time to respond back, Charlotte's head popped up from Gianna's lap. It didn't take her but a second to realize her mistress had returned. She looked at Gianna with a quick look that said, "I love you, but I love her more, so is it okay for me to go?"

Gianna ruffled her fuzzy head, and said, "Go on, silly goose, your beloved Elizabeth has arrived!"

Charlotte gave her a quick, wet kiss, jumped down to the floor, and came barreling around the desk towards me.

I bent down to catch her in my arms, grabbing her up as I received a torrent of puppy kisses, causing me to giggle with delight. Any make-up I had left after a busy day was now completely gone. Laughing, I finally got Charlotte to calm down a bit as Gianna rang up my bill and gathered Charlotte's things for me.

Charlotte was a six-month-old miniature sheepadoodle, and she looked like a living teddy bear: white face with a black left eye, black body, and white bands around her two front legs. I had been on a waiting list for a year, but one day I received a call that a sheepadoodle puppy had been given up by her owners who were moving abroad. *Was I interested? Absolutely!* And, we were a perfect match from the minute we met.

I named her Charlotte, after Queen Charlotte, royal consort to King George III of Great Britain and Ireland from 1761-1818. She was a huge patron of the arts, including Handel.

There were other musical connections that influenced Charlotte's name as well. One big connection involved Mozart. He visited Queen Charlotte and King George on his grand tour of Europe. The Mozarts had stayed from April of 1764 until July of 1765, being summoned to the court to play whenever they were in London. Another musical connection: Queen Charlotte's music-master was Bach's eleventh son. *Can you even imagine?* I get excited just thinking about all the connections — so naturally this miniature Old English sheepdog-poodle should be named Charlotte!

Charlotte the Sheepadoodle was herself a queen, for she ruled her domain with love, affection, and admiration for her Lady Elizabeth. Charlotte was easy to train, having her own repertoire of tricks that she loved to display for anyone who asked.

"Enough! Enough! Charlotte, I missed you, but we will never get home if you don't settle down and let me put your leash on you! Sit, pretty please!"

Charlotte obeyed while I fastened her pink leash to her pink collar. Having a docked tail meant her bottom was moving with excitement, giving the appearance Charlotte was doing the twist. Other clients in the waiting area were giggling, and one even asked to take her picture. Charlotte heard, conveniently striking a cute pose. Seriously, she was a queen. Given time, she would probably even master the queenly wave using her front paw. After paying the bill, we walked out to the car — well, I walked and Charlotte strutted. Putting Charlotte in the front seat, she calmly sat and looked out the front window as any normal passenger would do.

The ride home was uneventful. Since it was the rush hour, I had plugged into a Mozart station to peruse some repertoire for possibilities to use in the Prague gala. Joseph and I were meeting in the morning to settle on the program. *Three months...* I struggled to imagine how all of these pieces were going to come together.

I hadn't thought of Michael Holmes or Sherlock all day. That changed when I pulled into my garage. Smiling, I turned to Charlotte and said, "Let's go, young lady. I am curious if you will notice anything different."

Once inside with the security system disarmed, I reached down, took off Charlotte's leash, and hung it on the rack by the door. Charlotte waited for her command that she could go before running as fast as she could to her toy basket by her bed.

I watched with amusement as Charlotte reached into her toy basket for her favorite stuffed duck. She suddenly stopped, mid-prance, with the duck in her mouth. She looked around as if to say, "*Something is off. What is it?*" Shaking off the feeling, she proceeded to thrash the duck from side-to-side to show it she was still the boss. Still with the toy in her mouth, she now took off for her usual patrol of the downstairs area. I was in the kitchen watching her with a silly grin on my face, waiting... As she rounded the kitchen bar, Charlotte stopped dead in her tracks. She looked straight at Sherlock, who was calmly sitting next to me. She began barking, but had forgotten to drop her duck! The bark was muted like a jazz trumpet, and I just died laughing.

"It's okay Charlotte! Meet Sherlock, our guardian dog. He saved my life in Copenhagen, and has come to protect us from some not-so-nice goons that might try to hurt us."

I scooped Charlotte up in my arms, now aware that Sherlock was visible to her. Carrying her slowly over to the big, black giant of a dog, I introduced them nose-to-nose before putting Charlotte on the floor to get to know Sherlock for herself. Sherlock's tail was wagging so hard that when it hit the kitchen cabinets it sounded like a bass drum. These two were going to get along just fine.

Leaning up against the counter with a glass of water in my hand, and lost in the dogs' innocent play, I nearly jumped out of my skin when Michael Holmes came up beside me — appearing out of nowhere with a quiet "Boo!" in my ear.

"Quit doing that! Good grief. Now I am all wet."

I was now wearing the glass of water. Michael Holmes was laughing, and I figured I no other choice but to join in with him. After all, if you can't laugh at yourself, who will laugh?

"I am sorry, Elizabeth, but I just couldn't resist. You were in another world watching the pups play. Just so you know, not all dogs have seen Sherlock. Glad Charlotte can, so they can partner up to help you."

Michael Holmes stopped, saluted, clicked his heels together and said, "Here to report in, Dr. Stone!"

Elizabeth rolled her eyes and said, "Seriously? At ease. And just what are you reporting?"

"So far, Peter and Sophia are still in Vienna. I have been tracking 'Paparazzi' – the man who was taking pictures of you in Copenhagen and arranged for you to get Constanze's letters in the library. He was on the plane with you on the way over, and he is staying at a hotel near the university. He is on the good side, but I think he reports back to your benefactor frequently – like all the time. No harm intended, just observing you. The goons are not here, at least not yet."

"Are you aware of what happened at the university today?" I asked.

When Michael Holmes shook his head yes, I just had to laugh, "It's still a mystery to me what you do and don't know at any given moment. This 'angel' thing is new to me, after all."

Continuing, I queried, "So what do you make of it all? I honestly believe it is part of the plan, but I haven't decided if it's being arranged by my benefactor or by Peter. Prague is going to prove interesting indeed."

"You have a couple of months to figure this out. Remember – I know your comings and goings, but I am not aware of the outcome. You have to decipher this for yourself. Have you read the letters yet?"

"After dinner, I plan on curling up with them. Today has been a whirlwind, as you can imagine. The faculty is so excited about our invitation, which only added chaos to an already busy day."

"The letters are going to be a revelation to you. Read them well, for they hold a lot of the puzzle pieces you are missing. They were given to you for a purpose."

With that, Michael Holmes left.

At moments, I felt like I was inside a Dickens novel, except that Michael Holmes was all three of the spirits from *A Christmas Carol* – Past, Present, and Future.

"Alright you two," changing the attention to Charlotte and Sherlock. "Charlotte, you need to eat. Sherlock, you are welcome to join her if you desire," I smiled – until I imagined how much it would cost to feed a small horse, because Sherlock was the size of a miniature pony. Charlotte came up to the middle of his leg, and could easily walk under him.

I made a salad and ate it at the kitchen island while watching Charlotte eat. Sherlock lay at my feet, and I was relishing the comfort of the moment when my phone lit up with an incoming call. It was my best friend in the whole wide world, Amanda Kate, and I grimaced, realizing I hadn't checked in with her since returning from Copenhagen.

Amanda Kate and I met in grade school. Our adventures throughout the years are book-worthy – funny, sad, joyous – but in the end, they all led to one thing: sisterhood. Amanda Kate had gone on to follow her dreams as an interior designer, and had built quite a famous brand for herself. Her southern charm and good eye, as well as her classic beauty, had gained her both notoriety and popularity. Everyone clamored for an Amanda Kate make-over. Her blog, *Amanda Kate's Place*, had made her an instant internet star. Through it all, Amanda Kate and I remained friends and were each other's biggest fans.

Our other partner in crime was Amanda Kate's cousin, Peyton. Yes, her parents named her after the novel which had debuted the year we were born. Go figure. True to form, however, our Peyton was our proverbial source for anything that happened in our hometown. Because she still lived there, she kept up with everybody – even their dogs – and would call to fill us in on deaths, marriages, affairs, births, and the latest gossip.

"Amanda Kate! I was just going to call you!"

I crossed my fingers and hoped this would redeem me. Ever since I had been widowed, Amanda Kate had been even more concerned for my health and safety. I usually checked in with her before I checked in with my son, but all of this craziness with the Mozart treasures – and, oh, I don't know, angels and angel dogs in my life now – had somehow distracted me.

Grabbing a glass of water, I headed towards my reading chair. Charlotte was having a good time weaving in and out under Sherlock's legs. When he would look at her, she would run off. What a flirt.

"Izzibeth! I have been worried sick about you! You promised me this time you would call as soon as you got home. No call, no Izzibeth."

Amanda Kate had started calling me Izzibeth when we first met, and Izzibeth I was.

"Jet lag. Department meeting. New repertoire. Picking up Charlotte. Just got home. Do I need to make any more excuses? I love you Amanda Kate! More than chocolate!"

"You are not impressing me one bit," she retorted, but then laughed. "I have been a bit busy today, too, but have been checking to see if I missed a call. You know I worry. I can't help myself! If something were to happen to you – well, I would want to be the first to know!"

I bellowed. "I will rise from my coffin and shout – Amanda Kate! I tried to call you, but you didn't answer!"

We chatted for about thirty minutes. I gave her only small amounts of information about the trip to Copenhagen. I did tell her about meeting up with Benjamin, and Amanda Kate wanted to hear all about that.

Amanda Kate and Peyton had met Benjamin on a trip to New York City with me once. Benjamin had been in town conducting at Carnegie Hall. He had three tickets for us waiting at Will Call, with a note to meet him backstage afterwards. I recall that as Amanda Kate hooked my arm in the brisk New York City air that night, she wasted no time telling me that he was the man for me. I had blushed, but insisted I did not want another relationship yet in my life. Peyton agreed, although she couldn't hear the whole conversation. Coming down with a cold, she had Kleenex stuck in her ears to keep the chilly wind out, so she was only getting half of what we were discussing. What a fun trip!

"Amanda Kate. You will never believe! Today the University Choir and Orchestra were invited to play for a gala in Prague on New Year's Eve!" I quickly diverted the conversation away from Benjamin, hoping she would stop prodding me about him.

"What?! That is wonderful! Who is throwing the gala – anyone I know?" Amanda Kate's voice indicated her excitement was genuine.

"Are you free during that time? I would love to have you along to help. The dates are December 27-January 2. Talk to your sweet hubby and see if he will let you go!" Amanda Kate's husband was a real estate tycoon, and the two of them together made an amazing team.

"Thomas," Amanda Kate said, "I am going to Prague with Izzibeth for New Year's Eve!"

I heard a grunt as Amanda Kate had poked Thomas to tell him she was going. "So much for asking," I laughed, taking the grunt as a yes.

"I will send you all the details. Oh, and — I need to put you and your talents to work for me. However..." I paused, "I have some explaining to do to you, but it's better not to do it over the phone. Let me preface all this by saying that the invitation was very generous, covering all trip expenses to perform at this masquerade gala. Since I am asking you to be my design consultant, you will go like the rest of us — for free. We just got the invitation this morning, so details are not all worked out. I think they must have heard that I am a Mozart fanatic, because the gala is going to be at the famed Estates Theatre where Mozart premiered *Don Giovanni*. You game?"

"Izzibeth, since when am I not game for one of your adventures?"

"True. Do you think Peyton could get away, too? Hey, Charlotte needs to go outside, and I have some studying to do tonight. I love you, and I will send you information as soon as I have it all. Evidently, the mysterious benefactor of this invitation is setting up our whole itinerary."

"You're silly to even think otherwise — of course Peyton will be game! She will be giddy with delight since she has never been out of the country! What role will she play in this masquerade?"

"I have a very special job for her." I was already plotting Peyton's script for the gala, and she was perfect for the part.

"'Night, Amanda Kate. I love you more than chocolate and all the trips to Prague!"

With that, we said our good-byes. I imagined Amanda Kate immediately calling Peyton, and could hear the squeals across all the miles between them.

Charlotte had been staring at me for about five minutes. She finally stood up, walked to the door, and froze. Opening the back door for her, I went outside as well and stood on the deck. Sherlock followed, standing guard at the top of the stairs as Charlotte did her business below. The onset of dusk is my favorite time of day. I love seeing the stars just as they begin to awaken, taking their positions to watch over us for the night. That thought has always comforted me.

Michael Holmes had assured me that no one had followed me back home to the States except for Paparazzi, but I still asked BJ to watch the house for a few more nights. As Charlotte paraded back inside to get a drink, I calmly set the alarm system for the night. I had some reading to do.

20

Wolfgang and William

With Sherlock lying beside the bed, and Charlotte nestled by my side, I snuggled in to delve deeper into Constanze's letters. Finally — a chance to read them and search for more clues. I had the television on for company and for background noise. Almost as soon as I had placed the letters in my lap, Sherlock whined.

Uh oh. That usually means...

The television caught my attention. There on the screen was Vienna. My ears homed in on the sound of boots crunching on the snow-covered cobblestones. All I could see was the back of the man walking, but by now, I knew it was Wolfgang.

Vienna, December 1786

Wolfgang was walking briskly. He was humming the theme from the symphony he was working on, No. 38, which was to premiere next month in Prague. It would be his first visit there, and he wanted the symphony to be spectacular. He was almost finished, and was hurrying home from a rehearsal to work on it in front of the nice warm fire Constanze would have waiting for him. They were still in the rooms behind St. Stephen's Cathedral, facing Schulerstraße — rooms which had proven to be wonderful lodging for his small family.

"Wolfgang Amadeus Mozart!"

Wolfgang raised his head to see a man standing in front of him, arms open, apparently excited to see him. However, Wolfgang didn't recognize him at all — which wasn't uncommon. People would stop him all the time after they had heard one of his concerts.

"Yes, I am Wolfgang Amadeus Mozart. And you are?"

"Don't you recognize me? Lord William!"

Wolfgang apologized profusely that the name was not ringing a bell, and asked politely if he could refresh his memory of their acquaintance.

"London. 1763. Queen Charlotte's court. You played a concert there. We were both 7, and the Queen had invited my family to hear you. After the concert, you and I were introduced and left alone to play for a few minutes. As any young boys would do, we immediately ran to the courtyard and played a quick game of hide-and-seek with some of my other cousins. It didn't last long – your father came looking for you, reprimanded you for leaving the Queen's audience, and took you back inside. I never forgot that meeting, and have been a follower of yours ever since. I also know your dear, sweet Constanze. My family knew the Webers and were patrons of Aloysia."

"I remember that now!"

Wolfgang suddenly had recall of the very evening Lord William was referencing. Bach's youngest son, J.C. Bach, had been instrumental in getting the young Mozarts an audience with the Queen. It had been so refreshing to meet other young boys, but his father had not been happy. He also knew that Constanze had a childhood friend in England with whom she corresponded occasionally, but he didn't realize that he and Lord William were one and the same. What a small world!

"What brings you to Vienna in the winter, Lord William? Surely you must be freezing. Please, come with me to my home so we can all get reacquainted!"

Lord William eagerly accepted, but not until after he had explained that he had come to Vienna on family business and was very impressed with the city. The two talked as they walked the few blocks to Mozart's home. Wolfgang opened the door and called out: "Stanzi! Set out another bowl! We have a guest from England tonight, and you will never believe who it is!"

❧ ✳ ❧

And with that, the TV returned to its regularly scheduled programming. I was staring at the screen, Charlotte was staring at me, and Sherlock was resting peacefully.

"Wow. Both Wolfgang and Constanze knew Lord William in different contexts, and now those paths are merging into one! Fate brought them together! What a perfect prologue to the letters. Okay, guys, no more interruptions."

And, with that, I put my phone on the charger and set it to Do Not Disturb.

21
The Constanze Letters

December 1791

Dear William,

It is with great sadness that I write to tell you of Wolfgang's death. He died on December 5th. We had a simple service at St. Stephen's, which was attended by only a few. We were unable to afford a proper burial, so my beloved was taken to an unmarked pauper's grave, with me following solemnly behind the cart that carried his body.

What a blow this is to the world, William! I am going to make it my new mission in life to ensure he is not forgotten. Despite our desperate financial situation, I can't just put his music in a trunk and close the lid on his talents. I have been very protective of his scores, making sure he didn't lose them or give them away, so I have all of them in my possession.

As you know, we had a second son, Franz, who is just a tiny infant of five months. Karl is a mature seven-year-old and helps me out immensely with the baby. We are going to make it, but I know it won't be easy.

I don't write this seeking pity for my grief, but to make you aware of your friend's death. So young, and still so much music in his heart!

My plans are to stay in Vienna for the time being, and if you find yourself in this part of the world, please know that you are welcome in my home.

Sincerely,
Constanze Mozart

January 1792
My Dear Constanze,

I am heartsick upon hearing the news of Wolfgang's death. I wish I had known he was ill, for I would have made an attempt to come and see him and perhaps offer some help. Such a tragedy!

I am happy to hear you are going to make sure the world never forgets your very talented husband. If you ever need any help, I am at your beck and call. England has never forgotten the Mozarts' visit here.

It's been a bitter winter, but as soon as I can, I will come to Vienna to check on you and your boys. In the meantime, I have arranged some financial relief for you. I hope that it will help with your immediate needs, so please keep a portion for yourself. I hope it also allows you to move ahead with your efforts to maintain Wolfgang's music. Printing costs can be so expensive.

Thank you for writing, and I will see you sometime this spring. Give my love to Karl and Franz.

With love and sympathy,
Lord William

February 1792

My Dear Lord William,

Your generous donation to Wolfgang's cause and to our family made me weep! How kind of you! You were the first and only one so far to trust me with such an investment.

So much has happened since I last wrote to you. I do hope that you will find it in your schedule to come and visit, for I have things to ask of you. I need advice, and I feel that I can explain things better in person. I hate keeping this a mystery, but it is a mystery to me as well. Perhaps together we can solve the puzzle I have encountered while cleaning out Wolfgang's belongings and organizing his music. Do you know that he wrote over 600 hundred pieces of music in his short lifetime! Imagine if he had lived longer!

This is brief. The boys are doing well, and so am I. I will explain more when I see you this spring. I fear my letters are being read before they leave Vienna, so I am not taking any risks. Thank you for understanding.

Warmly,
Constanze

March 1792

Constanze!

I fear for you and the boys after your most recent letter! I am making arrangements to come to Vienna as soon as I can. I have immediate business to attend to with my properties, but will head your way very soon.

I have enclosed the name of a good magistrate in Vienna that I trust. If you feel the need to contact him, please present this letter to him.

His name is Peter Schultz. His office is located near St. Stephen's.

Sincerely,
Lord William

"PETER SCHULTZ!" I screamed, causing both dogs to jump to attention and shake the sleep off themselves.

"You have got to be kidding me! No wonder Peter is so interested in the treasures! If Constanze and William went to his great-great-whoever for help, there has to be some record of that. Peter most certainly has researched and uncovered this connection. Is he going to try to prove he has a legal claim to these treasures? Does he have a claim?"

Charlotte and Sherlock, who had their heads cocked, were focusing on her every word, as any good audience would do.

"That dirty rat knew this when he had our meeting in Vienna. Why didn't he just come clean? I think something must have transpired between 'Peter Past', William, and Constanze — something significant enough that it was recorded somewhere 'Peter Present' could find it. If Constanze's Peter was a well-respected magistrate, and William entrusted him with personal affairs, then records were kept or letters were passed down to our Peter. Smarmy jerk!"

I tousled Charlotte's head, and then reached over the side of the bed to do the same to Sherlock. Both dogs stretched and resettled into contented sleep, confident now there was no need for alarm.

My glasses were perched on the tip of my nose, so I pushed them up to look at the phone to see what time it was. I had an early meeting with Joseph to pick and order the gala repertoire. My instincts were to keep reading, but my body was hitting that jet lag brick wall. Satisfied that at least two clues had been uncovered tonight, I took off my glasses, settled in on my right side, fluffed my pillow, and let out a big sigh.

Right before drifting off to sleep, I itemized my findings tonight:

1. Wolfgang discovered in December of 1786 that he and Constanze both knew Lord William.
2. Constanze continued communicating with William in 1791 to inform him of Wolfgang's death. There may have been previous letters and meetings before Wolfgang's death, but the letters I had in my possession didn't indicate that.
3. Constanze was anxious to talk to Lord William in person about something concerning Wolfgang's estate.
4. Lord William gave her the name of a magistrate he used, who just happened to be named Peter Schultz.

Prague was going to be very interesting.

22
Obsession and Repentance

Arthur Adderly was not a happy camper. His obsession with the Mozart treasures just kept escalating. He thought about them 24/7, and he couldn't take his mind off how astute Dr. Stone ended up being. He thought she would be a pushover, selling him the snuff box and locket for a lark. But, oh no! The cunning Dr. Stone was anything but a pushover. She was clever, smart, and much tougher than she looked.

Adderly was sitting before a blazing fire, with Stanzi in his lap and Mozart blaring on his surround sound. Kristoph appeared from the kitchen and set a dinner tray and glass of chardonnay beside him. Adderly, still lost in thought, didn't acknowledge the meal, so Kristoph cleared his throat loudly. Adderly let out a big sigh, and Stanzi gave him a look that spoke volumes.

"Thank you, Kristoph. I am just so despondent over this Mozart affair that I lost track of time. Dr. Stone has been back in the States for only a few days, and I can't shake my disappointment. She rejected my charms and outsmarted us all. Peter is fuming, and Sophia is spitting mad. She apparently had a new home in the countryside picked out, and had to call the agent and cancel her appointment to see the property. Tragedy. Just tragedy." Adderly was shaking his head back and forth.

Kristoph sat in the chair next to his boss and faced him. "Sir, I know you are not happy, but you seriously need to snap out of this defeatist attitude. If we are to get the treasures, which is still our ultimate goal, we need to devise another plan. We can't do that if all you want to do is sit here and feel sorry for yourself."

"You are right, Kristoph, as always. The dinner smells delicious. Perhaps after some sustenance I will think more clearly. I want the locket. I have never wanted anything so badly, and I cannot believe Peter got us involved so deeply in these shenanigans. Usually my role in these transactions is much less...messy. Sadly, this has now become a game to see who can most effectively out-deceive the others. Mind you, I will again emphasize that Dr. Stone must not be harmed — that is not my intention."

Adderly was so preoccupied in his thoughts that he did not see Stanzi make a sneaky move towards his plate of fish. Just as she was about to pounce, Kristoph grabbed her up out of Adderly's lap and placed her on the footstool in front of the fire where she normally reigned. Her indignation showed as she curled up on her velvet throne. If cats could speak she would tell them a thing or two, or three...

"Sir, if anyone should be apologizing it should be me. You and Mr. Schultz devised a wonderful plan for me to steal the treasures at Tivoli. Dr. Stone was clearly frightened and handed over her bag freely. It all happened in a matter of a few minutes. I was in and out before she had a chance to even speak. I got out of the gardens unnoticed, taking the back streets, just as we had mapped out. When I got to my apartment, my heart was pounding. When I opened the wooden box and found it was empty, I was livid! I had put myself at risk, but more than that I had let you and Mr. Schultz down. My mind has so many questions... Everything we have planned has failed. How did she know? Dr. Stone is not the vulnerable woman I assumed she was."

Kristoph averted his gaze and wrung his hands in his lap. He had a good heart, and doing something this conniving had bothered him, yet he had agreed and failed. Until Dr. Stone's appearance in Adderly's life, his role had been simply a personal assistant, chef, and house sitter for his boss. This position was just temporary for him. He was saving money to open his own restaurant in Copenhagen, and the fact that Mr. Adderly paid him handsomely allowed him to save most of his salary.

Tivoli had been an exhilarating experience, but also frightening for someone who had always followed the rules. Mr. Schultz had added an extra bonus if he succeeded — enough for Kristoph to open his restaurant and live comfortably for many years. He had also threatened to expose Mr. Adderly for a "few shady art deals" in the past. Kristoph respected his boss and wished him no harm, so he agreed to the Tivoli robbery. When he saw the fearful look in Dr. Stone's eyes, he hated Peter Schultz even more. This memory would haunt him forever.

He remembered following Dr. Stone into the Hall of Mirrors. She had been standing in front of the mirrors in a trance, as if she saw something in them. He looked around, but saw only their reflections. She jumped when he asked for her bag and kept saying, 'No, not again!" What had happened before with her? He loosened his grip around her shoulders ever so slightly, hoping she would know he meant her no physical harm. She gave up her bag readily, just asking to keep her passport, which he quickly gave her before running out of the room.

Adderly's voice brought him out of the memory. Kristoph would never tell his boss about Peter's threats, but he knew there might come a time when it was necessary — especially if Peter got vicious or backed into a corner.

"Kristoph, I don't think any of us knew how clever Dr. Stone is, so please quit saying this is all your fault. True, I was hoping it would be over by now. I am troubled that we have had to resort to these means to get the treasures. Why didn't she just sell them outright and make a profit? What special hold do they have on her? Who is behind all of this? I still have so many questions, and perhaps we can figure it all out soon. Peter is supposed to be in Copenhagen again soon, and we will sit down to see what our next move is. How I would love to travel to the States and follow Dr. Stone around! But Peter feels it best to lay low. If we try again so soon, she really will be ready for us."

Adderly had been slowly eating during their conversation. Kristoph stood and asked him if he was ready to look at his mail. In all the chaos of the weekend, they had let other business slide. Kristoph thought that maybe getting his boss to focus on the real world would distract him from his recent failure. Adderly nodded his approval.

As Kristoph picked up his empty plate and headed for the kitchen, Adderly said, "Thank you, Kristoph. The meal was delicious, as always."

Mozart was still playing when Kristoph came back with the unopened mail. He had already sorted through some of the business correspondence himself, but he always left Adderly's personal mail unopened. He quietly set the stack on the table next to him and left the room.

Stanzi had raised her head when Kristoph left, and then jumped down to follow him to the kitchen to get her dinner. *Finally*, she thought, as she walked out with her head held high, purring loudly.

Adderly took another sip of his chardonnay, savoring the wine and the music before he reached for his mail. Mozart's *Requiem* was playing, and it was soothing his soul. He was a blessed man, but this obsession to get the treasures from Dr. Stone was warping his senses. It was as if he would not be whole until he had them in his possession. Why did he feel this way? He had many artifacts of Mozart's that he had acquired over the years, but they looked poor in comparison to what Dr. Stone was protecting. *Who was her mysterious benefactor that had contacted Peter? Why did they involve Peter? When was this all going to end?*

The *Requiem* ended and, after a brief pause, shifted to the *Prague Symphony*. Adderly reached for his stack of mail as the first movement made its opening statement. *Such a brilliant symphony*, he thought! But then again, all of Mozart's music was brilliant. He remembered the first time he had looked at one of his original manuscripts. Not one mistake! No erasures, no ink smears — just perfect notes. Beethoven, on the other hand, had cross-outs and ink smears all over his manuscripts, yet his music was just as incredible — just a different process to reach genius. It struck him how similar this was to his current situation! He and Peter had ink smears all over their plans as they worked out the way to finish their manuscript. *I am so brilliant*, he thought, but then laughed out loud for even putting himself in the same category as Mozart and Beethoven.

His mail really had piled up. He had thank you notes from grateful clients, who had also included of pictures of their artwork in its new home; numerous requests from private collectors looking for certain pieces to add to their collections; and several invitations. The last piece of mail in the stack was in a beautiful gold envelope with his name styled in elegant calligraphy. He paused for a moment, and turned it over and over again looking for the sender. Curiously, there was no return address! He was careful as he opened it, for he wanted to save the envelope that had obviously taken someone significant time and skill to address. It was an invitation, and he was delighted to see that it was also beautifully calligraphed by the same hand:

&><✳><&

You and a Guest Are Cordially Invited to Attend

The Mozart Masquerade Gala

New Year's Eve

Prague, Czech Republic

The Estates Theatre

8 p.m.

Choral and Orchestral Works of Mozart

Under the Direction of

Dr. Elizabeth Stone & Dr. Joseph Chamberlain

Please Come in Masquerade

No RSVP necessary but present this invitation upon arrival

&><✳><&

"KRISTOPH! Come quickly!" Adderly was shaking as he stood up. Kristoph ran into the room to see Adderly in a state of shock, holding a gold envelope in one hand, and its contents in the other.

"Are you okay, sir?"

Adderly didn't say a word, but turned and gingerly handed him the invitation. Kristoph read it, and re-read it, allowing the words on the beautiful paper to sink in. When he finally looked at his boss, he too was in a state of disbelief.

"Sir, do you think this has some connection with the Mozart treasures? What does this mean?"

"What it means, Kristoph, is that this whole escapade will finally come to a close on New Year's Eve in Prague. Get Peter on the phone. Don't apologize for the lateness of the hour. And, if he doesn't answer, leave a message for him to call me immediately!"

Adderly felt a new surge of energy replace the depression he had felt for days. A masquerade gala! Prague! A performance by the one and only Dr. Stone! Too many coincidences aligning here, and it was becoming obvious that her benefactor was also playing a game with all of them. He smiled as he paced the room with his hands behind his back, waiting to talk with Peter and plan their next chapter.

23

Peter Schultz

Vienna's weather was getting colder, and the days were getting dark earlier. Peter was working late at the museum, trying to catch up on business that had been ignored while they were in Copenhagen. He didn't like thinking about the trip, which ended up being largely a wasted effort. Dr. Stone had duped them and successfully held on to the treasures which he, Sophia, and Adderly had hoped would be in their possession by now. This was supposed to have been easy. Now work was piled up, Sophia was whining, plus they had nothing to show for their efforts except credit card debt for their travel to Copenhagen.

He had a nice fire going in his office, and Sophia was sitting across from him pouting and sipping on a glass of red wine. He had a glass as well, but he was still on his first one whereas she was on her second.

"Peter, when is this nonsense going to come to a close? You promised me it would be over in Copenhagen — that you and Adderly had the perfect plan — and yet here we are, empty-handed once again. Do you know how embarrassing and disappointing it was to call the real estate broker and tell him we had to postpone looking at the property?"

Sophia continued to whine, but Peter tuned her out. He was getting so weary of her demands that he wished he had not included her. Now she had a hold on him, leaving him no choice.

"Peter! You are ignoring me!"

"I am sorry Sophia — so much work to catch up on. I was focused on the letter of request from a school wanting to schedule a private tour this spring. What was it you were saying?"

"Oh, forget it."

She folded her arms, but then reached for her glass to take another sip of her wine. Hopefully he would be done soon and they could go and eat. As frustrating as all of this was, she really was fond of Peter. If they became rich from the sale of the treasures, she still considered that to be a side benefit of their relationship, so she needed to be careful and quit whining. She didn't want to lose Peter, or her job, so she settled for being quiet while he finished his business. She had stayed late to help him with correspondence, but had finished her tasks before him. The fire was inviting, Mozart was playing in the background, and the wine was superb.

Peter abruptly stood up. Sophia had been annoying with all her questions, so he almost ripped the beautiful gold envelope in half as he opened it. His hands were shaking as he read the contents of the gold envelope, but before Sophia had a chance to ask him what was wrong, his cell phone rang. Peter looked at the caller ID and saw that it was Adderly. He slowly sat down and answered the call, still holding the invitation in his hand. Sophia moved behind him to read what had obviously stunned Peter. As she read the invitation, staring at what she read in disbelief, Peter spoke on the phone.

"Adderly?" Peter asked.

"It's Kristoph, sir, but I am here with Adderly, who wishes to speak with you."

"Peter!" Adderly shouted. "I am assuming that you have received the same beautiful invitation that I received! What do you make of this? I hate to admit it, but this excites me after our failed attempt in Copenhagen! A masquerade with our dear Dr. Stone performing? Wonders never cease in this adventure!"

Peter finally heard Adderly breathe, so he interrupted him before Adderly could begin another excited soliloquy. "Slow down, Arthur! Yes, I just this very moment read the invitation. My brain is racing with a thousand questions, and yours obviously is as well. Who is behind the gala? Did Dr. Stone know about this when she was in Copenhagen, or is she just now finding out about it? Too many pieces of the puzzle aren't yet connecting, but my initial thoughts are that her benefactor is behind all of this."

"Me too, Peter! Do you know that Mozart's *Don Giovanni* was premiered at The Estates Theatre and that his *Symphony No. 38* is named the *Prague Symphony* because it was also premiered in Prague? It was

Mozart's first visit to the city, and the audiences loved him so much that they gave the symphony its name."

"Arthur, I run the Mozarthaus Museum — I know these things. It is my business, after all."

Sophia noisily sat back down to show her frustration. Peter gave her a look of "what can I do?" and continued on with Adderly.

"Seriously, historical facts aside, what do you make of this? It sounds as though none of us will know until we get there, and I plan on being in the front row. I want to see firsthand who is behind this charade. This is turning into a three-ring circus, and I don't want to be the main attraction! I want the treasures!"

With that, Peter hit his desk with his fist a little too hard, and his glass of wine nearly spilled. Sophia was quick to catch it before it stained all the papers on his desk.

"And there is no way to know ahead of time — no RSVP, no website, no sender address, not even a postmark! How did this person do this, and who is he?" Arthur said while pacing madly, talking like he had about twenty cups of coffee in him.

Peter and Adderly conversed on the phone for several more minutes trying to make sense of this new development. It was now the first of November, and the gala was two months away. Their biggest question was whether Dr. Stone was blindsided with the gala as well, or if this had been set in motion before her trip to Copenhagen. He and Arthur eventually decided that she probably didn't know about the gala until she got back to the States, but that she probably had already figured out they all would be there. Peter briefly considered contacting her, feigning politeness to say how much he looked forward to hearing the performance, but they decided it was better to leave their moves and motives hidden.

After all, it was a masquerade.

24

Paparazzi, Stateside

Paparazzi was enjoying himself in the States. It was his first time to visit, so he had searched online for the top ten things to do while he was here – in his spare time, of course. He loved the food, and he was finally getting the hang of driving on the righthand side of the road. He found Dr. Stone's campus to be beautiful, with many green spaces and communal areas for him to hang out while he was documenting her.

His job was to keep Elizabeth's benefactor informed, alerting him if anything seemed out of place. When Paparazzi took the assignment, it wasn't the first time he had worked for this prominent figure. He had been called again because he had done a good job and was trusted. Nothing – *nothing* – was to happen to Elizabeth. The Benefactor had made that very clear.

Now, he was sitting in a restaurant that boasted the best pancakes in town. He had a tall stack with a side of bacon, and the waitress was making sure his coffee cup was full. His hotel served breakfast, but he didn't always eat there. He enjoyed getting out and exploring, and he loved observing people. His job was a lonely one, so sitting in a restaurant with lots of noise and people made him feel like he wasn't so isolated.

His mouth full of gingerbread pancakes, he was annoyed that his phone began lighting up with a call. Swallowing quickly, he answered and spoke quietly into the receiver.

"Yes?" he asked, choking still on pancakes. He took a sip of water to help get the food down as he listened to the man on the other end of the phone

"How is it going? The boss wants to know how Dr. Stone took the invitation to perform in Prague. Any ideas yet? I know she just heard about it yesterday, but he wants to know if you've heard anything."

The man he was talking to was Mr. Brookshire, the Benefactor's lawyer. He was always the one who connected with him, and Paparazzi only knew him as Mr. Brookshire. They had met when the assignment was given, and reports were made directly to him. Mr. Brookshire then handed them over to the Benefactor.

Mr. Brookshire had been the one to explain the gala plans to him — at least the parts he was privy to know. Paparazzi was excited to see it all unfold, and especially excited to see all the players come together. A well written script!

Just as he started telling him that he planned to spend time on campus in the music building today, he looked up and saw Dr. Stone talking to the hostess!

"I need to go now. Dr. Stone just walked into the restaurant where I am eating. More later, Mr. Brookshire." As he signed off, he watched Dr. Stone and prayed that she would be seated near his table.

As luck would have it, she was seated in the booth behind him. Since arriving in the States, he had dressed very American. Jeans, blazer, turtleneck, and had added a ball cap to conceal his identity a bit. He didn't think Dr. Stone had ever seen him, but he didn't want to take the chance.

"Good Morning, Dr. Stone! How good to see you! It's been quite a while since you have been in. Could I get you started with some juice or coffee?" The waitress obviously knew Dr. Stone either through school or because she was a frequent client here.

"So good to see you, Lilah! How are your classes coming this fall? Still going to be a teacher, I hope? And yes — the biggest mug of coffee you have, black, no cream or sugar, please!"

Lilah laughed. "I remember, Dr. Stone. If we were late to your class, we had to bring you coffee. Not a bad trade off when the lunch lines were long. Remember that day when five of us were late, and we all brought you coffee? And, as I recall, it did not take you long to drink all five cups!"

Elizabeth put her hands on her cheeks. "Oh my, that was a good day! I thought I had died and gone to Coffee Heaven! I am waiting on Bradley — you remember him, right? He should be zipping in here shortly."

"He's your assistant, correct? Nice guy. I'll be right back with your coffee, and will keep an eye out for him." Lilah started to walk away, but then turned back to Elizabeth. "And yes, I am still going to be a teacher.

Your classes inspired me. Just trying to figure out which grade now, but student teaching will help."

Elizabeth clapped her hands with delight. "Come by my office any time if you have questions. And Lilah, we miss having you around. Just sayin'..." She winked and Lilah walked away a head taller than before. Lilah was putting herself through school, and she was the first in her generation to attend college. Some days weren't easy, but Dr. Stone just made her realize her goal was attainable.

Lilah came right back with her coffee. Elizabeth put her hand on Lilah's as she said a warm thank you, and then proceeded to take that cherished first sip. Her phone lit up, and she saw a text from Bradley. He was parking and was on his way in.

She turned to look at the door and saw Michael Holmes standing there. He nodded as she sipped, and pointed to the booth behind her. He made the motions of taking a picture — Paparazzi was in the booth behind her! Michael Holmes gave a thumbs-up, but also opened his eyes wide, pretending his fingers were propping them open, as a reminder to be vigilant. He then proceeded to make his way to that booth and actually sat across from the man. Must be nice to be an angel.

Elizabeth took her phone, put it on camera mode, and then acted as if she were using it to fix her hair. She could see Paparazzi, but not his face. He didn't have a clue an angel was watching him eat his breakfast, but the way he was eating made Elizabeth realize this was a chance encounter. He had no idea she was going to be here as well. Nothing seemed staged. She wished he would turn so she could get a look at his face! At least she would hear his voice; and, since Lilah was his waitress, she might be able to get some details from her later.

At that moment, Bradley came in through the front door in his true fashion — moving quickly and determined to get where he was going. He spotted Elizabeth and slid into the booth with a fast "Good Morning" before he settled in.

"And a good morning to you as well! So glad you could join me before we go to the office. I was hungry for gingerbread pancakes."

"Have you ordered yet?" Bradley was looking at the menu, but never looked up. When Lilah appeared at the table, he just said, "Coffee, please." He only looked up when Elizabeth cleared her throat. That is when he noticed Lilah standing there and recognized her from their class, Music Appreciation 101.

"Good Morning, Professor Bailey. How would you like your coffee?" Lilah was grinning, amused that she caught him off guard. Elizabeth thought she saw a few sparks fly when they recognized each other.

"Lilah, right? Music Appreciation 101 last spring. I remember the paper you wrote comparing Beethoven and Mozart. Very good." He nervously added that he would like his coffee black, no cream or sugar.

"Is drinking your coffee black a prerequisite for being Dr. Stone's assistant? I will be right back."

Lilah quickly left, but not before she gave a big wink to Bradley. This embarrassed him even more, so he buried his face in his menu.

Elizabeth laughed and laughed. Leaning forward on her elbows she asked quietly, "Do I need to ask her to bring water so she can put the fire out? Your face is beet red. I think you would like to get to know Lilah better. I can arrange that. Just give me the go ahead."

Her students knew she was never embarrassed to pre-arrange a chance meeting with someone they were too shy to do so themselves. Elizabeth had a stack of wedding invitations in her desk drawer to prove it.

Lilah came back with Bradley's coffee, and gave Elizabeth a fresh cup. Taking both their orders for gingerbread pancakes with a side of bacon, she cheerfully told them she would be right back. Elizabeth noticed Bradley watched her walk away this time.

"Lilah would be a good fit for you. Just come in here more often, and it will happen. She is pretty, smart, and will understand your profession." Elizabeth adored Bradley as if he were her own son. She leaned back in the booth, and noticed that when she did, the other side of the booth shifted a bit. Briefly forgetting that Paparazzi was there, she tuned in again and remembered to err on the side of caution in her conversation with Bradley.

"Thanks, Elizabeth," Bradley blushed. "What time is your meeting with Dr. Chamberlain? I barely slept last night. I couldn't stop thinking about Prague. What do you make of it?"

Elizabeth kicked Bradley from under the table. He gave her the oddest look, and she carefully put her finger to her lips and nodded to the booth behind her. He took the hint and nodded as he rubbed his shin.

"I mean," he continued, "do we have time to pick the repertoire and learn it? When will we tell the students?" He hoped he had made a good recovery, because he was going to ask if Prague was connected to the treasures. He only knew bits and pieces, but gleaned enough to know the situation could be dangerous.

"I'm meeting with Joseph at 9. I have a list I want to present to him that should suit the Chorale and Orchestra nicely. So much to choose from, but I need to know how long of a concert the event planners want us to prepare. Joseph probably has some ideas of his own as well. Chorale is this afternoon, so I thought I would let them know. They need to rearrange Christmas plans, or let me know they don't want to be a part of it all. I can't imagine the latter, but one never knows. I need to find out if family members can purchase tickets to the gala, how many seats are available, where we are staying, and the list goes on and on. Joseph said that once we accepted the invitation, his contact was going to get more information to him. And that, dear Bradley, is all I know." Elizabeth didn't say anything she didn't think Paparazzi knew, for Michael Holmes had already told her he was working for her benefactor.

Lilah appeared with their food. The pancakes smelled divine; the bacon cooked to perfection. She set Elizabeth's down first, making sure she made eye contact with Bradley as she set his plate in front of him. Bradley turned ten shades of red, and Elizabeth tried not to laugh out loud.

As luck would have it, Lilah stopped at Paparazzi's table and asked him if he wanted more coffee.

"Yes, please, and thank you." He tried to conceal his British accent, but Lilah had already commented on it when she waited on him earlier. She grinned and told him again how charming his accent was.

Elizabeth sat up taller. *British!* She and Bradley raised their eyebrows and gave each other the look of "interesting" that spoke volumes without words. In their teaching partnership, they had developed a silent language of looks to communicate with each other. Worked every time.

Breakfast continued with idle conversation, until Elizabeth checked the time on her phone and said she needed to get going. She got Lilah's attention, and then as she paid the check, she reiterated how proud of her she was and encouraged her to come by her office soon. And, she said, if I am not there, I am sure Professor Bailey can help you.

They gathered their things and walked out together. Both of them glimpsed back to where Paparazzi was seated and saw that Lilah had now given him his check. Elizabeth wondered if he paid with cash or by credit card. Cash, probably. Her benefactor seemed to have unlimited funds. Michael Holmes was looking intently at Paparazzi, as if to get a clue of his identity. *Surely he has a name!*

They were just walking out the door when Lilah ran out after them. "Dr. Stone! The gentleman in the booth asked me to give this to you." Lilah held out a folded note. Elizabeth thanked her, but her heart also skipped a beat. Was Paparazzi revealing himself to her? *Surely he knew this was risky!*

Elizabeth and Bradley moved into the shade of the restaurant's awning, and she nervously opened the note. In beautiful scripted handwriting was an address and phone number in Prague — of a masquerade shop. They both looked at each other and wondered what this meant, but both knew it was meant to be investigated. Bradley went back in to see if Paparazzi was still there, but he came back shaking his head "no." Lilah told him he had used the back door after handing her the note. Bradley jotted down his phone number and told Lilah to call him if the man came back to the restaurant.

Yet another clue.

Paparazzi had received a text with the instructions to give Elizabeth the information about the masquerade shop in Prague. He then slipped out after handing Lilah the note and a handsome tip. Scrunching down into his car seat, he saw Elizabeth and Bradley looking at the note.

"Happy solving, Dr. Stone!" He tipped his hat to her, even though he knew she didn't see him. She had her head buried in her phone, searching for information on this masquerade shop. Pleased, Paparazzi sent a text telling Mr. Brookshire the task was a success.

25

The Innocents

We were the Innocents — Amanda Kate, Peyton, and me — or Baby Boomers, as we are also commonly called. Products of the 1950s, we were raised by Southern mothers and fathers who instilled good manners, taught us to be kind and loving always, to respect our elders, and to be at the church every time the doors opened. We never ate at home on Wednesday nights, but instead took our share of roast beef, mashed potatoes, green beans, and hot rolls in the church's Fellowship Hall before we went to Wednesday night prayer meeting followed by youth groups and choir. Every Wednesday! Oh, those hot rolls! Amanda Kate always had as many as she wanted! On Sundays, we watched our mothers put on the pot roast before Sunday School, and then the same meal we ate on Wednesday night was ready when we got home from church promptly at 12:30 p.m. We were required to take a Sunday afternoon nap and then attend the evening service at 7 p.m. Families would rotate hosting an after-church fellowship at their homes on Sunday night. The adults played cards and dominoes while we either played outside or watched The Ed Sullivan Show.

In our hometown, everyone knew everyone, so we knew better than to get in trouble at school or our parents would hear about it from the whole town before we got home. We rode our bicycles or walked to neighborhood elementary schools, and we played jump rope after school until we were called in for dinner each night — smelling of grass and protesting that we weren't ready to come inside. Doctors still made house calls, and heaven forbid if we got the measles or chicken pox and had to watch our friends play from a bedroom window. If you had an over-protective mother like mine, you stayed home from school if you coughed or sneezed. Nothing to do while you lay in bed but read — books like *Nancy Drew* or *The Hardy Boys*, or others that are now children's classics.

We rode our bicycles with reckless abandon as our fathers cheered from the sidewalks and our mothers were inside fixing the evening meal. Those were the innocent times.

The three of us met in elementary school, and by the time we were teenagers, we were still kind, respectful, and innocent. We had fun, but we were the ones with the early curfews, whose fathers went looking for us if we were late. Those were the days before cell phones, but we were required to keep coins to use a pay phone to call home if we were going to be late.

None of us had our own car, as our parents couldn't afford to buy them for us. We took turns on the weekends asking to borrow the car, but we all had to pitch in to fill up the gas tank before we parked it back home in the garage. Normally we rode around "the drag" — a circle of blocks around the local drive-in — waving and honking at everyone we saw. At a certain point in the evening, we would reverse our direction and go the other way to catch anyone we missed. We were able to see who had dates, and how close they were sitting to each other. Guys would holler out the window and tell us to meet them at the drive-in, where they would hop in the car and order cokes and fries from the speaker phones that had tempting menus attached at the top.

Our local drive in was Murphy's, and it was the place to be on the weekends. They stayed open after the football games, and we made our way there hoping to catch a glimpse of the football boys who would be there to fill up on burgers, fries, and malts, with their faces still glistening from their locker room showers. Neither victory nor defeat kept them away from Murphy's. If we won, horns were blaring and kids were hanging out the windows all around the drag; and if we lost, horns were blaring and kids were hanging out the windows anyway.

In high school, the three of us spent our Friday nights going to the local dance, where a local band comprised of high school guys played. Every Friday night, I watched from the sidelines as Amanda Kate and Peyton danced the night away. Acne does that to you. No one wants to look at your festered face while dancing to cool music. So, I listened to the band and watched all the people. I learned the art of listening by being a wallflower — imagine that!

Since our parents were strict with curfews, we were picked up at the dance promptly at 10 p.m. We rotated spending the night at each other's houses — but often ended up at Amanda Kate's since she had an endless supply of Coca-Cola. We would spend the rest of the night lip syncing the Beatles and the Beach Boys, eating popcorn, and drinking Coke. We were the Innocents.

Life happened, but we remained supportive and strong through it all. Deaths, births, marriages — we held each other up.

On our most recent Innocents trip to New York City, we were sitting in the bar at our favorite boutique hotel. We had just come from seeing a show, and the wind was chilly on our rickshaw ride back to the hotel. We were warming up with a nice drink when I asked my two favorite friends in the world: "Have you ever thought about which one of us will die first?"

Peyton spilled her drink, and Amanda Kate gave me one of those looks. This was a topic we had not discussed, but I had thought about it a lot — especially since becoming a widow. What would I do if I lost my two best friends?

"Oh my, Izzibeth, what a horrible thought!" It was Amanda Kate. Peyton was cleaning up her spilled drink.

"Come on girls, I know you have thought about this, but it is one of those forbidden topics we were brought up not to discuss. It's been on my mind lately. You are my rocks, and even more so since Liam died. I just don't think I could bear it if one of you died. I keep thinking of Bette Midler and Barbara Hershey in *Beaches*. But seriously, we should discuss it. I want you to know I will always be there for both of you. I will take your dogs, but not your husbands."

I smiled a wicked smile as I said this, and Amanda Kate spit out the sip of her drink, which spewed all over the table. We all proceeded to laugh, and then the conversation was immediately forgotten as we turned to the menu to order a late dinner.

❧ ✳ ❧

I was reflecting on all of these memories as I was driving to my office after breakfast that morning. The conversation had crossed my mind several times since the attacks in Copenhagen. I wanted another chance to tell them both how much I loved them, and to take another trip together as the Innocents. The first attack in Copenhagen had traumatized me and made me realize I didn't want to die by someone else's hands. Just like in *Beaches*, I wanted them by my side, singing to me as I took my last breath.

Arriving at the Music Building, I picked up my cell phone and sent a group message to Amanda Kate and Peyton.

I love you both, and we need to talk. What weekend do you have free to come visit? I need to go over the Prague plans!

Within seconds, I had replies from both of them indicating they could come down this very weekend. The next texts confirmed they would arrive on Friday night and go back home on Sunday. That "sixth sense" we all shared had probably already kicked in, letting them know that something was amiss. Hooray for airline miles that afforded last-minute trips to see best friends in a time of need.

I was excited — and relieved. They need to know the whole story, and it was time to put my plan in action.

❧ ✳ ❧

Paparazzi was sitting at the bench near Elizabeth's parking spot. He had changed hats, pretending to look at a campus map. He snapped a few pictures with his phone and had noticed the thoughtful look on her face as she entered the building.

26

Mozart Travel Company

Joseph had been at the University for ten years now. The orchestra and the orchestral department had flourished under his direction, and the music faculty all looked up to him with great respect. He currently was sitting in his office with a notebook of detailed notes, sent to him via courier this morning, concerning the masquerade gala in Prague. He was noticeably stunned and excited by the generous invitation, but perplexed by the lack of names in any of the communications. No postmark, no indication where the material came from, and always hand delivered. Whoever had organized this event clearly wished to remain anonymous and was cautious every step of the way. Even when he sent his reply of acceptance, a courier picked up the contract he had signed. Strangest arrangement he had ever experienced.

There was a quiet knock on the door, and Elizabeth came in.

"Good Morning, Joseph. I hope I haven't kept you waiting."

"You are right on time, as usual, Elizabeth. Come on in and sit down. I just received an itinerary for the Prague trip. Whoever our benefactor is, well, let's say he is not sparing any cost. You, Bradley, the music faculty, and I all have First Class seats on all flights. All of the performers have upgraded seats in the economy section. A chartered bus with a full-time tour guide will meet us at the airport to take us to our four-star accommodation, The Mozart House. Breakfasts and dinners are provided, and a daily stipend will be given to everyone for their lunches. This is a lot of money being invested — a sum I can't wrap my head around! If we were having to finance this ourselves with our current budget, we would have had to decline. Amazing, Elizabeth! So, I am left wondering why — why were we chosen, and does it have something to do with you? I am just a bit perplexed."

Perplexed is mild compared to what it really is, Elizabeth thought. Putting on her best actress face, she said she was as perplexed as he was about the invitation, but had chosen to be more excited than perplexed.

"I am hoping," she said, "that once we get there, all of this will make perfect sense. I, too, want to meet this mysterious benefactor who is sponsoring us in such a generous manner. However, I feel it is best to concentrate now on what we will perform at the gala in order to provide our guests with a truly stunning experience."

"Agreed." Joseph took off his glasses and looked straight into her eyes. "Have you given it much thought? I explored some options last night, but I am interested to see if you and I are on the same page."

"Do the instructions say anything about the whole program needing to be Mozart? I was thinking it would be fun to open with a flashy staging of *Masquerade* from *The Phantom of the Opera*. I just received the name of a custom masquerade shop in Prague that I could contact about costumes and masks for the chorus. From there, we could go into the Mozart portion of the program. I was thinking of *Misericordias Domine K.222*. Wolfgang wrote it when he was nineteen. Psalm 88 is the text, and was premiered in Munich in 1775. Some believe Beethoven took his *Ode to Joy* theme from this piece, and when you listen to the *Misericordias* the theme is definitely present!"

Joseph was nodding in agreement with all that Elizabeth said.

"I have always loved that piece and the Beethoven connection. I like the opening idea too! Where did you hear about the masquerade shop?"

"My girlfriend, Amanda Kate, is a famous interior designer – you met her last year at the Fine Arts fundraiser dinner. She had donated the table decorations. Anyway, I was telling her about this invitation on the phone last night, and she mentioned the shop. In fact, she has agreed to come, along with her assistant, Peyton, to be the liaison with the shop and handle all of the costuming, etc."

"Interesting. Sounds good, Elizabeth. Any other repertoire suggestions at this time? We need to get the scores ASAP."

"I would also love to incorporate the *Requiem* and some of the *Vesperae solennes de confessore, K. 339* – perhaps the 5th movement? And...I have this wonderful idea, if you will agree. I believe with all my heart that Wolfgang would have been a rocker if he lived today. I think he would have been a pioneer today, just as he was then, out on the cutting edge. What if I take a chorus from either *Don Giovanni, The Magic Flute, or The Marriage of Figaro* and have Bradley arrange it as an a cappella piece with vocal percussion and all? I can envision it all now!"

Joseph had put his pen down and was listening with a big smile on his face. "I love it, Elizabeth! Brilliant programming! You've been to The Estates Theatre, correct?"

"Yes, twice. It isn't big. I saw a great production of *Così fan tutte*. It is a beautiful venue for our performance – so well preserved in its original state, and the acoustics are wonderful."

Elizabeth was talking so fast that she had to hold on to the edge of the table to contain her excitement. Programming was her strong suit, and she was excited that Joseph liked her ideas.

"Joseph, I was thinking perhaps you need to pick music for the guests to hear as they enter the theatre. There really isn't a lot of room in the foyer, except maybe for a small quartet, but it could create such an elegant ambience as the guests arrive! Maybe overtures from the operas? But, then, you know that repertoire better than I do."

"I definitely will come up with good pre-concert music. Oh, here is the itinerary and all the details that the courier delivered today. The envelope included your copy as well."

Elizabeth stiffened. "Courier? This is all so unusual. Is it a courier company, or the same individual each time? Have you had much interaction with this courier?"

"Beats me, Elizabeth. The deliveries have been waiting for me under my door each time, so I guess I am assuming it is a courier. No postmark, no address, nothing. The only info I have is the name you see on the header – Mozart Travel Company – and I am assuming this is the travel company arranging all our details. That is why I was hoping you knew more about this. Have you ever traveled with them?"

"Nope, not familiar with this one."

Elizabeth was shaking her head. Her knees were shaking as well, so she changed positions hoping it wouldn't show. *Mozart Travel Company, my foot*, she thought. This was clearly a bogus company her benefactor has concocted to conceal his identity. New Year's Eve couldn't get here fast enough!

"I know you have a class, Elizabeth. Thank you for coming in early to meet with me. Let's meet again in a few days to finalize the program. According to the note inside the packet, I need to have the program and all relevant details ready to send by Friday, when the elusive courier will pick everything up. There is also a page enclosed in your information, as well as mine, asking us to list all of our travelers by their passport names. No nicknames."

Elizabeth acted like she didn't already know this fact after years of traveling abroad with students and adults. She felt the need to play innocent for a while longer, since her benefactor has chosen to use Joseph as the main communicator. He probably knows she would camp out all night to see who picked up the envelopes on Friday — which wasn't a bad idea...

She and Joseph exchanged pleasantries as they ended the meeting. He returned to his computer to finish some work, and she headed down to her office. Students were already arriving, getting their folders, and greeting each other as only choir family could do. She loved these kids, and couldn't wait to see their faces when she told them about Prague today.

Her phone lit up as she stepped into her office, and it was a message from Benjamin. She hadn't talked to him in a few days, so she expected a question about how things were going.

Elizabeth — thank you so much for the beautiful invitation to Prague and the masquerade gala! My calendar is open, so I look forward to attending and hearing your chorale. On another note, how are things going?

Elizabeth was beginning to wonder who else had been invited. But, before she even had a chance to respond back to Benjamin, she had the same message from her banker, Matthew. And then her son. And then her brother in Copenhagen. She even heard from Amanda Kate and Peyton that they'd each received formal invitations, which was interesting because she'd already personally invited them. The scary thing was that they each received them in the mail, so the sender knew where they all lived.

Elizabeth felt a chill go up her spine as she thought of having everyone she loved at the gala. Even though she had faith they wouldn't be harmed, the attacks in Copenhagen had planted seeds of doubt in her mind – anything could happen at this point. Luckily, the treasures were still in the bank vault, and she couldn't think of a good reason why Peter and Adderly would try something at the gala – since they surely wouldn't think she would bring the treasures with her. She couldn't shake the chill in the air, even as she logically worked her way through everyone's motives. This was going to be tricky.

Chin up, she told herself. Elizabeth put on that million-dollar smile she was known for, and stepped on her conductor's stand.

"Choir, I have some very exciting news to tell you today. The University Chorale and University Orchestra have been invited to perform for a masquerade gala on New Year's Eve – in Prague."

Cheers erupted from the students, and they all began asking questions at once. Elizabeth raised her hand, and then proceeded to tell them all the details she knew up to this point.

"The main thing at the moment is for you to clear your calendars. Your families need to know so they can adjust holiday plans if necessary. So, if you would, please take the time right now to text or call whomever you need to verify you can go. The dates will be December 27th through January 2nd. And, if they ask – the cost of your whole trip is completely covered by an anonymous donor who is sponsoring the gala!"

This caused an uproar of emotions, and some students even burst into tears. College was an expensive investment, and many were putting themselves through. This gala was the opportunity of a lifetime for them all, and for that, Elizabeth was grateful to her benefactor. She just prayed he had everyone's best interest at heart and had planned for every contingency.

Bradley was going around answering all the questions he could answer. What a dear. Once things had died down a bit, she got the group's attention again.

"This trip is happening really quickly. I just learned of it yesterday myself. We have two months to learn the repertoire — which will be mostly Mozart because we are performing at The Estates Theatre. In order to meet the tour operator's deadlines, I need your passport names today. Bradley is passing around a clipboard for you to print them on. If you don't have one yet, your passport name will be what is on your driver's license or birth certificate. For example, mine is Dr. Elizabeth Mayme Stone. No nicknames. If you have questions, please ask. It costs a fortune to change a name on an airline ticket, and you don't want to be left waving good-bye to us through your tears when you can't board the plane with us!"

Everyone in Chorale got the go ahead from their families, passport names were recorded, and then Bradley gave copies of Mozart's *Requiem* to the section leaders to pass out. Luckily the library already housed multiple copies, so we were able to immediately begin working.

"Okay, choir, let's warm up and get to work — we are going to Prague!"

27
Things Get Personal

What a busy day! After class, Bradley and I put the names of Chorale members into a spreadsheet to take to Joseph, who had been doing the same with his orchestra and other faculty members. I had also added the information for Amanda Kate and Peyton. He was told by the "tour company" to put all the participant travel information in an envelope and leave it in the Fine Arts main office for someone to pick up. It all seemed tedious, the lengths that my benefactor was taking to remain anonymous. However, I was reminded of the safety of everyone involved, so I shook off the desire to hide out in the office all day and night to see who picked up the envelope. If I were a betting woman, I would put all my money on Paparazzi.

Meanwhile, I was happy to get home and see Sherlock and Charlotte. They, in turn, were more than excited to see me walk in the back door. For Charlotte, it meant she could now go out and sniff around the backyard before dinner, and for Sherlock it meant he could watch over his earthly mistress from the comfort of her home. If dogs could talk, he would tell me everything. Every night I sat and quizzed him, trying to pry answers from him, but he just stared right back at me with his big, black, soulful eyes.

I went outside with the dogs and took in the beautiful evening. The birds were beginning to settle in for the night, and their chatter was expressive and comforting. The trees were turning, and fall was definitely in the air.

Hands on my hips, I began taking in deep breaths when Michael Holmes appeared beside me.

"Good Evening, Elizabeth. How was your day?"

"Need you ask? I thought you were aware of my every move." I laughed as I turned to face him.

"True, but it doesn't mean I can't ask how you felt about the day. Well — aren't you going to ask about mine?"

"Good evening, Michael Holmes. How was your day?" I winked, and Sherlock came bounding up the stairs behind Charlotte to greet Michael.

"I think we probably need to go inside for our daily briefing, if you catch my drift."

"Why can't we talk outside?" I asked, furrowing my brows.

"No cause for concern. I just think you will be more comfortable inside. Your neighbors might see you talking to yourself, causing some alarm for your sanity."

"True. And as usual, you are looking after my best interest."

My neighbors could see me on the deck from their back porch, and I definitely didn't want them to worry any more than they already did.

Closing the door behind us, Michael Holmes sat at the bar while I fixed Charlotte's dinner. Charlotte sat like a queen while she waited.

"Charlotte, let's give thanks for your dinner."

Michael watched with amusement and wonder as Charlotte bowed her head while I said a quick prayer for her food. As soon as I said "amen," Charlotte stood and began eating.

"That is so cute." Michael said. "How clever of you, Elizabeth."

"I saw it online and taught her — can't take the credit completely. There are dogs all over the world saying grace right now. So, cut to the chase Michael Holmes and brief me on your day." I grabbed a cold water from the refrigerator and sat down next to him.

"You are correct about Paparazzi. He is the courier for your benefactor, and he reports in every day to a Mr. Brookshire. I haven't been able to see the phone number to catch where the call is from, but I overheard him call him by name today. Paparazzi has a name, but I haven't heard it yet. He is extremely clever, and very good at what he does. He changes his look frequently, and is a man who wears many hats — literally. He was scared this morning when you and Bradley were eating near him, yet he was thrilled to be where he could overhear your conversation. He's a good guy and has your best interest at heart. I wonder what he would think if he knew he wasn't your only guardian angel." Michael smiled.

"Oh no, Michael Holmes — I forgot to contact the masquerade shop today!" I got up and reached for my purse to dig out the note that Paparazzi had given Lilah at the restaurant that morning. Finding it, I sat back down next to Michael Holmes and used my phone to search for more information about the shop. According to their website, they were located near Old Town Square, which was very close to The Estates Theatre. A seven-hour time difference, it was futile to call now, so I texted a reminder to myself to call tomorrow during my conference time.

"May I see the note?" Michael didn't know what difference it would make, but he wanted to check the handwriting. "So, I guess you noticed it is the same writing on the invitations?"

"I did — that is what made me think Paparazzi is the go-between. Oh, also, what is up with everyone I love in the world being invited to the gala? I got seven texts today at the same time thanking me for inviting them! It is worrisome that their addresses are known."

"Paparazzi and Mr. Brookshire seem to be the only ones who know them, so you don't need to worry. Maybe you could find some information about Mr. Brookshire and see where he is located?"

"Good idea." After several internet search attempts, nothing obvious had turned up. "Drat! I cannot believe how much care has been taken to hide their identities!" I laid my phone down and let out a huge sigh.

"Need I remind you, Elizabeth, that the journey is often the best part of an adventure, and you are doing a great job putting all the pieces together. Someone cares very deeply about you, but also has a great sense of humor in the way he goes about showing you. Not to mention the money he is spending!"

"I know, right? Extravagant. But, I also believe he is protecting the Mozart treasures because he didn't know Peter and Adderly would try to steal them and harm me — it wasn't in his plan."

Michael lowered his head.

"What?" I noticed a change in Michael Holmes' demeanor.

"Adderly, Peter, and Sophia all got invitations as well. The gala will be filled with their goons, so we'll all need to plan accordingly. From what I gather, your benefactor is taking extra precautions, but is also enjoying the intrigue behind all of this. He has loved seeing Peter and Adderly's plans foiled. I believe there is some history behind them."

"I do too — especially since 'Peter Schultz the Present' had a magistrate ancestor with the same name, referenced in Constanze and Lord William's letters."

Michael looked up. "Have you finished the letters?"

I shook my head, "No. That is the agenda tonight. The last letter I read was from Lord William in March of 1792, and he was making arrangements to come to Vienna to see Constanze. It is interesting to me that the letters given to me aren't all from her Copenhagen days."

"Your benefactor knew that you were interested in that time frame, but he also wanted the earlier correspondence to get into your hands. Copenhagen was just the right moment to do so."

"Something else is bothering you, Michael Holmes. Can you share?"

"Not at this time. Let's just say that I have been dealing with Simon. He can be unpleasant, to say the least, and he is working on two of the same cases I have been assigned to. He's very persistent, and that only makes my work more difficult."

"I am sorry to hear about Simon. You don't deserve that. But, I do want to emphasize that I appreciate all of the effort you are putting in for me, and for whomever else you are protecting right now."

"Thanks, Elizabeth. I just feel sorry for him. Simon created his own existence, and unfortunately, he has followers who strive to gain power in this world alongside him. Fortunately, you are not one of them."

"Thank goodness for that! Well, it's been such a long day, and this gal needs to start reading more of those letters so we can solve this case." I stood up and made my way into the living room, both dogs following me. Lying on the table was a stack of mail that my housekeeper, Olivia, had set there earlier in the day when she was in to clean and help with Charlotte. Obviously, she was not able to see Sherlock, or she would have been out of there in a heartbeat.

Picking up the mail, I sorted it by junk, bills, and personal correspondence. Halfway in the stack was a beautifully embossed envelope. Having so many former students, I received lots of wedding invitations, but this did not have the usual return address. I had the thought that perhaps I was receiving my own personal invitation to the gala like everyone else. Hesitant to open it, I turned to look at Michael Holmes — who was not there anymore, thank you very much. I was on my own. Careful not to rip the paper, I slowly opened the flap on the back. Sherlock was near, and he was not warning me of any danger, so I pulled out the contents of the envelope.

Sure enough, it was my own invitation to the gala, and I saw why everyone who received one was excited. It was beautiful. But, there was something else in the envelope as well. A folded piece of cream-colored linen paper had fallen in my lap. No one else had mentioned getting instructions, directions, or anything else except the invitation. I hoped this was another clue to who my benefactor was, so I was excited as I opened the letter.

Dearest Elizabeth,

I am thrilled that your choir and orchestra have accepted the invitation to perform at the masquerade gala in Prague on New Year's Eve! I know Prague is one of your favorite cities to visit, and it is especially beautiful during the holiday season. Plans are being finalized to show you and your guests an amazing time! I am anxious for you to contact the masquerade shop, if you haven't already, as the owner is a personal friend of mine and is preparing some beautiful costumes and masks for you, your choir, and your friends who are attending.

I will be at the gala, but it will be up to you whether you meet me or not. You will be busy, and I merely will be enjoying watching what you do best — making beautiful music.

On a different note, I am glad you are finally reading the Constanze letters and getting closer to putting this puzzle together. The clues are in front of you, Elizabeth, including some very close

*at hand that you have overlooked. I also hope you are enjoying the
necklace I sent.*

Keep up the good work, Elizabeth, and I will see you in Prague!

No signature. No real answers. Just more intrigue. I slowly read the
letter again. Several things stood out:

1. Contact the masquerade shop — a new ally?
2. There was no guarantee I'd meet my benefactor at the gala.
3. There are more clues in the letters.
4. Clues right in front of me? Why did he mention the necklace?

Laying the letter in my lap, I contemplated all the information I had
gleaned in such a short correspondence. I folded the letter and put it back
in the envelope with the invitation. Looking at my phone to check the
time, I was shocked that it was nearly 8 p.m. I realized I hadn't eaten since
breakfast that morning. *Was that just this morning that Paparazzi handed
Lilah the note? Good grief.*

I needed to contact my son, my friends, Benjamin — but I was
extremely eager to read some more of the correspondence between
Constanze and Lord William.

After making a sandwich, with a side of raw veggies to balance out my
pancakes from this morning, I picked up the folder with the letters and
settled in my recliner. Both dogs settled at my feet, content. Taking a bite
of the turkey sandwich, I opened the folder and began reading. I wondered
if Constanze had contacted Peter Schultz, or if she had waited for Lord
William to arrive in Vienna...

28
Filling in the Gaps

April 1792

Dear Lord William,

I appreciate you giving me the name of Mr. Peter Schultz. He has helped me immensely and given me some sound advice. I have not revealed all to him, however, as I am awaiting your arrival in a few weeks before I do. I am strong, but I do not want to be taken advantage of with Wolfgang's estate. My family's future depends on the decisions I make, and so I must walk cautiously through this process. We have food and lodging for the time being, but I am not sure how much longer the funds will last.

Please let me know where you will be staying while you are in town. I will leave a letter with the staff there containing information on how to contact me. We must be careful — Vienna is a town that loves gossip, and I don't want to add fuel to the rumors already going around about Wolfgang and me. Antonio Salieri has been a huge help, but I only give him snippets of information regarding the manuscripts Wolfgang left behind. I do not want our estate to get in the wrong hands.

Sincerely,
Constanze

April 1792

Dear Constanze,

Your letters have concerned me, and I am anxious to meet with you in person. I plan on arriving by coach in a week's time. I plan to stay at Hotel Stefanie, located on Taborstraße, only a few steps from St. Stephens.

I will see you soon, dear friend. Please be careful until then.

Sincerely,
William

ॐ✳ॐ

I stopped to contemplate the two letters I had just read. I was once again thankful to whomever had translated the letters from German to English so I didn't have to rely on my poor German language skills. I had been keeping all the facts and questions in a journal, so I added:

1. Constanze spoke enough English to carry on a conversation with Lord William, but he seemed fully conversant in German.

2. Antonio Salieri was helping Constanze. He was the court musician for the Habsburgs. He would have been 42 years old in 1792, and Constanze 30, so there was a reason why she looked to him for advice and help. Good girl for not giving him Mozart's manuscripts! Not that he would have used them for his own, but if she had handed them to him, they might have been given to the monarchy out of his loyalty and faithful service to them (1774-1824).

3. Constanze had gone to Peter Schultz, but it sounds like she only went to make the connection without giving him details.

4. What was Constanze holding that she didn't want anyone to know about? The snuff box and locket, more than likely. Constanze knew they were rare.

5. The letter from Lord William in reply to Constanze said that he would be there in a week's time. Considering the modes of transportation in 1792, the timing seems rushed. Was he already on his way when he wrote the letter? Did he get Constanze's? Hurry and get there William!

The next letter was dated June of 1792. *Wait a minute! What happened while he was there with her in Vienna?* I frantically flipped through the folder to make sure I wasn't missing something that had gotten out of order, but my hopes were in vain.

Filling in the gaps was becoming the theme of this adventure. Frustrated, and wanting to speculate on what happened during Lord William's visit to Vienna, I closed the folder and went in to wash my dinner plate. Olivia had also left a plate of chocolate chip cookies on the island. Staring at the cookies, my favorite, I knew I shouldn't, but I think better when eating chocolate of any kind — so I bit into a cookie for inspiration and comfort.

The letter I had received from my benefactor today was the second one I had received — the first one came with the beautiful treble clef necklace in the beautiful box. Grabbing another cookie, I walked to my bedroom, where I had put the jewelry box when I came home from Copenhagen. Wiping my hands together to dust away any stray crumbs, I picked up the beautiful box. The letter today had said clues were right in front of me... *What did he mean?* Still holding the box, I heard Sherlock whimper ever so slightly. Looking down at him and smiling, I realized he was trying to tell me something. He nudged my leg, and I almost dropped the box. *The box!*

"Sherlock, is there something in the box?"

I was already opening it, and Sherlock was wagging his tail in affirmation. My hands were shaking as I reached inside for the first note that accompanied this special gift. Not taking the time to read it again, I set the note aside and I inspected the box more thoroughly. The satin necklace holder lifted up easily, and voila! There was another note, much smaller in size and folded twice to fit its small hiding place. Needless to say, I could barely contain myself as I unfolded the note that had been right in front of my face all the time. Opening it with great anticipation, I read:

1778

Saying it out loud, more than once, still did not answer any questions — it only created more. *What is the significance of 1778? Mozart and Constanze married in 1782, so what happened in 1778?* I looked down at Sherlock.

"Do you know what happened, Sherlock?"

Totally understanding what I had asked, Sherlock began waging his huge tail so fast and so hard that he knocked over Charlotte, who gave him a look of indignation.

"No time for hurt feelings, Charlotte, so shake it off. Time for one more trip outside, you two, before I settle in to research the significance of 1778."

I picked up my journal on the way to the back door. While the dogs were outside, I flipped through the pages. I remembered having put together a timeline of events in Mozart's life on one page of the journal. Running my finger down the page, I landed on 1778:

1777-78: Resigned job in Salzburg. Traveled to Mannheim, Augsburg, Paris, and Munich. Fell in love with Aloysia Weber. Rejected a job as organist at Versailles. Fell into debt. His Mother died. Offered a job as Court Organist and Concert Master in Salzburg.

I had underlined "fell in love with Aloysia Weber." Aloysia was Constanze's sister, and a famous singer of their time. She was also very beautiful. Mozart got his heart broken by Aloysia, but he met Constanze as a result.

Deep in thought, I heard Charlotte bark. Both dogs were staring at me through the glass door, but I could have sworn that Sherlock was smiling at me — and it all had to do with 1778.

Letting them in, I looked at Sherlock and said, "Help me out here, buddy. 1778. What happened then?"

Still contemplating 1778, I settled in for the night. But, unlike most nights, tonight I fell asleep instantly.

Sherlock whimpered.

29
July 25, 1778

Wolfgang really disliked Paris. This was his third visit here, and the worst. He detested calling on potential supporters who allowed him to play, said thank you, and sent him out the door with no payment or further appointments scheduled. He felt it was a waste of time, and would rather be composing – which is when he was his happiest.

His mother had accompanied him this time. They had arrived from Salzburg in March, very low on funds, hoping that this visit would result in a job. Meanwhile, his father had stayed behind in Salzburg, trying to find Mozart a position there. Living conditions in Paris were horrible, and food was scarce. Baron von Grimm, whom he had met on the Grand Tour when he was seven, had secured introductions for him and was acting as a pseudo-manager. However, no one was paying.

As if the trip wasn't miserable enough, his dear mother, Anna Maria, died on Friday, July 3rd, in their rooms at No. 8 rue du Sentier. Alone, he had arranged for a modest grave in the cemetery of Saint-Eustache.

Grimm was kind enough to invite him to come and live at the ducal manor, where he resided as personal secretary to the Duke of Orleans after his mother's death. However, this wasn't a very pleasant arrangement. Grimm nagged him all the time about getting out more to promote himself, and had even written his father to say that Paris was not a good place for him to be.

Wolfgang was ruminating on his situation while he endured the twenty or more miles to Versailles, where he had a scheduled audience with the Queen. He had been shocked when he received a handwritten invitation from Queen Marie Antoinette to visit her at the palace! He had not seen her since they were children, but he remembered her fondly. She was making a name for herself in history, and Wolfgang couldn't help but compare her situation to his – a poor, struggling musician that no court wants to hire. He was working on a new composition that he hated to leave, but one must not turn down an invitation from the Queen of France!

It was a hot summer's day. Wolfgang had loosened his cravat, thankful for the light breeze dancing its way into the carriage through the open windows. He had on his best suit, but it was showing signs of wear and tear. He had pawned yet another snuff box yesterday, but had only received enough coins to buy dinner and a new shirt.

He was grateful that he had brought so many trinkets along with him on this trip. He and his sister, Nannerl, had received many of these items when they were on their Grand Tour as young prodigies. His poor father! How he had hoped the tour would bring riches! Instead it only brought little suits of clothes and many, many snuff boxes.

He smiled as he remembered the blue and gold snuff box Marie Antoinette had given him when he visited the Habsburg Court as a child. It was one of her own personal boxes, engraved on the bottom with her name. He had no intention of ever pawning that one, so it remained in a safe place back in Salzburg. She seemed to feel so genuinely sorry for him when he fell all those years ago. He wondered what would have happened had they met in a different time and under different circumstances — but, he knew she was way above his station in life!

So why had she invited him to Versailles today? Despite his current circumstances, the outcome he most desired was to laugh and experience some joy for the first time in what seemed like ages.

He already felt better, just by leaving Grimm behind. Wolfgang felt like an imposter when he put on the smiles and airs necessary to call on society in Paris. It gained him nothing, but Grimm felt he should keep trying. Grimm just did not understand the happiness Wolfgang experienced when he was composing. Even now, Mozart had a musical theme he wanted to explore on manuscript paper, and couldn't wait to put the notes on paper!

The carriage was approaching the main gate to Versailles. It was a massive wrought iron gate covered in gold leaf, and Wolfgang could not help but shield his eyes as the sun reflected its brilliance. A gatekeeper stepped out to the carriage driver to see who was entering the main courtyard, and after a brief exchange, the carriage entered. The horses' gait on the cobblestones created an interesting rhythm, to which Wolfgang instantly added a melody. He grinned, and hoped he remembered this one when he returned home that evening.

Home. Where was home? Not Paris. Not Versailles. He longed for Salzburg, but dreaded facing the wrath of his father when he did return. His mother had always intervened and defused his father's impatient demands, but she wasn't here to support him anymore. His heart sank again into grief.

He snapped out of his solemnness when the footman opened the carriage door.

Wolfgang nodded to the footman as he stepped out and stretched his back. He reached inside for the small bouquet of flowers he had picked up from the corner flower stall. Not as elegant as what the Queen would be accustomed to, but he wanted to present her a small token of his appreciation for the invitation to the palace. A gentleman must never come empty-handed to call on the Queen!

A gentleman approached Wolfgang with his hand outstretched to greet him. Wolfgang shifted the flowers to his left hand so that he could return the greeting.

"Monsieur Mozart! Welcome to Versailles! I am the Queen's personal porter for the Petit Trianon — the only one who holds the keys. I have not seen her this excited in a long time. I have been instructed to take you personally to the Petit Trianon. She prefers the smaller palace, and because you two have known each other since childhood, she wishes to visit with you there."

As he was speaking, the carriage he had ridden to Versailles had been replaced with a smaller horse-drawn cart. The horse was anxious to go, as if he sensed the Queen's excitement to see Wolfgang, and both gentlemen let out a laugh.

"After you, Monsieur."

Wolfgang stepped into the open cart. The porter explained to him that they used the smaller, open carts and the younger horses for the short jaunt to Petit Trianon. The colt was spirited and pranced over the cobblestones as if he were gliding on air, tossing his beautiful white mane with his head held high. He knew he was in the Queen's royal stable.

The gardens were in full bloom, and the Grand Canal hosted courtiers picnicking or boating. Wolfgang admired the beautiful ladies he saw, holding parasols to keep the bright sun off their delicate skin. The porter, whose name was not disclosed to Wolfgang, kept him entertained with stories and gossip about who was attending court these days.

"Monsieur, we have up to 10,000 courtiers at the palace year-round, so you can imagine how nice it is for the Queen to get away from the constant demands of a busy court. It is my duty to let the Queen's Lady-in-Waiting, Princess de la Lamballe, know who wishes to hold court with the Queen. She, in turn, speaks to the Queen, gets back to me, and then I bring them to Petit Trianon. Monsieur, I understand you have been here before? Do you notice the changes made? Monsieur?"

Wolfgang was about to fall out of the carriage as he gawked at the sights along the Grand Canal. He felt a slight touch on his jacket that brought him back to reality.

"Pardon, Monsieur. You were saying? I am just enjoying the many beauties one sees in the Gardens of Versailles."

The porter let out a huge laugh, wishing he were a young man again like this spirited fellow, Wolfgang Mozart. He had heard of him, and had actually gone to the recent Concert Spirituel at Tuileries Palace on June 18th, where his latest symphony was played. Mozart's symphony began the concert, and received rave reviews. The concert goers loved it, and Parisians were already calling it the Paris Symphony. Such a brilliant musician! Talk was that he was in Paris looking for employment, and while here his beloved mother had died — such a sad story. The porter was inwardly smiling and hoping the visit with the Queen would bring some happiness to this young man's life. He certainly needed some.

He continued. "Just chit chat, Monsieur. We are almost to Petit Trianon. I hope you have a pleasant and enjoyable time with the Queen. I understand you were last here during Louis XV's reign, and you were but a seven-year old prodigy."

Wolfgang let out a sigh. "Yes, my father was certain we would become rich and powerful from our visits to Royal Courts all over Europe. Our stay here was enjoyable, and the King was very kind to us. He rewarded us nicely and sent us on our merry way after a sixteen-day stay at the palace. The gardens were not as brilliant as now, because it was winter, and I remember thinking the gardens were full of ghosts – but it was only that the gardeners had covered all of the statues with cloths to protect them from the weather!"

"Ah, I would love to hear more stories of your stay here sometime, but I understand you are just here for tea with the Queen. Perhaps on your next visit we will have coffee, and I can hear all about your adventures! I heard your symphony at the Concert Spirituel – a true hit, Monsieur. Bravo!"

Mozart turned his head to the porter. "You were in attendance? Thank you for your kind words. I was hoping it was well received by everyone."

"Indeed, it was. And now, Monsieur, our short journey and time together has come to an end – at least until the end of your visit. We have arrived at Petit Trianon."

The footman stepped out to hold the bridle of the frisky colt and steady the carriage. Wolfgang noticed he whispered in the horse's ear, more than likely affirming he did a great job. It was nice to see the humanity behind the scenes here. The porter then stepped out and took the keys from his pocket to open the gate leading into the courtyard of Petit Trianon. This gate was similar to the main gate into Versailles, beautiful wrought ironwork adorned with gold leaf, but on a much smaller scale.

Once the gate was open, the footman stepped back onto the carriage and the driver gently guided the horse through to the courtyard. The porter locked the gate and rejoined Wolfgang in the carriage.

Wolfgang was unimpressed on his first glimpse of Petit Trianon, because the courtyard was simple and unadorned compared to the beautiful main entrance to the palace. The porter reassured him that the back of the palace was more than grand, and gave him a sly wink.

The carriage came to a second halt. After the horse was steadied, the porter and Wolfgang stepped onto the cobblestone courtyard. Mozart looked over his shoulder to see the footman again whispering in the young horse's ear as he patted his head. The footman looked to be about fifteen years old, and was indeed taking his job seriously, with heart and passion. Wolfgang longed to do that with his music instead of constantly having to impress royals or other patrons who might influence a steady-paying job that would please his father. *I bet this young footman's father was proud of him and told him so,* Mozart thought.

A servant had appeared and opened a door off the courtyard, and the porter gestured for me to follow him. We entered the ground floor and began our ascent to the first floor, up a grand staircase. Wolfgang was used to royal dwellings – he had certainly seen many in his quest for royal court appointments – yet he still took time to notice the beauty of the small palace. The porter gave him time to admire the green marble floor and the wrought iron staircase with the Queen's monogram. The main color of the palace was green, to bring together nature and architecture.

After reaching the first floor, the porter led Wolfgang into the Grand Salon. Wolfgang instantly took a liking to it. The Queen's harp was the focal point of the room, but there was also a beautiful harpsichord just begging to be played. Spacious, the room had ample seating for guests and musical gatherings. He was admiring the view of the gardens from the window when he heard his name.

"Wolfgang Amadeus Mozart!"

Wolfgang turned to see Marie Antoinette standing there with a big smile on her face. Dressed in pink and green, to match the room, she was a vision of loveliness. Wolfgang bowed a graceful low bow, making a grand gesture with the bouquet he had brought.

"Your Majesty! How lovely to see you once again!" he said in German.

"We both have changed a little, don't you think? And you broke your promise to me! I remember you promised to marry me. You ran off all over

Europe, and I tired of waiting on you, so I married Louis, heir to the throne of France."

It was so nice to speak in German with the Queen, and seeing her made him smile. She indeed had changed!

"Ah," replied Wolfgang, "I believe you fared much better by not waiting on me."

By now, Marie Antoinette had invited him to sit with her in a set of two very exquisitely carved arm chairs. She thanked him for the beautiful flowers. Wolfgang knew that a meal would not be served, for queens were not to eat with gentlemen without the king present, but he was hoping for perhaps tea and cake. The Queen was fanning herself with a beautiful fan, and Mozart was benefiting from some of the breeze she was creating. Thankfully, he had remembered to tighten his cravat before he entered.

For several minutes, the conversation centered around family. The Queen expressed her condolences for the death of his mother, and inquired after his father and sister. He in turn asked about her family back home in Vienna.

"I miss Austria. I miss the coolness of the mountains and the fresh air. I miss the quietness of the countryside. That is one reason I asked Louis to allow me to retreat to Petit Trianon and make it my own. It was originally built by his father for his mistress Madame de Pompadour, but I love the solitude I have here as well as the control I have over whom I entertain. The main palace has thousands of courtiers there round the clock — 'What is the Queen doing? What is she wearing? What is she eating?' I tell you, Wolfgang, they exhaust me." Marie Antoinette fanned harder, for dramatic emphasis.

"I met Madame de Pompadour when I visited here as a child," Wolfgang said. "I whispered to my father that she looked like our cook."

Marie Antoinette laughed so hard that several maid servants poked their heads in the door to see what was causing the ruckus.

"I love that, Wolfgang!"

"And to make matters worse," he continued, "they sat me by her at dinner one night. My father kept giving me a stare from the other end of the table as a warning not to say a word. I do remember she was very nice to me, even though she made me miss our cook back home."

At that moment, a maid entered the room, curtsied to the Queen, and set down a small tray with an assortment of cakes and two cups of tea. Marie Antoinette picked up her cup of tea and told Wolfgang to please help himself to the cakes, as he must be famished. They chatted while they enjoyed their tea, and the Queen told him of her plans to build a theatre at the Petit Trianon, and that she intended for her and her friends to put on the very latest plays and operas.

"I want a mechanical engineer to design a way for us to change scenery quickly. Who knows, maybe we will be performing one of your operas one day! I hear great things about your works, Wolfgang. The courtiers that went to the Concert Spirituel loved your latest symphony!"

"You are most kind, Your Majesty, and I would be honored for you to sing the leading role in any of my operas. I hear you have a lovely voice, and that you play the harp better than most who play for a living. Bravo, Your Majesty!"

"What are your plans, Wolfgang? I hear you are in Paris seeking employment." The Queen took a sip of her tea and looked to Wolfgang for his answer.

"Indeed. I have been seeking employment — and it seems I have been seeking employment all my life. I came here from Mannheim, where I had hoped to be employed. Paris has offered some wonderful experiences, and Baron von Grimm has introduced me to many people. Alas, nothing has turned into gainful employment."

"How about coming here to be the chapel organist at Versailles?"

Wolfgang almost spit his tea out when he heard the Queen say this.

"I am sorry, what did you say? The chapel organist? Here at Versailles?" Wolfgang was dabbing his chin so that tea would not drip on his new shirt...or embarrass him further in front of the Queen.

"I can make it happen, Wolfgang. Louis goes to Chapel at the same time every day. *Every. Day.* The current organist hurts my ears, and I hear he might be on his way out the door anyway. I can certainly use my influence to get you the position. Please, Wolfgang! You would be such an exciting addition to the Court!" The Queen had put her cup down and was pleading with her eyes.

"My dear Queen, this is one of the most generous offers I have had in months. But, I must let you in on a bit of a secret."

Wolfgang leaned in towards her as he whispered the last words. In return, the Queen leaned in towards him to hear what he had to say. She loved secrets.

"I am in love," Wolfgang proclaimed in a dreamy voice. "I have met someone who has stolen my heart."

"Tell me, Wolfgang! Who is the lucky young girl? A Princess? A Lady?" The Queen was clapping her hands quietly in delight and in great anticipation to hear more about the young lady who had stolen the famous Wolfgang Mozart's heart.

"Her name is Aloysia Weber. She is beautiful, a singer I admire, and she lives in Mannheim. I am enamored with her beauty and her talent, and I plan on going back to Mannheim to ask her to be my wife. Paris has been difficult, and holds too many sad memories for me now. I thank you, Your Majesty, for the offer, but I must follow my heart."

"Oh yes, Wolfgang, you must! You must write to me when you return and let me know what Aloysia says! I will just have to continue to carry on here at Court without you." Marie Antoinette hid demurely behind her fan as she spoke these last words.

The young maid came in to retrieve the tray, and Wolfgang noticed she was probably around the same age as the footman. The Queen was kind to her, and thanked her for the tea and cakes. Wolfgang would miss the cakes in Paris — in fact all the pastries and breads were divine — but with his funds so depleted, today's tea and cakes with the Queen was a true luxury.

"Wolfgang," the Queen continued, breaking his thoughts about cakes, "I am curious. Do you still have the little blue and gold snuff box I gave you when I was seven and you were six? I believe you had fallen on the marble floor, and I gave it to you to soothe your pain. That is also when you promised to marry me, if memory serves."

"As a matter of fact, I do still have it! I was just thinking about that on the carriage ride from Paris to Versailles. Father took it immediately from me and put it in a small wooden box. He made the comment that one day this would be a special gift to have, so it did not go on the shelf with all the others we had received. I wanted to play with it, but he wouldn't allow me to." Wolfgang was not about to mention that he had begun pawning off snuff boxes in order to live — not to the Queen! He was so thankful he knew that the snuff box was still in a small wooden box in Salzburg. His dear mother, when she heard it was a gift from the young princess, made a special blue velvet pouch with a gold drawstring to hold the snuff box.

"Have you ever looked inside the snuff box?" The Queen put her fan down and awaited Wolfgang's answer.

"Inside the box? No. My father wouldn't let me touch the clasp for fear of breaking it. Why? Is there something inside?"

At that very moment, a huge black dog bounded into the room, followed by a very embarrassed young servant girl.

"Beau!" exclaimed the Queen, as she ruffled the head of her furry friend. "Wolfgang, meet Beau — my giant furry companion!"

30
More Surprise Connections

"BEAU!" I sat straight up in bed and looked to the edge of the bed, into the eyes of my big, black, furry friend, Sherlock. His tail was beating so hard it sounded like thunder, and he looked like he had a huge smile on his face. If dogs could talk, he would be asking, "What took you so long?"

"You were Marie Antoinette's dog?!" I exclaimed, truly surprised.

"What time is it? I must have fallen asleep reading the letters," I said, glancing at the stack of letters on the pillow as I rummaged for my glasses on the nightstand.

"That dream sure made sense of the note in the jewelry box. 1778 was a pivotal year in this mystery. And Mozart had not ever looked inside the snuff box!"

"Ugh. 4:30 a.m. Too early to get up, but too late to go back to sleep. C'mon, Beau, let's go make coffee and try to write down the details of that dream."

Charlotte didn't budge, but she did at least open one eye before going back to her queenly sleep.

Still wearing my readers, which seemed to end up in every room of the house these days, I stumbled sleepily into the kitchen to turn on the coffee maker. Normally it began auto-brewing at 5:15 and was ready when I woke up. Nice to just press ON and have it start this early so I didn't have to deal with spilling water while my eyes adjusted to being awake.

I reached up and grabbed one of my favorite mugs, one I picked up in England, and leaned up against the counter while I waited for the coffee maker to brew enough to pour one mug. I was still reeling over the dream of Mozart visiting Marie Antoinette at Petit Trianon. It makes sense that Mozart would not have looked inside the snuff box to find the locket because he was only six, but did his father know the locket was there? I can envision a young child trying to open the delicate clasp and his father scolding him as he took it away from him. How long had the treasures been housed in the wooden box and blue velvet pouch?

A warm mug of coffee in my hands, I grabbed my journal and headed back to my bed. Charlotte begrudgingly moved over so I could get in, and Beau settled in on the floor at the side of the bed.

Beau. What a dog. I was still flabbergasted that my dream showed my beloved Sherlock bounding into the salon at Versailles. First, finding out Holmes was Michael; now, Sherlock is actually Beau. Good thing musicians are flexible and can adapt easily to change.

Adjusting my glasses, I opened my journal and titled the clean page, "Mozart's Visit to Queen Marie Antoinette at Petit Trianon," and began writing down what I remembered.

1. Mozart was in Paris in 1778 seeking employment and staying with Baron von Grimm after the death of his mother.
2. Mozart was unhappy in Paris. He felt meeting and playing for people only took time away from his composing – which was when he was the happiest.
3. Mozart met Marie Antoinette (MA) at Petit Trianon, a small palace that Louis XV had built for his mistress Madame du Pompadour. When MA became Queen, Louis XVI gave the palace to her. She liked the smallness of the palace and only received guests when she wanted to.
4. The Maison du Suisse, or porter, held the only keys to the palace and only he let guests in by the Queen's orders.
5. MA met Mozart in the Grand Salon, where she and guests would play musical instruments and sing. Her harp was the central focal point in the room.
6. MA offered Mozart a job as Chapel Organist.
7. Mozart told her he was in love with Aloysia Weber and wanted to go back to her in Mannheim.
8. MA mentioned their first meeting in Vienna, and asked him if he still had the snuff box and had ever looked inside. Mozart replied no, that his father had snatched it up before he had a chance to.

9. Beau bounding into the room, interrupting their visit.

I realized as I wrote all of this down that Marie Antoinette must have been happy to have a German-speaking guest at the palace, but not as happy as Mozart must have been to converse with her in his native tongue. I read somewhere that he said he had trouble with the French language, but obviously was conversant enough to get by.

Mozart was anxious to get back to Aloysia in Mannheim. He will be so sad when he gets there and learns she has not waited for him! BUT — it's during this time that he meets Aloysia's sister, Constanze, who is a much better fit.

Wait a doggone minute! Think, Elizabeth, think! I flipped back to the first of my journal and pulled out the copy of the letter that Peter had given me, which I had placed in a pocket of the journal. In the letter, Constanze had written to Aloysia that she and Georg had discovered the snuff box when they moved from Vienna to Copenhagen, but Constanze had written to Lord William before that — right after Mozart's death — saying that she had found something that might be a game-changer in her handling of the estate.

Something else was bothering me. I started at the beginning of my entries, and bingo — there it was! In Copenhagen, the first vision I had of Mozart revealed him lifting the snuff box out of a trunk after Constanze was asleep! So, wait... If I had not awakened from the dream with Marie Antoinette, I might have seen her tell Mozart about the locket. He would have then gone back to Salzburg and asked his father to see the snuff box, discovering the locket for himself! I bet his mother even knew about it — why else would she have made a special velvet pouch to house the snuff box? She didn't do that for any of the other trinkets! When Mozart's father died, he made sure he got the treasures and hid them in the trunk with the little outfit. He was protecting his family's future!

These new revelations were awakening suspicions that the first letter Peter had given me in the Mozarthaus Museum was a fake. I jotted a note in my journal: *Peter Schultz, counterfeiter — check authenticity of his copy of Constanze's letter to Aloysia.*

Time was getting away from me, so I stopped to get ready for class.

"Charlotte, you must wake up and go outside. It's almost time for me to go to work." I ruffled her pretty head, and she reluctantly obeyed.

The normal routine of the morning allowed me to take my mind off of the dream and my new revelations to focus on what needed to be done at work today. First on my list is to call the Masquerade Shop in Prague. Amanda Kate and Peyton will be here in a few days, and I need to have all the details lined up before their arrival.

My phone lit up with a message from BJ, my street guard.

Are you okay, Dr. Stone? I noticed your lights on earlier than usual.

Yes, just a rough night. Couldn't sleep well, so I just got up. Street clear all night?

Yes Ma'am. I will be taking off as soon as you leave for the university. Do you think you need me tonight?

If you are available, I would love for you to stay through the weekend. I have guests coming. Can you do that?

Yes Ma'am. Be safe today.

I was so proud of BJ for the direction he had taken in his life. Always a good student, he at one time felt he wanted to teach. He realized during student teaching that he wasn't ready to make a lifetime commitment to the classroom yet, and that he wanted to follow his dream of becoming a police officer. The cool thing is that he started a Police Community Choir. They meet every week and sing at various community ceremonies and events. They are called The Singing Blues, and my favorite concert is their Veteran's Day concert in the Veteran's Park.

It was time for me to leave, or I was going to get stuck in traffic. I texted Bradley to see if he could stop and pick up coffee and meet me in the office at 7:30. He replied and said he was already ahead of my game. I smiled and wondered if he had gone back to the restaurant to see Lilah. Charlotte had eaten, gone outside, and was now settling into her daybed, with Beau close by.

I was still amazed at this revelation about Beau. It was hard to believe that just a few days ago, Michael Holmes had sat in my hotel room in

Copenhagen and explained why he and Beau would be known to me as Holmes and Sherlock. Now I understood why they didn't reveal their true identities right away. Was that only five days ago?

Filling up my mug for the road, I punched the garage door opener and said good-bye to the pups. No telling what these two do while I am away. I should ask Michael Holmes sometime.

I looked in my rearview mirror in time to see BJ pull in behind me as I left my neighborhood. He deserves a medal for this one, and maybe one day I can explain all of it to him. I need to check-in with Matthew at the bank today as well. I am curious if anyone suspicious has come in. I can't leave any stone unturned.

When I arrived at my office, it was 7:05 a.m. That would make it 2:05 p.m. in Prague. I fumbled to find the card with the phone number, and nervously dialed the number. In Czech I heard, but didn't understand, "Good Morning. Masquerade Mystique, Eduard Doubek speaking."

Taking a risk, I replied in English.

"Good Morning. This is Dr. Elizabeth Stone, and..."

Before I even finished my sentence Mr. Doubek replied, "Dr. Stone! At last we speak! I have been anticipating your call!"

Relaxing as I heard a distinctive British accent coming through in his flawless English, I realized Mr. Doubek was more than likely connected in some way to Lord William and my benefactor. Interesting though, since his name sounded Czech. At times, I think I am the only person in the world who only speaks one language, something I'd like to change.

"Mr. Doubek — "

"Please, Dr. Stone, call me Eduard!"

I could tell he was enjoying the call and was very excited to speak to me. *Oh, the questions I have for him!*

"Eduard! How lovely to finally speak! I had to calculate a time when I knew you were open. It is still early morning here. I understand you have some information to give me about the New Year's Eve gala?" I grabbed pencil and paper to jot down any info he gave me as we spoke.

"I do, Dr. Stone, indeed I do! I have been contacted by the chairman of the gala regarding the costuming the committee wishes you to have. I am supplying special masques for everyone in your group, and for you, Dr. Stone, I have designed a special gown for you to wear. I need a list of your group as soon as possible, notating female or male, choir, orchestra, directors, etc., so I can begin making the masques. They are going to be fabulous!"

I was writing as fast as I could, but Eduard was talking quickly. When he finally stopped long enough to take a breath, I jumped into the conversation.

"Eduard, would I be able to include my family and special friends who are attending?"

"Of course! I am also to tell you we are planning a Red Carpet with a photo op, as well as a separate photo booth. The Estates Theatre doesn't have a huge lobby, but oh my, the plans they have to decorate! You will be in such awe, Dr. Stone!"

"Eduard, you are getting me excited as well! I was wondering if my good friend, who is an interior designer, could possibly help with the decorating for the gala. Perhaps you have heard of her — Amanda Kate?"

Amanda Kate will be so proud of me for thinking on my toes, and I can already imagine her and Eduard hitting it off. No one will be able to get a word in edgewise! Maybe they can partner on other projects as well.

"Not THE Amanda Kate? I find that fabulous! I already have a detailed list of decorations, as well as some images of the table decorations for the lobby. The colors for the evening will coordinate with the interior of the theatre — blue, gold, and white. Wonderful, wouldn't you say?"

I detected in that last statement that Eduard Doubek knew more than he was letting on, and wasn't afraid to subtly let me know.

"Dr. Stone? A delicate question — what size gown would you wear? I need to get started on this immediately. In fact, if you trust me, would you please send your measurements? I know this is awkward, but you see, I am a fashion designer and want this gown to be yours — totally yours. Wait till you see it!"

"Well this is a first! I usually find my gowns on the sales rack. What a treat! I trust you completely, Eduard. I also trust you to design this with my age in mind – not too much cleavage, ok? And my back will be to the audience while I conduct, so don't accent my bottom in any way – please!"

Laughing, Eduard told me he would take all of this into consideration. He also suggested that someone take a full-length picture of me to send. I asked about shoes, telling him I never conducted in shoes with over a three-inch heel for fear of falling over during a conducting gesture. I had him laughing so hard now that I'd bet he had tears streaming down his face. I liked him, and couldn't wait to meet him in person.

We were concluding the conversation just as Bradley walked in the office door bearing sweet gifts of black coffee and pumpkin bread.

"Eduard, it has been charming to talk to you, and I cannot wait to meet you in person! I will get all of these details to you by the end of the day if possible. What is a good email address for you?"

Prepared to write it down, I was stunned when he said, "Oh no, Dr. Stone. Please do not send this info via email. Mozart Travel Company will send a courier to pick it up – just as they have done with your other details. These were the instructions given to me to give to you."

Now I knew for sure he was in on the escapade! Still not letting him know I was on to him, I agreed to do as he said. My benefactor feared emails were being hacked and read, and was taking every precaution to keep things under control. This was also a warning to me to be cautious with my correspondence. Advice noted and received.

Bradley had set my coffee and pumpkin bread beside me, and I reached for them as I wished Mr. Eduard Doubek a good day – with a promise that I would collect all the information he had asked for.

Looking at Bradley, I said, "Wow. You won't believe the latest developments." I began telling him, and he stopped in the middle of spreading cream cheese on his pumpkin bread.

"That's wild, Dr. Stone! This just keeps getting more and more mysterious, yet so exciting! I will get another document started with the information Mr. Doubek needs, including the orchestra roster and all the faculty chaperones."

"Don't forget to add my family, Amanda Kate, Peyton, Benjamin, and Matthew... Matthew! I need to call the bank and make sure the treasures are still safe and sound!"

Swallowing my coffee, I dialed the number of the bank and asked for Matthew. He wasn't in yet, and the receptionist said she would have him call me as soon as he arrived.

"Bradley, we have work to do. Shall we begin?" And with that, we turned to the computer and began putting together the program for the gala.

31

Mr. Eduard Doubek

Eduard put down his cell phone and clapped his hands in delight after chatting with Dr. Stone. She was everything he was told she was — charming, witty, and very smart. Even though she didn't let on that she knew, he sensed she was well aware that he knew more than he was letting on. She played along with the charade quite beautifully, just as he was informed she would!

Picking up his phone again, he dialed a number he knew by memory. Hearing the party on the other end pick up without speaking, he simply said, "Dr. Stone called. I should have all of her information soon. Any other details I need to know? She is as delightful as you said she would be."

Eduard was personal friends with Dr. Stone's benefactor. They had made acquaintance while working on another gala. That one was in Vienna, and was so magnificent that he was called upon several more times to help produce galas in London, Paris, and Florence. But, those previous galas were charity events, and none was as special as this one. The Benefactor was sparing no expense for this extravagant affair!

Eduard had been born in Prague, but had studied fashion design and art in London. He loved London, but felt a calling to go back to his homeland and work from there. His designs had been worn and displayed on Red Carpets all over the world — even the Oscars! He loved meeting the stars when they would fly in for fittings, but he could tell he was really going to enjoy getting to know Dr. Stone.

In pictures he had seen, she was fairly typical for her age, with a sort of understated, but charming style. Designing gowns for women of Dr. Stone's age, a young 60-ish, was challenging, but fun. He looked at his sketches and smiled. He expected her to be a bit shy a first, because this was more glamorous than her typical approach, but he wanted her gown to reflect elegance from top to bottom.

Eduard picked up the sketchbook that had the masques detailed. Everyone was going to look spectacular! For the orchestra, he even designed special masques that were dramatic, but mostly transparent, so they wouldn't obstruct the players' line of sight. He had completed most of the initial designs already. Several were ready to be created, so he headed back to his design shop and handed the book to his assistant, Pavla.

Eduard had discovered Pavla selling her artwork in the Old Town Square in front of the Old Town Hall. He was so impressed that he asked her if she would care to apprentice with him at his shop. She proved to be a welcome addition, and he was now considering hiring her full time. Her imagination and creative designs were coming in handy for the masques. She was referencing colorful birds in the designs – peacocks, parrots, hummingbirds – but using luxurious golds and blues to meet the Benefactor's design requirements. Every masque was to be based on characters in Mozart's opera, *The Magic Flute*.

Eduard had seen the opera several times, and was always enthralled with the colors and the sets. He had even seen the production that was performed with marionette puppets. The plot sang like a fairytale, with its deceptions, trials, and victories, leading to a happily-ever-after ending of courage, wisdom, and virtue. Set in a fantasy land, where birds talked and the Queen of the Night makes an appearance by flying in on the moon, the opera is one of Mozart's finest. Sadly, he died only two months after its premier on September 30, 1791. Eduard read that his friend, Schikaneder, had written the libretto, and the opera was premiered at his theatre in Vienna – the Theater auf der Wieden. The theatre was for the people, and Schikaneder wanted Mozart to see how much the real people of the world loved his music.

So, when the Benefactor suggested that the set, the foyer, the masques, and costumes be designed as if the participants were part of the opera itself, Eduard gladly took on the challenge. But, he had told Dr. Stone an itty-bitty lie: the main colors were not blue, gold and white, as he described on the phone. The Benefactor wants the actual design, inspired by *The Magic Flute*, to be a surprise – and, oh, how Eduard loved surprises!

"Pavla, have the fabrics and accessories all come in? My supplier in Paris assured me they would be sent out immediately."

Pavla looked up from the sketchbook, pushing a lock of her blue hair behind her ear. "They are trickling in," she said in Czech, "and the ones that have arrived have been sorted and inventoried, put in bins, and are ready for assembly."

"You are magnificent! I should have the number of masques soon. If I calculate correctly, we are looking at making close to 100 masques. Thankfully we still have time, but none to spare!"

"I will begin making patterns. I can't wait to see them all come to life!" Pavla gleamed.

"Oh, darling, if only you knew the half of it!"

Eduard winked at her. He was instructed not to tell anyone any of the details, or about the Mozart treasures involved. He knew because he had earned his friend's trust. Pavla still had friends on the street, and he wanted the shop to remain free of any drama that might accompany this escapade if information got into the wrong hands. He shivered just thinking about it. He had been advised of the goons in Copenhagen and that Peter Schultz was willing to stoop to violence to get what he wanted. While the Benefactor was less concerned about greedy Arthur Adderly, he was unsure if Adderly's assistant, Kristoph, intended further trouble, especially after the Tivoli Hall of Mirrors attack. They were taking extra precautions with the gala preparations to avoid unnecessary risks.

Pavla watched as Eduard looked at neatly organized inventory. She loved how excited he got when he held fabrics in his hands or ran his fingers across the accessories, imagining them in their final design. She was being paid well for her assistance. She had plenty of questions about the gala, but she knew better than to ask or snoop around. She really liked Eduard, and the money he was paying her kept her coming back each day. She had already made in one month's time what she usually made in a year selling her art in the square. This was good gig, and she wasn't going to blow it. So, when Eduard asked her to design bird masques or sort fabrics or whatever, she jumped at the chance to please. He had promised her permanent employment if she did an excellent job for the gala. She knew his professional reputation, so she really wanted to make this a permanent gig.

Eduard's phone rang, and he walked out of the design room as he answered it. It was the courier with Mozart Travel Company letting him know he had the names of the participants in Dr. Stone's group, as well as Dr. Stone's picture and measurements for her gown. The voice on the other end of the line told him he was faxing it to him right now. Eduard walked over to the fax machine just as it started up. Soon, he had the pages necessary to really begin work on the gala. He waited until all the pages had arrived, and then thanked his caller. He had never been told who the courier was, and he didn't ask.

"Pavla! We have the information for our guests! We can now begin designing the masques for the gala!"

Eduard and Pavla sat together at the drawing table and made cards with each participant's name and gender. They taped them all to the wall; and then, as each masque was finished, they would take a picture, attach it to the card, and label the masque. Each finished masque was going into a beautiful gift box with the participant's name in a beautiful script. They had cleared a shelf to store them once they were completed.

The two worked diligently and quickly. It was almost closing time, and both were very hungry. Eduard had a very nice apartment above his shop, but Pavla had to take public transportation home each night. Eduard never asked about her personal life. He was only concerned with the artistry of her finished products. In turn, Pavla never asked him about his personal life, nor had she been in his apartment. He always served tea and cake in the afternoon from the small kitchenette in the shop. He always had classical music playing, which she had surprisingly grown to admire and enjoy as a soundtrack for her work. However, the moment she stepped back out into the square, she put on her headphones to listen to her own music playlist, which was much edgier.

She had never mentioned — and Eduard didn't need to know yet — that she still lived with her grandmother, who had basically raised her. Pavla had been born to her loving gypsy parents in the hills outside of Prague. They often brought her into town to visit her grandmother. One day, when she was six, they asked her if she would like to live with her grandmother and go to school with other children her age. Her parents were performers, and they felt she needed the stability of a home while they were on the road. It was hard at first, but she adapted. She always loved it when they would come back into town, bearing wonderful stories of their adventures on the road. Now, she sees them frequently — and enjoys sharing stories of her own adventures with them.

Pavla and Eduard exchanged "Good Nights," and then Pavla stepped outside and plugged in her headphones. She heard Eduard lock the shop doors, and watched as he turned the Open sign to Closed before waving good-bye to her. She wasn't certain, but she thought she saw him mouth the words "Be Careful" to her before she headed across the square towards the tram. She thought to herself, *Why do I need to be careful?* Shaking her head, she turned up her music and hurried on her way.

32

Liam Stone

I miss Liam.

We met in high school when we were both seniors. He was the captain of the football team, and I was the choir geek. He was strikingly handsome and smart; and I was, well, average – high on talent and low on looks, with my acne-ridden skin. I would see him in the hall, but if he looked my way, I would scamper away with my head down low, embarrassed that he saw me. He always had a bevy of cheerleaders hanging out at his locker, and I envied how at ease they all were. Beautiful people talking to each other.

One glorious autumn day, I was eating lunch outside at one of the cement picnic tables they provided for those of us who didn't go off campus or home for lunch. I had my transistor radio blaring, head buried in my musical libretto, memorizing my lines, munching on my peanut butter and jelly sandwich, and waiting on Amanda Kate and Peyton to join me. My mouth was full of food when I heard a male voice say, "Is this seat taken?" Not looking up, I shook my head no.

Stopping mid-chew when I did look up, I realized that Liam Stone was sitting across from me. I subtly tried to get the peanut butter off the roof of my mouth so I could say something, but it wasn't cooperating, so I just stared. I was staring into the most beautiful blue eyes I had ever seen. I was doing my best not to look like an idiot, mouth coated in peanut butter, still unable speak to this gorgeous creature sitting across from me.

Laughing, he asked, "Do you speak?"

I managed to mumble a very weak "Yes" while nervously nodding my head at the same time. So embarrassed, I looked down at my libretto again. I had just forgotten every line I had learned. I think the pounding of my heart erased my brain.

"Hey, if I am bothering you, I can go somewhere else."

Gathering my courage, I looked straight in his beautiful baby blues and said, much stronger this time, "No, please stay," as I smiled and closed my libretto. To hell with the acne.

He reached out a hand to me, "Hi, I don't think we have formally met. I am Liam Stone."

I wiped the jelly off my hand before I took his, and said, "No, but I know who you are. I am Elizabeth Grey with an 'e', not an 'a'."

Oh God, I would never wash my right hand again, I thought. Then, I cringed when I noticed him nonchalantly wipe away a smudge of strawberry jelly I'd transferred to his hand.

I wasn't prepared for his genuine laugh at my quirky introduction, or for what he said in response.

"THE Elizabeth Grey? The one who has more talent in her little finger than this whole student body? I heard you at the talent show, and you are amazing. I also plan to come and see the musical next month."

Stunned. *Liam. Stone. Just. Complimented. Me. Wow.*

"Thank you. That is quite the compliment coming from the star of the football team. I come to all the games, by the way. I don't understand all of it, but I enjoy the atmosphere and the revelry of it all. I am afraid you caught me studying my lines for the musical." I held up my libretto.

"Do you always study by listening to the radio?" He was eating his sandwich by now, and neither of us felt awkward anymore.

I couldn't help but notice that he was eating a ham and cheese on white, with about an inch of mayonnaise slathered between the slices. No lettuce, no tomato. *Why of all days did I choose to fix a peanut butter and jelly sandwich?* In order to save myself from any more embarrassment of trying to talk through peanut butter, I put the sandwich aside and concentrated on the chips. *Slow and easy, Elizabeth, I thought.*

"Yes, I find I concentrate better when I have noise. Probably similar to you — do you always play football with full stands of yelling fans?"

He guffawed and said, "Two points, Elizabeth Grey with an 'e', not an 'a'."

From there out, we chatted like we had always been close friends. The bell rang and startled us both. Gathering our trash, I realized Amanda Kate and Peyton never did show up — and I was so glad they didn't! Wait till I tell them I ate lunch with THE Liam Stone!

Before he walked back into the school, Liam turned to me and said, "Thank you, Elizabeth. I really enjoyed talking to you. You are so real." With that, he left me standing there with my mouth open.

I started walking to my next class, and Amanda Kate and Peyton came running up to me.

"Izzibeth!! We saw you eating lunch with Liam Stone. THE Liam Stone! And you were talking! And laughing!" Amanda Kate was as stunned as I was. Peyton was echoing everything she said, and they both wanted to know what we had talked about.

"Oh, you know — football and music, what else?" I had arrived at my class, and I walked in confidently, leaving them begging for more information.

Amanda Kate hollered, "I am not through asking you questions, Izzibeth!! I want to know everything!"

I just winked.

From that day forward, Liam and I met at least once a week in "our spot" at the cement table. He usually found me, as it wasn't proper back then to "go after" a crush. He seemed to enjoy talking to me about everything, but mainly about science. Liam was brilliant, and wanted to make a difference in the world by finding a cure for cancer or other diseases. I nodded my head as he spoke in terms I didn't really understand, and I never got bored with hearing him tell me about his dreams and interests.

In return, Liam would help me memorize my lines. He had a brilliant speaking voice, and was patient with me when I made a mistake. On warm days, we would practice my stage directions under the big oak tree, while he kept his head buried in the libretto. On cold days, we would find a spot in the hallway. He didn't even care when his football buddies walked by and teased him. Thankfully, there were more warm days than cold.

He sat on the front row every night of the musical. At first, I thought it would distract me, but then again, I knew he would mouth my words if I messed up. After each show, he came by and complimented me on a great performance.

Liam and I understood each other. I also knew that we had a sincere friendship rather than a budding romance. He currently was not dating, since it was football season, but I knew he might start dating again once that was finished. And I was fine with that.

The seasons changed, and we still met once a week for lunch. I was busy rehearsing for college music school auditions, and he stayed busy with studying for college entrance exams.

Prom season came around, and I wasn't surprised when he asked the head cheerleader, Ruthie Jones, to the prom instead of me. Both had been nominated for Prom King and Queen, so it made sense that the Royal Court go together. I stayed home.

One day in April, Liam sat down at lunch and pushed an envelope towards me. "Read it, Elizabeth."

I noticed that the envelope was from Johns Hopkins University, and I looked at him quizzically.

"Go ahead, you can read it." He was expressionless.

Nervously, I opened it and read that he had been accepted into the prestigious school on a full scholarship.

I screamed, and then he screamed.

"YES!" I exclaimed. "Congratulations! I knew you could do it, Liam! Now all of your dreams will come true!" I was sincerely happy for him.

"I know, right?" he said. "My parents are thrilled, needless to say. But I have to tell you, Elizabeth, the bad part is that I am going to leave the week after graduation to start their summer program."

My heart sank, but I knew this day would come. He would go his way, and I would go mine. I was waiting to hear about scholarships, and knew I would be staying in state to go to school. Liam would now be across country in Maryland.

But I smiled, "That is wonderful, Liam! Wow! This just made my day, so I can't imagine the joy you are feeling right now — that, and the stress is off. Johns Hopkins your first choice, right? Are you still waiting to hear from other schools?" Inwardly, I was hoping he would say that an in-state school had also offered him a scholarship.

"Yes, it is my first choice because of the research they are fielding. I am really excited, Elizabeth."

And I was excited for him.

Graduation came. Graduation went, and Liam went with it. He promised me he would write, but I knew better than that. June, July, August, and nothing. I was accepted into my first choice of music schools, so in the fall my parents drove me with a car loaded with clothes and minimal dorm accessories.

It was amazing how quickly four years went. I would go home during the holidays, but the first visit home I found out that Liam's parents had relocated to another city. So, life went on, and the years passed. After I finished my undergraduate studies, I chose to take a couple of intensive classes on Opera and Choral Conducting in Vienna. The classes spanned just one semester — not quite long enough to become proficient in the language, which is why my German is still so elementary today. The '70s were a musically exciting time in Vienna, and I was spending most of my time at the Statsopera. When I wasn't studying, rehearsing, or performing, I was doing any and every job they allowed me to do there. I worked on stage design, costuming, and even sang in the Chorus several times. I loved it.

One cold winter day, as I was heading from a voice lesson towards the opera house, I heard my name. I recognized that voice and froze before turning around. *Liam?* Turning, and hoping I wasn't dreaming, I saw The Liam Stone coming towards me the doorway of a restaurant.

"Elizabeth Grey, with an 'e', not an 'a'! It is you!" Liam picked me up off my feet and turned me around in circles before lowering me back onto the cobblestones.

"The Liam Stone! What are you doing in Vienna, of all places?" I still had my arms on his, as we both gave each other a look-over to see how the years had treated us.

At that moment, we heard a knock on the window from inside the restaurant. Looking over, I saw a table of his friends, male and female, pointing to the table and motioning that his food was ready. He shrugged them off and turned back towards me. I knew he must be freezing without his coat, but he didn't act like it.

"I was about to ask you the very same thing! I am doing graduate work at Oxford. However, my friends and I try to take as many weekend trips as we can. I am so thrilled to see you again! You look WONDERFUL!"

That last comment made me happy — that he had noticed the acne was gone, and he was happy for me.

"Thank you, Liam. You are a sight for sore eyes. How long are you here? I am on my way to the opera house for a performance and need to get going."

"Sadly, only until tomorrow. We have to head back to Oxford tomorrow because we all have classes on Monday morning."

"Do you have plans tonight? Say, around 10 p.m.? Or breakfast?" I was crossing my fingers that something would work out, and secretly hoping the girl glaring at me from the inside of the restaurant wasn't a fiancé or something like that.

"Do you think I could get a ticket to the performance tonight, or is it too late?" he asked.

To say my heart skipped a beat is an understatement. I was in the chorus! We were doing a performance of Mozart's *The Marriage of Figaro*, and tonight was the last performance.

"I will have a ticket for you at Will Call. Be there by 7 p.m. to pick it up. Do any of your friends want to go as well?" I nodded towards the window where the blonde was now glaring at both of us.

"Nah, I want to come by myself. There wasn't anything planned but bar hopping, and what good is being in Vienna if you don't enjoy the music as well? Can you go out for a drink afterwards?"

Beaming, I said I could, and told him where to meet me after the performance. We hugged each other. He watched me walk down the street, and I turned just as he stepped into the warm restaurant. *LIAM STONE in Vienna, no way!* We hadn't seen each other in nearly 5 years, and we meet as I am walking down the street in Vienna, of all places?

The rest is history. I think I fell in love with him on that cold, blustery night after the opera, and I would like to think that is the moment he also knew we were meant to be with each other. From that night forward, we wrote to each other faithfully. We both knew we were not anywhere close to reaching our dreams yet, and neither of us pressured the other towards making a commitment. He was able to come to Vienna one more time, and I was able to meet him in Paris one weekend when he went with friends. We never kissed, never had any physical contact other than the initial greeting hug, which was rather obligatory.

Liam eventually went back to the States to begin Medical School, and, ironically, I went on to Oxford University to complete a doctoral degree. We continued to stay in touch, and then one day, over a quick lunch in New York while I was there, he blurted out his true feelings for me over dessert and a cappuccino.

"I love you, Elizabeth Grey, with an 'e', not an 'a'. I believe I have loved you from that first meeting at lunch in high school, but I was afraid to tell you. I still have one year of med school left, and then medical residency, but will you wait for me?" Liam had my hands in his, and I was overwhelmed with love.

I began to cry, and I don't cry pretty. I cry huge crocodile tears that spurt out my eyes, and my eyes go instantly puffy. Liam looked at me, stunned, because he had never seen me cry. Oh boy, I thought, as I dabbed my eyes — this might be a deal breaker.

"Are you okay, Elizabeth? Did I say something that upset you?"

"No," I sobbed. "I cry when I'm happy...I cry when I'm sad...I cry when I'm mad. I am very happy! I have loved you silently for so long, and when we lost touch, I knew it was never meant to be. I am ecstatic right now."

The seasons changed again, and then one day in early September, four years later, we said our vows to one another in front of family and a few close friends. Amanda Kate and Peyton cried the whole ceremony, but flitted around during the reception being their gracious, charming selves to our mixed guests of musicians and doctors.

Surprisingly, we both found jobs in the same city before the wedding. I was an Associate at the University, and he began doing research at the University Hospital. It wasn't long before the University heard about his research and asked him to join the faculty as an adjunct while he still worked at the hospital.

Life happened. We had a son, Grey (yes, with an 'e'), juggled professional careers, and yet always supported each other in our endeavors. We didn't step on each other's dreams — we walked side-by-side. We were happy.

One day, two years ago, I got the call no one ever wants to get. My sweet, wonderful Liam was rushed from the University to the ER, and had been admitted with an apparent heart attack. I dropped everything, and had Bradley drive me right to the ER door while I texted Grey.

Staying calm, I walked into the ER bay where they had Liam hooked up to every machine imaginable. All the staff knew and loved him, and they looked sadly at me as I made my way to his bedside. Taking his hand in mine, I squeezed it ever so gently, and he squeezed back.

"I love you, The Liam Stone."

"And I love you more, Elizabeth Grey, with an 'e', not an 'a'." Liam was so weak that I begged him not to talk.

The doctor came in, and I stepped out in the hall with him as Liam was sleeping.

"Liam needs surgery, Elizabeth. Two of his coronary arteries have collapsed, and if we don't put in stents, he will die. However, I want you to know that putting in the stents carries its own risks. He needs to get a little stronger before we can attempt the surgery, and we are monitoring him very closely."

The doctor was a personal friend of Liam's, so I knew he would be doing everything in his power to make sure Liam lived. Hugging me before he left, he promised he would check back in and told me to call him if I needed to talk.

Grey arrived just as the doctor walked away, and suddenly the mom in me kicked in for him. Before we went in to see his father, I explained to him the risks the doctor had just told me about. We discussed all the options, realizing that with Liam's critical condition, there were few.

Grey begged me to go home and get some rest, but I refused. He stayed with me through the night in Liam's room. I pulled one of the chairs next to his bed, and held his hand. Grey slept in the other chair, on the other side of his father. We both knew it was crucial that his dad make it through the night.

He didn't. And our world changed when we heard the sound of the monitor flat lining.

$$\approx *\approx$$

I recalled all of this while sitting here on my bed with Constanze's letters and my grandfather's wooden Prince Albert cigar box. That is where I have kept all the letters Liam wrote me over the years. Whenever I open the lid, the sweet smell of cedar always carries the sweet fragrance of our memories.

I hadn't read his letters since he died, but tonight I missed him. I opened the letters, one-by-one. Charlotte didn't know Liam, but she sensed something special and snuggled closer to me. Beau was looking at me, understanding my tears, for he, too, knew loss. Soon enough, though, I was laughing, crying, and laughing again. I closed the lid, feeling better that I had read them.

Liam was my voice of reason. He balanced me, and I hope I balanced him. His scientific mind would have had all these puzzle pieces figured out by now, and he would be helping me approach the gala with joy and confidence.

After reading his letters, I felt a renewed strength — as if Liam were actually there, telling me to carry on with courage and confidence. I breathed in deeply, and felt my mind become peaceful again.

As I was putting Liam's letters back into the cigar box, Beau whimpered, bringing me out of my solace. When I looked over at him, I noticed that my tablet screen had come to life, flashing the date "April 1792" before settling into the scene.

33

Lord William Arrives

April 1792

Lord William stretched his tired legs after he descended from his coach. Weary from traveling for days, he thanked his drivers, and asked them to wait for a few moments. Henry and John were his personal drivers, and fine young men. Both jumped down to soothe the horses, who were ready to eat and bed down for the night. They had taken a boat to the mainland, and then hired a coach with a strong team of horses. The journey had taken weeks, stopping every night to give the horses a much-needed rest or to hire new ones to take the next leg of the journey. St. Stephen's bells tolled five comforting chimes as he stepped into the lobby of the Hotel Stefanie. He was hungry, and he knew from previous visits that the hotel had an excellent menu — but first he must see if Constanze had left a message. The purpose of this visit was to make sure she was safe and determine what she had been so mysterious about in her letters.

"Good evening, Lord William! How nice to see you again!" The clerk recognized him from his previous stay and stepped out to greet him.

Lord William returned the enthusiasm, and again marveled at the warmth the hotel offered upon arrival. The Hotel Stefanie had been in existence since the 1600s, originally under the name of The White Rose. Located in the 2nd District, on Taborstraße, he could get anywhere within a matter of minutes.

Speaking in German, in which he was fluent, Lord William asked if he had any messages.

The desk clerk, named Hans, went back behind the counter and picked up a stack of notes from the mail slot.

"You have several, Lord William," he said as he sorted, and then kindly handed them across the counter. "Your room is also ready. Shall I send someone out to get your bags?"

"Yes, please. And my drivers, Henry and John — do you have their accommodations ready as well?"

"Yes, their room is ready as well, and the stable is ready for your horses. Will you be needing a wainwright?"

"Not immediately. The coach did a fine job, but we will have it checked out before our return."

Anxious to look through his messages, but not wanting to appear rude, Lord William thanked Hans again and headed back out to the coach to speak with Henry and John. Before stepping outside, he found the message he was looking for — a simple envelope bearing his name, Lord William. Opening it, he saw an address only. But he knew who it was from: Constanze, being cautious.

"Henry or John, I need one of you to go to this address and simply tell the lady of the house that we have arrived in Vienna. Find out where she would like to meet in the morning, and what time is best for her. According to the address, it is a short walk from here. Whoever doesn't go on this errand needs to go with this fine young man from the hotel and bed the horses down. Once you are both done, come to my room and let me know your assignments are complete. Then we will share a nice warm meal together. You both deserve it."

The horses, two beautiful white stallions, neighed in anticipation of their evening meal. John said he would take the horses, and Henry set out immediately for the address on the note. He took the original message to show that he indeed was representing Lord William.

The coach was emptied of its bags, and Lord William went upstairs to settle in his room. He walked to the window, which faced the street, and saw Henry turning a corner. What was Constanze going to tell him in the morning?

It wasn't long before he heard a knock on his door, and he opened it to find Henry and John standing there.

Henry spoke, in English, "Sir, the message was delivered as you requested, and the lady of the house sent this back to you." He handed Lord William the new note.

Opening it, Lord William read the name of a nearby café and a meeting time — Café Frauenhuber, on Himmelpfortgasse, 10 a.m.

"Thank you for your service, Henry and John. Let's go and have dinner. I don't know about you, but I am famished."

Lord William locked the door behind him, after making one last quick inspection of the room. The three of them then headed downstairs.

Meanwhile, a short distance away, Constanze tucked her children into bed. Kissing them both on the cheek, she told them that things were going to be okay now, for Lord William had arrived.

Both Lord William and Constanze slept restlessly that night. The morning light crept through the windows as the bells of St. Stephen's began to toll. Constanze dressed her boys quickly and fed them a small breakfast before taking them to her kind neighbor who had offered to keep them for a few hours this morning.

Lord William had asked for a strong coffee to be delivered to him at 7 a.m., and the knock on the door brought with it the delicious smell of Viennese coffee. He thanked the young man, who set the steaming pot on the small table in his room. Sitting, Lord William enjoyed his coffee before he got up and finished dressing to meet Constanze.

Constanze was the first to arrive, and asked for a table for two near the back. She was clutching a small bag, and thanked the waiter as he pulled the chair out for her. She had fond memories of this place, but also sadness — Wolfgang frequented this café, and his last public performance was here on March 4th, 1791. Her mood changed when she saw Lord William walk in the door, and she smiled as he made his way back to her.

Kissing her on both cheeks, Lord William noticed how frail Constanze seemed.

"Constanze! Finally, I am here! How are you and the boys?" Lord William and Constanze exchanged casual conversation for a few minutes while the waiter took their order and brought their food.

Leaning in once the waiter finally had them served, Lord William asked, "So, please tell me what this is all about, dear Constanze."

"I am so sorry, Lord William, for causing so much concern, but I needed your advice. I cannot trust the advice of the ones here in Vienna who were working against Wolfgang."

She fumbled for the small bag she was holding in her lap. "You mustn't tell anyone about what I am going to give you. Please, I beg of you!"

From inside the bag, Constanze reached for a small wooden box and handed it to Lord William.

"Look inside, but please don't exclaim anything once you do." Constanze was searching the room as she spoke. "I need you to take this back to England with you, and keep it under lock and key."

Lord William stared at Constanze before opening it. The clasp was delicate, and he gingerly opened the box to reveal a small blue velvet pouch housed inside. Without making a big scene, he placed his hand inside and pulled out the small gold and blue snuff box housed inside. He looked at Constanze.

"Constanze, this looks like every snuff box I see in shops here. I don't understand."

Still staring intensely at him, she said, "Look at the inscription on the bottom and then look inside. Go ahead. It is not ordinary."

Lord William had chills when he saw the inscription on the bottom of the snuff box, but nothing had prepared him for the treasure he saw inside.

ക്ക**ക

I awoke with a start, still clutching one of Liam's letters in my hand.

"So, I was right — Peter did lie to me! Surprise of all surprises," I said looking at Beau and Charlotte. "That letter was a fake to throw me off the trail. Well, I might be old, but I am not stupid, Mr. Peter Schultz."

I retrieved Peter's letter from my journal again and shook my head in utter disbelief.

"Silly, silly me!" I held the letter first in Charlotte's face and then in Beau's, as if they could read it. "I was so naïve in the beginning. It says at the bottom, 'Translated by Peter Schultz'. I should have asked for the original to verify the authenticity, but he didn't want me to compare the two. What a creep — not to mention a crook! Agree?" Both dogs were looking at me a little strangely, but I felt empowered.

I also had a clearer idea of how this all connected to me. Lord William — who was a Grey with an 'e', not an 'a', just like me — was the person Constanze entrusted with the treasures. Mozart had kept them hidden in a trunk without Constanze knowing, but Constanze had discovered the them when she moved out of the house behind St. Stephen's. He knew that one day she might need them, but I'm sure he had no idea how many ripples these treasures would cause so far into the future!

I was so relieved the pieces were all starting to come together, but my mind was racing and it was still too early to call it a night.

I had a crazy idea...

34
Diva Scheduled

Contacts still in, I could see across the room to the clock – plenty of time. I picked up my phone. I had a truly mad idea about an addition to the gala program, but I needed to make one very important phone call to make to see if it was even an option.

"Elizabeth!"

"Emilia Rose! Where in the world are you, and do you have your calendar handy? I have a deal for you that you can't refuse."

"I am presently in NYC doing an evening Master Class for the Met. Just what is this deal I can't refuse?"

"Well... What are you doing New Year's Eve this year? Say, from December 27th through January 2nd?"

I heard her thumb very loudly and quickly through her planner, which she always had handy. I held my breath and prayed.

Finally, she came back and said, "Nothing on the calendar. I was planning on a quiet holiday at home with the grands. What's up?"

"How would you like an all-expenses-paid trip to Prague with a chance to sing at The Estates Theatre with my chorale?"

"You have got to be kidding! All expenses paid? No one does that without a catch, Elizabeth, so what's the catch?"

I took a deep breath. "You need to brush up on 'The Queen of the Night', be able to sing in a masque, and be willing to fly in on a moon to sing."

"As in the scene from *Amadeus*?"

"Umm, sort of, yes."

"Elizabeth, how are you going to pull that off at The Estates? It's not a big stage."

"I have my ways, Emilia Rose, and surely you remember that they filmed the actual scene for the movie on that very stage. I just need you to agree so I can get you a flight to Prague and get 'my people' started on your costume and masque design. I *neeeed* you. And, I will explain all of it later — if you say yes."

"You have me hooked and curious, but yes, count me in. I expect answers soon, please!"

"I will. I promise. Also, I need you to sing the *Laudate Dominum* from *Vesperae solennes de confessore*."

"If I weren't on break, out of class right now, I would insist you tell me what is going on."

"I promise I will," I said. "It's complicated."

I heard voices in the background, and someone called her name.

"Elizabeth, I will be back home in three days. Call me." And without a good-bye, Emilia Rose was gone.

Diva scheduled.

Amanda Kate and Peyton arrive tomorrow. I wonder how they're going to react to everything...especially Emilia Rose.

I stayed up a couple more hours researching and planning, but things were finally coming together. When I finally did get to sleep, I slept more soundly than I had in months. Even the dogs slept quietly all night.

🔊 ✳ 🔊

I awoke feeling rested and refreshed. Even the morning coffee felt more like a bonus than a necessity today.

The first thing I did this Friday morning as I hit my office was to call Eduard Doubek at his shop. This time a female voice answered, and she identified herself as Pavla, Eduard's assistant. *Ah, so he's not alone in his office.* I was thankful she knew a bit of English. She sounded as if she knew who I was, so I assumed that Eduard was using her to prepare for the gala.

"Dr. Stone!" he exclaimed as Pavla turned the call over to him. "I was not expecting to hear from you so soon! Thank you for getting us the information we needed to begin making the masques. You should see them! The forms are all laid out on tables, fabrics are being cut, and there seems to be an abundance of sparkles in my shop these days!"

Smiling from across the world, I loved hearing his excitement. I knew he was in on at least some of the behind-the-scenes planning with my benefactor, and possibly knew him personally. But, it was fun playing coy for the moment.

"Eduard, I cannot wait to see the finished products! Before I forget, I hope you let me know when and where to pick up all of the masques and costumes once we arrive."

"Oh, darling," he inserted. "All of your masques, costumes, and final instructions will be awaiting you at the theatre! You are not to worry about anything! "

"How thoughtful, Eduard! And it sounds as if Pavla is of great help to you, so I will not worry myself about the masques in the least. But, I really called to add a name to the list. Are you familiar with the name Emilia Rose?"

"Not THE Emilia Rose, the one who has sung on every opera stage in the world? Of course I am!"

"She is a personal friend, and I have asked her to be a part of the gala program. Here's the challenge for you — I have asked her not only to sing the solo in the *Laudate Dominum*, but... I have asked her to sing 'The Queen of the Night's aria' from *The Magic Flute*." I held my breath, waiting for his reaction.

"Dr. Stone, you just catapulted my career into another league! This is going to be fun, and my mind is already designing her costume. I think," he said turning to Pavla, "that I also have the crew to build the moon for her to sing from."

"Awesome! I realize we will have to do it on a much smaller scale, but I completely trust your design judgement. Amanda Kate and Peyton will be there to help you in any way they can. They also know Emilia Rose's little quirks before a performance, which should reduce some of the stress for you."

We ended the conversation, but not before I gave Eduard the size for Emilia Rose's gown and the promise to call and check in periodically. I hung up as Bradley walked in the door, questioning the Cheshire cat grin on my face.

Bradley and I spent the rest of day conducting classes and working hard to learn all the repertoire. He had the a cappella arrangement I had asked for, and the choir loved singing Mozart with a beat. I was a stickler for memorization, scores out of their hands, and I reemphasized that their deadline to be off books was coming up soon.

35
The Innocents Unite

As I drove home, I started to get very excited. Amanda Kate and Peyton were in the air, on their way to see me. They would take a car service to the house, and I expected them around 8 p.m. I would stop at the grocery store deli and pick up a light supper. We had details to discuss, and we didn't need to be in a busy restaurant where they couldn't hear.

Table set, a fire going, music playing softly in the background, and the doorbell rang — just after 8 p.m. Both dogs raised their sleepy heads and instantly jumped to their feet to help me greet our guests. I heard their happy chatter before I reached the door. Opening it, I grabbed my friends in a huge group hug.

Hugging me tightly, and looking towards the fireplace, Amanda Kate said, "Since when have you had TWO dogs?! Who is that giant?"

Peyton also chimed in the same question. I froze. *They could both see Beau!*

Acting as nonchalantly as I could, and without giving away all of the details, I said calmly, "Friends, meet Beau — my latest rescue dog. I could not resist, and it happened right before I left for Copenhagen, so I guess I sort of forgot to tell you. He is a gentle giant, a great companion for Charlotte, and a great guard dog — almost like he is my guardian angel."

Satisfied, they both took off for their rooms upstairs to put away their suitcases, then headed back down for dinner. We sat by the fire with a nice glass of wine, Mozart playing in the background, dogs at our feet, and carrying on casual conversations about life in general.

As if on cue, Amanda Kate said, "So, Elizabeth, why did you really call us here? You said you had things to discuss about the gala that couldn't be discussed over the phone." With a grand gesture, she concluded, "Here we are, and we are all ears. It's been all we can talk about since you summoned us, so please, do fill us in!"

Peyton had gone into the kitchen to open another bottle of wine. "Don't start before I get there! I don't want to miss anything!"

Once we all settled in, I began with the attack in Copenhagen, and told them everything. *Everything*. I think we went through two more bottles of wine as they quietly let me tell my story. I noticed they were looking at Beau differently. I did leave out one detail — but that was soon to be revealed.

"Good evening, ladies, you must be Amanda Kate and Peyton. I have heard a lot about you."

I thought Amanda Kate and Peyton were going to jump out of their skins. It was Michael, and he had just suddenly put himself into the storytelling, without any introduction. My, how he loved the look on their faces!

"Elizabeth, I don't think you told us everything! Would you care to explain who this is?!" Peyton exclaimed, unable to take her eyes off Michael Holmes.

"Friends, dear friends, meet my guardian angel, Michael Holmes. He has saved my life more than once during this adventure, and he is here to guide me so I won't get hurt as I work to solve this mystery I've literally inherited. We are the only three people, as far as I know, who can see him or Beau. And, up until just now, I was unaware that you two would be able to see them. It pleases me, because it shows we are united, but it could also mean that you might have cause to call upon them."

Peyton and Amanda Kate both said together, "Danger?"

"No, not necessarily," Michael Holmes said. "But you might need an expanded sense of awareness, especially at the gala. My job has been to sort of shepherd all the players involved, but even I don't know how this is all going to end. Elizabeth is the only one in control of the ending. As Elizabeth has explained, Peter, Sophia, Adderly, and Kristoph are very motivated to acquire the treasures, and they've already resorted to violence on multiple occasions. They have not come here to the States, so that means they're not on the offensive at the moment. But, they are *all* invited to the gala, so we need to put a strong plan into place to make sure

Elizabeth remains safe. It will be interesting to see what kind of trouble, if any, they cause at the gala, but I'm also very curious to see if they work as a team or as independent agents."

Amanda Kate and Peyton were nodding their heads along with each and every word, ready to hear what their role would be.

Deciding it was as good a time as any, I calmly threw out there, "And I called Emilia Rose."

Setting down their glasses, both of their heads turned sharply to me, and in unison they chimed, "You didn't!"

"I did. And she is in. Wait until you hear what I have planned for her at the gala!" I was watching their reactions. We all knew that when Emilia Rose was involved, our schemes didn't always run smoothly.

"What, exactly, is she going to be doing?" Amanda Kate asked, "And why do I get this feeling that Peyton and I are directly involved? The last time we helped her with a performance, I had to run all over the city to find the stinkin' chicken livers she *has* to eat before each performance. They were disgusting, and my car smelled like them for days!"

"Yes, Elizabeth, and I had to darken all her windows at the hotel so she could sleep. We thought we were helping with the gala preparations! Does Emilia Rose know about, um, Michael and Beau?" Peyton took a sip, no a gulp, from her wine glass, and reached over to refill my glass as she waited for my reply.

"Emilia Rose knows nothing, and will not know anything — not even about the treasures. As far as she knows, she has been hired to sing in my program, nothing more."

"What is she singing?" Amanda Kate leaned in closer to me as she asked. Emilia Rose is a bigger-than-life star on the stage, and wouldn't be helping Elizabeth just for some mediocre solo or even for a free trip to Prague.

"I have asked her to sing the *Laudate Dominum*," I said. Both girls gave a huge sigh of relief.

"And... She will also be doing 'The Queen of the Night's aria' from *The Magic Flute*." I waited with bated breath for their reactions, and I didn't have to wait long.

"Wait — the iconic one, right?" Amanda Kate asked. "Surely you are not having her duplicate that scene from *Amadeus*, where she swings from a moon above the stage? Please tell me she isn't. You know she is afraid of heights!"

"She is doing exactly that." They both looked at me like I was crazy. "I have a plan, girls, and that is why you are here. Have I ever let you down?"

They looked at one another before shaking their heads no, even though I had led them on some pretty wild adventures during our friendship.

Peyton looked at me seriously, "Elizabeth, you know that if you have invited Emilia Rose to sing and wear a costume, then you had better enlist the help of Frieda. Is there room on the plane? If not, you had better figure out a way to get her there."

Amanda Kate put her glass down. "Izzibeth! I implore you to ask Frieda to come and help with Emilia Rose! Please! I couldn't deal with doing her hair and make-up on top of all the other details I will be overseeing!"

As I looked at both of my lifelong friends pleading with me in front of the fire, I laughed and agreed to call Frieda first thing in the morning. Frieda was a hairdresser and make-up artist we had known since high school. They were right, Frieda would be a good addition to our team. I would also call Eduard and tell him, for I am sure he would get the word to Mozart Travel to add her to the passenger list - although I'm pretty certain that Mozart Travel Company and Masquerade Mystique are one and the same. Either way, I loved talking to Eduard, and couldn't wait to meet him in person.

"Did you both bring your planners? We need to get planning!"

I had distracted them so much by telling them about Emilia Rose, that they didn't notice Michael Holmes whispering in my ear before he left our fine company. What he said had put chills up my spine: "Simon. He has something up his sleeve, so be on the lookout." And with that, he vanished.

Simon. Trying to keep my composure, I told myself: *Smile, Elizabeth, keep smiling.*

"What?" Peyton asked, "Michael left without saying good-bye?"

I reassured her that she would get used to his comings and goings, like I had. But for now, we have work to do in preparation for the gala.

"Amanda Kate, could you make me an inventory of what you would need for the Red Carpet? Also, I need to put you in contact with the designer in Prague who is our liaison with the event planners. That way you two can get busy finalizing the designs. He did tell me the main colors are blue, gold, and white to match the interior of the theatre."

We were off and running — still writing and plotting, even as the fire died down. We had christened our plans The Stanzi Project, in honor of Constanze. Our minds and intentions seemed to sync up perfectly as we planned. The Innocents had once again united.

The clock struck midnight, and as if we had lost our glass slippers at the same time, we all put our pencils down and said our goodnights. We had all day tomorrow to finish.

ॐ ✳ ॐ

The first words out of Peyton's mouth on Saturday morning were, "Elizabeth, I swear — if you haven't called Frieda by noon her time, I'm going to call her myself!"

I reassured her it would all be fine, and poured some more coffee in everyone's cups. Secretly, though, I was crossing my fingers.

When I called a few hours later, Frieda was between clients and sitting in her office.

"Elizabeth! I haven't heard from you in months! What's the holdup, girlfriend? How are you doing?"

Frieda's enthusiasm made me smile.

ॐ ✳ ॐ

When you sit in Frieda Becker's stylist chair, you are in for the ride of your life, so you'd better hang on with both hands. Once she had whipped the beauty cape around your neck and snapped you in — you were hers. She would spin the chair around and look at you from every angle. You would hear her saying, "Yes. Maybe. Hmm..." as she perused your head of hair. You would hold your breath, not knowing if you were about to get a trim or if you were about to be her guinea pig for a new style she'd seen in a magazine. No matter what, you were in for a wild ride. Not only was Frieda good at what she did, but she was an amazing storyteller and vocal impressionist. You'd be laughing so hard that she would have to scold you to sit still so you didn't mess up her creation.

She never revealed her clients' stories, but could write a book about the things clients had told her while sitting in her chair. Frieda knew everything, for she also was skilled in the art of listening. She knew about divorces before husbands did; she knew due dates of babies; she knew wedding plans and parties and happenings around town. Frieda's clients weren't just any clients — she was a stylist to the stars. Yes, Hollywood stars.

She had moved out to L.A. on a whim after high school, much to her parent's chagrin and their constant reminder that she was going to go hungry. "Wouldn't you rather rent a space in the mall at home?" they would ask. No, Frieda had a dream, and nothing, including hunger, was going to stop her.

Success hadn't come easy. Her first job was receptionist at a famous Hollywood salon. She had pounded the pavement for days before wandering into this salon with her best smile and smoothest southern accent to ask for a job — any job. The owner had a brief break between clients, so he gave her five minutes. He listened intently as Frieda told him all she was capable of doing. She had even brought along a portfolio. Enchanted by her determination, and her accent, the owner asked if she was willing to start as a receptionist and work her way up. Frieda accepted and said she could start that day. As she started to get her footing, she also started beauty school, and then worked up the ranks — next stop, shampooist.

Everyone wanted Frieda to shampoo their hair. They would even wait for her to finish a previous customer if necessary. She would compliment their hair, even when it was a dirty mess, and gave great scalp massages. She was genuine, funny, and charming; and the stylists loved the mood the clients were in once they were in their chairs. Frieda made their job easier.

The stylists in the shop were the best around, and Frieda watched everything they did. They took her to shows, and she would help them dress the models and touch up their make-up before they hit the runway. Gradually, Frieda earned her own stylist chair in the salon, and was hiring her own shampooists. When the owner was ready to sell and go live in the tropics, Frieda bought his famous salon outright. She was in demand all over Hollywood, but never forgot her roots – or her longtime friends.

⸮✱ⸯ

"Frieda, I am sitting here with Amanda Kate and Peyton. They are on speakerphone."

Everyone screamed with excitement, which led to laughter when Charlotte began howling.

"Frieda. We need you. Desperately. What are you doing from December 27 through January 2?"

She was flipping through her appointment book, and we were all holding our breath.

"Let me see," she said. "Nothing. Not a thing. That is a slow time for me. I have learned I can say no to doing New Year's Eve hairdos and take some time off. I was considering going to Paris for a few days, but I haven't booked anything yet."

Frieda heard everyone let out a huge sigh of relief, in unison.

Confused, she asked, "Uh, what do you three have in mind? Do you need me to come and fix some bad hair or something?"

Laughing, I continued. "Maybe, Frieda, maybe. How about an all-expenses-paid trip to Prague?"

"Well that's a no-brainer. But I sense there is a catch to this deal," Frieda quipped.

"There is, Frieda, but nothing you can't handle."

"Okay," she said, "give it to me. What are you three really up to?"

"We need you to help with Emilia Rose."

Dead silence on the other end.

"Frieda, are you ok?"

"Excuse me, but something must be wrong with the connection. I thought I heard you say you needed my help with Emilia Rose."

"You heard right, Frieda. Please say yes! I know she is picky and demanding, but you are the only one she totally trusts, and this is huge! My University Chorale and Orchestra have been invited to play for an extravagant masquerade gala at The Estates Theatre on New Year's Eve. You know, the famous theatre where Mozart premiered his infamous *Don Giovanni*. This program, upon the request of the organizers, will be totally Mozart. Emilia Rose is singing 'The Queen of the Night's aria'."

I held my breath and looked at my friends sitting on the couch with me. They both had their praying hands lifted high as we waited for her to answer.

"Not the iconic scene from the movie — Elizabeth you wouldn't!"

"I would, and I have. You just have to help backstage and make sure she stays happy. And, you know, do her hair and make-up... She trusts you, Frieda, please say yes! I am afraid she will chew up and spit out anyone else!"

"Okay, I'm in. Something tells me there is more to this than meets the eye — I know you, Elizabeth, and when you get all of us together, there is always adventure involved. Put me down, and send me details — flights, etc., since I will need to fly out of L.A. I love you all, but I need to go. I have a star waiting."

Frieda couldn't see the fist pumps and high fives going around Elizabeth's living room, but she was suspicious about what The Innocents were really up to. Shaking her head and smiling, she penciled in her appointment book: *Masquerade Gala, Prague for Dec. 27 - Jan. 2.*

❧ ✳ ❧

By the time the weekend ended, the girls and I had finished our plans. I waved goodbye to Amanda Kate and Peyton from my front porch as their car left for the airport.

Before crawling into bed that night, I looked out my front window to see BJ's vehicle down the street. As I set the security alarm, I wondered what Simon was up to. Whatever it was, I was determined he wasn't going to beat me. Let me rephrase — he wasn't going to beat us!

36

The Final Players

It was nightfall in Prague when Pavla finally stopped working on the masque she had begun that morning. She and Eduard were making progress, and the shop was coming to life as the masque forms took personality. It was invigorating and satisfying work, and Eduard was paying her well. She loved arriving to work in the mornings, and hated it when he finally convinced her each evening to go home and get some rest. This evening wasn't any different. Eduard had to beg her to stop.

"It's getting dark, Pavla, and you must go home or go out and have some fun with young people your age!"

"I will, Eduard, I will. By the way, Monday morning I should have a list of friends who want to help with the production end of the gala."

"Splendid! I knew with all your artistic connections you would know exactly who to ask! Are some of them willing to build the swinging moon, by any chance?"

"As a matter of fact, yes. You will be pleased. They even have a place to build it and store it until we need it for the gala. Are you doing the design, or do you want me to do it?"

"How about you, Pavla — this could be your stage design debut! Just watch the movie to see what Dr. Stone is envisioning, and then put your stamp on it. She will be happy."

Pavla could not believe her ears. She held her head high when she left the shop. Tonight, she was on a special mission: she was going to visit her friends and talk to them about helping with the gala. If she timed it right, she would arrive at Palac Savarin just as they were finishing their first show of the evening at the Black Light Theatre Srnec. Pavla knew the cast well, as they had all started out on the street, busking in the Old Square. Now they were performing nightly to a crowded theatre, and she had a nice job with a famous designer. Hopefully, she can convince them to be a part of the gala — especially adding a bit of black light and magic to "The

Queen of the Night." Dr. Stone might even like to have some effects in her opening number. Pavla had seen from the repertoire list that the Chorale was performing *Masquerade* from *The Phantom of the Opera.*

Pavla took the metro to Mustek, and arrived at the theatre just as a noisy audience was piling out of the theatre front doors, raving about the show. The Black Light Show originated in Prague, and is one of a kind. It is pure magic – a spellbinding smorgasbord of visual delight. Pavla never tired of going to the performances, and was very proud of her friends for becoming a part of the cast.

Pavla entered the theatre, politely going against the flow of the outgoing crowd as she made her way to one of the ushers.

"Pavla! What brings you to the theatre tonight? Did you see the show?"

"No, Nikolas, I am here to see if I can go backstage for a few moments. Could you check with Lukas, please?"

It wasn't long before Nikolas came back and told her that it was okay – Lukas was waiting for her.

After hugging and kissing each cheek, Lukas kept his hands on Pavla, holding her in front of him at arm's length. "Pavla, you look different to me. You look happy!"

"I am very happy, Lukas. The job at Masquerade Mystique is more than I expected it to be. Eduard Doubek allows me to be creative, and he is the reason I am here to see you tonight."

"Oh? And what would a famous designer such as Eduard Doubek need from a lowly black light theatre actor? You intrigue me, Pavla, but we must hurry – the next show starts in an hour, and I am famished. Come – sit with me while I eat in my dressing room and tell me why you are here."

Lukas began eating his cheese, bread, and fruit while Pavla began telling him about the gala. As she got more in depth, he put his food down, and was listening with great intensity.

"Yes, Pavla, we will be a part of this! I get the feeling that you sense there is more to this gala than meets the eye, and I definitely do not want to miss out on it! Are you going to get your parents involved as well?"

"Yes, at least I hope they can. They're next on my list. I plan on visiting them tomorrow. Who all do you think will join us? I need set designers, builders, and crew during the actual performance."

Lukas looked at her and confidently listed several names — Adela, Dominik, Emil, Adela — and himself, for sure. He asked if that was enough.

"Only time will tell. We need to start soon, as December is just around the corner. I will stay in touch. And yes, I will stay for the show."

"Join us for a beer afterwards, and then I will see you home." Lukas headed for the stage, and Pavla was shown to an empty seat in the theater by the usher so she could watch the show.

The show was fabulous, the beer refreshing, and the company delightful. Adela, Emil, Blanka, Dominik and Emil all had agreed to join, so they began the plans for the gala around the table. Midnight came and went, and Pavla finally suggested that she needed to go home before her grandmother worried. Lukas rode on the metro with her and saw her to her door, where he gave her a hug and waited until she was safely inside. He had always felt protective of Pavla, even though she usually didn't need his help.

The morning came, much sooner than Pavla wanted, but the smell of coffee and sizzling bacon from the kitchen got her up and moving. Her grandmother spoiled her, and Pavla never complained.

"Good morning, Babicka. This smells heavenly!"

Babicka is a term of endearment commonly given to Czech grandmothers. Her Babicka returned the kiss Pavla had planted on her cheek.

"You need your strength. You are too skinny, Pavla. And today especially, as you go to see your parents. I have made a basket of food for you to take to them. Full of breads and pastries! Tell that daughter of mine not to hoard them all!" Babicka's laugh radiated throughout the room as she set a plate of food in front of Pavla and brought her a steaming mug of coffee. She lovingly touched Pavla's head, smiling at her dyed-blue hair, thinking it brought out her blue eyes even more. Hair is hair, and it will grow out. Pavla had her mother's dark blue-black hair and deep, piercing blue eyes. She had her father's creative spirit — and his stubbornness. However, despite her strong and independent exterior, Pavla's Babicka saw her softer side as well. She had also noticed a change in Pavla recently. Ever since she had begun working for Eduard Doubek, Pavla had walked taller and was happy all the time. Miracles of all miracles!

"Babicka, would you like to go with me today? We could have a picnic on the hillside. I promise not to stay all day, but I would love to have you with me. It has been too long! I know mother would love it too."

"No, you go. I am meeting friends in the Square to go see a new exhibit at Prague Castle. We will meet for lunch and then take the tram to the castle. They have Mucha and Klimt paintings on display, and the price of the tour includes a tea in the Palace Café. Please give them my best, and I will make my way there soon."

Pavla's grandmother was herself a former artist at The Prague National Theatre. She was known for her scenic backdrops as well as her costume designs. She had retired a few years earlier, and was enjoying working in her garden, visiting with friends, and taking in as much of the Prague art scene as she could. The theatre still occasionally called upon her for advice, and she would oblige them in any way she could. Pavla remembered as a little girl going backstage and sitting there amongst the canvases and paints, her Babicka giving her a small canvas to paint while she was busy with a backdrop scene for the upcoming opera production. The whole process from start-to-finish was magical for Pavla.

Dedecek, her grandfather, had died a few years earlier. He and Babicka had met at the opera house. He was Stage Manager, overseeing many details of each production. He would lift Pavla onto his shoulders and walk out with her on the stage.

"See this? Tonight, magic will happen. The audience will be transformed to another place in time, with music filling the air." He walked very carefully over to the orchestra pit and let her look down.

"Here, Pavla, the orchestra will play. At precisely 8 p.m., the concertmaster will walk out, bow, turn to his orchestra and give them all a pitch to tune to. What sounds! Violins! Violas! Cellos! String bass! Winds!

All instruments tuning to a single pitch to join as one. Satisfied, the concertmaster will sit, and the Maestro will walk out to thunderous applause! Oh, the joy one hears when he lifts his baton and the overture begins. Pavla, it is magical. And my heart jumps with joy, no matter how tired I am from a busy day of preparation!"

Pavla grew up listening backstage to opera after opera. She had her favorites, and Mozart was top of the list. To say she was excited to work on the gala was an understatement.

Babicka and Dedecek had one daughter — the beautiful Susanna, named after the character in Mozart's *The Marriage of Figaro*, which happened to be the opera performed when she was born. Dark haired and blue eyed, Susanna had grown into a beauty, but a rebel. When she was 20, she ran off with a handsome Romani named Pavel, and joined a band of performers. Pavla was named after her father. When their high-flying act took to traveling all over Europe, Pavla went to live with her grandparents for some stability in her education. Inheriting art, music, opera, drama — Pavla was a mixture of all who raised her.

Looking back, Pavla was grateful she was in the right place at the right time when Eduard approached her in the Old Square. Trying her hand to see if the tourists would buy her artwork, which they did, she grew fond of the other buskers, or street performers. At night, she was taking art classes, with plans to join the artistic team at the National Theatre once she had her certification. Eduard complimented her work, telling her she would be of great benefit to him in his shop, if she was interested. She was, and the rest is history.

Back to her parents and the task at hand, she must convince them that she needs them for the gala production. Somehow, she knew they would be up for the challenge, especially since Pavla was sensing other excitement might take place during the evening.

Kissing Babicka on the cheeks, Pavla grabbed the basket of food and headed for the hills, unaware that Michael Holmes was accompanying her.

Pavel was waiting for his daughter at the final tram stop. Together they would walk up the hillside to their modest house nestled among beautiful old Norway Spruce, Scots pine, and Sessile oak trees. Susanna was on the porch waiting for them, and once she caught sight of them on the trail, she ran to greet them.

Pavla loved her parents, and she was proud of what they did. They were well known throughout Europe as the most daring aerial acrobats. Their specialty was aerial silk, and their performances were stunning and beautiful. Audiences were mesmerized, and the love the two had for each other was transmitted through their act. Pavla knew better than to ask them when they would stop traveling and performing – but she knew the day would come. They could afford a nice home in the city, but they chose to live off the grid when they were not on tour. They did have a studio built to practice and design, but their home itself was modest. They told her it was good for their mind, body, and soul to create among the trees.

"Pavla! I love your hair!" Susanna was turning Pavla around to get a better look. "I love how it is highlighted to match your eyes. And, wait a minute... Something is different about you. Let me look – oh my, I see peace and happiness in your face! Tell us all about it!"

Arm-in-arm, the three walked up the porch steps and went into the kitchen. Pavel was unloading the basket of food Susanna's mother had sent, and they were all devouring and talking at once. Pavla told them how happy she was working for Eduard Doubek, and then filled them in on the masquerade gala. As she told them about the performance, she could see the wheels turning in their heads. She also told them that she was getting a sense that something else was going on with this gala – perhaps danger, and that she particularly needed their help to pull it all together. Pavel and Susanna, never ones to turn down an adventure – or disappoint their only daughter – said they would be happy to join the gala team.

Pavla showed her parents the scene from *Amadeus* on her phone. For the rest of the afternoon, the trio sat around the kitchen table planning and designing. Pavla had her sketch pad, and by the time she and her dad walked back down the hill, she had a good plan to give Lukas.

Pavel kissed his beautiful and talented daughter goodbye at the tram station, and stood there waving as long as he had the tram in sight. He then walked back up the hill to rejoin Susanna, who was already waiting for him in the studio to begin practicing their role in the gala.

Michael Holmes quietly sat there while the others planned and sketched, pleased with the direction it took. He was amazed that all the players were connected, and all were on the same track for the gala — despite being unaware of so many other facets of the story or how things would play out in the end. He watched as Pavla studied their design all the way home, taking notes and sketching more ideas. Yes, she was a good addition to Eduard's team. This was all coming together nicely. Very nicely.

37
Vignettes of a Season

November. A season of many changes: the brilliant backdrop of autumn foliage, crisp mornings reminding one that winter is on its way, and busy preparations for the holiday season. But, for those anticipating the Mozart Masquerade Gala, this particular November was special.

Copenhagen

Copenhagen was a flurry of activity as the city prepared for its annual Christmas markets. Tivoli Gardens transformed from a festival of frights to a wintery wonderland by mid-November. Sixty wooden houses resembling gingerbread houses lined the illuminated gardens like a fairy village — selling foods, sweets, hot drinks, crafts, Christmas decorations, and other delights. The lake by the Chinese Pavilion reflected thousands of lights, and choirs sang carols throughout the holiday season. Santa Claus, better known as Julemanden in Denmark, is present with his reindeer at Tivoli to the delight of the children. The sweet smell of sugar-roasted almonds fills the air, accompanying the festive spirit the entire park embraces.

Nyhavn also sets up stalls along the canal, and the harbor area's colorful houses are dressed in holiday decorations and lights. One can also travel to Odense by train to experience the Hans Christian Andersen Christmas Market on Kultorvet Square. All the stalls are named after his fairy tales, there's a nostalgic carousel for the children, and of course there are thousands of holiday lights and sweet delights.

Arthur Adderly conducted business as usual, but nothing overshadowed his excitement to go to Prague for the gala, not even this — his favorite time of the year. Normally, he was out and about visiting the various markets, but this season he and Kristoph spent their evenings finalizing costumes, masques, hotel arrangements, and flight plans. Adderly would sit in the evenings with Stanzi in his lap, listening to Mozart, and imagining the gala. He wished he could find out what the program was to be for the evening, but in the meantime, he would close his eyes and dream about finally holding the priceless locket in his hands.

Kristoph followed through with all his employer's instructions about the gala, and their costumes would be ready for a fitting by the first of December. Adderly had told him not to tell anyone, not even Peter, what they would be wearing. He wanted it to be a total surprise once they arrived in Prague. Kristoph kept in touch with Peter, who kept pressuring him to make things happen at the gala. Kristoph was filled with mixed emotions. His first loyalty was to his boss, but he feared Peter. Therefore, he tried to appease him as much as he could when he called with unreasonable demands.

Kristoph finally managed to get Adderly to the market on Nyhavn, enjoying the festive atmosphere and sampling the food and drinks. It took their minds off the gala, off the treasures, and off Peter. On the rare nights he did ask off, Kristoph met friends and enjoyed being away from the pressure the gala was putting on him and his boss. He didn't confide in anyone – but once he was alone, he felt a heaviness in his heart about the awkward position in which Peter had placed him.

Vienna

Vienna was busy transforming into a Christmas playground as well. Its various holiday markets were scattered throughout the city, full of festive music and holiday goodies. The most traditional market of them all was the Old Viennese Christmas Market on Freyung in the city center. This market was first held as early as 1772, and a visitor today could easily feel transported back in time as they browse glass decorations, ceramics, handicrafts, and traditional nativities amid the sea of festive lights.

Peter grew more and more disgruntled with his job at the Mozarthaus. Tourists and visitors were steady, especially with the markets opening, but the confines of his office were stifling. He was restless, and wished many times over that he had not contacted Dr. Stone, but had kept the treasures to himself. He knew from the beginning that his embezzlements from the museum would be exposed if he did not follow through with the instructions Mr. Brookshire handed him — that, and he had hastily signed a contract.

Peter thought he had been so clever to give Dr. Stone a fake letter from Constanze! *How easily she had been duped!* However, she has since then proved to be more clever than he anticipated. He and Adderly had to up their game for the gala or the treasures would never be theirs.

Adderly and Kristoph were becoming more difficult to work with, questioning everything he suggested, especially since the failed efforts at Tivoli. He grew impatient, and realized he had to come up with a secondary plan that didn't involve them. He put together a specialized team for the elaborate scheme he was hatching. He would sit at his desk for hours plotting, but because he was blind to facts of the actual event, he had to plan for many different scenarios. He felt like he was closer to coming up with a winning plan, but he was constantly stressed.

Sophia watched Peter closely. She didn't dare question his moods lately. She just went about her mundane job at the Mozarthaus with a fake smile on her face for all who walked through the door. At night, she tried to comfort Peter as much as she could, and kept the conversation light if she did have questions about the gala. Peter had asked her to take the lead on getting their costumes and masques for the event, so she turned her attention to that and had fun finding the perfect outfits for them. They would, of course, go as Wolfgang and Constanze! Sophia wanted the treasures as much as Peter and Adderly, but she wanted them for the money and the ticket out of Vienna. She adored Peter, but she feared he didn't share the same feelings for her. So, she remained cautious — and kept her eyes and ears open.

Prague

Prague was bustling with Christmas markets. Shoppers could go from wooden stall to wooden stall sampling hot food and hot drinks or buying hand-carved toys, puppets, glass decorations and other traditional Czech handicrafts. The Old Town Square was even more spectacular with its huge Christmas tree lit by thousands of lights. There also was a live Nativity scene, with animals and actors portraying Mary, Joseph, Baby Jesus, and the Three Kings, accompanied by beautiful Christmas music being performed by choirs from all over the world.

Eduard loved this time of the year, and he loved that his shop was right on the Square, where he could enjoy the festivities even while he was working. The gala was taking most of his time — there were plenty of late nights as they finished up the gowns for Elizabeth and for the infamous Emilia Rose — but he and Pavla were meeting all their deadlines. He kept a flowchart in the shop, and they checked off items as they were completed. He was pleased to see they were right on track to finish production on all gala-related items by his target date of December 24th. He did want time to visit the market and go to church before Dr. Stone and everyone else arrived on the 28th.

Eduard had the ground transportation all taken care of, and the tour guides would meet the participants at the airport and take them to their hotel. They were in for such a surprise! No expense was being spared for Elizabeth and her entourage, and Eduard was making sure that the details under his supervision were indeed spectacular.

In addition to the design studio, Masquerade Mystique maintained a store front operation with unusual masques for tourists to purchase. The holiday season was a particularly busy time for the shop, so Eduard was glad they were as far along as they were for the gala.

On this particular day, however, as the bell on the front door jingled, it signaled the entrance of a very special guest. A big smile grew across Eduard's face when he realized who had just entered the shop, and he happily went and hugged his long-time friend — and Elizabeth's benefactor. Saying very little, as there were other customers browsing, he and his friend went back to the design studio office. Pavla took her cue, and went to help the customers.

An hour later, Eduard's guest left the shop. He was pleased with the masques, the gowns, and the other details of the gala that Eduard shared with him. Taking his leave from Masquerade Mystique on this chilly day, Eduard's friend was excited to see his plan coming to fruition.

Eduard watched his friend nonchalantly walk through the Square, occasionally stopping and viewing items in the stalls so that anyone observing would think he was a regular tourist visiting the famous Christmas Market. No one saw his two guards in front clearing a path, or the two in the rear, covering his back. Eduard knew. Eduard smiled.

Pavla didn't question who the visitor was. In all honesty, she was busy working. But even when the two walked back to front shop, she didn't take the time to look at his face — which was partially covered with a scarf, and partially obscured by the brim of his hat. Pavla just knew that customers needed to be assisted. After the mysterious guest left, she went back to her work on the masques, knowing that if she were supposed to know who the guest was, Eduard would tell her. Although, she did hear his voice — a deep, rich, British accent that traveled to the storefront as low-murmured tones from the back shop. She made note of it, just in case she ever needed to know.

Pavla had been extremely busy with the masques, but she had visited her parents every Sunday in order to see what they had planned for *Lacrimosa*. When she had shown them the musical selections being performed at the gala, they all agreed that this haunting Mozart composition was the one they most wanted to choreograph. Their aerial dance was stunning, and she continued to be in awe of her beautiful and talented parents.

The set was coming along nicely as well, and she tried her best to stop by her friends' workshop to pitch in whenever she had a chance. They would be able to move the sets to The Estates Theatre on the 26th, and Eduard had rented a moving van for them to carry the pieces there safely — and incognito. Lukas, Adela, Blanka, Emil, and Dominik had created some incredible black light scenes for the performance. Now, if all players did their parts, this was going to be a gala to remember.

That evening after Eduard's guest left, Pavla left the shop and stopped for a mug of hot chocolate at one of the stalls before heading home. Her grandmother kept dinner warm for her, and understood her late nights without questioning her. Babicka would always sit with her while she ate, and they would talk about the gala preparations. Pavla had filled her in that Susanna and Pavel would be involved, and Babicka had offered to help backstage if necessary. But Pavla knew better than to break Eduard's trust — she wouldn't speculate, even to Babicka, about the mysterious man who visited the shop today. That must remain a secret.

The States

Paparazzi

Paparazzi was not at all familiar with the Thanksgiving traditions in the States. He had heard and read about Thanksgiving, of course, but it was only celebrated in Great Britain by US expats. He loved that it was a time of gathering for families, and the meal looked scrumptious. The television food networks were filled with episodes showing the proper way to bake a turkey, broast a turkey, smoke a turkey, and even fry a turkey. Then, there were all the traditional sides to go along with whatever turkey you chose to serve. Oh, and the desserts! The days leading up to Thanksgiving had him wishing he had family or friends there to celebrate with. Because the university was closing for the holiday and Dr. Stone would be spending time with family, he called his boss to see if he could fly home for a few days. Mr. Brookshire agreed, and made arrangements for him to fly out on the Wednesday before Thanksgiving and return on the Monday after. Thankful, Paparazzi informed the hotel clerk of his plans, but that he would not be checking out and would like to keep the current room he was in.

Until then, Paparazzi continued to observe Dr. Stone. She was very focused with the gala program preparations, and had called evening rehearsals with the choir and orchestra. He was able to slip unnoticed into the back of the rehearsal stage once for a few moments before he feared being recognized, but in those few moments he was mesmerized by the beauty of the music. Dr. Stone and Dr. Chamberlain were both so passionate about their work, and they collaborated well on this program. Her students were respectful, and the rehearsals were run smoothly, yet on task. He noticed before they left for Thanksgiving that most of the students were singing off-music, or off-book as he heard her say once to them. She looked tired, but was dauntless. Paparazzi was glad she would get a few days off.

As much as he needed some family time, he hated leaving Dr. Stone. He had grown fond of her comings and goings — and several times they had landed at restaurants at the same time, usually for morning meetings. She seemed to prefer to eat at home in the evenings.

Paparazzi packed a small bag to take home with him, leaving behind no trace of business in the hotel room to be found by cleaning staff. It was a large, upscale hotel, and he loved that he could come and go without being noticed in the busy lobby. However, when the elevators doors opened onto the lobby that morning, he was not at all prepared to see Dr. Benjamin Watson asking the desk clerk a question. Pulling his hat down lower over his face, he proceeded to the entrance where his driver was already waiting for him. Goodness, Elizabeth must have invited him here for Thanksgiving, and he must have arrived last night. As thankful as Paparazzi was that he was taking a break, he was a bit disappointed that he wouldn't be around to see the interaction between Elizabeth and Dr. Watson. Not taking any chances, he texted Mr. Brookshire and let him know of the recent development. Mr. Brookshire was grateful for the info, but told Paparazzi to continue with his plans. No one seemed to think Dr. Watson was a threat.

After his connection in NYC, Paparazzi checked in to his British Airways flight, first class of course, and settled in for his flight to London. His beautiful wife had also been on an assignment, and they were looking forward to a few days together. The attendant came around, interrupting his thoughts, asking him if he would like something to drink. While sipping his coffee and awaiting departure, he thumbed through his journal, reviewing his findings since he had been in the States. As part of the deal letting him come home for the holiday, he was to have a personal briefing with Mr. Brookshire, where he get further instructions for the gala. Looking out the window upon take-off, he paused for a moment to think, *Take care, Dr. Stone.* And with that, Paparazzi was off.

Benjamin

Benjamin arrived quite late on Tuesday night, so he hadn't seen Elizabeth yet — only texted to let her know he had arrived safely. He was pleased, yet surprised, when she had invited him for Thanksgiving with her family. He already had plans to be with his family, but worked it out so he could spend Wednesday with her. Benjamin's daughter worked, so he wasn't expected until dinner on Thursday. He had been in Dallas for a concert tour, so the journey to see Elizabeth was easy. His flight to Boston was later tonight, which would give him a night in his own bed before driving to his daughter's home. Elizabeth was picking him up for breakfast, so he wanted to go ahead and check out before she arrived. They were going to spend the day together, and then she would drop him off at the airport for his flight.

Just as he was thanking the clerk and folding his bill, he heard his name. "Benjamin!"

Turning, he smiled as he saw Elizabeth bound through the door. She looked wonderful, and he greeted her with a hug.

"Elizabeth! You are a sight for sore eyes! And I am starving! Where are you taking me for breakfast?"

"I hope you like pancakes — because I am taking you to the most famous pancake house in Texas. Their specialty is gingerbread pancakes, and this time of the year they also have a pumpkin spice pancakes. Are you game?"

"Totally!"

They turned to leave, and Benjamin thanked the clerk again. He was anxious to hear any updates about the treasures and about her progress with the music for the gala.

Over a plate full of gingerbread and pumpkin pancakes, with a side of sizzling bacon and mug of hot coffee that Lilah kept full, Elizabeth filled Benjamin on all the latest. He didn't know about Amanda Kate, Peyton, Emilia Rose, and Frieda joining the team.

"THE Emilia Rose? How in the world did you convince her to do 'The Queen of the Night'? I hear she is also afraid of heights, so how is all of this going to work?" Benjamin was astonished.

"I think she has overcome those fears to a certain degree. Besides, it might make her reach the high notes easier as we lift her high above the stage." They both laughed at the thought of this, but in truth both of them loved Emilia Rose and all of her quirks.

"Elizabeth, you continue to amaze me. I love all your production ideas. Tell me more about Masquerade Mystique." Benjamin settled back in the booth as Elizabeth excitedly told him about all the masques and costumes Eduard Doubek was supplying for the group.

Benjamin set his coffee cup on the table, "I haven't even begun looking for a masque yet, so I may be a rather boring guest at the gala and come with a simple masque. The tour is keeping me on the road, and I didn't realize how full my calendar was with guest conducting until you had me check to see if I was busy New Year's."

"Well," Elizabeth said slowly, "I turned your name in as a guest of mine to Eduard, so he is making your masque. No worries for you, Maestro!"

Benjamin was stunned that Elizabeth had taken care of so many details for him, and he expressed his gratitude several times.

Lilah brought the bill, and Benjamin paid for breakfast. They spent some time in Elizabeth's office, where she asked him some opinions about her approach to the program. He agreed with her score study, gave her a few tips that she was excited about, and then he watched as she conducted to a recording of the *Requiem*. A skilled conductor is never afraid to have an extra set of eyes offer a critique, and Elizabeth was pleased that Benjamin felt she was right on-target with her interpretation.

Totally involved in their music, the two were stunned when they realized it was nearly time for Benjamin to go to the airport.

"Are you hungry? I know a place close by where we can grab a quick bite." Elizabeth was collecting her scores in her briefcase to take home.

"I think I am fine after the huge breakfast, and I hear the traffic is awful to the airport." Benjamin had stood up and was stretching his legs.

"Awful is an understatement, so we will just go straight there. You know me, I like to be early, and you can always grab a bite in the airport if need be." Elizabeth locked up her office and turned to look at the handsome Benjamin Watson who was waiting patiently for her to finish. She smiled, and together they walked to her car. The drive wasn't terrible, and the goodbyes at the curb were quick.

"See you in Prague!" Benjamin shouted as she began to drive away. Elizabeth managed a thumbs-up before pulling into the lane of traffic, pleased to see Benjamin still in her rearview mirror, standing there waving.

Emilia Rose

Emilia Rose spent every spare moment she had rehearsing for this mysterious Mozart Masquerade gala where Elizabeth had asked her to perform. She was excited about going back to Prague, for it had been at least ten years since she had sung in The Estates Theatre. Between her current calendar of performances, master classes, and teaching, Emilia Rose had very little time to brush up on "The Queen of the Night." She had performed it many times, as well as the *Laudate* from the *Vesperae solennes de confessore*, but it had been a while. She was a little concerned after re-watching the iconic scene from *Amadeus*, but Elizabeth had promised her it would be safe.

Emilia Rose cringed as she remembered her horrible experience at the Met several years ago. She was playing the role of Senta in Wagner's opera, *The Flying Dutchman*. In the last scene, Senta and the Dutchman ascend towards heaven after Senta throws herself into the sea, having declared her undying love for the Dutchman. The young director at the time thought it would be grand if the two singers literally ascended, instead of the traditional staging where the ascent is implied. The director called in the experts, and she and the male lead practiced several times before opening night. They had a mechanically rising platform that represented the deck of the ghost ship, and the background was made up of panels that digitally showed a crashing ocean around them.

Opening night arrived, and the opera was going along as rehearsed — until the last scene, that is. In rehearsals, Emilia Rose had not looked around to see the crashing waves around her. As they ascended, she made the fatal mistake of looking, and vertigo set in. She felt the whole stage spinning, and instead of looking out at the audience as she had rehearsed, she did the unthinkable – she fainted. Her partner felt her hand relax, but kept in character and held on to her tighter. The stage crew had seen what happened, so they did an unrehearsed curtain pull in order to get her down without panicking the audience. She was only out for a moment, and when she came to, she revived herself long enough to help them get her out of the safety harness. Emilia Rose was not going to miss her curtain call, and so the audience never suspected a thing when she took her final bow. The cast praised her as they led her to her dressing room, proclaiming how brilliant she was to finish the show. A true artist they raved!

That night she read up on vertigo, and they mentioned that foods with Vitamin B6 helped reduce the dizziness and nausea that she had experienced. They listed chicken, pork, salmon, tuna, peanut butter, beans, etc. So, the next night, about four hours before her call time, she ordered chicken livers from a restaurant nearby and had them delivered to the backstage door. Chicken livers were high in iron, B6, and B12. They worked beautifully. She got through the whole show, even the end, without incident. From then on, she ordered chicken livers before every performance – just in case.

She prayed that Prague had chicken livers. But, she knew Amanda Kate and Peyton would be on top of this and would make them magically appear for her. That's what friends are for.

Matthew

Matthew had ordered a tux to take with him for the gala. The bank had plenty of formal events, but a suit was usually sufficient. At a Halloween clearance sale, he found a very nice black cape with a red lining that would go well with his new tux and be all the costume he needed. Elizabeth had emailed him that his masque was being handmade in Prague, and he was thrilled to hear he didn't need to hunt one of those down. All the ones he had seen were flimsy, and he didn't want to take the risk of it falling apart.

He and Elizabeth had met one morning for breakfast, and she quietly told him her plans to take a decoy box to Prague containing fake treasures to try to lure out Peter and Arthur Adderly. She didn't want Matthew to freak out when he saw her with them, knowing that he had not taken the real ones out of the safe. He was to act as if they were the real treasures, but she also wanted him to act like the keeper of the box for the gala. Elizabeth explained he would be watched, and she wanted him to talk loudly about the treasures during all the social events. She described Peter, Sophia, Adderly, and Kristoph to him, but reminded him that they would be in costume and masque. He was to carry the treasures in a sling bag that matched his costume, and just notice if anyone moved towards him when he was bragging about the treasures. Elizabeth assumed, from previous experience, that they would try to steal the bag, so she and Matthew planned an elaborate scene as a response if they did snatch the decoy treasures. Matthew couldn't wait.

Frieda

Frieda had lost count of how many galas, movie premieres, and red-carpet events she had done hair for this month. She was thankful that the holiday gave her a day off to rest her weary hands. She also needed time to absorb all the information she was getting from Elizabeth about the gala in Prague and her job with Emilia Rose. Frieda was reading between the lines and figuring there was more than meets the eye with this gala.

Elizabeth would educate her, in due time, but in the meantime, she spent her off hours looking at new hairdos for Emilia Rose. At least Emilia had great hair to work with, even though she was a diva. Divas were no match for Frieda, and that is why she was highly sought after as a stylist.

Frieda had done quite a bit of online research about the solos Emilia would be singing. She really fell in love with the 5th movement of the *Vesperae solennes de confessore*, the beautiful *Laudate Dominum* solo. Frieda was intrigued by "The Queen of the Night's aria," and she had some fun ideas about wig styles to give Emilia Rose dramatic hair even while wearing a headpiece. However, she knew enough about the stage to realize it was going to be a feat to pull off this performance — especially knowing Emilia Rose's background and personality quirks. At least she would have Amanda Kate and Peyton by her side. None of them wanted to let Elizabeth down, and they all knew this was an important event for her.

Frieda sent Emilia Rose several choices of hairstyles for the gala. She was pleased when they both liked the same ones, but Frieda knew that liking it was just the first step — Emilia Rose had been known to have her stylists change her hair several times before she went out on stage. Frieda was determined not to play that game, and she hoped to keep her focused on the ones they agreed to ahead of time. After all, she was going to wear it for all of ten minutes, and then rush backstage to put on the headpiece!

Frieda had also started packing a make-up and supplies kit to take with her. Everything was brand new and still in its packaging so Emilia Rose couldn't question who had used it before. Surely, they could work through this smoothly. Surely...

Now she just had to get through the rest of the holiday season and then get on the plane to Prague. There were hundreds of holiday parties in Hollywood, so Frieda stayed very busy right up until Christmas Eve. Before heading to bed that evening, she sent Amanda Kate a text:

Hi girl, so what is really up with the gala?

Frieda didn't expect an honest answer, but she hoped she had planted a seed with Amanda Kate that would result in Elizabeth getting back to her.

Ping.

Honestly, Frieda, you must ask Elizabeth if you really want to know. She will fill you in.

Thanks, Amanda Kate — I will do just that. Looking forward to Prague!

Frieda smiled. There *was* something else going on with the gala! She would follow through with Elizabeth soon, but for now, she had fun imagining what Emilia Rose would do if she sprayed her hair a rose color on the evening of the gala. Fun to think about, but she valued her life, so she just imagined it.

Amanda Kate

Amanda Kate's clients began calling her in early November to start decorating their houses for Christmas, and some wanted Thanksgiving and Christmas both. Her team worked steadily to get them all done, but she had been so busy with designs that she hadn't had a chance to catch up on her blog. She was writing about how to make holiday wreaths when she received the text from Frieda. Afterwards, she realized that she had just verified to Frieda that there was something else going on with the gala. Oh well, she knew Izzibeth would tell her soon enough. She might need to know, just in case someone tries to sabotage the backstage area. Heaven forbid if that happens, but in this case, it is a big possibility!

She retrieved her gala design notebook from a drawer in her desk. This was a dream assignment − Eduard was a joy to work with, he loved her ideas, and she only needed to oversee set up on the day of the gala. Eduard had his team working on production, and promised to have a team there to do all the actual set-up. Amanda Kate was especially proud of the picture backdrop she had designed for the Red Carpet. It was 12'x8', Prussian blue background, with "Mozart Masquerade Gala" in fancy gold script across the top. Black music staves from one of Mozart's manuscripts spanned the breadth of the backdrop. Simple, elegant, and to the point. The plan was to have Peyton there to greet guests and pose them on the Red Carpet for pictures. This way, she could interact with most of the guests and be on the lookout for anyone suspicious. Good grief, with all the guests in masques, that was going to be a challenge!

Peyton

Peyton was reading all the information she could find on Prague. She had her list of sights she wanted to visit, foods to try, and items to buy. She had read that the Christmas Market would still be going on in the Old Town Square, and she knew she and Amanda Kate would have fun shopping and stocking up on Christmas items for next year.

Peyton had never been abroad, so she had to apply for her passport. She was so excited when it arrived in the mail. Not fully knowing what might take place at the gala just added more excitement to the trip. She had been given descriptions of all the known villains — Adderly, Kristoph, Peter, Sophia. Her job was to start scoping them out from the moment they arrived on the Red Carpet. For now, she could only imagine how the escapade would unfold. Elizabeth was known for her productions, but this would be her finest and certainly her most exciting!

In the meantime, however, Peyton continued her holiday baking. The church was having a bazaar, and everyone expected her pumpkin spice cake balls, spiced cupcakes with orange crème frosting, and pecan tarts. She usually brought her famous iced shortbread Christmas cookies as well. She found herself joyfully singing and baking in the warmth of her kitchen every evening. Amanda Kate was coming for the bazaar that weekend, and she was bringing her notebook with all the gala designs.

The oven timer went off, and Peyton pulled out a tray of pumpkin spice cake balls. She would let them cool and then sprinkle them with powdered sugar. She had a cookie tin all ready to load up and mail to Elizabeth. The Stanzi Project had contributed a new layer of adventure to her small-town life, and she was loving it.

38

Elizabeth

Burning the candle at both ends seemed to energize me. I was pleased with the progress of the music before the students went home for Thanksgiving, and I knew they would continue to study it while they were off. That's the kind of students I taught. They never wanted to do anything less than spectacular. I had given them a date to be off-book, and that deadline was coming soon. I would feel so much better when they were, because that was when the real magic started.

I'm so happy I had contacted Benjamin on a whim about Thanksgiving. We had a wonderful visit, catching up on our careers and planning for Prague. I was sad to see him go, but enjoyed our time together immensely.

Thanksgiving with Grey's family was wonderful. I was fortunate that he and his sweet family lived within miles of me, so we could get together easily at any time. We laughed and ate — a lot. After dinner that evening, while the grandchildren, Ellie and Liam, were quietly playing, I poured us a glass of wine. Nonchalantly I told Grey and his wife, Emma, we needed to talk. Ignoring their quizzical looks, I waited until they had settled in on the couch before I began my tale.

I spared a few details — like Michael Holmes and the big, black dog cuddled up next to Charlotte. I didn't think they could handle all of it at once. They sat there in stunned silence, taking it all in, and then I began to tell them what I might need them to do at the gala. The plan caused great excitement, and they began chatting at once, elaborating on the scheme and asking to see the treasures. I explained that they were in a safe place, for the time being, and that they would get to see them in due time. They stayed the night because it had gotten so late by the time we finished talking.

When I kissed them goodbye the next day, I smiled to think how far I had come since my husband Liam's death. Two years ago, right after his death, Thanksgiving was heartbreaking. This year I was still sad he was missing from the festivities, but I was looking forward to a quiet cup of coffee and second piece of pumpkin pie by myself.

Beau and Charlotte were waiting for me inside after waving goodbye to my family from the porch, and behind them was Michael Holmes.

"Well done, Dr. Stone. Your family is as amazing as you are. They took the news well, don't you think?"

"Hopefully they won't have to get involved on the night of the gala, but I wanted them to be informed. I really thought they would be able to see Beau, so I was surprised. What's up with that?"

Michael smiled. "I prevented them from seeing him tonight. But the next time he will be visible. I think the children knew — especially your granddaughter. You might have missed it, but she was looking right at him several times throughout the evening, as if she was trying to figure him out."

Michael filled me in on everything he had observed in Prague. I got really excited and couldn't wait to meet Pavla, her parents, and the Black Light crew. He was gone as fast as he came, promising to keep me informed. We both agreed that I had collected most of the clues I needed from the letters, visions, and dreams. The only thing left now was keeping the treasures safe from Peter and Arthur Adderly.

I spent the rest of the weekend practicing my conducting. I liked to use my scores, but usually had them memorized so my head wasn't down during the concert. This program had more than its fair share of challenges, so I needed to be confident with every note and every page turn. I had a playlist of my favorite performances of this repertoire, which I used as a backdrop for my score study. I put my headphones on and really immersed myself in the music. If anyone looked in my window, they would think I was some crazy lady waving my arms in front of my fireplace. Little would they know that I was training my hands to respond to my heart as I experienced the spirit of the music.

Thirty-three days until departure, with Christmas in-between. I can do this. I have to.

I ran my fingers over the diamond treble clef and remembered the words of my benefactor: *Keep the integrity.* I planned to do just that — not only for myself, but for Mozart and Marie Antoinette.

With that thought, I closed my scores and headed for the kitchen. In honor of Mozart, Constanze, and Marie Antoinette, I pulled up a recipe for Sachertorte that was trending online. I remembered seeing Michael Holmes looking at me through the window at the Hotel Sacher in Vienna just last spring, and he startled me at the time. With Mozart playing in the background over the wireless speaker, I made the famous cake — all the while thinking of how one little snuff box and one small locket had brought us all together.

Sachertorte Recipe

Cook time: 50-65 minutes. Makes 8-10 servings

Ingredients:

Cake

5 oz. softened butter
½ C sifted confectioner's sugar
8 egg yolks
8 egg whites

5 oz. bittersweet chocolate
2/3 C of flour
1/2 C sugar
2 T apricot jam

Glaze

8 oz. bittersweet chocolate
2 T butter

Garnish

Whipped Cream

Directions:

Cake

Preheat oven to 375.
Cream together butter and confectioner's sugar. Add 1 egg yolk at a time, mixing until creamy. Melt 5 oz. bittersweet chocolate in a double boiler or microwave; then gradually add to the creamed mixture. Fold in the flour. In a separate bowl, beat the egg whites and sugar until stiff. Fold this mixture into the chocolate mixture. Pour batter into a lined 9-inch springform pan. Bake for 50-65 minutes. Remove from the pan and cool on a wire rack. Heat apricot jam and smooth over the entire torte, including the sides.

Glaze

Melt the 8 oz. bittersweet chocolate with the butter, let cool slightly, and then frost the cake. Serve with whipped cream.

39
The Visitor

I was pouring a cup of coffee when Beau growled and leaned in strongly against me.

"What's wrong, buddy?" I continued filling my mug, and then bent down to talk to him.

As I turned, I froze, for there standing before me was the biggest man I had ever seen. Michael Holmes was tall, but this man was at least a foot taller than him. The ceilings in my kitchen were 12 feet high, but he was clearing those, so I guessed he was about 10 feet tall. My eyes went to his face. His shoulder length hair was jet black, as were his eyes. His skin was a pale white, smooth as ivory, and his features finely chiseled. He was wearing a black shirt with a mandarin collar, black jeans, and black boots. Beau stayed close, but had quit growling. However, I honestly was more intrigued by the man than afraid of him at that point.

"What a pleasure it is to finally meet you, Dr. Stone." His voice was not as deep as I had expected it to be, but it was very musical. I would have put him in my Bass 1 section. Maybe even Tenor 2.

"And you are...here to grant me three wishes?" I quipped. I was surprised how calmly I spoke, even though my heart was pounding. Mentally, I was yelling for Michael, but he had not yet made his appearance.

This giant laughed, and it shook my house. My coffee filled with ripples so strong they had white caps on them, like waves crashing against the shore. I had to hold on tightly to keep it from spilling.

"You are as charming as everyone tells me you are, Dr. Stone! I am Simon — surely Michael has told you about me? By the way... You can quit calling for him, because he cannot hear you. I have put a shield around you, preventing Michael from hearing you or Beau call for him. Remember the Fun House at Tivoli?"

"I do, Simon. As I recall, Michael couldn't hear me then either. Nice to have that mystery solved. That wasn't a pleasant experience."

"Ah, but you tricked us, Dr. Stone. I didn't like that, but I do admire your cleverness."

Simon had not moved once during our conversation. He kept his gaze straight on me, so I returned the favor.

Simon continued. "I know a lot about you, Dr. Stone. I know today is your group's departure for your big trip to the masquerade gala in Prague. Bizarre — this whole event — when it would just be so simple for you to turn over the treasures."

"And to whom would that be, Simon? Who is your human protégé?"

Simon didn't particularly like my use of terminology, and I thought I saw a smirk on his face.

"Haven't you solved that yet? As clever as you are, I would have thought you immediately figured out the mastermind behind this escapade."

"All clues point to Peter, so he's my guess. But — he's so ineffective and sloppy thus far, I just wanted you to confirm it's really him."

Simon laughed again, and I held on the counter this time.

"You amuse me, Dr. Stone! Yes, it is Peter, and we are getting impatient. I don't like to lose, Dr. Stone, or to be out-tricked. Why don't you just tell me where you have the treasures, and all of this will be over with?"

"Don't you know, Simon? I thought you knew everything. Please don't take this as sarcasm, as I truly find it intriguing that you don't know where the treasures are. I have my plans, too, by the way. Perhaps you and Peter will just have to be patient long enough to see them unfold in Prague. That is all I am going to tell you."

I could see Simon digesting my words. He didn't like it, but he didn't react.

"I have not come to harm you, Dr. Stone. I have come to warn you before someone really does get hurt. If you don't comply, then Peter and I will have to resort to extreme means to get the treasures. You don't want to see Arthur Adderly or Sophia hurt now, do you? Kristoph? Or what about your precious family? Bradley? Your friends? Your colleagues? Think about it, Dr. Stone. You have a couple of hours before you board the plane to Prague. Bring the treasures. This is your last warning."

With that, he vanished.

I surprised myself with how calmly and confidently I handled his visit. His words didn't scare me, and neither did his threats. I already had a plan in motion that was going to work. I just knew it would.

As I stood there reflecting on the encounter with Simon, I felt Beau's tail start beating against my leg. I looked up from taking a sip of coffee to see Michael in the same spot that Simon had just been standing. What a difference between these two! Michael was like a breath of fresh air, like night and day.

"Well *that* was interesting," I stated sarcastically as I refilled my cup.

"I see you met Simon."

"Let's rephrase that, Michael Holmes — Simon met me." I winked and gave Michael a confident tilt of my head. Two months ago my life was pretty routine, and now I am entertaining angels in my kitchen.

Suddenly, though, I froze, and chills went up my spine. I set my coffee mug on the counter. I had been drinking out of a mug that said Copenhagen, and I had a flashback to that night when I was attacked.

"Oh my gosh, Michael — I recognize those eyes. Tonight wasn't my first time to meet Simon. It was Simon who attacked me that night, wasn't it?!"

"Yes, that was Simon who attacked you. That is why we were able to apprehend him ourselves. He was not a happy camper that he let his guard down long enough for Beau to knock him off you." Michael spoke calmly and assuredly.

"Well, part of me is relieved to finally know who it was. But, unlike tonight's encounter, I did feel fear that night in Copenhagen. Would he really have killed me if you two had not come along at the right moment?"

Michael nodded a confirming yes, but then smiled. "I hate to admit it, but that was one of my finest moments. Seeing Simon's reaction when Beau knocked him over was priceless."

"But he didn't seem to be as tall that night in the street. He is at least 10 feet tall, but that night he was more like 6 feet tall."

"Simon is tricky. He can take whatever form he needs in order to achieve his ends. Above anything else, he's obsessed with winning. His goal that night was to get the treasures, no matter what. Evidently, he and Peter have a friendship such as ours, where Peter can visibly see Simon. Simon overstepped a boundary that night when he attacked you. That was against our rules, but Simon doesn't think rules apply to him. We are to advise you, guard you, but not do your dirty work for you."

"That puts a new twist on things if he's willing to get involved that directly," I said with a new concern in my voice. "It means Simon's willing to carry through on his threats, and he obviously has the means to do it. I was mainly focused on Peter, and he doesn't scare me anymore. We have to make sure our plans for Prague are perfect. You're up-to-date, correct?"

Michael nodded, and then was off.

40
Prague

Prague. Praha. The City of a Hundred Spires. The capital of the Czech Republic, with a population of 1.26 million people at last count, and the 15th largest city in the European Union.

My first visit to Prague, several years earlier, was a whimsical adventure in a city that was new to both Liam and me. I was thrilled when he decided to travel as my companion on this tour, pleased that he took the time off from work. The group had been picked up at the airport by a very vibrant and young tour director by the name of Pavel. In his short briefing at the airport we learned that he and his wife enjoyed snowboarding, surfing, roller blading, and were living out of an old VW van. After our tour, they had plans to go to the coast of Spain.

After a quick shower at the hotel and a dinner of lentil soup followed by svickova, a popular Czech dish of beef sirloin in a cream sauce served with bread dumplings called knedliky, we loaded up in taxis and headed to The Estates Theatre to see a production of Mozart's *Cosi fan tutte*. The taxi ride was wilder than a taxi ride in NYC. The group had filled three taxis, and when we all piled out, we were laughing and comparing drivers.

We then walked inside the famous Estates Theatre, and oh my, I wanted to cry. Mozart, the Wolfgang Amadeus Mozart, had been in this very theatre! The stage itself was not very wide, but it was adorned from floor to ceiling by a huge blue curtain and encircled by incredibly ornate theatre boxes. The orchestra pit was relatively large compared to the size of the stage. We sat in white French country chairs with blue velvet cushions. I looked up at the luxuriously decorated ceiling and the beautiful chandelier hanging right above me. Built in classical style, Pavel told us that the theatre is preserved in its original state.

I was enthralled, but I had imposed an opera production on jetlagged travelers. I was on the edge of my seat, but when I looked down the row, my group was nodding off at different times. I elbowed Liam next to me, fearful his snoring might not fit in with the music. The orchestra and cast did a wonderful job presenting the opera. I could only imagine them talking backstage about Row 11 being asleep.

Afterwards, as if being in the same theatre where Mozart had been wasn't enough, a magical moment occurred. We were so tired, but Pavel said, "Give me ten minutes." He then led us out into the street.

It had rained during the performance, and the night air perked us up a bit as we followed Pavel down a narrow street. His legs were so long, and we laughed trying to keep up with him, but we were all anxious to see where he was taking us. Suddenly we were there, and we all froze as our mouths dropped open.

Pavel had taken us to the Old Town Square. The buildings were wet and glistening from the recent rain, and the lights of the Square just added to the fairyland atmosphere. Pavel explained that we were seeing Gothic, Medieval, and Baroque architecture. The blend was stunning.

Pavel allowed us a few moments to take in the splendor, and then asked us to follow him again. A short distance from the square was the famous Charles Bridge. There, reflecting in the waters of the Vltava River, atop a hillside, was the most beautiful castle I had ever seen — Prague Castle, lit up with what looked like a thousand lights dancing off the stonework. I had never seen anything so beautiful in all my travels. We would begin our tour there in the morning, and on the ride back home, we were all abuzz about the adventures awaiting us in Prague.

Pavel didn't disappoint us. The sights, the smells, the foods, the shops, and definitely the history were all new to me, and I was like a sponge absorbing everything I could. He began the tour at the castle, in a small courtyard next to the Writers' College, giving us a quiet history lesson away from the throngs of tourists starting to gather at the main entrance. We learned from him that the castle is the largest in Europe, and it took about five hundred years to complete. It is so stunning that one might think it is a cathedral instead of a castle!

He then led us through the Royal Gardens, which hadn't been open to the public for very long at that time. We walked through the wonderful, woodsy gardens to our goal – the Singing Fountain in the Summer Palace of Queen Anne. King Ferdinand I had commissioned the court painter and a master bell-caster to create the fountain for his wife, Queen Anne. It was finished in 1568. Water falls into metal basins through spouts emerging from various human and animal heads. As the water hits the metal, it produces a symphony of musical tones. If you hold your ear near the base, the water even makes a singing sound, hence the fountain's nickname. Lucky Queen! I remember Liam sticking his ear close to the base of the fountain and smiling as he heard the fountain's song. There was so much history to take in!

The guards at the Prague Castle are famous for their beautiful baby blue uniforms, which were designed by the costume designer who created the costumes for the movie, *Amadeus*. We were told that many movies were filmed here because it doesn't cost a lot for this fabulous backdrop: *Yentl*, *Les Miserables* with Liam Neeson in 1998, *Immortal Beloved*, *Mission Impossible*, and *Amadeus* – just to name a few.

Finally making our way into the center of the castle, Pavel explained that it is made up of three courtyards – the middle being the oldest. Surprisingly, there was no admission to the castle grounds, but there was a separate fee for entrance into the various buildings on the grounds. Our group opted for the free portion, but even it was great. The St. Vitus Cathedral was a beautiful example of Gothic architecture, with mosaics and a beautiful rose window made of 27,000 pieces. The big attraction, however, was a 1931 stained glass window by Alphonse Mucha, the famous Czech Art Nouveau artist. The window portrayed St. Wenceslaus in the center with his grandmother, St. Ludmila, and it was surrounded by panels depicting the lives of Saints Cyril and Methodius. As intriguing as the history depicted in the window was, what caught my eye was the beauty Mucha portrayed in his faces of his subjects. I couldn't wait to see more of his work.

The castle tour just kept getting better and better, and Pavel was an excellent guide. We looked in Vladislav Hall, a large hall that Pavel said was used to crown the kings and hold banquets. He explained that you would ride your horse in and then be lifted off and carried to the banquet table! Pavel also pointed out a bit of gross trivia, that they even had a special room for you to go and tickle your throat with a feather, so you could vomit and then go back out to eat more food. I wouldn't want a job involving anything to do with that room!

Prague Castle, like the Old Town Square, showcased many significant styles of architecture, and Pavel was so good at helping us understand their main features and history. He had us make a human arch with our hands, and then had others push on our shoulders to illustrate how flying buttresses support Gothic windows. Pavel pointed out that Gothic windows look like praying hands and that the tall towers were designed to draw your eyes upward, to look to God. We also saw buildings in Baroque and Romanesque styles. When it takes five hundred years to build a castle, styles do change!

We passed by the Golden Lane, where supposedly the King hid all his gold in an Alchemist shop, but we didn't go in. No, our ears were being drawn to a Russian band giving a free concert nearby, so we all stopped and listened. They were great, and so were their singers, but my favorite memory was Pavel demonstrating the Russian dance for us and the thousand other tourists who stopped to watch our very talented guide. What a jewel he was!

We walked down the very steep Kings Road to the Charles Bridge. Pavel had us all get out a piece of paper and write out the following: 135797531

These lucky numbers were given to King Charles IV by court astrologers, and they indicated when the first stone was laid to begin the bridge – the year 1357, the 9th of July, at exactly 5:31 a.m.

Another interesting legend was that the bridge's wooden pillars were held together with mortar that had been mixed with eggs!

Artists, buskers, and many tourists meandered along the bridge, and the atmosphere was happy. I remember one busker played guitar while dressed as a marionette clown. We also walked past a statue that everyone rubs for good luck. Of course, we all took our turns! I laughed as Liam rubbed it once, then went back to rub it again.

Pavel spared no details when relating to us the brutal history of the Czechs. When someone was executed, they would first cut off their hands, then their arms, and then whatever else — while they were alive — and they made the person's family pay for each part in order to bury it. Only then would the head be cut off. But you couldn't buy the head — it was displayed on the tower for SEVEN years! Needless to say, we all were grimacing with this Pavel story, and we weren't quite sure we were ready to go to lunch in Old Town, especially after such an unappetizing story.

I quickly discovered that I would lose Pavel if I stopped to gawk in the beautiful shop windows we were whizzing past at lightning speed. I swear, he must have run marathons on the weekends! There was so much to look at. Prague's shops have Bohemian crystal, Praha Blue art glass, hand-painted pottery, Russian nesting dolls, and Prague's famous marionettes. Being my first visit, I was window shopping and scouting out places to go after lunch. I had to buy souvenirs of this fascinating city!

Lunch was goulash, but not the "goulash" my mother made (which wasn't really goulash at all). Czech goulash consisted of several pieces of stew meat in a brown sauce with Bohemian dumplings that had bits of bacon in them. It was served with a side of bread dumplings, which were crustless circles of sourdough bread. I must say, it was very good.

After lunch, Pavel gave us free time to shop, and then we met just before 5 p.m. by the Astronomical Clock. This clock, first installed in 1410, is older than the famous Glockenspiel in Munich's Marienplatz, but not as fancy. Pavel was just full of interesting stories, and he was so good at making them come to life for us. According to Pavel, the government officials didn't want anyone else to duplicate their clock, so they went and blinded the clock maker so he couldn't make anymore. However, his dying wish was to visit his clock one more time. When he did, he took out a piece of the clock's mechanism! As a result, the clock was silent for 150 years. Surely a legend, but it was repaired and back up and running in 1552. Like Munich's Glockenspiel, Prague's Astronomical Clock has figures that tell a story on the hour. Exactly at 5:00, The Walk of the Apostles came out to our delight. True to Czech fashion, a skeleton representing death strikes the time.

As if we hadn't already seen so many interesting things, we then took a walk through the famous Jewish section of Prague, which was not destroyed during the war. They have a fascinating stacked cemetery, where they would just keep adding layers of bodies in this small amount of land. On another visit, I would like to spend more time here.

We kept moving while we looked, because Pavel had bought us tickets to the Black Light Theatre, which was all the rage there at the time. We loved the show, which was over at 9:30 p.m., but our evening of entertainment was not over. Pavel next took us by tram to see The Singing Fountain show. That night's show featured Andrea Bocelli's recordings as the fountain danced and changed colors to the music. When that was over at 10:45 p.m., Pavel took us to an outdoor pub where we heard a woman who sounded like a man sing. Her husband ran the sound, and their thirteen-year-old danced and sang as well. They were quite good, and very entertaining! We had fun singing and dancing, and then literally had to run to catch the tram, which would take us to the Metro and the bus, and then a short walk to our hotel. Whew, what an incredible day and introduction to Prague!

In the morning, we would depart for Vienna, and I must say, Pavel did a great job maximizing our one day in Prague — not an easy chore. I'd say we easily walked 10 miles that day.

❧ ✳ ❧

I fondly recalled all these memories while I rode on the deluxe coach that was transporting us from the airport to our hotel, lost in the memories of Liam and me. I was watching the landscape and buildings whizz past me, but I was lost in my own thoughts as our new tour director gave a brief overview of Prague for my weary choir. Our group had been picked up by three coaches and three tour guides.

Amanda Kate brought me back to reality. "Are you okay, Izzibeth? I know Liam was with you the last time you were here." She took my hand, and I laid my head on her shoulder for comfort.

"Thank you, sweet friend. I have just been recalling that trip, and it is full of happy memories, so I can't be sad!" I squeezed her hand to emphasize how thankful I was for her support.

We drew our attention back to Dusan, our guide for this trip, but my thoughts couldn't help but think about Pavel and where he might be now. And what was his wife's name? Oh yes — Susanna.

41

The Mozart House

Mozart Travel Company had given us a detailed itinerary for our trip, except they left out the most important detail — where we were staying. I had my suspicions while we were driving that we weren't staying at just any hotel. We had arrived at 10 a.m. that morning, and amazingly, all the bags had also arrived. We were loaded up by noon to make our way into Prague, taking in the view from our comfortable coach seats. Dusan was great with his overview, pointing out the landmarks and giving brief explanations of each. My students and friends were glued to their windows, gawking at the new sights. My sweet family had made it in as well, and we were all on the coach now. Peyton was sitting with Emilia Rose, listening to her recall all the times she had been to Prague; Frieda had spread out in her own seat; and Amanda Kate was sitting with me. Grey and Emma were behind us commenting on the landscape, and I was one happy camper — for the moment. Benjamin was arriving on a later flight because he had a performance in Boston today.

I couldn't shake what Simon had said in the kitchen yesterday. I turned around to see Bradley sitting with Matthew, and they both waved at me. Just as we had planned, Matthew was carrying a briefcase with a fake snuff box and locket inside a small wooden box placed in a blue velvet pouch. A big, impressive looking lock secured the bag to make it look really important. The plan had to work. All the players were on this coach, except for the ones Eduard had hired to help with the production. *I couldn't wait to meet Eduard and Pavla and to see the masques and costumes!*

I could see Prague Castle and the Charles Bridge, but instead of heading toward the city center, the coach continued along the river. Soon, we were in the immediate countryside. The coach slowed, turning down a beautiful tree-lined, two-lane road. Horses were grazing near the fences along the road, and cows were grazing the fields further out. It reminded me of the road leading to Muckross House in Killarney, Ireland. A mile or two down the road, the coach pulled into a huge circular drive in front of a stately home that would put Downton Abbey to shame. It was huge, and from its stone exterior rose at least fifty towers, which were a mixture of Gothic, Romanesque, Baroque, and Renaissance — just like Prague Castle. It reminded me of Chambord Castle in France, but the grounds were much more exquisite here.

You could have heard a pin drop on the bus as Dusan said over the microphone, "Ladies and Gentlemen, we have arrived at your residence for the next few days. Welcome to The Mozart House. The estate is privately owned, and its owner is a lover of Mozart, so he named the house after the famous composer. I think you will find your stay elegant, but comfortable!"

Amanda Kate just stared at me in disbelief, and I heard cries of "Mom!" Elizabeth!" and "Dr. Stone!" from everyone else on the bus. I think the castle is a hit. I couldn't take credit for securing it, but I certainly could relish in everyone's pleasure. I silently thanked my benefactor for making me look better than I really was. A castle!

Joseph and Ian stepped onto our bus. Joseph looked at me and said, "Seriously, Elizabeth? Surely this is a joke."

"No joke, Joseph. This is our castle for a few days. An experience to remember, for sure." *Hopefully, a good experience*, I thought. We were tired from our journey, so the two men didn't notice the nervous laugh that accompanied my response.

I stepped out of the coach carefully, overcome by a wave of uncertainty, with multiple questions flooding my already muddled brain. I looked resolutely at the marvelous Mozart House, wondering who was really behind all of this. *Why were they going to such great lengths to protect the treasures, and what was waiting for me here in Prague?*

The air held an ominous chill, prompting me to tighten my wool scarf even more snugly around my throat. Singers always need to keep their throats warm, so when we are out in the brisk air, it is important to wear protection. I was watching Emilia Rose, who had a valid reason for staying well since she was the soloist for our gala performance. She had enlisted the help from one of the young men in the choir, who gladly rolled his and her luggage across the courtyard. Emilia was clinging to her coat, her scarf, and had pulled her wool-brimmed hat down below her nose. She held on to his arm while he gingerly led her to the front door.

The rest of the group breathed in the crisp air as if it were liquid gold, reviving them from the long flight and bringing a sense of great anticipation about the events ahead. A group that had been rendered silent under the weight of a jetlagged stupor was now alive with chatter.

I could smell snow in the air, bringing back memories of my days studying in Vienna during the winter months. A warmness filled my heart. I had stopped briefly to take in the scene, when a gentleman approached me. He was wearing a beautiful black top coat with black leather gloves.

"Dr. Stone, I presume?" He had a charming accent, and a smile that would win over anyone's heart.

"Indeed I am." I extended my hand for a welcoming handshake.

Taking my hand, and then placing his other hand over both of our hands, he introduced himself. "I am Anton, and I will be making sure your stay here at The Mozart House is beyond your expectations. I have been given the pleasure of being your personal attendant during your stay."

"Anton," I said with my hand over my heart, "I am completely honored to meet you, and I look forward to getting to know you better during our stay."

Anton took my luggage, silencing all protests that I could manage on my own. On our short walk to the entrance, I took in the beauty of courtyard. The circular drive was lined with linden trees – national tree of the Czech Republic and symbol of friendship, love and loyalty. Most of their leaves had fallen to the ground, but here and there, as the sunlight danced across them, I caught a glimmer of the brilliant golden color they turn during the autumn months. I also noticed the trees were strung with lights. As I paused to ponder how each tree's personality must light up when its lights are switched on, Anton, sensing what I was looking at, interrupted my thoughts.

"In just a few short hours, Dr. Stone, The Mozart House will be lit up as if it were taken from the pages of a magical fairytale." He had a huge smile on his face, showing he took great pride in the estate.

"I cannot wait, Anton, and I am sure it will be beyond expectations. I might never want to leave." I returned his smile as he we continued on to the front entrance.

As we approached, as if there were sensors telling them we were there, two men in tuxes opened the two enormous wooden front doors. I stopped in my tracks.

Framed by the doorway was the most beautiful Christmas tree I had ever seen. Anton did not bother to interrupt my moment of awe. The tree was at least twenty feet tall and was nestled in the foyer between two grand, winding staircases, which were decked in garland, bows, and lights. I stepped over the threshold, but couldn't take my eyes off the beauty of this grand foyer. I wasn't the only one in a daze. I looked around, and everyone – I mean everyone – was silent and looking.

"Izzibeth, is this for real, or are we in a dream?" Amanda Kate whispered in my ear.

"I don't know, Amanda Kate, but for now it seems like a dream."

The tree was adorned in gold and white, with a touch of red. It was covered in lights; delicate gold ribbon with a hint of white; gold ball ornaments; and clusters of red berries tied onto branches. The simplicity of the decorations made it even more elegant. The tree was there to enhance the beauty of the grand foyer, not take away from it. I easily could have stood there mesmerized for hours, taking in every detail, but suddenly a familiar voice broke our silence.

"Greetings to my very honored guests! I am Eduard Doubek. I have been anticipating your arrival for many months, so it is a great pleasure to finally have you here in my house."

I heard gasps echoed throughout the foyer. Eduard and I made eye contact, each giving the other a big smile of approval. I suppose I wasn't really surprised that The Mozart House was his estate. Nothing about this project should surprise me now. He had said that he lived above his shop in the Square, but obviously that was just his work hideaway. I could see that he had ample staff here to run the estate in his working absence.

Eduard was all that I had imagined: tall, thin, dark-haired, and meticulously dressed in a beautifully tailored suit. His blue eyes twinkled as he spoke, while his hands made elegant gestures to compliment his words. His face was sculpted in handsome, yet delicate features. I figured he was in his early 50s, and looked to be in excellent physical shape.

"I hope you had a wonderful flight, and I know you must be tired and very hungry. My goal is to get you settled into your rooms quickly, as my chef has prepared a delicious welcome dinner in the main dining room. The staff is set up at tables around the foyer to assist you in finding your rooms. Your keys look like this —"

Eduard held up a skeleton key attached to a tag shaped like an eighth note. "Your room name is engraved on the note. How boring it would be to have common keys or ordinary room numbers in The Mozart House! The rooms are named after characters in his operas or names of his family. On each door, you will see a plaque with the room's name. For instance, Emilia Rose, you will be staying in The Queen of the Night's room. I thought that was fitting since you will be our Queen of the Night in a few short days."

Emilia Rose acted shy, but we all knew she was enjoying every moment. I couldn't wait to see which room Eduard had put me in and to go exploring on my own.

With a quiet clap of his hands, his staff sprang into action while we all got in our rooming groups. The foyer suddenly became a buzz of activity as everyone began their quest to find their rooms. The stairs were marble, with beautiful red and gold tapestry stair runners, held down at the base of each stair by a golden rod to keep the carpet from buckling. I presumed that it was Carrera marble from Italy, as every little detail in this beautiful mansion was exquisite.

Everyone had their keys and their rooms except for me.

I couldn't wait to see if the rooms reflected the characters. The staff provided us with a list of room assignments, along with a very convenient map. I planned on doing a little tour once I got settled in. I wanted to explore every inch! I was looking at my map, lost in thought, when I heard a voice from behind.

"Dr. Stone, we finally meet!"

I turned to be embraced by Eduard, and we exchanged the traditional greeting of kissing on each cheek before he held me out at arm's length.

"You are even more beautiful in person, and as charming as they all said you were!"

This statement was one I was hearing a lot, from varying sources, so I wondered who "they" were.

"Eduard, I am stunned by all of this!" I waved my hand in a gentle gesture around the foyer. "Truly beautiful, and we're all in shock that this is our residence while we are here. I think you and I have a lot of catching up to do — you are more a man of mystery than I imagined!"

Eduard was dying laughing. "Indeed, we have many stories to share. In the meantime, please allow Anton to escort you to your room so you can freshen up before dinner."

As he said this, I heard the rattle of a key in Anton's hand. "Follow me, Dr. Stone."

Eduard stood at the base of the elegant stairs and blew me a kiss. "See you in a bit, darling!"

And so began my ascent on the winding staircase to the second floor. At the top of the stairs, I could almost reach out and touch the top of the Christmas tree. I paused on the landing overlooking the grand foyer to admire the view. Anton kept walking, so I rushed to catch up. He had turned to the right from the landing, but I noticed the hallway was very long on both sides. After about two minutes of walking, he paused at a door and began to put the key in the keyhole. I caught a glimpse of the name — The Constanze Room.

"I hope you find your room pleasing, Dr. Stone. Mr. Doubek wanted you to have the very best."

"Oh, Anton, I believe he came through alright!"

I stepped over the threshold, into a sitting area warmed by a cozy fire in a marble fireplace. Two Queen Anne chairs in blue and gold were set in front of the fireplace, with a table in between. I let out a small gasp, because there on the hearth was my beloved Beau! Not knowing if Anton could see him, but assuming he couldn't, I didn't move towards him as I wanted to, and Beau just wagged his tail.

Anton had opened a beautiful whitewashed antique wardrobe and placed my luggage inside. I turned to see an enormous white French Provincial bed with large carved spindles that looked to be at least six feet tall. There was a blue velvet bench at the end of the bed. The bedding was also blue and gold, and the pillows extra fluffy. Had I been by myself, I would have run and jumped on it. It was difficult, but I contained my excitement and tried to remain as elegant and as classy as this room.

"This is absolutely beautiful, Anton, and I feel so special. You and your staff have gone above and beyond to make us feel very welcome."

"The bathroom is through these doors." He opened two French doors to reveal a huge porcelain tub in the center of the room with a chandelier hanging above it. The vanity was a double vanity of marble, with gold fixtures, and there was a private room for the toilet. The towels were thick Egyptian cotton in sparkling white with a gold monogram MH on the border. Anton had turned on a switch, and suddenly the suite was filled with Mozart's music.

"You will see that you have a bar available, with many fine choices, if you would like to invite your friends in to visit after dinner. There is plenty of water in the refrigerator here, and some fruit for you to snack on."

Anton went over and pulled the drapes, revealing a French door leading out to a balcony overlooking the back of the estate! I might never want to leave. This room just keeps getting better and better! I felt like I had stepped back into the 18th century – like Constanze and Wolfgang would come laughing through the door at any moment.

"I will leave you to relax, Dr. Stone. Dinner is in two hours, which gives you plenty of time to freshen up. Don't worry – we will check on the students. I know you always like to do that, but please allow us the joy of attending to them at The Mozart House so you can also enjoy your stay.

Anton set the key on the table between the chairs by the fire, still giving no indication that he saw Beau. Beau, meanwhile, was being a silent giant – that is, until Anton shut the door behind him, and then Beau almost tackled me to the floor.

"It's only been one day, Beau! But, it sure is great to see you. Where's Michael?" I looked all around the room, but he was not there. Strange. I thought at least he would check in with me once we arrived.

The two hours provided enough time for a long, hot bath. As tempting as it was to fall asleep after the refreshing bath, I resisted. I was hungry, and curious to see what the house chef had prepared for our welcome dinner. The thought of food perked me up, as I continued to put myself together for the evening.

With time remaining before our six o'clock dinner call, I stepped out onto the balcony. I was greeted by the crisp night air, but it was the sight took my breath away. The back of the estate was even more lit up than the front. There were millions of tiny white lights everywhere – in the trees, along the balusters of the back fence, outlining the brick courtyard, and on the gazebo. The fountain in the middle of the courtyard was turned off, but lights accented the fountain's sculpture, which just happened to be Mozart. I could hear the Vltava river beyond the trees. The water was calming to hear, and I was mesmerized by the Winter Wonderland in front of me.

Suddenly and quietly, from the within the thicket of trees in my view, stepped a beautiful and enormous white stag. He slowly turned his regal face towards me, and stared me in the eyes. It was as if I knew him and he knew me. We looked at each other in silence, and during that time, I felt a comfort in my soul that I had not felt since losing Liam. His gaze gave me confidence and filled me with courage to stay strong, and I believe he knew the next few days were going to be challenging. His beauty was beyond any I had ever seen in an animal. But it was his spirit that captured my heart. I was trying to wrap my mind around all of it – all the things I had heard about the white stag and what he symbolized – but all I wanted to do was stay connected with his gaze and feel the peace he was sending my way.

I finally found a voice and whispered, "Liam, if that is you, please know I am okay. I miss you dearly, but I am carrying on. You taught me to be strong, to be myself, and stay true to what I believed in. I can do this. I am not going to let harm come to me, to our family, or to the treasures."

A quiet knock on the door broke the moment, and the stag gave me a nod before turning around to bound quietly back into the woods. I watched him as long as I could, and now my heart was racing from the experience. Beau had been beside me, and now he was nudging me to go and answer the door.

"Mom? Are you okay?" It was my son, Grey, and his wife, Emma.

"Yes! I was just out on the balcony enjoying the beauty, and didn't hear you knock at first." I gave them a big hug. It was great having them here.

The door had been left open, so right behind them came Amanda Kate, Peyton, Frieda, Emilia Rose, Matthew, and Bradley. They all piled into my enormous sitting room, all talking at once about The Mozart House and how incredible their rooms were.

Matthew came by and quietly whispered in my ear, "Eduard put the briefcase in a safe place."

"Thanks, Matthew," I smiled. Our plan was already in the works.

At exactly six o'clock, a huge clock in the foyer began chiming, and we knew we needed to make our way down to dinner.

We chatted as we descended the elegant stairway, joining the others already gathered in the foyer. My students came bustling up to me, with exclamations of "Oh my gosh" and "Wow" and "This is amazing, Dr. Stone." I was beaming, but inside, I still had that little bit of anticipation about what was going to happen at the gala.

Suddenly, two huge doors opened, and once again, we were all silent. The Dining Room was a banquet hall. I had imagined a room set up like a restaurant, with multiple tables to seat us all. No, this had a long banquet table that would seat the entire group. Candles were lit everywhere, but what caught our eye was they had brought the outside to the inside — the whole dining room was decorated like a forest, with at least forty different shapes and sizes of evergreens decorated with white lights and delicate gold ornaments. A huge fireplace was situated at the opposite end of the hall. It was magical.

The table was set with white linens, a gold runner down the length of the table, and candelabras situated about every ten chairs. Simple, yet elegant. When you looked up, the ceiling was a fresco painted like the sky, with stars that seemed to be illuminated. It reminded me of the Gothic ceiling in Sainte-Chapelle. That one took my breath away, and this one does too. I tried to count the number of crystal chandeliers that were hanging like delicate icicles, but someone touched my elbow. My gaze lowered to meet the sparkling eyes of my host, Eduard.

"Do you like The Mozart House, Dr. Stone?" he asked as he began leading me to my seat.

"Oh yes, Eduard. I believe 'like' is not the correct word. I am stunned, overwhelmed, in awe, speechless. Yes, speechless. I think we are all waiting to wake up and find that this is just a dream."

He laughed, pleased, and pulled my chair out for me. "I am glad, Dr. Stone — very glad indeed."

Once Eduard was seated, it seemed that more magic happened. A string quartet appeared and began playing — Mozart, of course. Then, seemingly from nowhere, came a dozen or so waiters in tuxes and white gloves bearing our first course.

A steaming ceramic bowl of Bramboracka, or potato soup, was set in front of me. The aroma was wafting up to my nose, and I couldn't wait to dip my spoon to get my first taste. I turned to Eduard and asked what the main ingredients were.

Pleased that I asked, he began to tell me that the soup is normally served in a bread bowl, but due to the nature of the tonight's meal he chose not to mess with the crumbs. Carrots, celeriac root, cabbage, leeks, onions, garlic, vegetable broth, sea salt, black pepper, marjoram, and flour. A small sprinkle of bacon and parsley finished off the presentation. Small rolls were individually served with small pats of creamy butter in the shape of a snowflake.

"But, Dr. Stone, the key to this soup," he continued, "is the flavor that the dried forest mushrooms provide. Without them, this would just be a plain potato soup."

"Why Eduard, I do believe you are a chef. When do you have time to cook?"

"It is my passion to create fine foods, just as I create fine fashion. It all goes together if you truly think about it."

Once everyone was served, we all began our soup, and it was as delightful as it smelled. I was glad I had taken one of our trip meetings to go over fine dining etiquette with the group. No one dipped into their soup before service was done – a proud moment.

The next course was a small salad with mixed greens and a cranberry vinaigrette delicately drizzled in an artistic way across the greens.

The third course was beef tenderloin, roasted potatoes, dumplings, and white asparagus tips.

Eduard leaned in as I was marveling at the meal and explained to me that normally the Czech dishes are served with sauces and gravies. But tonight, he said, he knew our stomachs were jetlagged and we didn't need any upset tummies for our artists. He had such a fun way to describe everything, and I felt very relaxed around him. I told him I appreciated that, but that we also wanted to experience the Czech foods he was describing.

As if the meal couldn't get better, dessert arrived. I had heard about the fruit dumplings here, and now, a most beautiful example was being set in front of me. I could tell it was warm, and I smelled the butter and cinnamon.

"Apricot and strawberry," Eduard whispered. "My favorite. It is always served with a side of farmer's cheese, and a dab of jam made from the fruit that is inside. I hope you enjoy it as much as I do."

And I did. Every bite. I looked around, and all I saw were happy faces enjoying a wonderful meal – such a stark contrast to our meager airplane meal. As the waiters began clearing the dessert dishes, and the quartet continued playing quietly in the background. My stomach was happy, but my nerves were still on the edge of uncertainty. This was all too easy, too good to be true and too well scripted. I kept waiting for the chandelier to fall, disrupting the fairy tale dinner.

Eduard stood up, and the quartet stopped. He tapped on his water glass ever so lightly to get everyone's attention.

"Good evening! I hope you enjoyed your meal!" He was greeted by a round of applause and cries of bravo, to which he had to tap his glass again to get everyone's attention.

"Thank you, thank you! We have a wonderful chef and staff here, and in the next few days we plan on spoiling you even more. Chef Antoine sends his apologies for not stepping out tonight to greet you, but he assures me you will get to meet him while you are here."

Another round of applause, and another tap on the glass.

"Tomorrow is a busy day for you all. When you go back upstairs to your rooms, you will see that our staff has laid out tomorrow's agenda for you. Please make sure you look it over tonight, take a picture of it, put it in your daypack for tomorrow, and set your alarms. We don't want to leave anyone behind. I hope you all enjoy a good night's sleep tonight, trying your best not stay up too late."

Laughter. College kids...late nights...hmm. More laughter.

"Tomorrow we have a brief sightseeing tour planned first thing. We will go to Prague Castle and walk the Charles Bridge, ending up in Old Town Square. After a short lunch, for which you are on your own, you will meet at The Estates Theatre for a walk-through of the program. I believe Dr. Stone and Dr. Chamberlain have a rehearsal planned for the day after tomorrow, but we wanted you to get a visual of the beautiful venue and to see the work already underway for the gala."

He turned to face Amanda Kate and Peyton. "Amanda Kate, I know you will want to see what is happening. I hope we have followed your instructions! You have designed beautiful décor for our gala!" Amanda Kate blushed, but she loved it.

More light applause, and one last tap on the glass.

"So, my dear friends, having enjoyed our exquisite dinner, as the clock now strikes nine o'clock, I think it is time to let you retire to your rooms."

I swear Eduard must be a magician, for the clock began chiming nine, just as he said this.

"I bid you a good night. If you need anything, please come down to the foyer and someone will assist you. I hope you have enough water and snacks to get you through the night. Breakfast is on the other side of the foyer in the Morning Room. We will begin serving at 6 a.m. Dr. Stone, your coffee will be served before you come downstairs." He grinned, and everyone laughed, for they all knew I liked my coffee first.

With these words, the quartet picked back up again, and we all began to make our way out of this beautiful banquet hall. I was full to the brim. My goodness, what a welcome dinner! This trip was not my typical student tour — no, not typical at all.

Upstairs, my family and close friends and I said our goodnights with hugs and kisses. As much as we wanted to stay up and visit, we knew better than to overdo it. As I shut my door, I was greeted again by my faithful Beau. I knew it was nearly impossible, but I went back out on the balcony to see if the white stag would show up again to tell me good night. I looked everywhere, and stayed out wishing it would happen, but he was nowhere in sight. As I turned to go back inside, a light snow began to fall, dusting the landscape with a fine powder.

A perfect ending to a perfect day.

Not wanting this peaceful feeling to end, I changed into my bedclothes and crawled under the oversized duvet to review the agenda that was on my nightstand. Eduard had thought of everything — even a small piece of chocolate on the nightstand. It looked like the type of chocolate wrapper that sometimes has a message written on it, so I looked inside.

ELIZABETH, KEEP THE INTEGRITY

You have got to be kidding me! I laughed out loud — a deep, wonderful laugh that cleansed my soul. Yes, I planned on keeping the integrity, and we were off to a great start.

Beau and I settled in, and as I turned out the light, I marveled at the moonlight shining through the French doors. The snow was still falling lightly as I fell deeply into the best sleep I had experienced in a long time.

42

December 29th

Benjamin was sitting in the breakfast room when I went in to have more coffee and a bite to eat. He must have arrived after we all went upstairs last night.

"Benjamin! You made it!" I was greeted by his warm smile as I sat down across from him.

"I did! Dog tired, but here. Elizabeth, how did you score this place? I thought the taxi driver had dropped me off at the wrong address. Anton met me at the door, showed me up to my room, and reassured me that I was, indeed, in the right place. I have never in my life been treated like this!"

"You should have seen dinner. And, oh my, this breakfast buffet looks amazing too."

I went over to the sideboard and spooned a couple of yummy looking dishes onto my plate. Then I went over and got another steaming cup of coffee. True to their word, an attendant had delivered a small carafe of coffee to my room, promptly at 6 a.m., on a silver tray with a delicate blue and gold china cup and saucer. *I could get used to this.*

Benjamin and I caught up on his tour, details of today, and other miscellaneous topics as all the other guests in our entourage began making their way into the Morning Room for breakfast. Our itinerary detailed our morning's tour in Prague, and we were to be ready to load the coach at 8:00. I was pleased that everyone was prompt and excited about our day. I went back upstairs to grab my briefcase with my music and my crossbody bag.

The morning was spectacular: the skies were blue, and a light dusting of snow covered the earth, adding a delicate, icy lace to an already beautiful setting. Dusan was very knowledgeable. He gave us an informative and entertaining narrative about the history of Prague before we arrived at Prague Castle. Even though I had been twice, I learned new information and retained more of the history. I spent time gazing at the Mucha window, marveling yet again how blessed I am to feast upon the splendor revealed in this stained-glass masterpiece.

We lunched in Old Town Square, and then on to the moment I had really been waiting for — a walkthrough of The Estates Theatre. My heart was pounding as we stepped inside the foyer, already bustling with workers setting up small cocktail tables, hanging garland, and adding glimmer everywhere. Amanda Kate squealed — yes, squealed — with delight as she watched her sketches coming to life. She ran over to the Red Carpet area and tried out several glamourous poses while Peyton took pictures with her phone. I stepped back and enjoyed watching their dreams come true.

The students were gawking, and Eduard had joined us in the foyer. Standing on the stairs, he clapped his delicate hands to get our attention yet again.

"Well, what do you think? I hope you are as excited as we are for the gala to arrive. In just two short days, this theatre will be filled with guests coming to hear your marvelous performance! They are coming from all over the world, and I know they will be amazed at your talents. The purpose of this gala is to raise funds to support the arts, so I hope the guests are not only amazed, but generous!"

Everyone gave Eduard and his team a round of applause.

"Today, I would like to give you a tour of the theatre so you can get your bearings backstage. I will show you the dressing rooms, the green room, and the bathrooms at your disposal. Come, let's begin!"

Eduard came down the stairs and took my hand to personally lead me into the theatre. When we stepped inside, I stopped dead in my tracks, out of shock, to drink it all in — *we are here, in this very room where Mozart played, with the chairs his actual audiences sat in, and the original curtain...and I just can't get enough of this.* Eduard almost fell when I stopped so abruptly, but he understood and gave me my moment while we kept walking.

"It's beautiful, isn't it Elizabeth," he said as he looked back at me. "I never tire of its beauty nor its history. But now it is your turn — time for your dream to come true. You will be onstage, directing your choir, feeling the presence of the great Mozart."

"Okay, Eduard, now you have me crying. This just can't be happening. I do not deserve any of this recognition — especially for simply loving what I do."

Eduard leaned in and hugged me as he whispered, "Oh, but you do deserve it Elizabeth. You deserve it more than you know. You have worked hard, stayed diligent, and your reputation is renown. Embrace these moments and stand proud for the opportunity."

Others then started coming into the theatre area. We walked around, touching the chairs, looking at every detail. There were workers still painting and installing as we toured. Eduard then took us up to the stage, and we all stood there looking out to where our audience would be sitting. Unbelievable.

Eduard showed us the props I had requested. The two winding, twelve-step staircases that will come out stage left and stage right for *Masquerade* were perfect. We then saw where the moon swing for the "The Queen of the Night's aria" was being installed. Emilia Rose went over to make sure the paint would be dry before the performance because she "didn't want paint all over her butt." Her words, not mine. The poor workers spoke no English, so they just stared at her and smiled and kept right on painting gold and black paint. There were some ropes on either side of the moon, but Eduard was vague with what those were for, so I didn't question him anymore.

Backstage, there were two nicely sized dressing rooms. One for the men in the choir and orchestra, and one for the women in both groups. The dressing room walls were lined with large mirrors and make-up lights, and each room had an area of hanging racks for costumes and uniforms. The students were excited to have such classy accommodations, since they normally just stood backstage before getting onto a set of risers for each performance.

Down the hall from the students, there were three more dressing rooms. Emilia Rose and I each had our own, and Bradley and the orchestra directors would share one. Frieda was glad to see she had lots of working room for Emilia Rose's pre-show routine. Amanda Kate and Peyton would be floating around out front with the guests before coming back to assist me and Frieda.

Joseph was delighted with the orchestra pit. He then had gone to check out the instruments that Eduard had procured for him. String bass, harp, timpani – all the larger instruments that don't fly very well. He was very pleased, later telling me that they were top of the line. I smiled, for I expected nothing less than the best.

Before departing the theatre, I asked the choir to come and stand on stage. We sang through bits and pieces of a few songs, unaccompanied, to get the feel of the acoustics, and they were excellent. Tomorrow, we were to have a full day of rehearsals with short breaks for shopping in Old Town Square. I was pleased to see how excited everyone was to come back to rehearse. Bradley kept pinching himself, literally. I took his arm in mine and told him how much he meant to me, and that I appreciated all he did to get us to this point. He had worked really hard and deserved much more attention than I did. I was very blessed to have him.

I spotted Amanda Kate talking to Eduard. They were in their element, discussing details and decorations. Peyton was already snapping pictures, as I had also asked her to be the historian of the trip so I could make a book of our adventures.

I stepped to the edge of the stage one more time and looked down to where I thought perhaps Mozart had sat during the premiere of *Don Giovanni*.

"Pretty overwhelming, isn't it?"

I turned to see Benjamin doing the same. I had wondered if he was at all jealous that it was me getting to conduct here.

"Very." I turned and looked at him. "Benjamin, you are happy for me, right?"

He looked startled. "Why wouldn't I be? This is your moment, Elizabeth, not mine, and I am here to support you, not gloat or pout that it isn't me."

"I still can't believe it is happening! Of course, on the other hand, I'm still praying my plan works... As much as I am loving all of this, I can't seem to put it out of my head that something awful might happen at the gala. I have a lot of people here who are counting on me, and I just hope I can live up to my end of the bargain — with a little help, of course." I smiled, and knew that Benjamin understood.

"Elizabeth!" Eduard was coming towards us. "I want you to meet my assistant, Pavla!"

A beautiful young woman was standing next to him, and as she reached out her hand to me, I felt an instant connection.

"Hello, Pavla, I am so excited to meet you! I hear you have been very busy getting ready for the gala, and I cannot wait to see your beautiful work. Thank you for all you have done for us!" I put both of my hands around hers and gave her a little squeeze.

"Thank you, Dr. Stone. It is a pleasure to meet you after hearing so much about you."

"I also hear you have been instrumental in getting me some special effects? On my first visit to Prague, I attended a Black Light Theatre production and was enthralled. I am so pleased we are incorporating this into our program."

"My very talented friends are the ones who will make it spectacular for you, Dr. Stone. They have had a lot of fun choreographing the Mozart pieces you requested, along with *Masquerade*. However, their favorite so far is 'The Queen of the Night's aria'. I think you will be stunned at what they have planned."

"Now you have piqued my interest! I hope I can conduct while I am being stunned!"

Eduard cleared his throat, a clear sign our tour was over and he must hustle us back to The Mozart House.

"Elizabeth, when we return, you and Emilia Rose will find your custom gowns in your rooms, ready for you to try on. I will send a seamstress to help you with the fitting and make any necessary adjustments that might need to be made.

"I should not have eaten those dumplings at lunch. Thanks, Eduard. I thought I had at least one day to enjoy myself."

Eduard was laughing, but I was serious. I can eat one tiny thing these days and swell up like a toad. A big, fat toad. Middle-age belly fat was real, and no laughing matter.

The coach ride back to The Mozart House was full of noisy excitement. Anticipation was in the air, and as prepared as the choir was, I had the sense that rehearsals should go well the next few days.

The sun was already setting as we approached our castle in the woods, and the trees were casting strange but beautiful shapes on the road. The Mozart House was all lit up, making us feel like we were coming home.

Anton and other staff were waiting in the drive for us, and Anton reached out his hand to help me descend the bus steps.

"How was your day, Dr. Stone?" he asked as he gently led me to the front door.

"Lovely, Anton, but not as lovely as it is to be back here with your gracious hospitality."

I thought I saw Anton blush, but surely that was just a reflection of the lights as we passed through the entryway.

Beautiful music was playing — Mozart, of course — and we were told dinner was at 7 p.m.

I went and found Amanda Kate and Peyton, asking them to meet me in my room. I also asked Frieda to go to Emilia Rose's room with her so she could help with her fitting.

I was nervous and excited to see the gown created especially for me. I had no idea what Eduard had envisioned, but I would have been perfectly comfortable in my black dress so as not to draw attention away from the singers. I cautiously opened the door to the Constanze Suite. A crackling fire and Mozart's music greeted me, along with a very happy Beau. I had barely hugged his big furry neck before Amanda Kate and Peyton came bounding in the room. They saw Beau, and soon the three of us were on the floor being overwhelmed by his sweet kisses. Still no Michael, which was beginning to concern me.

We were interrupted when a timid young girl knocked lightly on the door. Because she couldn't see Beau, I bet she thought we were crazy! We were overcome with laughter as we awkwardly tried up from the floor. What a sight we must have been — getting on all fours and helping each other up. Several minutes later we were finally standing up to introduce ourselves.

The young seamstress' name was Klara, and she led me to the huge walk-in closet off my bathroom. When she opened the door, the three of us just stood there in awe, our jaws almost coming out of their hinges. Hanging in the closet was the most gorgeous gown I had ever laid my eyes on.

"Izzibeth. It is beautiful. You will look like an angel on stage. The angel you really are."

Peyton started crying, and blew her nose. "Elizabeth, this makes me so happy," she wailed.

The dress was a deep blue, the color of twilight — my favorite time of day. *How could Eduard possibly have known that?!* It was woven throughout with delicate, subtle gold threads that gently caught the light, as if they were capturing the last moments of daylight before it slipped away. It also was studded gracefully with small crystals that looked like delicate stars emerging from the darkness. The gown had long, delicate sleeves made of lace and a modest boatneck bodice, with more tiny crystals at the neckline. The style was a simple, modified A-line, appropriately loose, to allow me to conduct without ripping the shoulders or looking like a T-Rex flailing its arms. The gown flowed to the floor, but only close enough to kiss the ground. I had never conducted in anything but black, but this was simple, elegant, and so me.

I was nervous as Klara slipped it over my head. Amanda Kate and Peyton had been holding their breath, but once the gown was over my head, they let out a gasp. Turning slowly, I looked in the mirror. *It. Was. Perfect. How did Eduard do this?*

"Dr. Stone," Klara had zipped me up, and had moved to the closet where a shoe box was stored on the shelf, "Mr. Doubek also designed some shoes for you to wear."

She opened the shoebox, picking up the first shoe wrapped in a gold-colored tissue paper. *Good grief, even the shoes come beautifully wrapped.* We all were watching with bated breath, and we were not disappointed. Klara held up a satin three-inch-heel pump that seamlessly matched the subtleties of the gown. On the toe of the shoe was a crystal treble clef. I happened to be wearing the diamond treble clef my benefactor had given me, and I looked down at it. The treble clefs on the shoes were exactly like my necklace.

Peyton broke the silence. "Elizabeth, I don't think those are crystals."

"I don't either," echoed Amanda Kate.

"Neither do I," I chimed.

Klara was over at the dresser now, and when she turned back toward me, she was holding a box that looked exactly like the one the treble clef necklace had come in. She handed it to me.

I was nervous opening it, and Amanda Kate and Peyton were crowded in, watching over my shoulder.

I was moving slowly, caught in a dream. The box was so beautiful that I hated opening it. Amanda Kate hit my arm. "Open it, Izzibeth! We can't be late for dinner!"

So, I did. And there, nestled in blue velvet, was a pair of gorgeous diamond treble clef earrings that matched the necklace that matched the shoes.

I think we stared for at least five minutes before Klara gently cleared her throat.

"Dr. Stone? If you could, please try on the shoes so I can tell Mr. Doubek whether they fit. And yes, he will be unhappy if you are late for dinner."

We all giggled as I tried the shoes on. They fit perfectly. I was known to be a klutz, so I was glad the heels were sturdy enough that I wouldn't trip on stage. Klara then helped me out of the gown, put the shoes back in the shoe box, and placed the earrings back in the drawer — pointing out to me where they were, so I wouldn't forget to wear them. *As if I was in danger of forgetting about those!*

Right at that moment, Emilia Rose bolted into the room with Frieda and another young girl right behind her.

"Elizabeth! Eduard is a genius!" She took in the moment, swirling in her beautiful gown that flattered her tremendously. I didn't get a close look at the fabric, but somehow it gave the effect of storm clouds bathed in moonlight. Her shoes were a dramatic silver, like bright-burning stars, befitting the Queen of the Night.

Frieda was smiling. We never knew how Emilia Rose was going to react to fittings, but this had been a huge success.

Suddenly, the big clock struck 6:30. We had thirty minutes to get our act together and get downstairs for dinner, so my friends all scrambled for their rooms to get ready.

After dinner, and then an after-dinner drink, I returned to my room — and again to the balcony. The white stag never appeared, even though Beau and I stayed out for quite a while, looking intently for any sign of him. Michael Holmes was nowhere to be seen, either. When the cold finally started getting to me, I went inside and crawled into bed with my scores for a quick study before rehearsal tomorrow.

I was in the middle of the *Lacrimosa* of Mozart's *Requiem* when Beau whimpered.

43

Lord William and Constanze

Lord William was staring in disbelief at the locket inside the snuff box.

"Constanze, is this what I think it is? A miniature of Marie Antoinette as a young girl?"

"Yes," she whispered. "William, I don't think it is safe here. When I went to speak with Peter Schultz, he acted as if I should give him the snuff box and locket so that he could turn it over to the authorities. But I didn't trust him, for I could see the greed in his eyes. Ever since Wolfgang died, I have dealt with the greed of men trying to claim his works – and now, a treasure. What am I to do? I have been followed, and my children might not be safe."

"This definitely is monumental. Wolfgang must have known how special it was, which is why he held on to it. Perhaps he hoped it would help you and the boys if something happened to him."

"He left a note inside the wooden box. I found all of this in a trunk when we moved after he died."

Constanze reached into her bag and looked all around her before handing him the folded-up note. It read:

Dear Constanze,

 In the event of my death, I want you to guard these treasures with your life and keep them from getting into the wrong hands. When I was six, Marie Antoinette gave these to me after I had fallen in her palace. Her parents probably didn't even realize she had given them to me. She was wearing the locket at the time, and simply took it off her neck and put it inside the snuff box. It didn't mean a thing to me in that moment, and I just handed the gift over to my father. It was my sweet mother who recognized the value of the gift. She placed the treasures in a blue velvet bag she had made, and then enclosed them in a small wooden box. She tucked this plain wooden box in with a suit of clothes also given to me on that day. In 1778, I visited Marie Antoinette in Paris, at Versailles, and it was there that she reminded me of the snuff box and locket. Mother had died while we were in Paris, and I was distraught. When I returned to Salzburg, I found the treasures one day while my father was out. My heart stood still! I held on to them because my mother had held on to them — and also because I felt they were important. During our rough days, when we had to pawn so many of the gifts I had received, I just could not bring myself to depart with these. Hopefully, they will help you, my dear Constanze. I love you with all my heart.

Lovingly,
Wolfgang

Constanze broke the silence. "Wolfgang died in 1791. I found the treasures, and now Marie Antoinette is going through a terrible revolution as Queen of France! Please help me, Lord William. I am hoping that you will take these treasures back with you to England and keep them safe until you deem it necessary to bring them out into the world. My family is okay now financially. I don't need them for the money. It is the history of these objects that needs to be protected."

Constanze suddenly gave Lord William a look of fear, and he quickly put the wooden box into the leather messenger bag he carried. He hid the note in his hand and picked up his coffee cup, as did Constanze.

"Lord William, Peter Schultz has just walked into the café", Constanze whispered as she took a sip of her coffee. "He sees us, and is heading our way."

"Act normal, Constanze. After all, he knows both of us, and we don't want to act suspiciously."

"Lord William! What a pleasure to see you here in Vienna! Hello, Frau Mozart, it is nice to see you again as well! What brings you to our fair city, Lord William?" With that, he just made himself comfortable at our table.

"Peter! A pleasure to see you as well. Please, join us. I have some business to attend to, and I wanted to also check on Constanze. I have not seen her since Wolfgang died, so it does my heart good to see her doing so well!"

Peter, Constanze, and Lord William maintained a constant stream of uncomfortably polite chit chat — all while this despicable man attempted to ingratiate himself. Constanze did a good job hiding her fear of him, and Lord William was glad the treasures were safe within his bag now. Hopefully Peter wouldn't put two and two together and figure out the treasures had changed hands.

Finally, after what seemed to be ages, Peter stood up to go.

"It was good to see you, Peter," Lord William said as he stood to shake Peter's hand. "Perhaps on my next trip I will have more time to visit with you. I am leaving in a few short hours, due to the long journey home and the unpredictable weather."

After Peter was out of earshot, Lord William quietly said, "Constanze, keep talking normally as we leave the café. Peter might have people watching us." With that, Lord William signaled for their check, and they gathered their things to depart. As he was helping her with her coat, he stealthily placed the letter from Wolfgang into her coat's right-side hand pocket. It was a memory that he knew she would want to keep.

"Constanze, it was good to see you again." Lord William leaned in to hug her and whispered in her ear, "I will take good care of your treasures, making sure they never come into the wrong hands."

She managed a timid, yet believable smile as she squeezed his hand.

"I trust you completely, Lord William."

"Constanze, I am going to send some funds to you before I leave. Please don't say no. Just accept them as a guarantee that I will keep the treasures safe. Do not hesitate to let me know if Peter Schultz threatens you or bothers you in any way."

With that, she hurried down the street, looking both ways. Lord William stood there watching her until she turned the corner.

"Henry," Lord William spoke to his driver who had just appeared in front of the café. "Please follow Mrs. Mozart to her apartment. Let me know if she arrives safely."

Lord William walked the short distance back to the hotel to prepare to leave. It wasn't long before Henry knocked on the door, reporting that

Mrs. Mozart had arrived safely home. Lord William was relieved to hear she was safe — at least for the time being.

44
Dress Rehearsal

The theatre was filled with a glorious cacophony: strings tuning; the excited chatter of the choir as they found their places on the stairways; and the steady, percussive beat of the stage crew making final improvements to the set design. Eduard, Amanda Kate, and Peyton were out front finishing up the foyer, and Frieda was in the dressing room with Emilia Rose, tweaking the styling of the wig she would wear with the headpiece in "The Queen of the Night."

I stood center stage, giving directions, answering questions, and taking deep breaths. Dress rehearsal had arrived.

Joseph tapped his podium to get the orchestra's attention, and I turned to face him. Looking out on the theatre was thrilling, no matter where you were — but in this moment and from this perspective, it was mind boggling. The choir took the cue from Joseph as well, his baton taps focusing their attention. All choir members were quiet, standing in their places. In the few seconds of sheer silence, I felt an uneasiness I couldn't put my finger on.

"Let's do this from the top," I said as I gave Joseph the cue to begin the overture. The stage was empty, except for the stairs, with the choir waiting offstage for their first number.

We began working our way through the program, and each piece had gone well so far. Soon, I was raising my hand to begin the *Lacrimosa*, one of the most haunting and mesmerizing melodies Mozart wrote. Out of the corner of my eye, I saw Pavla move stage right. The music started, and from above the choir a man and a woman descended, dressed in shimmering white, performing an aerial silk ballet. I gasped, but kept conducting; and the choir, though they were aware that something was going on, stayed in character. It was beautiful. Fluid, graceful, elegant. It was so beautiful that I found myself crying. My hands held on to the last beat, as I watched the couple freeze in a final pose. My hands went down.

I wanted to stop, but we couldn't. We needed to do a run-through, so we kept going. Finally, when Emilia was done with "The Queen of the Night," I spoke.

"Brilliant, everyone! Dr. Chamberlain, Orchestra, Mr. Bailey, Emilia Rose, Choir — we have a show! Take a break, get some water, then regroup out in the audience for afternoon instructions."

Eduard was rushing towards me. "Dr. Stone! Everyone! I need you to go to your dressing rooms. Your masques have been delivered! You will find yours labeled with your name. Please try it on and let Pavla or myself know if any alterations need to be made!"

Eduard hugged me, gloating over the brilliance of the programming, and then over his shoulder I noticed Pavla coming towards me with the two aerial ballet performers.

I pulled away and looked at them. "That is probably the most beautiful aerial performance I have ever witnessed! What a surprise — a glorious one — but wow, it caught me off guard for a moment! Who do I have the pleasure of thanking for that visual delight?"

It was Pavla who spoke. "Dr. Stone, I would like for you to meet my parents, Pavel and Susanna. They are very famous..."

"Pavel?! Susanna?!" I interrupted, screaming with delight. They both looked at me like I was a crazy woman. I am crazy, of course, but not the type of crazy they are thinking right now.

"Pavel, do you remember me? You led my tour group about ten years ago. You took us on the wildest tour of Prague I have ever had! Right after my tour, you and Susanna were leaving in your minivan for the coast of Spain!"

Pavel now was hugging me so hard I could not breathe. "Elizabeth! I thought you looked familiar. But I guess I didn't recognize the blonde hair." He was smiling.

"Well, getting older does that to a woman. When one doesn't want to go gray, go blonde! You, on the other hand, haven't changed a bit!"

We stood there reminiscing, and I just couldn't get over my good fortune to see them again. For some reason, I got great comfort from knowing they would be onstage with me, sharing in this wonderful evening.

I invited them to join me for lunch, but they had plans with Pavla to sort out more details of the show. I hugged them again, introduced them to everyone, and then turned to talk to the choir, who had now gathered in the theatre.

"You have the afternoon free. Please enjoy a nice lunch, but remember we have another four-course dinner awaiting us at The Mozart House tonight, so don't overeat! This is your only time to shop for souvenirs, so take advantage of the Christmas Markets. You are to be back in front of the theatre by exactly 5:30 p.m. Travel in pairs or groups, and text me if you need anything. I am going to shop as well, so I will be nearby. Thank you for a wonderful rehearsal. Go! Embrace Praha!"

My steps were light and quick as I entered my dressing room. I heard the girls before I stepped in, and I found them hovered over something on the dressing table. They jumped when I came in.

"Izzibeth! Look!" Amanda Kate held up the most beautiful masque I had ever seen. It was the fabric of my dress, but instead of having elastic to hold it in place, it was fashioned like a pair of designer glasses to fit over my ears. Dear Eduard, he knew how important it was for the back of my head to look good while I conducted. He has thought of everything. The masque was delicate, fitting nicely over my eyes without interfering with my field of view (a very important factor for the performance!). I was beyond pleased with it.

Emilia Rose and Frieda came bustling in, already in full conversation when they entered. I was thrilled they were getting along.

"Elizabeth, Eduard is a genius. Pure genius! What do I do to get him to come work for the Met? I have never had an engagement where everything has been so perfect! This diva is a happy diva!"

We all cracked up. Emilia Rose, hard to please? No, she just knows what she wants and what is best. We were all happy that she was happy.

We left the theatre arm-in-arm to go eat, shop, and meet up with the rest of our group. As we entered Old Town Square, the smells stopped us in mid-step. Cinnamon, chocolate, spices, meats... And, music filled the air. Everywhere.

We looked at each other, nodded, and all chimed in unison, "GO! Embrace Praha!"

I caught movement to my right, and I saw someone take a picture. *Ah, Paparazzi! Nice to see you!* I nodded his way, and then gave him a fun pose. A happy pose. He put down his phone and grinned. The bill of his cap was pulled down, so I still couldn't really see enough of his face to form a memory, but we acknowledged each other for the first time. He touched his hat and tipped his head, and then turned to lose himself in the crowd.

45

Angels and Gargoyles

The day of the gala was finally upon us. After a quick and quiet breakfast, everyone kicked into high gear.

The Mozart House was a flurry of activity — Eduard directing traffic from the foyer; his assistants scurrying with armloads of items to the coaches; students bumping into each other on the stairs, laughing with excitement as the day we had been preparing for had finally arrived. I stood at the top of the stairs, with Beau at my side, looking down from the balcony with pride.

"It's going to be fabulous, Elizabeth."

Michael Holmes startled me. I hadn't seen him in a few days. Without turning my head, I nodded a gentle 'yes.' It *was* going to be fabulous.

"Keep on watching downstairs. I just wanted to see you before tonight because I might be busy. They have plans, Elizabeth, so stick to yours and always be aware of your surroundings. Give Peyton and Amanda Kate a heads-up, and warn them to watch their backs. I don't think Adderly and Kristoph will make a move tonight, but I do think Simon and Peter are up to something. I need to go to the theatre and check on one more thing before the event. Just be careful and stay strong."

"I feel more confident than I've ever felt, Michael, and at least some of that is because I know I have you guarding over me. Please take care of yourself, too, dear friend. With Simon, anything could happen, even to you. I will see you at the theatre. I have the best seat in the house reserved for you."

With that, Michael vanished. It hadn't been the right time to ask, but I still had plenty of questions about his absence since we had arrived in Prague. Perhaps he knew I was surrounded by my entire support network of friends and family. Perhaps angels know exactly when and where they're needed, and I was covered for the moment. Perhaps he was just detained.

"Dr. Stone!" It was Eduard from below. "It's time to depart! Do you have everything?"

Jolted out of my spiritual state, I replied, "Ready! And yes, Klara took care of everything for me! Let's get this show on the road!"

I leaned down and gave Beau a big pat on the head. "I will see you later tonight. I know I can count on you as well!"

Everyone knew what to do once we arrived at The Estates Theatre. But first, we needed to get dressed, so we all headed back to our dressing rooms. We had three hours before guests started arriving, and I needed to do a warm-up with the choir before we opened the house. It was hard not to stop and gawk at the foyer. It looked amazing. The Red Carpet area was the best I had ever seen, and the cocktail tables set around the foyer were elegant and beautifully dressed. The event staff were setting up the bar and food service, filling the air with sounds of clinking glasses and clanking metal. *This was the real deal — the gala was going to happen. Deep breaths.*

"Peyton — could I speak with you for a moment?"

Peyton sidled up next to me, and I spoke quietly so no one else could hear. "I spoke with Michael before we left. He asked me to give you a heads-up as you watch the crowd for us tonight. He said Adderly and Kristoph wouldn't likely make a move, but Peter probably would. Take lots of pictures, and text if you see anything out of the ordinary. Also, remind Amanda Kate and Frieda to watch their backs. Emilia Rose will be focused on her performance, so we'll all need to watch out for her."

"Will do, Elizabeth. I have never been so excited in my life. Never did I dream I would be living a life of mystery and drama! And fame, too! You are the best, Elizabeth Stone, and no one is going to get past me tonight."

"Thanks, Peyton, I knew I could count on you."

Closing the door behind me as I entered the dressing room, my mind flashed back to the events that had led up to this very moment, and it all still seemed surreal. My gown was hung neatly, my shoes laid out on the counter, and the earrings placed carefully by my make-up bag. Klara was taking excellent care of me.

I sat in my dressing chair and gazed in the mirror. This time I saw a strong, capable, beautiful woman in her own way looking back at me and I smiled. "Good job, Elizabeth. Tonight's performance is going to be stunning."

A gentle knock on my door. "Come in."

It was Bradley. "Are you ready, Dr. Stone? I am so excited! I just wanted you and I to go over the program step-by-step again before I got dressed. I will gather the students for their call time and have them ready for warm-ups for you as well. I know I keep saying it, but I can't thank you enough for this amazing opportunity and this awesome trip!"

We went over everything — twice — and then he gave me a pat on my arm and left to go get into his tux. From a musical standpoint, I had no doubts about the performance at this point.

ॐ ✳ ॐ

Michael appeared at the theatre just as the guests were arriving. Swooping in from above, he could see colorfully dressed attendees emerging from cars that were dropping them off at the theatre entrance. As he enjoyed the festive atmosphere and the people watching, something else caught his eye.

Sitting on top of the theatre, perched like a gargoyle, was Simon. Like Michael, he also was intently watching the guests arrive. Michael hesitated before joining him, but knew it was destined that he must.

"Well, well, Simon," Michael said as he landed on the roof, folding his wings before approaching him. "What have we here? It's not like you to sit idly on a roof and watch the crowd go by. You are usually walking amidst them, whispering doubt in their ears."

"I am in a Victor Hugo mood, what can I say," Simon retorted.

Michael bust out laughing.

"I am sick of this mickey-mouse assignment," Simon continued.

"Bored with it, eh, or are you sick of being defeated?" Michael asked as he braced himself for what was surely to follow.

"Don't humor yourself, Michael," Simon said as he stood and faced Michael. "Tonight, I will put an end to this tedious ordeal. Peter will get the treasures, and you won't be able to do anything about it."

"What makes you so sure of that, Simon? Elizabeth has foiled all your plans up to this point. Of all nights, what makes you think she'll suddenly let her guard down tonight – at *her* gala?"

Simon's posture was becoming more aggressive. Michael was hitting all the right points to irritate him. This wasn't the first time they'd faced each other, nor will it be the last.

Simon began walking towards Michael, but Michael didn't cower, which made Simon even madder.

"You are a second-rate guardian, Michael, face it. What makes you think your 'goody two shoes' Dr. Elizabeth Stone is going to keep Peter from getting the treasures tonight? He has me, Simon, the strongest in all the heavens, helping him!"

Simon was getting closer to Michael.

"You will have to go through me to get to her, Simon. If you hurt one hair on her head, or anyone else associated with her, I will unleash forces like you have never seen before."

That did it. Simon stopped dead in his tracks.

Michael didn't know what hit him. It happened so fast that he didn't have time to defend himself. He suddenly found himself unable to move. It's like he was trapped in an invisible web. His head was free, but everything else below his neck was bound. When he tried to speak, he realized Simon had also frozen his vocal cords, prohibiting him from calling out for help.

Simon raised his hands, lifting Michael about two feet above the roof.

"That's awfully tough talk for you, Michael. Too bad you don't have what it takes to back it up. Go ahead, try to use your 'spirit' voice to call for backup. You've never learned how to break through my defensive shields. No one will find you tonight, Michael. Not Elizabeth; not your angelic allies. You lose. Come on, let's enjoy the show now. I will show you to your seat. You have the best seat in the house!"

Simon pointed his long, bony finger towards Michael, and then unfolded his black wings. As Simon rose, so did Michael, as if he were on a leash. Simon flew to the back of the theatre, to the open backstage door. No one saw him placing Michael backstage, high in a corner, suspended in space.

Michael indeed had the best seat in the house. He could see and hear everything. The stage was in full view, so he knew he would be facing Elizabeth as she directed. He also knew that if Peter tried to steal the treasures or hurt Elizabeth, he couldn't do anything about it. He was powerless.

46
The Mozart Masquerade Gala

Out front, things were starting to get busy. Guests were arriving, and Peyton was in the Red Carpet area snapping pictures and helping people pose. She was great, and didn't let anyone slip past her. No language barrier was going to keep her from getting the shots she needed.

"Excuse me, sir. Could you please step over here?" Peyton felt a chill run up her spine when the gentleman turned to face her. She recognized him as Peter, and Sophia was on his arm. Even dressed as Wolfgang and Constanze, she recognized them. And what a lame costume idea... There were only going to be a hundred Wolfgangs and Constanzes tonight. But they were different. Sophia had on very expensive diamond jewelry – a huge diamond brooch perched on her bosom, which was extremely low-cut in Peyton's estimation. It had to have cost a fortune, so where did they get it? Also, Peter's masque looked comical, as if he were mocking Wolfgang instead of honoring him. Peyton continued to coax them in front of the backdrop, helping them pose as she took at least ten shots of them. They were getting annoyed with her, but she was persistent – just like she meant to be. She was told to rile them up a little to aggravate them, so they would be talking about all the annoying event staff instead of focusing on Elizabeth and the other guests.

Peyton finally let them go, and Amanda Kate took her cue. Except, as she was walking towards Sophia with a glass of champagne to welcome them, her foot slipped on the Red Carpet and she tumbled forward. Her eyes got wide, and she watched in slow motion, as the glass of champagne went right down Sophia's bosom.

"I am SO sorry!" Amanda Kate's hand went immediately to help wipe off the champagne, which made for an even more awkward moment. Sophia's German started flying.

Peyton didn't have to understand German to know this wasn't good. Of course, there was no shortage of waiters rushing over to help her wipe off her bosom... At least four eager young men offered to dry her off before she pushed them all away, storming off towards the ladies' room. Guests were chuckling, and Peter, unbeknownst to all, had slipped away by himself.

Peyton and Amanda Kate scoured the room trying to find him, but by then another ten Wolfgangs had come in, and Peyton needed to continue taking pictures.

"Where did he go?" Peyton put her smile back on her face, and kept on clicking.

Amanda Kate made her way to the ladies' room to apologize to Sophia. She found her at the sink wiping herself off. Luckily, champagne doesn't stain.

Sophia looked up when she saw her come in. "Of all the nerve! What do you want now? You have done enough damage, thank you. That was embarrassing, and you, my dear, are a klutz."

Amanda Kate looked her square in the eyes and said, "I just wanted to say I am sorry again. I certainly didn't mean for this to happen. These are new shoes, and my heel got caught in the carpet. Please accept my apology. You look beautiful tonight, by the way. That diamond brooch is stunning!"

As usual, Amanda Kate had the magic touch, and Sophia softened. "It is, isn't it! My boyfriend presented it to me tonight. He is a very important museum curator, and he said this was a special brooch that had belonged to the Mozart family."

They walked out of the ladies' room laughing. Amanda Kate guided her over to the bar and handed her a new glass of champagne.

"Enjoy your evening."

"Thank you." With that, Sophia picked up her skirts and started scouting the room for Peter, who had magically reappeared. She ran to join him, seemingly in a good mood again.

Peyton was waving her arms trying to get Amanda Kate's attention from across the room. Amanda Kate, finally seeing her, nonchalantly walked over to see what the panic was about.

"Adderly and Kristoph have arrived. Look to your left, at the cocktail table by the front window," she whispered.

Turning, Amanda Kate saw Adderly and quietly exclaimed, "Leave it to Adderly to wear all gold..."

He was dressed in an 18th century gold brocade suit with a shimmering gold cravat. He wore a gold three-cornered hat, and his wig had a delightful pigtail braided down the back with a gold bow dangling at the end. He wore white tights and very fancy looking gold shoes. He accessorized it all with a gold walking stick. Even his masque was gold. But, he wore it well, with his robust figure filling out the jacket as if he had walked right out that era. Kristoph, on the other hand, was dressed in all black. From what Elizabeth had told them about Tivoli Gardens, this was the costume he was wearing that night as well. A chill went up their spines, and they gave each other a look. Peyton took more pictures and then returned to her post at the Red Carpet. Amanda Kate approached Adderly.

"Good evening, gentlemen. Welcome to the gala! May I get you anything? You both look wonderful, by the way!"

"No thank you, my dear," Adderly said in his delightful English accent.

Amanda Kate wanted to comment on how charming he looked, but she knew she needed to keep this formal and not give herself away. Kristoph nodded without speaking, but Amanda Kate felt him checking her out from behind the masque. It gave her the creeps, but she kept her composure.

"Please, enjoy yourselves. I know for a fact you will enjoy the program! I heard some of the rehearsal, and it is going to be wonderful. Where are you seated, may I ask?"

"Third row, center." It was Kristoph, sounding like Darth Vader through the masque.

"Those are great seats. Enjoy, and please, have more to eat and drink!" They both gave her a friendly nod and thanked her for her kindness. She found them to be pleasant, but of course, didn't trust them past her nose.

Amanda Kate moved away, and then sent Elizabeth a quick text with their seat location. She knew Peter and Sophia would be nearby, so that would give her a focal point for keeping her eye on them while she was on stage.

There had to be at least six hundred guests in attendance already. The theatre held six hundred and fifty-nine, so they were almost to capacity.

Frieda showed up beside her, looking a little concerned.

"Just where am I supposed to find chicken livers for the diva here in Prague? And why is she just now asking — *an hour before curtain* — for her beloved chicken livers? 'Frieda, darling, please be a dear and go get me an order of chicken livers. You know I can't perform without them!' Amanda Kate, you and Peyton promised me..." If looks could freeze, Frieda could have frozen the Sahara with the look she was giving Amanda Kate.

The rant wasn't over. "This was in the middle of me fixing her hair, my mouth full of bobby pins. I spat them out all over the counter, which irritated her because one fell in her precious cup of tea with honey. She threw her hands up, hitting me in the face and making me drop the curls I was pinning. So now, not only do I have to find chicken livers, but I also have to redo her hair! Ugh! Amanda Kate!!!"

"Honey," Amanda Kate said, "didn't we anticipate all of this when you signed on? We all knew beforehand that Emilia Rose is a 'little' difficult right before a performance. Now, I wouldn't bring you all the way to Prague to deal with her if I hadn't also done some proper planning for this very moment."

Frieda gave her another not-amused, quizzical look, saying, "Go on. I am listening, but it better be good."

"Follow me. I never know if she is going to be demanding or compliant before performances, so I plan on both."

Amanda Kate went to the caterer, said something, and instantly was handed a silver tray with a plate full of chicken livers from out of the warming oven.

"Amanda Kate, I love you, but heavens, couldn't you have done me the decency of telling me you were prepared?"

"But I did, Frieda. Did you look in your tool box of combs and pins and see the note I left you?"

Frieda froze. There had been a small, folded-up piece of paper when she opened her tool box, but she had tossed it aside to pick up the bobby pins.

"Yes, and — "

"And you tossed it aside." Amanda Kate flicked her hand in a dramatic gesture. "You were too focused on your client to take a look. Oh Frieda, I tried saving you. The note was telling you that if Emilia Rose happened to ask for her 'beloved chicken livers' that I had them up front in a warming oven." Amanda Kate gave Frieda a grin, and then they both burst out laughing.

"Now I know why they call you Queen of Events, Amanda Kate. I am going to walk proudly backstage with these stinky chicken livers and act like I am Queen of the Day. Thank you for thinking of everything." Frieda took the tray of chicken livers and gave Amanda Kate a peck on the cheek.

Holding her nose as she walked away with the tray of chicken livers as far from her body as she could, she nasally proclaimed, "Why chicken livers, of all things? Divas..."

Laughing, Amanda Kate rubbed her hands together, and then turned back to her crowd. She checked on the caterer, making sure the food and drink were holding up. She knew that donors paid more when they were happy, so she went around the room once more greeting and thanking guests for coming. She didn't even act like it was weird that she was talking to faces behind masques of all shapes, sorts, and sizes. She found it fascinating. She loved the mixture of different languages she was hearing, as if the chatter and activity in the foyer was its own performance.

Peyton was still snapping pictures. Elizabeth had asked her to keep an eye out for Paparazzi and for someone who might be her benefactor. English accents were her clue, and tonight there were plenty, so any one of a dozen or more people could be who she was looking for.

"Excuse me, Madame, could I bother you to take a picture of us with our phone?"

Peyton turned to see a couple dressed as Papageno and Papagena, with the most beautiful masques she had ever seen. Their English was broken, but she couldn't place the accent.

"Of course! Are you enjoying yourselves? You look fabulous, by the way, and if I were giving out a prize I would give it to you!"

The couple smiled, took their phone, and then posed for Peyton on the Red Carpet.

Interesting, thought Peyton, and she clicked more pictures of them as they walked away. Through her lens, she saw them approach Adderly and Kristoph! *Goons!* Click. Click. How did they get in without an invitation? She got Amanda Kate's attention by waving her arms profusely and pointing in their direction. Amanda Kate got the message and went over to Adderly's table again. When she walked away, she texted Peyton and Elizabeth that they were indeed goons, and sounded like the ones Elizabeth described from Copenhagen. She found out they were sitting with Adderly and warned everyone to be on the lookout.

Matthew Finley was having the time of his life. A drink in one hand, and a velvet bag securely fastened underneath his jacket, he couldn't wait to get this show on the road. He was dressed as the infamous Plague Doctor, so he had to be careful not to hit people with the masque's nose when he turned his head. No one recognized him, but he had identified Adderly, Kristoph, Peter, and Sophia from behind his cover. There were several Plague Doctors in the foyer, so he didn't stand out – and he made an effort to keep his anonymity by not socializing too much. Taking another drink from the tray being offered to him, he took a big swig and said, "Let the games begin."

A bell rang, indicating the house was opening. The guests scurried, taking advantage of getting one more drink before going in to be seated. The excitement built even more. The small string quartet that had been playing for the cocktail hour stood up, packed up, and moved to their place in the pit with Dr. Chamberlain.

Ushers at the door checked every invitation and either showed guests to their floor seats or directed them to their elaborate box seats upstairs.

The orchestra was tuning, and the lights were dimmed, giving one final warning that the program was about to begin. The major players were in their seats — Adderly, Kristoph, Peter, and Sophia — but as Peyton watched them be seated, she didn't see the bird couple sit with them.

Where did they go? She scouted the audience, but they were nowhere to be seen. She reminded herself not to panic — that all bases were covered, and maybe they were simply wrong about their seats when they talked to Amanda Kate earlier. *Ah!* There they are, in a box on Stage Left. *Interesting. Birds in a box,* she thought, as she sent a text update to the girls. But then, Peyton looked Stage Right, and directly across from the first bird couple was another couple dressed exactly like them. *A flock of goons. Oh dear!*

This didn't look good, and certainly didn't fit into the plan. She desperately looked for Amanda Kate, but when she couldn't find her, she headed off backstage by herself. Something is rotten in Prague, and they had better be ready for Plan B.

47
The Performance

"May I come in?"

I was looking over my scores, one last time, but the sound of Benjamin's gentle voice at my door calmed my pre-performance anxiety.

"Benjamin! Of course! I was just reviewing – again. I want this performance to be perfect."

"It will be, Elizabeth, because you are a wonderful director, you've planned an incredible program, and your students have worked very hard to make this special. I brought you these."

From behind his back he produced a beautiful bouquet of lilies and roses.

"My favorites! Thank you for being here, Benjamin. It means a lot to me."

What a cliché romantic moment we were having, I thought. His flattery still made me feel a bit awkward, especially since nothing had felt normal for months, but his gesture was nice all the same. Thankfully, my watch came to my rescue.

"Oh dear, would you look at the time!" I said, feeling a bit like a schoolgirl. "I need to get dressed. I had them give you the best seat in the house, one I am sure even the maestro Mozart would have approved of."

"You are going to do great. Just remember – keep the integrity."

We briefly hugged, then I was once again alone.

I reached with shaky hands for my beautiful gown. I had told Eduard that I'd rather be without Klara tonight because, despite her impeccable service so far, the extra attention would just fluster me before I went on stage.

"Deep breaths, Elizabeth, deep breaths." Calming my nerves, I gently took the gown off the hanger and pulled it over my head.

Amanda Kate knocked on my dressing room door just as I was trying to zip up my gown.

"Just in the nick of time, as always," I said as she finished zipping me up. It was then that Peyton burst in with a look of disdain on her face.

"Goons. A flock of goons. Everywhere!" she said breathlessly.

"Peyton, what are you talking about?" I looked at my friend, who was noticeably shaken.

Peyton continued her rapid-fire update: "To your right and to your left, Elizabeth. The box seats by the stage are full of Peter's goons, dressed in look-alike Papageno and Papagena costumes. I saw a pair of them talking to Adderly and Kristoph, so I sent Amanda Kate over to talk to them. They told her they were Adderly's guests and would be sitting with them, but then I couldn't find them at first when the house opened. Once I found them, I noticed more of them filling the box seats. Oh, Elizabeth! Be careful out there!"

Peyton took out her camera and showed us pictures of everyone so that we could have a visual.

I reassured her, "You did great, Peyton. And, you know what? We are going to be the winners tonight, not them. You can count on that, ok?"

Peyton had taken a couple of slow, deep breaths to calm her racing heart, giving me a reassuring nod that she was okay now.

"Remember to keep your heads about you during the performance. Don't let these goons rattle our plan. You can do this, Peyton. *We* can do this!"

Amanda Kate looked at a text that had just come through — all was well with Emilia Rose. "Thank heavens for small miracles!" we all quipped in unison before breaking out into laughter, easing the tension in the room.

I noticed the orchestra had stopped warming up and the audience had started clapping, meaning the concertmaster must be taking his place to give the final tuning.

"It's time." I was excited, yet nervous.

"We are just so proud of you we can hardly stand it, Elizabeth," Peyton said with tears in her eyes.

I took a moment to look in the mirror one last time and give myself one final pep talk, and then I opened the door and stepped out to take my place

Stage Right. The choir kids were in place, each one giving me a fist bump as I passed. I looked across to the group Stage Left, waving a big thumbs-up and blowing kisses at them. They looked stunning in their beautiful masques.

The stairs were in place, stage lights down, and all the Black Light crew were in place for their parts in the music. I felt a hand on my shoulder. It was Pavel. No words were spoken between us as I placed my hand over his.

The orchestra was tuned and silent, which was Joseph's cue to take the podium. There was applause, and then the overture to *The Marriage of Figaro* began resonating with brilliance throughout The Estates Theatre.

Applause. Downbeat to *Masquerade*. I watched with great pride as the choir totally blew the audience away. The choreography was crisp and spotless; chords in tune; gestures dramatic, and voices strong. Between the staircases, the Black Light cast performed their own intricate routines. They were in shapes of giant masques that illuminated from within, and I was mesmerized.

Segue into Bradley's a cappella arrangement of the Kyrie's allegro section from the *Requiem,* and you could hear gasps from the audience as the genius of Mozart finally filled the theatre.

Applause. For the stage change, Joseph and the orchestra played a portion of *Symphony No. 40 in G minor.* Choir in place, stage lights up. Everything was going as rehearsed. My turn. Deep breaths.

Where were Amanda Kate and Peyton? They should be bringing Emilia Rose backstage right now. I have no time to worry, as I take my cue to walk on stage.

I walked on like Vanna White. Tall, poised, and aware of the beautiful gown I was wearing as I looked out confidently to the audience. I stopped center stage and took a small bow. As my head came up, I scouted the audience. I located Adderly's group on the third row, and I as turned to face the choir, I saw the flock of goons in the box seats above me — just as Peyton said.

Where is Michael? I didn't see him anywhere.

Joseph took his cue from me when I raised my arms. It felt good to be making the magic at last. I love looking into the faces of my choir as we connect: from my heart to my hands to their voices. The *Misericordias Domini, K. 222* was flawless. I dropped my hands, turned to acknowledge the choir and orchestra, and then turned Stage Right to welcome Emilia Rose.

She was standing there as Frieda touched up her hair, straightened her gown, and gave her silent words of encouragement. I saw her take a deep breath offstage, and then she made her entrance. While I make every effort to float out onto the stage, Emilia Rose enters with heavy feet. The audience could hear every footstep as she took her place beside me. She told me once that stomping her way onto the stage gives her the confidence she needs, and it also reminds her to "breathe low." Whatever – it worked for her, and that's all that mattered, graceful or not. We smiled at each other, clasped our hands, and bowed to the audience as they applauded enthusiastically for Emilia Rose.

The audience went silent again as I turned and raised my hands for the *Laudate Dominum* to begin. Just as I expected, Emilia Rose stunned her audience with her beautiful lyrical voice. She floated to the top effortlessly, and was so musical with her phrases. I didn't want it to end. I felt like I was conducting a chorus of angels. It was so breathtaking that I didn't hear one peep of audience noise during the whole piece. When I lowered my arms, there was a moment of total silence before the audience began clapping. They didn't want the song to end either, but once the applause started, it was thunderous. I gave her a look, reminding her that she had a quick change, and then she was off, waving to the audience in true Emilia Rose fashion. They loved her, and she loved them.

I braced myself to be strong. I could not wait to see how the audience was going to react to the *Lacrimosa* aerial silk ballet. I wasn't disappointed. The introduction began. There are only two measures before the haunting melody comes in. *La-cri-mo-sa*, and then out float Pavel and Susanna.

The ballet fit the words, and the audience had the translation in their program:

A day of tears is that dread day,
O which shall rise from ashen dust to judgment true each guilty man.
Then spare this soul O God, we pray,
O loving Saviour, Jesus Lord,
Grant Thou to them Thy rest.
Amen.

It was the most beautiful three minutes and twenty-one seconds ever. I could hear weeping from the audience as Pavel and Susanna interpreted the text with their beautiful movements. They came together as one on the Amen, and held the pose as if they were embracing the souls of all the world. I couldn't move. I couldn't breathe. Somehow, I lowered my arms, and the audience erupted. Pavel and Susanna took their bows from the silks, and then gracefully descended to Center Stage to join me for a bow.

The lights dimmed, the platforms spread apart a bit, and suddenly we were all a flutter with the Papageno and Papagena duet. Black light characters from *The Magic Flute* were dancing among the choir members, and the interaction was electrifying. I had walked offstage with Pavel and Susanna so Bradley could conduct this one.

I still found it strange that Amanda Kate and Peyton were not backstage watching. Maybe they changed their minds and found seats in the audience. Pavel and Susanna walked away, and I looked out toward the boxes Stage Right. *Where were the goons? There were no birds in the boxes!*

I looked out onstage, and I saw them — they had the audacity to come onstage behind the Black Light cast and were choreographing their own moves as they placed themselves around the outside of the stage area. *What are they up to?? They don't seem to be doing anything harmful, so why then are they on stage? How did they get past the Stage Manager?*

There was no time to panic. The song was over, and as quickly as the goons were onstage, they were off again with everyone else. I moved into my place as the orchestra immediately began the introduction to "The Queen of the Night's aria." I watched with relief as Emilia Rose was gently lowered on her moon, ready to sing. She always said her fear of heights just made her sing the high notes better, and she was nailing them tonight. The moon suddenly tilted a bit, but the crew holding the ropes straightened her back to center. She never missed a beat. Underneath her, another black light presentation, and the choir giving her background vocal support. It was better than the movie. Truly. The last note was approaching, all leading to the grand finale...

Brilliant! Applause. And more applause.

Time for curtain calls. I saw Emilia being lowered to the ground, where two gallant young men took her by her hands and led her Center Stage. The audience was on their feet, shouting, "Brava! Brava!"

I walked out to join her, and we took our bow. I gestured to Joseph; his orchestra; called Bradley out to join us; acknowledged the choir; and asked the other performers to join us on stage. After the applause died down, I stepped Downstage to get closer to the audience. The moment had arrived.

"Ladies and Gentlemen! Distinguished guests! Dr. Chamberlain, Mr. Bailey, and all of us involved in tonight's gala wish to thank you for coming to our performance. It truly has been an honor to be invited to perform in this historical venue, and we only hope we made Mozart and Prague proud tonight."

Applause.

Deep breaths, Elizabeth, deep breaths.

"Before we leave tonight, I have a special presentation to make. So, if you would kindly take your seats, I would like to call Mr. Matthew Finley to join me on stage."

There was hushed chatter in the audience, as people wondered who in the world Matthew Finley was, and I saw Adderly and his entourage jerk their heads towards each other. But, I didn't see Peter.

Matthew met me Center Stage, looking ridiculously happy — even with the daunting Plague Doctor masque — and I smiled. He was living the moment.

"Several months ago, I was given a very special gift. Tonight, I would like to..."

And then I blacked out.

48

The Awakening

I woke up to the sound of a monitor beeping in my ear. I tried opening my eyes, but they wouldn't move. I could hear low, hushed talking in the distance, and felt a warm hand embracing mine. Slowly, I managed to open my eyes halfway, but my eyelashes were blurring my vision. My head hurt, and it felt heavy. Very heavy. Blinking my eyes, I began to focus on my surroundings. Amanda Kate was holding my hand, but her head was down, and I could hear her softly weeping. I made out Grey and Emma at the end of the bed, and could tell that everyone I loved was gathered in this room. The murmured conversations seemed to suggest everyone was afraid I might wake up and hear them talking about me. I finally managed to open my eyes fully, and I took in more of my surroundings while I found my voice. I was screaming to everyone from the inside, but I couldn't make a sound.

This was not a normal hospital. The room looked more like a hotel suite, not the sterile environment of a public hospital. I could make out light blue walls with big crown molding. The light fixtures were elegant, and the light was soft and dimmed instead of fluorescent. People were standing, sitting, talking in small groups, and holding cups of coffee. It smelled so good.

I tried to squeeze Amanda Kate's hand to send a signal, but it didn't seem to be working. My left hand was sore, so I figured I had an IV attached. My legs felt heavy, and try as I may, nothing moved.

"Did I tear my dress?" I had suddenly found my voice. The whole room gasped and turned towards the bed, where I had also managed a weak smile as they all stared at me. Not just staring — they all froze mid-sentence, mouths open.

I felt like a goldfish in a bowl.

I cleared my throat, and asked, "Will someone please say something and tell me what happened? Where am I? How long have I been out?" My voice was cracking, it was so dry. I sounded like a teenage boy going through a voice change.

Amanda Kate still had her hand on mine, but had begun crying louder. Peyton joined her, putting her hands on Amanda Kate's shoulders, both of them weeping beside my bed.

A very good-looking doctor made his way through the crowd and asked everyone to please move back. He patted me on the arm and softly said, "Welcome back, Dr. Stone! We have been quite concerned about you. It has been three days now since you were hurt at the gala."

He turned to everyone and asked them go to the waiting room while he checked my vitals. Still not saying a word, the crowd in my hospital room nodded their heads and moved quietly out into the hallway. Grey patted my arm and kissed me on the cheek. Amanda Kate squeezed my hand while continuing to sob loudly. Peyton was sniffling as they walked out arm-in-arm. Frieda gently smoothed my hair. Even Emilia Rose was quiet as she blew me a kiss and walked out. The room cleared, and then I found myself looking into the doctor's baby blues. He then shined a very bright light in eyes. I tried to smile.

"Don't try to talk, Dr. Stone. You have had a nasty head injury that put you in a coma for a few days. Luckily, it didn't require surgery. You aren't out of the woods yet, but I am very happy to see that you are awake and still have your humor! Your family and friends have hardly left your side since it happened. I am Dr. Dvorak, and have been with you since they brought you in."

Cool - a doctor with a composer name, I found myself thinking. All I could hear was *New World Symphony* in my head.

He and his nurse continued to check my heart rate, my breathing, my reflexes, my temperature, my blood pressure, my ears, and so on. I remained silent, but I had a thousand questions. However, I knew Dr. Dvorak wasn't the person who could answer them all. Finally, he sat on the edge of the bed and took my hand in his.

"Dr. Stone. You gave us all a scare. I know you want explanations, and you will get them. It has been an exciting few days around our quiet little hospital! You are quite a celebrity now, and I have had to turn away reporters and even some paparazzi. One gentleman, in particular, has been hanging around with his camera and notepad, refusing to leave. He sits outside on a bench under the chestnut tree, and when I walk out to my car he jumps up and asks me questions about how you are."

Paparazzi. That made me happy. This time, I managed a smile.

He continued. "Your vitals look pretty good, all things considered, and I am very pleased with your progress. You have some sutures on your head – eight, to be exact – and your left arm was also broken in the incident. It was a nice clean break that I was able to set without surgery. We will need to run some more tests to make sure everything is healing properly, and I would like to keep you here for a few more days for observation and to help you manage your pain. But, I'm optimistic. In other words, Dr. Stone, you are one lucky lady."

"What day is it?" I asked. He said I had been out for three days. I would have come in on December 31st. It wasn't midnight yet when the gala ended.

"January 2nd."

"But we are supposed to go home today!"

"I am going to let Eduard come in for a moment and speak to you, okay?" Dr. Dvorak patted me on the arm, and nodded to the nurse to go and get Eduard. They evidently knew each other very well since he called him by first name.

In a few moments, Eduard was by my side. He pulled the chair Amanda Kate had been sitting in closer to me and took my hand in his.

"Elizabeth, my dear, we are all elated you have rejoined us! I hear you were asking about your flight home today. Bradley, Dr. Chamberlain, and the rest of the faculty chaperones escorted all the students home today. Their flights left early this morning. They didn't want to leave, but we knew that you would need more time to recover, and they have families and obligations waiting for them back home. They have kept candlelight vigils for you ever since you were brought to hospital. Please don't worry about your own flight home. I have arranged for that departure to be determined depending upon your recovery. The last thing you need to do right now is get on a plane."

"Did I tear that beautiful gown you made me?"

Eduard chuckled out loud. "No, you didn't. Surprisingly. But that was the least of our concerns."

I managed another weak smile. I was getting tired again.

"I don't remember anything. What happened?"

Eduard frowned. "A lot. I am going to let all the players involved tell their pieces of the story — when you are better. It is going to be a lot for you to take in."

I closed my eyes and nodded. "Okay. But I want to know soon. Very soon. I don't want to lie here in this bed and speculate about what transpired. It will drive me crazy."

"I will talk to Dr. Dvorak to see if we can arrange that. After you get out of the hospital, we want you to come to The Mozart House for a few days before we send you back home. Your friends and family have arranged to stay behind with you. Well, really, they refused to leave without you. Hopefully you will be on your way by the end of the week, but you take all the time you need. Dr. Dvorak has gone out to tell everyone to return to the house so you can get some sleep. They are exhausted as well."

He leaned in and kissed me gently on the cheek. "Get some rest, dear Elizabeth. We all love you."

Eduard had barely been out of the room for five seconds when I heard a very quiet knock on my door. Amanda Kate and Peyton didn't come in, but they did stick their heads in far enough for me to see them.

"Izzibeth," Amanda Kate said softly, "I wouldn't have been able to stand it if anything had happened to you. We love you."

And with that, they blew me a kiss and shut the door quietly behind them.

The nurse was still in the room and watched them close the door. Making sure no one else was coming in, she then dimmed the lights even more. After letting me chew on some ice chips and sip some water, which tasted so good, I fell asleep to the steady beat of my heart monitor. The moonlight gave a soft glow to the room. In my dreams, my white stag visited me.

49

The Music Room

The fire was blazing as we all gathered in the Music Room at The Mozart House. Eduard had a dessert bar set up with small pastries and sweets, coffee, and other after dinner drink options. Those who had stayed in Prague after the gala were invited to a welcome home dinner in honor of my recovery, and now we were stuffing our faces with fancy desserts while we laughed and embraced life with family and friends. Pavel, Susanna, and Pavla had also joined us for dinner, and it was nice to get reacquainted without the stress of the gala bearing down on us. Benjamin, unfortunately, had to return to Boston yesterday to perform, but he had stopped by the hospital on his way to the airport to say goodbye, with a promise of seeing me again soon.

꘎ ✳ ꘧

I had arrived back at the house from the hospital around noon this morning — making it a total of five days that I was pampered back to health by Dr. Dvorak and his staff. My head was feeling normal, well, as normal as it could be, and the sutures were healing nicely. My arm was now sporting a beautiful pink cast.

I had gasped when I looked in the mirror for the first time — black eyes, shaved part of my head, bruised cheeks. Not a pretty sight, but no one ever said a word. Vanity aside, I was glad to be alive. No joke. Having never personally experienced a major illness or traumatic injury like this, it was all a new experience for me. It was all quite different from that time when I cut off my big toe with a band cymbal. I always jokingly call that my "most symbolic experience." However, this was proving to be more humbling.

Anton had cried when he came to help me out of the car. I didn't expect that, so I cried too. He and Klara helped me up the stairs, even though my legs were fine, and I didn't resist. I smelled roses as Anton opened the door. Upon entering, I saw that my room was filled with several dozen red roses. The fire was low, and the bed was turned down. On the chair in front of the fire, I noticed a beautiful music-themed afghan throw, which hadn't been there before.

"Klara and I found this afghan and wanted you to have it." Anton and Klara were smiling as I walked towards the afghan. It was made with a wonderfully soft velour yarn, with Mozart's music woven on both sides. "You two must come home with me! What am I going to do without you?" I hugged them gingerly before Klara helped me settle into the chair.

They all were spoiling me, and though I was ready to be my independent self, I didn't deny them the joy of caring for me.

"Dinner is at six, Dr. Stone. The chef has planned a welcome home dinner in your honor. Klara will assist you down to the Dining Room. For now, Dr. Dvorak said rest — and resist visiting with everyone until dinner time. In fact, we sent them all on a brief sightseeing cruise so they wouldn't distract you. Now, get some rest and we will see you soon."

Klara fluffed the afghan one more time before she left the room. The door had barely shut before Michael Holmes and Beau were beside me.

"Michael Holmes! Beau! What a sight for sore eyes — literally!"

Beau put his head in my lap, and Michael Holmes sat in the chair beside me. I think he was waiting for me to start quizzing him, because he didn't say a word — just sat there with his head down and his hands clasped.

"Are you okay? I really have missed you guys." I continued rubbing Beau's head.

"I failed you, Elizabeth." Michael finally said.

"Excuse me? What did you just say? Fail? I don't think so — I am here, aren't I?"

"You weren't supposed to get hurt. That was my job. I was to make sure that no harm came to you, and harm did."

"First of all, I am alive. A little bunged up, agreed, but alive. These injuries will heal, so no — no harm done, not in the long-term. You did your job. End of discussion."

"I know you haven't heard what happened yet. When you do, which I think is on the schedule tonight, be prepared. I don't know that I'll ever get over the feeling that I let you down, but it is encouraging to hear you try to reassure me. I have some explaining to do 'upstairs,' and I'm very curious to learn the outcome of that case briefing. Mistakes were made, but I think I'll be vindicated. I am so sorry, Elizabeth. I watched over you in the hospital, and kept telling myself this should have never happened."

"You are forgiven, Michael Holmes. End of discussion. I get answers tonight? Good. All I have done is wonder. When everyone came to visit, they always steered the conversation to pleasantries or mundane topics, avoiding any questions I asked. It was like I was talking to air. Peyton wouldn't even budge. Eduard must have bribed everyone. I look forward to the truth tonight, and I am strong enough now to hear it."

With that, Michael nodded and left. He did smile, but he still seemed defeated. Beau remained by me, and once alone, I realized how exhausting the day had been. The next thing I knew, Klara was gently touching me on the shoulder.

"Dr. Stone? It is time to get ready for dinner."

Good, I thought. I was so ready to hear the truth.

❦✳❧

And now here we were in the Music Room. I was waiting for a cue to begin, but thankfully, I didn't have to initiate it. Eduard walked briskly into the room. I don't think he ever walked slower than an allegro.

Walking to the hearth, he stopped and cleared his throat.

"I think we all know why we are gathered here after dinner, and I know that Elizabeth has many questions about the night of the gala. If you all will be seated, I believe the best way to tell the story is for each of you to share your perspective — one at a time, or alongside the others directly with you as events unfolded. You have had a few days to let it all sink in and to script your story so that it makes sense to Elizabeth. You all were players, and you each have a story to tell. Let's see... If I am not mistaken, based on what I've heard from talking to all of you, the drama began before the actual performance began. In that case, I believe Amanda Kate and Peyton need to begin and tell what happened to them first. Ladies, the floor is yours."

Nervously, they both came and stood in front of the hearth and faced me. The room had plenty of comfortable seating, and I heard everyone take a big breath as they settled in to hear the whole story as it was retold to me.

"First and foremost, we are all so glad you are okay, Izzibeth, and that you are here with us tonight. We have been so worried about you. The last several days have been such a shock. Now, going back to the events of the gala... Peyton and I had spent the evening scouting out the guests, and we recognized Adderly and Kristoph right off the bat. Peter and Sophia were also easy marks. I even managed to spill a whole glass of champagne down Sophia's dress. She was showing off a diamond brooch, but that wasn't' all."

Everyone laughed.

"I followed her into the ladies' room to apologize, but she began bragging about how her boyfriend was this all-important person at a Mozart museum and that the diamond brooch had belonged to some Mozart descendants. That raised a red flag with me, so I came backstage to tell you about it in your dressing room. Once I got there, you needed help with your dress, so I zipped you up. I got distracted and forgot to tell you about Sophia's brooch. Peyton rushed in to tell us about the 'bird goons,' and the next thing we knew, the orchestra had finished tuning. That's when it got really weird."

While Amanda Kate was beginning her story, I noticed Michael was in a corner in the room looking at me.

"*Elizabeth,*" he said in the voice only he and I could hear, "*I am going to tell you my story as well so you can get the whole picture. I'll interject details via spirit voice when necessary. I don't want you to think I abandoned you.*"

I smiled warmly at him, and listened as the story continued.

50

The Gala Saga, As It Happened That Night

As the others began recounting their gala experiences, Michael added: "*I was already in trouble by this point. Simon and I had an encounter on the roof of the theatre when I arrived before the gala. I was pushing all his buttons. And then I questioned his powers, so he blindsided me — bound me in some sort of web and rendered me powerless. He hung me up backstage, suspended, where I watched the evening unfold like a fly caught by a spider.*"

❦ ✳ ❧

"Did you tell her about the brooch?" Peyton asked.

"No," Amanda Kate said, "we got busy with her dress. I can't believe I forgot! Did you get a good picture of it?"

"I did. I got some great shots of everyone tonight." Peyton was looking for the brooch on her camera.

"Show me your pictures again — especially all the couples you got that came in dressed as Papagena and Papageno. They are all strategically seated around the theatre. Something is up!"

They were huddled together around the dressing table, looking at pictures, when they heard a click. Looking into the mirror, they each let out a gasp and froze. Standing behind them in the dressing room was the biggest man they had ever seen. His head almost reached the ceiling, he was dressed in the ghost costume that is traditional for productions of *Don Giovanni* — and was wearing a death mask. Slowly, they turned to face him, clinging on to each other.

"Hello, ladies, what a pleasure to finally meet you." His voice was unnerving, but not loud. "I am Simon. Surely Elizabeth has told you about me, so don't act so shocked. I am well aware that you are key players in her plans tonight. However, I am afraid that you will be, shall we say, indisposed. Your little plan is going to fail, and I will come out on top tonight."

With that, he vanished. They heard another click.

"Did you get a picture, Peyton?" Amanda Kate managed to squeak out. "Because no one is ever going to believe this."

"I tried. I don't know if it worked or not."

They looked at her camera, but all that showed up was a screen of smoke. Very eerie looking smoke.

"What are we doing? We need to warn Izzibeth before she goes out on stage!" Amanda Kate ran to the door. It was locked. Simon had locked them in the dressing room.

They heard the orchestra begin the overture, realizing the program had begun and they just had a few minutes to get to Elizabeth.

"Peyton, text Frieda. Emilia Rose doesn't go out for a little bit, so they should still be in their dressing room." Amanda Kate frantically continued trying to pull the door open.

"I don't have any service, and neither do you. Simon must have done something to our phones!" Peyton joined Amanda Kate, and they both began pounding on the door.

"Help! Somebody let us out!"

No one was near their dressing room. All the performers were in place for their numbers, and the sound of the music was drowning out their cries for help.

"We are not giving up, Peyton," Amanda Kate said. "That is not in our vocabulary. Let's try beating on the wall — surely Frieda will hear us!"

Their fists were getting tired, and they were beginning to really panic when they suddenly heard Frieda out in the hall.

"Emilia Rose, if I have told you once, I have told you twice — you look gorgeous and you are going to be wonderful tonight! Didn't you have your chicken livers? It's your turn, so go out and be stunning!"

Applause.

"FRIEDA!" Amanda Kate and Peyton yelled through the keyhole of the door. "HELP!"

"Amanda Kate? Peyton?" Frieda rushed to the door and tried to open it.

"Someone has locked us in! Something bad is going to happen! You have to get us out!"

"I'll be right back!" They heard Frieda run down the hall. She was back at the door in a flash.

"I have bobby pins! Give me a minute — I have done this before. One of the stars I worked with in Hollywood managed to get locked in her dressing room all the time, so I learned how to pick the lock. Steady, Frieda, steady."

Click.

"She did it!" Amanda Kate and Peyton said in unison. Luckily it was an older style of lock, much easier to pick.

Opening the door, the trio didn't waste time talking. They ran down the hall toward backstage to warn Elizabeth. But it was too late. Elizabeth was already on stage. The three of them stood there watching in horror, wondering what was going to happen.

Emilia Rose had finished her first piece, and was heading offstage.

"Frieda, let's go! 'The Queen of the Night' awaits."

Amanda Kate and Peyton told her how wonderful she had been, and mouthed to Frieda, "Don't tell her what happened!"

Frieda took the cue and hustled off to get Emilia Rose ready for her grand finale.

Amanda Kate looked beyond Elizabeth to the audience — and the third row in particular. Everyone of interest was still in their seats, thankfully. The music had begun for the *Lacrimosa*, and she and Peyton both stood there mesmerized as they watched Pavel and Susanna do their aerial ballet. Peyton took some pictures, getting some great backstage shots of the choir and Elizabeth on stage. The program was winding down, with only two more numbers left — the two from *The Magic Flute*.

Applause. So far so good. Backstage was a flurry of activity as now the Black Light troupe was getting in place for their part in the *Papageno, Papagena* duet and "The Queen of the Night's aria." Peyton was snapping pictures, and Amanda Kate was trying to stay out of everyone's way. When things had settled down a bit, she looked out to the audience again.

Something was wrong on the third row. Sophia looked different — or rather, the diamond brooch did. It wasn't there on her dress. And, the gentleman seated next to her looked heavier than Peter was.

"Peyton!" she quietly got Peyton's attention away from snapping a picture. "Peter and Sophia are MIA. Those are imposters in their seats!"

"What?! How do you know?" Peyton was stumped.

"The brooch. Sophia had the brooch on. Look out at the girl who's supposedly Sophia. The brooch is not there. They were careless and left out that very important detail. But, where are they?"

Amanda Kate felt something in the small of her back.

"Why, ladies, I am right here — and you both need to come with me. Quietly. We wouldn't want to spoil Dr. Stone's precious gala, would we?"

Sophia and a female goon led Amanda Kate and Peyton down a hallway, all the while twisting their arms behind their backs. They were then forced into a custodial closet, the door locked behind them.

"Try getting out of this closet, girls. By the way, nice try with the champagne earlier. I hope you don't think you were too clever." Sophia and her goon girlfriend laughed as they walked away.

Amanda Kate and Peyton could not believe their good fortune — locked in, twice in one night. They looked at each other. They could hear applause and knew it was grand finale time. They didn't want to miss it!

Suddenly, Amanda Kate looked at Peyton and started grabbing at her head.

"Ouch! What are you doing, Amanda Kate?"

"Bobby pins! Frieda pinned your hair up tonight, remember? Let's get to cracking — we have a lock to pick!"

With that, they both got down on their knees and began to work on the closet door's lock. The first pin broke, and Peyton pulled another one out of her hair.

"There are plenty more where this came from. Remember, giving up is not in our vocabulary." Peyton's hair was falling in her eyes by now, having taken most of the pins out.

"What time is it, Peyton?"

Without hesitating, Peyton checked her phone.

"Amanda Kate! I have service!"

She began texting Frieda while Amanda Kate kept picking at the lock.

We are locked in a broom closet. Help! Stage Right hallway. Quick!

Send.

What? After the dressing room? Again?

Reply.

Just come and get us, quickly! Will explain later.

Amanda Kate was intense and focused as she worked on the lock.

"I think I have it..."

Just as she heard a click in the lock, the door flew open. There stood Frieda with one of the stage crew who had unlocked the door with his key. Amanda Kate tumbled forward, with a disheveled Peyton right on top of her.

"Hurry!" Amanda Kate yelled as she picked herself up off the floor and began running toward the backstage area. "We have to warn Elizabeth! Something is about to happen!"

Just as they were getting backstage, Elizabeth was calling her banker, Matthew, onto the stage. The trio watched in horror as Peter ran on from the other side of the stage, knocked Elizabeth down, and then grabbed the small wooden box out of Matthew's hands before running back offstage. It happened so quickly. Elizabeth wasn't moving, and there was blood everywhere.

Amanda Kate, Peyton, and Frieda ran to Elizabeth. They discovered that Peter had knocked her so hard that she fell back on one of the platforms, hitting her head on the sharp corner. Her left arm appeared to be broken as well. Eduard was onstage now, calling an ambulance. Chaos erupted at the gala. Guests screamed in horror, and people backstage were running all directions to go after Peter. In what seemed like the blink of an eye, he had disappeared when everyone's attention was turned to Elizabeth.

Suddenly, Simon appeared in a flash of smoke onstage, and everyone froze. Deep, creepy laughter filled the theatre as he outstretched his arms and began to speak.

"Victory is ours!"

While Simon was distracted by his own gloating, Pavel and Susanna swung out on their silks from both sides of the stage. They swung back and forth, and he began swatting at them like flies as he tried to get them out of the way. Everyone watched in silence as the lights then went out in the theatre and the Black Light troupe appeared at Simon's feet, distracting him even more. These "gnats" were persistent, and they were throwing him off his game. After about five minutes, he gave up and disappeared in the same flash of smoke in which he had appeared.

The lights came back on, and the audience burst into applause. From Stage Left, two policemen came onstage toting a handcuffed Peter Schultz. A weeping Sophia was behind him, followed by the flock of bird goons. They went up to Eduard.

"Mr. Doubek, is this the gentleman you are looking for? We caught him, his very dramatic accomplice, and a flock of birds running out of the back door of the theatre where you had asked us to station ourselves."

The policeman handed Eduard the wooden box, and the audience burst into applause again. The officers led the two villains out, and at about the same time, the paramedics arrived to take Elizabeth to the hospital. She was still unconscious.

What the audience did not see was Michael Holmes standing behind Elizabeth.

At this point in the story, Michael added, "*When Simon was distracted by the performers, he lost focus on me as well — releasing me from my bindings. He flew off in a fit of rage like I've never seen before. I was able to come to your side at that point, but it was too late to prevent the harm they'd caused you.*"

Amanda Kate, Peyton and Frieda had seen Michael Holmes on stage. He looked overcome with grief. They stepped beside him while the paramedics gently raised Elizabeth on a stretcher. They all walked alongside the stretcher to the waiting ambulance. Grey rode with her to the hospital. Eduard informed everyone she was being taken to a private hospital nearby.

On cue, the orchestra and choir began singing the *Lacrimosa*, and Pavel and Susanna encored their beautiful aerial ballet. The encores put the audience back in their seats, calmed everyone's nerves, and brought a slight sense of peace to the situation after all the chaos. Emilia Rose had stepped up to direct, and there were tears in everyone's eyes.

Once the choir had finished singing and everyone was a bit calmer, despite all they had just witnessed, Eduard stepped Center Stage.

"My dear friends, tonight we have witnessed a beautiful performance. Let's give all our performers one more hand."

Everyone in the audience jumped to their feet and filled the theatre with roaring applause. The orchestra, choir, soloists, artists, Black Light cast and crew, and everyone else involved in the evening took one last bow.

"I cannot at this moment explain the phenomenon you witnessed, nor tell you why the gentleman ran on stage and attacked Dr. Stone. Those answers will be revealed after a thorough investigation has taken place. What we do know is that Dr. Stone was injured tonight. Please keep her and her family in your prayers. My accountant tells me your generosity tonight has been overwhelming. I would like to ask that Dr. Joseph Chamberlain join me onstage."

More applause as Joseph, looking confused and shocked, joined Eduard.

"Dr. Chamberlain, thank you again. As much as we both wish Dr. Stone was here on stage with us, I know her well enough that she would want you to press forward in her absence. Your groups were invited here to perform for us tonight, but what you weren't told is that donations have been taken up to support the arts — not only at your university, but for the arts here in Prague. Through generous donations tonight, I am pleased to announce that your university will be receiving a gift of one million dollars toward arts education."

Joseph about fainted, and thunderous applause once more filled the theatre. Eduard reached into his inside coat pocket, and then handed Joseph and envelope as he shook his hand.

"In the envelope, you will find a letter addressed to you and Dr. Stone. It gives you the details of the funding and ideas for how we hope you will use it."

"Thank you," Joseph responded, in a slightly flustered voice, "this is all a wonderful surprise. On behalf of Dr. Stone, our colleagues, and most importantly our students, we thank you very much."

Eduard then called Pavla, Pavel, and Susanna to the forefront. Looking confused, they joined him.

"Distinguished guests, you witnessed beautiful art tonight. We also saw the courage that these two fine performers, who just happen to be my assistant's parents, had in the face of danger. The foundation I am representing tonight wishes to award a monetary gift to Pavel and Susanna so they can build a studio to teach their art to young performers here in Prague."

Eduard reached for another envelope and handed it to a very stunned Pavel. It had been a secret desire of theirs to start a studio, but they realized they could never afford it. He turned to look at Pavla, who had tears running down her face. She shook her head to let him know she had never told Eduard their dream.

The audience continued to applaud until Eduard silenced them once more.

"Pavla, stay with me. Lukas, would you and the Black Light cast and crew come and join us?"

More stunned looks as they joined Eduard Center Stage.

"The art of the Black Light Theatre is unique to Prague. I personally attend your amazing performances on a regular basis. You are innovative, and truly love your art. On behalf of the foundation I represent, we are also presenting you with a monetary gift to further advance your black light performances here in Prague. Our benefactor would love to see you be able to reach a larger audience, and all the details are listed in this letter. I think you will be pleased."

The audience was on their feet once more as Lukas took the envelope. How did Eduard know the troupe had been looking for a bigger venue and wanted to do outreach to the school children in Prague?

"Now, ladies and gentlemen, there are more surprises, but due to Dr. Stone's injury, they will have to wait until she is better. For the moment," he looked at his watch, "it is five minutes to midnight!"

On cue, waiters appeared at each aisle and on stage with trays of champagne and gave each guest a glass. Everyone laughed when Emilia Rose took one for each hand.

"Dr. Chamberlain, are you ready?" Eduard looked down at the orchestra pit where Joseph was.

Eduard looked at his watch once more. "Ten, nine, eight..." The audience joined him in the countdown. "seven, six, five, four, three, two, one. HAPPY NEW YEAR!"

The orchestra began playing *Auld Lang Syne*, and the theatre erupted into song — singing in their own language, but relaying the same sentiment.

"A toast!" Eduard cried. "To a healthy and prosperous New Year for all."

Glasses clinked as everyone for the moment forgot all that had happened earlier in the evening.

Everyone's masques had come off at midnight, and Amanda Kate looked down to row three. Arthur Adderly and Kristoph were still there, and she smiled. They caught each other's eyes briefly, and she raised her glass to them. It was nice to know they didn't run when Peter was caught. Now she knew for sure they intended no harm to Elizabeth. She couldn't wait to tell her in person.

Eduard got the audience's attention for one last time.

"Please join us out in the foyer for coffee and some light refreshments. Please be safe as you go home tonight. If you need to arrange transportation home, please ask the attendants out front. We have made arrangements with local car service providers. Thank you, again, to everyone for attending tonight!"

The audience began to empty into the foyer. Everyone on the stage was huddled together now, and their emotions were finally coming out. The students were being consoled, and the coach drivers and tour guides had come in to help organize them so they could get back on the coaches to go home. Bradley was right on top of it all, and soon the students were headed outside. Eduard's staff at The Mozart House had a late-night meal waiting for them.

Amanda Kate was visiting quietly with Eduard, when Adderly walked up beside them onstage. She stood a little taller when he approached.

"Mr. Doubek," he spoke with a lilting British accent, "I am Mr. Arthur Adderly. Perhaps Dr. Stone has mentioned me to you?"

Eduard reached out to shake his hand. "No, I am afraid she hasn't, but your reputation in the art world precedes you."

Amanda Kate was impressed, because Adderly instantly warmed up to Eduard. She was beginning to think Eduard had many resources that they didn't know about. She saw Kristoph behind the two gentlemen, and she went over to him.

"You must be Kristoph. Elizabeth has told me about both of you. Despite all this unpleasantness, she still had some good things to say about you."

Kristoph's head raised to meet her eyes. "Thank you for sharing that with me. I am worried about her."

"Me too," Amanda Kate consoled. "She and I have been friends forever, and I just don't know what I would do without her. I also know that she would want us not to waste too much energy worrying about her, but to think instead about her students and others who were affected by tonight's happenings. Don't you agree?"

She and Kristoph talked for a bit, until Adderly motioned that he was ready to go. He paused for a moment by Amanda Kate.

"Please convey my concerns to Dr. Stone."

"I will, Mr. Adderly. She will be pleased to hear this."

With a tip of his hat, Adderly walked proudly offstage and out to the foyer, with Kristoph by his side. Amanda Kate wondered if she had seen the last of them. Probably not, she thought to herself with a smile.

Eduard had arranged for drivers to take the remaining people back to The Mozart House, since all the coaches had left earlier. The core group had stayed to make sure the guests left happy, and finally, at 3 a.m., they were on their way back to The Mozart House.

Amanda's phone buzzed, and she looked down to see a text from Grey.

Mom is stabilized. Emma and I are staying here tonight with her.
She is not conscious, though, so continue to pray.

As she read the text, there in the relative privacy of the car, Amanda Kate finally let her guard down, and the tears began flowing again. Everyone was exhausted − emotionally and physically − when they arrived back at The Mozart House. The students all had waited up for them in the Breakfast Room, as they were hoping for news about Elizabeth. Amanda Kate shared Grey's update, and then the chaperones encouraged the students to go and get some rest. Begrudgingly, they made their way upstairs to their rooms, many of them still very emotional.

❧ ✳ ❧

And that is how the gala saga played out that night.

The Music Room fell silent as the story ended. I sat for a moment, letting it all sink in. I had listened intently as they collectively told the story of the gala. We had laughed and cried as the story unfolded, enjoying the full range of emotions wrapped up in the events of the evening.

Carefully, I rose and went to stand in front of the fireplace. Several had offered to help me, but I shooed them away. I needed to do this all by myself to get stronger.

I stood silently, head slightly bowed, as I tried to find the right words. Finally, I lifted my head and spoke.

"Thank you. The gratitude I feel right now truly is beyond words. I love each and every one of you for what you did that night after I was hurt."

I looked towards the back of the room and saw Michael Holmes standing there. He still looked defeated, and my heart just broke for him.

"Our initial plan for the evening was designed to keep everyone safe — but also to catch Peter as he made a play to steal the treasures. I need each of you to realize that we did succeed in the end. Peter was caught. He will not escape punishment for his actions. But, even if he had gotten away, he would not have done so with the treasures. Matthew and I had planted fakes in the wooden box..."

The whole room gasped and broke into exclamations of "WHAT?!" as Matthew and I gave each other a sly wink.

"In order for the decoys to work, we had to keep everyone in the dark. If, somehow, Peter had overheard someone talking about the fake treasures, then he might have abandoned his plans and never have been caught. He needed to be caught. His crimes extend far beyond what you witnessed at the gala. We just never anticipated him rushing onto the stage so brazenly. It was sloppy, even for him.

"None of us knows how the drama would have unfolded if I hadn't been hurt. But, it happened. The important thing I am hearing tonight is how you all came together in a split second to show your strength. Pavel and Susanna — you reacted brilliantly and quickly, and got everyone else to participate! I would have loved to have seen it all. Clearly you met Simon. There's much more to that story...and I promise I'll fill you in.

"For now, I just want to say I am extremely proud of each of you. It was because of your love for me that you all sprang to action, and that means more to me than the treasures — which, by the way, are still safe and sound back in the States."

I paused.

"I began this journey when I received the snuff box and locket, and very soon I will see that journey through to its completion. I was broken, but I am alive and mending. Peter and Sophia were caught, and they both are under investigation for fraud and embezzlement. We have made new friends and experienced the time of our lives here in Prague and at The Mozart House. Soon we will all go back to our respective lives with a story to tell, and our lives *definitely* are more exciting than they were a couple of months ago!"

Everyone laughed.

"There are still some pretty amazing desserts on the table, and I, for one, need chocolate after hearing your incredible stories of courage. Eduard, I want to personally thank you for all you have done from the very beginning of the adventure. You and your staff here have outdone yourselves. I know you weren't prepared for us to stay as long as we have, but thank you, my dear new friends. We hope that you will come to see us in the States, and I personally plan to return here soon!"

With that, we finished the evening with laughter — and lots of chocolate.

Epilogue

I realized in the end that Sophia's diamond brooch at the gala had belonged to Mozart's mother. The brooch — not the locket — was the final item Constanze had given to Lord William in Copenhagen, since she had given him the locket in Vienna. I believe that my benefactor used the brooch to lure Peter further in. One day I will ask him how he pulled it all off.

Peter and Sophia were charged with fraud and embezzlement after further investigation revealed that they had been stealing artifacts that had been donated to the Mozarthaus. Investigators found jewels, letters, more snuff boxes, and even some music manuscripts hidden in his secret vault at the Mozarthaus Museum. Peter also had stashed millions of euros in a Swiss bank account from sales of stolen artifacts. Peter had been at this game for years, and Sophia had become his willing accomplice. They were tried in Criminal Court in Vienna, and were currently awaiting sentencing.

I still don't know exactly how deeply Arthur Adderly was involved, but he hasn't yet been caught up in the legal actions. I think he's got a good heart, at the end of the day, and that seems to be confirmed by Amanda Kate's encounter with him and Kristoph after the gala. I decided to reach out to Arthur and thank him for his concern. I truly did enjoy his personality, and who knows — I might just encounter him again.

It made me sad that people could descend into such behavior, but I was glad we had been instrumental in catching them. A lawyer had called me to ask questions about the recent events, and the conference call had ended with me being given a more thorough understanding of Peter's scheme.

Peter's ancestor was indeed the Peter Schultz that Constanze and Lord William had mentioned in their letters. I had faxed copies of the letters to the lawyer working on the case, and he researched them quite extensively to verify all the facts. Peter's great, great-whatever had left behind a journal, and Peter's father had given it to him on his twenty-first birthday. Peter was clever, and being the opportunist that he was, even at an early age, he devised a plan to become involved with the Mozarthaus right after he graduated from university. The day that Mr. Brookshire brought in the snuff box and locket, Peter was elated. He had read about it in his grandfather's journal and could not believe his good fortune. The plot simply thickened when I was dragged into it.

The important thing is that the treasures did not fall into Peter's hands. I believe they were used — no, *I* was used — to bring justice to all who had been defrauded by Peter and to return Mozart's artifacts to their rightful place in history. My benefactor knew these particular treasures would entice him to his breaking point, and in turn, bring his escapades to an end.

Speaking of which, I still don't know who my benefactor is. I was hoping the gala would bring him out of hiding, or that he would magically appear at the hospital and introduce himself — leading to a lifelong friendship.

That obviously didn't happen. And, as I sit here with Charlotte in my lap and Beau at my feet, I still have many questions about Lord William and his connection to my benefactor.

Michael Holmes came to say goodbye a few days ago. I reassured him, once again, that he didn't fail. Everything had happened for a reason.

He has been assigned to a new case, but he promised he would pop in every now and then. I knew that if I ever needed Michael Holmes again, he would be there.

Beau was now a permanent guardian and companion for me, which made me believe my adventures were not over yet.

I had healed, and was being a good patient by continuing to go to therapy for my arm. I kept telling my physical therapist that conducting was the best therapy, but she didn't believe me.

Benjamin and I kept in touch, but for the moment that relationship wasn't going anywhere romantically. I was good with that, and so was he. We chose to remain good friends and colleagues, and to take it easy if we moved forward.

Family and friends kept in touch with me daily, even though the gala was months ago. I love their thoughtfulness and concern, and I'm still so very happy we shared such an amazing adventure together.

And the treasures? Before returning to the States, Eduard helped me get in touch with Mr. Brookshire, my benefactor's barrister. We all concurred that the snuff box and locket should return to Marie Antoinette's family in Vienna, to the very place where the young girl had given the items to the young Wolfgang. Mr. Brookshire made the calls, and once I am done with this current semester, I am going to meet him in Vienna, where we will deliver the priceless treasures to the Hofburg Palace Museum. Mr. Brookshire was drawing up a contract, and I was to be listed as the donor, despite my protests. In the meantime, Matthew and I are the only ones who know where they are being kept safe.

I think Paparazzi is back in the States. I haven't spotted him yet, but I have this feeling that my benefactor is still watching over me closely.

I didn't hear the doorbell ring, but the dogs did, jolting me out of my pensive state. I wasn't expecting anyone, nor had I ordered anything to be delivered.

I opened the door to find a delivery man with a package that required a signature. I thanked him, closed the door, and went to the kitchen to open the package. *Wait!* There was a familiarity about the way the delivery man tipped his hat! *Paparazzi!* I ran back to the door, but the truck had already driven off. With a big sigh, I went back to the kitchen to open the mysterious package.

My hands were shaking and my heart was racing. Out of the shipping box, I lifted another blue case like the one my necklace had come in, except this one was a bit bigger. I held it in my hands for a few moments before going to my chair to reveal what was inside. Sitting, with both dogs staring me down, I slowly untied the big white bow and lifted the lid.

Inside was a blue velvet lining. Laying on top was a beautiful envelope with my name written in calligraphy — just like the other notes I had received from my benefactor. I don't think my heart could have beat any faster as I opened it. It read:

My Dearest Elizabeth,

Brava! The Mozart Masquerade Gala was a huge success. Your program was outstanding, and I was so proud of you and your groups. I knew if anyone could bring Peter Schultz to the forefront and expose him, you could. Tell your friends I am quite impressed with them as well — especially the way they handled themselves after you were assaulted. I was horrified, as no one was supposed to get hurt. But, that is behind us now. I am so glad you are on the mend! You handled this case so well that I thought you might like another adventure. Enjoy this token of my gratitude. And again, my sincerest appreciation to all involved in the gala.

No signature — again. I looked all over the envelope for clues, and as usual, there were none.

Laying the note aside, I looked at the blue velvet. Folding it back, my heart pounding, I was surprised to see a shiny, gold drawstring bag. I carefully untied it. Inside were pearls.

"Pearls?" I said out loud. Both dogs cocked their heads to one side as if to echo my question.

Reaching inside, I pulled out a strand of exquisite Baroque pearls. Baroque pearls have an irregular shape — not spherical like the pearls you see in later periods. I reached back inside, and there was another strand of pearls, these from a more modern era, again exquisite. These were not costume jewelry, but the real deal. I reached my hand back inside, and there were earrings to match each strand. My hand touched a piece of paper at the bottom of the bag. Pulling it out and opening it, I read:

No one can have enough pearls. Just ask Queen Margherita. Your next clue will follow soon.

I picked up my phone to search for information about Queen Margherita. Finding what I needed, I turned and looked at the dogs.

"Queen Margherita loved pearls. Looks like I will be planning a trip to Italy for my next adventure..."

I turned, and there in my chair was a familiar red scarf. Michael would be back.

Mozart's Timeline from Elizabeth's Journal

Born: Jan. 27, 1756, Salzburg, Austria

1761: First public performance

1762: Trip to Court of the Prince-Elector Maximillian II of Bavaria in Munich, Germany; Imperial Court in Vienna; Imperial Court in Prague

1763: Grand Tour begins. Leopold and his wife Anna Maria take his musically gifted children Nannerl and little Wolfgang on a 3-year tour through Western Europe.

1766: Tour ends

1767: Performance in Vienna

1768: Mozart writes his first opera, *La Finte Simplice*

1769: Italy — met Giovanni Battista Martini in Bologna and became a member of Accademia Filarmonica.

1770: Milan, where he wrote *Mitirdate, re di Ponte*

1771-73: Visited Milan for premiers of *Ascanio in Albe* (1771); *Lucio filla* (1772) and "Exulatate, jubilate" (first work)

1773: Salzburg. Court of the Ruler of Salzburg, Prince Archbishop Hieronymous Colloredo. Wrote 5 Violin concertos and Piano Concertos.

1777: Resigned job as a musician at the Salzburg Court and travels to Mannheim, Augsburg, Paris, and Munich composing music. **Falls in love with Aloysia Weber. Rejected a job as organist at Versailles.** Fell into debt.

1778: His mother dies so he leaves Paris in September. Here he had written the "Paris Symphony No.31" and the beautiful "A minor Piano Sonata". Offered Court Organist and Concert Master job in Salzburg.

1781: *Idomeneo* was premiered in Munich. Invited to the Court of Archbishop Collerdo in Salzburg. Quarreled over salary, he resigned, but resignation refused. He was later dismissed.

1781: Settled in Vienna as freelance composer and performer.

1782: *The Abduction from the Seraglio* premiered. Moved in with the Weber family in Vienna who had moved from Mannheim. **Aloysia was married, but Mozart got involved with their younger daughter, Constanze.**

1782: Married in St. Stephen's Cathedral on August 4, 1782. Mozart had trouble getting his father's approval of the marriage.

1783: Mozart wrote what some believe to be his greatest piece, Mass in C minor

1784: Became a Freemason. Mozart also meets Franz Joseph Haydn and the two become friends.

1786: *The Marriage of Figaro* premiered in Vienna

1787: **Don Giovanni premieres in Prague at the Estates Theatre**

1787: Appointed by Emperor Joseph II as his chamber composer, but it was just a part time job

1787: Meets the young Ludwig Von Beethoven who hopes to study with him. Unfortunately, this never happened.

1789: Leopold dies.

1791: Fell ill in Prague at the Sept. 6 premiere of his opera *La clemenza di Tito*. Continued his public functions despite being ill and conducted the premiere of The Magic Flute on Sept. 30.

He was in the middle of composing the *Requiem*, commissioned by an anonymous stranger.

December 5, 1791, Mozart died in his home at age 35 at 1:00 am. Due to financial constraints, he was buried in a pauper's grave outside of Vienna.

Wolfgang and Constanze had 6 children, but only two survived:

Karl Thomas Mozart, Sept. 21, 1784

Franz Xavier Mozart, July 26, 1791

The Mozart Masquerade Gala Program

The Marriage of Figaro Overture ....The University Orchestra

"Masquerade"
from The Phantom of the Opera ....The University Chorale

"Kyrie" from the Requiem ....The University Chorale

Symphony No. 40 in G minor, K 550 ....The University Orchestra

"Misericordias Domini", K 222 ....The University Chorale

"Laudate Dominum"
from Vesperae Solennes De Confessore ....The University Chorale
Soloist, Emilia Rose

"Lacrimosa" from the Requiem ....The University Chorale

"Pappageno, Pappagena"
from The Magic Flute ....The University Chorale

"The Queen of the Night's Aria"
from The Magic Flute ....The University Chorale
Soloist, Emilia Rose

Dear Readers,

I sincerely hope you take the time to read more about Wolfgang Amadeus and learn more about him than what I have shared with you in this book. I have not altered the basic facts of his life, but I have stepped inside his timeline to create a story that "could have been."

The gala program features only a handful of his 600 works. I encourage you to find recordings of these wonderful pieces and listen along as you read the book. If you're new to Mozart, I hope you'll find his musical genius as captivating as I do.

The next Dr. Elizabeth Stone adventure takes us to Italy. I hope you will join me.

— Wanetta Hill
Author of the Dr. Elizabeth Stone Travel Adventures

Made in the USA
San Bernardino, CA
14 October 2017